# UNTETHERED

# UNTETHERED

## SWEET, FUNNY, AND STRANGE TALES OF THE

## PARANORMAL

Edited by
Marianne H. Donley and Carol L. Wright

# BETHLEHEM WRITERS GROUP, LLC
### Bethlehem, Pennsylvania

# UNTETHERED

Published by Bethlehem Writers Group, LLC
Bethlehem, Pennsylvania
http://bethlehemwritersgroup.com

Cover design and print book layout by Carol L. Wright
e-book layout by Marianne H. Donley

Cover image © Fotosearch.com

ISBN: 978-0-9892650-4-1 (paperback)
ISBM: 978-0-8982650-5-8 (e-book)

Library of Congress Control Number: 2018952492

Printed in the United States of America

*for Sal*

# TABLE OF CONTENTS

# Sal's Cookies

*Emily P. W. Murphy*

It hit me like all the clichés, the news of Sal's death. Scrolling through Facebook last thing before bed, the post from her daughter looked unremarkable. *That's not funny . . . oh wait, it's not her . . . wait, yes, it is.*

The impossibility of it sent my mind jumping through all the imagined misinterpretations. All the creative explanations. Until it settled on the truth. It was Sal's daughter. She was saying what it seemed she was saying. Somehow, impossibly, Sal was gone.

Before Sal, Death had always knocked politely at the door. Certainly, Death came before we were ready, in his own time, but he had always given us the opportunity to say goodbye before entering. Whether the loved one lingered for months or for days, there was always that *warning.*

Not so with Sal. Of course, she had cancer, but she was fighting it—and then the anger hit. *How could they not tell me she'd turned for the worse?* I called my mother. She was as shocked as I. She hadn't been warned either.

I hung up the phone as a wave of nausea swept me up, threatening to carry me away. It was a tsunami of the feeling I experienced five and a half years earlier, when I woke to her email. The one that said "4th stage cancer."

That February morning, Mom was visiting me in Maryland. It was very early, so I chose to take a shower before waking her up with bad news. I remember choosing my shower gel thinking, *This scent will always remind me of the morning I learned Sal has cancer.* It always has. Juniper Breeze—Sal has cancer.

That sort of observation is so much more like her than it is like me. She is—was—an observer. She noticed everything. New glasses, small injuries. She'd notice things about you that you hadn't even noticed yourself. She possessed a natural talent for observation that writers work decades to develop—and a tin ear for dialogue. I suspect this was because she put everything into the experience of her conversations with others, leaving nothing to analyze the words and natural rhythms of how people speak. At least it meant I could bring something to the equation.

Even when Death has knocked at the door, my response to the finality of his actions has always been to examine my heart for regrets. I wish I had visited my grandmother before that trip to Minneapolis. Even though she wouldn't have known it was me. Death knocked a few days later, and I made it to her bedside in time to hold her hand as she passed . . . but still.

In Sal's case, I didn't feel regret just . . . confusion. When you live far away from loved ones, when you don't speak to them on a regular basis, their passing isn't obvious in your day-to-day perceptions. And yet every day I felt the strangeness of her absence. It was particularly strong as I watched those around me grieve in their own ways, posting their tributes to the woman they knew. Sharing their perceptions of who Sal was. How I longed to meet her for coffee and hear what she thought of it all. I could only imagine.

As Christmas approached, the first real regret started to niggle at the back of my mind. Sal's cookies.

Every Christmas Mom and I made a variety of cookies. The same recipes year after year. And Sal made chocolate chip. Chocolate chip cookies that put our colorful variety to shame. Years ago, before the cancer, I begged her for the recipe. We were visiting her in the home she built. The one she wrote about in *From Scratch*. Together we were enjoying the quiet noisiness of nature on the back porch. "I'm serious," I said. "Your cookies are incredible. Could I please have the recipe?" She led me into the house, to the kitchen pantry, took out her recipe box and thumbed through the cards. "Here," she said, passing me a large white card with pictures of fruit. "I have two copies. . . . I don't know why. I'll keep this one because it's my mother's handwriting. You can have the other."

My regret—sometime in the years since, my recipe card met with a few drops of water. The ink ran, obscuring some crucial measurements. "Mix . . . add 1 teas . . . +1 . . . water . . . cup . . . lour . . . sp soda . . . 1 " van . . . chips + . . . ts."

When Sal knew something was wrong, but before she knew for sure it was cancer, she confided in my mother. Mom asked if she could keep me in the loop, and Sal agreed. She wrote at the time, "The reason I chose not to include her in the emails to you is only because she is *young* . . . but tough, I know. And I love her optimism. She is one of my most favorite loves of all time, and I didn't want her to have to feel the sadness." After the news of her passing, I wondered whether, in her final days, Sal knew the end was coming. Whether she'd hidden the fact from me for that reason. She didn't want me to feel the sadness.

But if I'd known, I certainly would have taken the opportunity for one last hug. One last cup of coffee. One last clarification of her cookie recipe.

*Regret.*

Christmas ticked closer, and it was time to commence the annual baking. My preschool-aged children were finally old enough to *get* things. They were eager to be my kitchen assistants.

I went to the cupboard for my recipe box and pulled out the usual family favorites: Spritz Cookies, Snowball Cookies, Christmas Fudge (of course), Peanut Butter Kiss Cookies, Cherry Cake, "Good" Cookies. I looked for that white card with the pictures of fruit. It wasn't there. I heard my mother-in-law's voice in my memory. She had helped me pack up the kitchen in our last move and, when it was too late to do anything about it, mentioned: "I found a recipe card that was beyond saving, so I threw it away." Was that Sal's card? There was no way to know.

I pulled the remaining cards out of the box to flip through them one by one. A small neon yellow index card escaped the stack and fluttered down, landing face down on the floor. None of my recipes are on neon index cards. What could it be? I bent to pick it up and turned it over.

"Sal," it said in her handwriting in the upper right-hand corner. It was her cookie recipe.

I felt her words around me, almost as if she were standing in the room. "I didn't want her to have to feel the sadness."

Holding the card to my heart, I whispered, "Thanks, Sal."

# THE BEAST

*Kidd Wadsworth*

The road is deserted. It's 1955, and he's driving an old, yellow Buick somewhere in Arizona, trying to make California before morning. Seeing movement out of the corner of his eye, he glances out the passenger side window. A man is running alongside the car, keeping pace with it. Shock jerks the driver backward in his seat. He checks his speed—sixty miles an hour.

"A mile a minute," he whispers. Again, he glances out the window. The man is wearing buckskin, moccasins, and a feather. He turns and smiles, revealing war paint, the top half of his face red, with vertical white and black lines extending downward. As the driver watches, the man's head morphs into the head of a wolf, his pointed canine teeth growing until they are four . . . six inches long.

The driver steps on the gas. The thing jumps—over the car—and lands on the driver's side, still running, still keeping pace. Frantically, the driver floors it. It's August, in Arizona, yet ice crystals are growing on the windshield. The driver reaches down to turn on the defrost, but his fingers don't work. They're too numb from the cold. He blows on them. Still, they don't work. He can't see the road. He puts his index finger and his thumb in his mouth, furiously sucking until his fingers thaw enough to turn on the defrost.

He peers through the thawing ice, searching for the lights of another car, praying that someone will come along in the opposing lane and kill the thing. He gets it up to eighty, and it's still beside the car. The driver is violently shivering; the tips of his pinkies are black. Fear has him gripping the steering wheel so hard he almost breaks his own fingers. A high-pitched whine, like a dog in pain, is coming from the engine. The right front wheel is vibrating furiously.

The needle creeps up to ninety. Still, the beast is beside the car, running effortlessly. The driver comes to a town, small, real small, but it has one of those Old West-style saloons with a long front porch and two rocking chairs out front. Suddenly, the heinous creature vanishes, so the man gets out and runs for the door, smashing it open.

Inside are some guys at the bar, two shooting pool, and some others sitting at tables. It's a rather peaceful place. The theme from Marlboro Country is playing in the background. The driver looks behind him, sighing with relief. He's alone. No one followed him in. Everyone in the bar is staring at him. Still panting, he smooths down his sweater-vest and tries to stop shivering. His fingers throb like they've been run over by a semi.

Relieved, he goes to the bar, orders a beer, changes it to whiskey, then two whiskeys. "Leave the bottle," he says. As he drinks, as his hands slowly stop shaking, when he's able to talk again without stuttering like an idiot, he tells the bartender the story about the wolf-thing running alongside his car. Maybe if he'd been less scared, or if the Navajo were given to more showy dress, he might have noticed that everyone in there is dark-skinned but him. As he talks—not loud, mind you, just in a normal voice—the whole place goes quiet, and the dudes shooting pool come over and sit at the bar. When the driver finishes telling his tale, the bartender looks toward the end of the bar where a guy is pretty well drunk and says, "Better bring the boy in—now." Then he pulls a shotgun out from behind the bar, hands it to another fellow, and says, "Go with him, DT."

"You think a gun's going to help?" DT asks.

"If you don't want it . . ."

DT takes it. He and the drunk, plus two more, go out and bring in a sleeping child. Seems the drunk had his four-year-old waiting for him in his car.

By this time, Buick-guy is losing it. Every man in the place is locking windows. Two go to check the windows in the kitchen and lock the back door. Behind the bar, the bartender calls his wife, tells her he won't be home until morning. Then he whispers a name into the phone.

"What's going on?" Buick-guy shouts.

Finally, the bartender tells him. "You were being hunted."

"By what?"

"Something old."

The drunk guy—someone's given him a gun, and he's loading it—says, "In my grandfather's day, the tribe got a Catholic priest to hold an exorcism."

"You believe that?" DT asks. He shakes his head; rolls his eyes. "The tribe never called a priest."

The drunk guy finishes loading the gun.

"So what happened?" Buick-guy asks. "You know, with the priest?"

The drunk raises one hand in the air—half of a shrug. "Haven't seen the priest."

"Will locking the doors will keep him out?"

Now DT shrugs. He glances over at the bartender and back at Buick-guy. "You rather we unlock them?"

They all bed down in the bar, loaded guns beside them. As Buick-guy tries and fails to fall asleep, DT whispers, "You were lucky, White Man. Not many survive who have seen the Beast."

〜

As I grew up, I tried to dismiss the tale. After all, I'd been a Brownie at Girl Scout camp when I first heard it. Our counselor had gathered us around the campfire, put a flashlight under her chin and said, "I swear this is true." Then she'd scared the bejeebers out of me. I remember shivering in my sleeping bag in the middle of June. Trouble was, I couldn't forget the tale because I kept hearing it, and each time it was a little different.

When I was sixteen, Charlie Crabtree took me out for pizza and a movie. On the way home, he decided we should park. I guess he thought a scary story would have me clinging to him.

"I swear this is true," he said. "My brother's roommate in college knew the dude."

~

It's 1985, and two Olympic skier wannabes rent a helicopter to take them, at night, to the top of a mountain in Arizona. The pilot gives them a thumbs-up; they jump. Landing flawlessly, they begin to race. Without light pollution, the Milky Way is dazzling above them, reflecting off the snow. They ski through the tree line, entering the sparse pines, swishing between the trunks effortlessly. Joy has them whooping and hollering.

As the forest thickens, they swerve away from the cliff face and onto the broad slope cleared of trees. Beside the skiers, a man appears—running on the snow—wearing a buckskin loincloth. Covering his head, is the head of a wolf. It's not a mask, it's the head of a real wolf, like you might see hanging as a trophy on a wall. The skiers are easily pushing seventy miles an hour. One of the two is a real idiot. He thinks wolf-dude is super cool, so he smiles at him. The wolf turns, and his wolf mouth smiles back. Then his wolf head morphs. Now he's not a man wearing a wolf head, he's a man with a wolf head. Shock careens the Idiot sideways; he breaks a ski on an outcropping of rock and tumbles down the mountain, crashing into the trunk of a tree. When he can open his eyes through the pain, he sees his friend frantically racing the wolf. The wolf is literally running in circles around the skier. Using the side of a rock as a ramp, the wolf runs up it, and jumps over the skier, rotating 360 degrees before landing on the other side, plunging into the snow. The skier sees his chance to get away—the wolf is stuck in the snow—and he points his skis directly downhill. His knees bent, his legs together, poles at his sides, he picks up dangerous speed. The wolf jumps out of his snow hole and howls. At first, as the wolf begins to run, he sinks into the snow with every step, but the faster he runs, the more he runs on top of the snow, the more the snow's icy crust holds him up. He catches the skier. Again the wolf jumps, this time he crashes his feet into the skier. They somersault down the mountain, out of view of the Idiot.

Fumbling, the Idiot unzips his backpack, gets out his radio and calls the helicopter for help. Rescuers search the mountain for three days. They use infrared. They never find his friend.

~

Charlie Crabtree didn't get any smoochies. He found it difficult to kiss me because my teeth were chattering.

The third time I heard the tale, I heard it from my undergraduate American Lit prof. She had a grant to study urban legends. Her thesis: Urban legends exist because they tell us something fundamentally true about ourselves or our world. Her version had the Beast going after a woman. I remember sitting in the class, trying not to laugh. I was absolutely *not* shivering.

~

A waitress is coming home, on her Harley, from her job at the IHOP. It's three in the morning. She lives just outside of Sedona. She's known around town for her lip and her Harley, because although Sedona may appear to be full of nothing but liberal, do-gooder artists, she knows the men who come into the IHOP at two in the morning looking for a waffle. She's wearing her light-blue waitress dress, white sneakers, and her helmet. Tucked in her saddlebags is her purse, filled with the night's tips and a small revolver.

She's flying down Arizona State Route 89A when a man runs up beside her, keeping pace with the Harley. He's wearing a buckskin loincloth and a single feather. He's barefoot.

She leans forward, whispers to the Harley, "Come on, Chris," and gives Chris the gas. The man increases his speed, keeping abreast of her. He's running along her right side, so she sneaks her left hand down her left side, pulls up her dress, pushes upward slightly with her feet, and slips the knife she has hidden against her inner thigh, into the palm of her left hand. Meanwhile, Chris is doing 102 miles per hour. The waitress glances sideways. The thing running beside her now has canine teeth so long they extend below his face. Nights of watching men for signs of trouble has her seeing his intent in his eyes before he acts. She swerves to her left as he punches out his fist, intending to knock her from the bike. They pass a closed Circle K. She swerves toward him; he jumps over the bike. As he passes overhead, she slices upward with the knife in her left hand. He yelps like a dog; she loses the knife in his gut. Burning rubber on both wheels, she breaks and turns in a wide arch, leaving the freeway, sliding on the rocks and the sand of the desert. Maneuvering back onto the road, she heads for the Circle K, flying through the front window. She lands in the candy aisle and somehow stumbles, with four broken ribs, into the restroom and locks herself inside.

The next morning, the police find the unconscious waitress still locked in the bathroom. In the back of the store, in a cramped office, they find a computer, payroll receipts, and inventory rolls covering a small desk. They guess that the owner of the Circle K had been in the back office doing the taxes when someone crashed through the front window. Now she is dead, lying on the floor next to the soda coolers, with a knife plunged into her chest. She is wearing a light blue dress and white sneakers.

~

This urban legend, my prof said, had her baffled. Her question to the class—and our homework assignment— "What does this story teach the reader?"

I was twenty-two years old, and I was done being scared. I wrote: This story tells me that American Lit profs get paid for doing stupid stuff.

# THE BEAST

When I was twenty-six, in graduate school at the University of Michigan, the Beast decided to race me.

∾

Andy sat down on the edge of my desk. "Did you comb your hair today?"

"Thanks, I needed that."

"Really, J. You look awful."

"Leave."

"Three of us are going climbing. Wanna come?"

I channeled my inner teenager and rolled my eyes. "I don't climb."

"J, you need a break."

"Why?"

"Because you haven't made a lick of progress in—let me guess—two weeks."

He was wrong. Two weeks was a cake walk. I'd been stuck for three months.

He put his hand over my screen. It didn't work. I had a twenty-seven-inch monitor. I could still see my graphs clearly showing that my equation in no way predicted my data. I wanted to scream. I'd retaken the data—four times. I'd checked and rechecked the entire system until I was convinced that nature was indeed operating correctly. It was my equation that was wrong, but why?

Andy leaned in. "Trust me," he whispered. "A little time in the great outdoors and you'll find the problem."

Three days later we set off for somewhere in Arizona. I spent thirty hours in a car (they slept and drove in shifts) with two physicists and an astronomer. I gave up trying to work. They had dedicated themselves to naming all the stars, comets, quasars, nebulas, galaxies, planets, moons, and other heavenly phenomena whose names contained all the letters found on passing license plates.

We arrived, exhausted, in the late afternoon. I found our small cabin, tucked away in a corner of the park, idyllic. I even enjoyed drifting off to sleep to the unfamiliar sounds of three guys snoring. The next morning Andy loaded me up with pancakes and bacon.

"You know," he hesitated, "we didn't charge you for gas."

I stopped stuffing my mouth.

"The guys . . ." He ruffled his own hair and looked at the ground.

"Spill," I said.

"The guys sort of expect you to video our climb."

I looked around at the morning, sans buildings, sans street noise, sans the bustle of students, and mostly sans my own inflated expectations of my worth to the scientific world. "I'd love to film you guys."

"Did you bring your camera?"

I grinned. "Yes, Andy, I brought my ultra-cool camera."

The next morning we drove to the mountain and took a seldom-used trail to the starting point of a north-side ascent. The fellows intended to climb until sunset, sleep suspended, and ascend to the peak the following day. There they'd camp. On day three, they'd rappel down.

"Rappelling goes quickly; we should be back here by noon," Andy said.

After some initial filming, I turned off my camera and settled down to work. I'd brought my equation, calculus books, papers, mechanical pencils, calculator, etc. I knew I couldn't count on cell reception. Every hour, I'd find the fellows again with my binoculars and film about five or ten minutes of video. Late in the afternoon I became engrossed in my work; I forgot about the promised videoing.

Night fell with a suddenness that surprised me until I realized it wasn't night, I was sitting in the shadow of the mountain. In front of me, it loomed dark, backlit by the setting sun. "What am I doing? I've let five hours go by." Quickly, I took out the camera. It was hopeless. They were in shadow.

I'd hiked about halfway to the parking lot when the moon rose, full and bright. I looked back at the mountain. "Maybe." I turned around. By the time I got back to the base, my flashlight was superfluous. The moon and stars had the place lit up so bright I even saw a toad. "Better watch out, little guy. Predators come out at night."

The fellows were clearly visible in the moonlight hanging from their ropes near an outcropping of rock. "Yes!" I recorded them as they set up their suspended beds. When completed they looked like Chinese lanterns lit from the inside, bubbles of light. I was about to call it a night when, to their left, I saw something move. Wondering if it was big horned sheep, I continued recording, hoping to surprise Andy with some footage of truly awesome climbers.

It wasn't sheep. Instead, I saw two men, climbing, the second moving at a furious pace. The first was dressed in typical fashion, khaki shorts, T-shirt, backpack, boots with spikes. The second wore buckskin and a feather, no shirt, no shoes, no ropes. He crawled up the mountain like an arachnid. And he wasn't simply climbing. He was toying with the first man, climbing around him and jumping over him, with amazing speed.

I froze, my breath reduced to tiny, trembling gasps. Around me the forest went quiet, even the frogs stopped their croaking.

"What are you doing, girl?" I whispered. "You're totally alone. If you scream, the fellows won't hear you. Even if they do, it's not like they can help you."

Panic thawed my frozen legs. I ran for the car. On the road on the way down, I took one of the switchbacks so fast I almost became part of the breath-taking scenery. I locked myself in the cabin and didn't come out. Inside, I had running water and some food—three Twix candy bars, a Dr Pepper, and an orange. The next morning, I remembered Andy's pop tarts. They were just outside the door on the backseat of the Land Rover, along with the charger for my phone. The fellows had taken the rest of the food with them. I was supposed to buy supplies for myself in town.

Flattening myself against the cabin wall, I reached to the side and opened the curtain. I tried to force myself to look out the window. "He's just a myth. He's just a myth." I couldn't do it, I couldn't even look out. I thought I'd see the Beast, and if I did, and if he saw me . . .

Two days later the fellows came back. They laughed at me. "You've been hiding in this cabin this whole time?"

"Hey," Andy held up a hand, "give her a break, guys."

He hustled me into the Land Rover, drove into town, and treated me to a fancy vegetarian feast complete with a dessert that included five kinds of chocolate. Later, when the others were asleep, I whispered to him, "Would you sleep next to me. I mean . . . I'm not asking you to . . ."

He lay down beside me. "I get it, J. No one with a metabolism like yours, starves in a cabin for three days, with a full box of frosted strawberry pop tarts eight feet from the door, unless they're scared witless. I'm so sorry. I wanted this to be fun for you."

The drive home to Michigan was blessedly uneventful. Andy wouldn't let the others tease me. I sat in the backseat of the Land Rover and tried to forget about what I'd seen by reading license plates . . . D Y R 3 9 7.

*Hmmm . . . quasars that contain the letters D Y R . . .*

D Y R . . . SPYDER. In my mind, I saw him again . . . crawling up the mountain.

～

We'd been home two days when Andy sought me out.

"So," he paused, looking sick to his stomach, "you know that dude you saw on the mountain?"

A cold wind blew over me. We were inside, in the computer lab. I was in the process of creating an algorithm to run on Michigan's highly parallel computer.

"I got a call from the ranger. I reported your sighting when I checked out. He wants to take a look at your video."

"Why?"

"A man went missing on the mountain over a year ago."

"A year ago?"

Andy shuffled his feet. "There were some unusual circumstances."

He loaded the video onto my computer and sent the email. I couldn't stop shivering. Afterward, he gave me a ride back to my apartment. I locked the door, shut off the A/C, dug out my electric blanket, turned it on high, and tried to sleep. About 10 p.m., I got a call.

I didn't want to answer the phone like I hadn't wanted to look out the window, but maybe, I thought, maybe it's Andy calling to check on me.

I picked up the phone. Unknown caller. I answered it anyway.

"This is Julie."

"Ms. Raichart? My name is Hannah Wilcox. I'm calling you about my husband."

"I'm sorry, I don't know who you are."

"You got video of my husband on the mountain. Please, I need you to help me."

My finger hovered over the red hang-up button. All I had to do was touch it, and I could forget about her, about arachnid-guy, about everything.

"Please. I think you can save him."

"I don't know him, and I don't know you."

"But you saw him. Please. I think if you came back, you'd see him again."

"That doesn't make any sense."

"I know, but he's been missing over a year. Please, you saw him. No one else has seen him. I can't see him."

I shivered out the next words. "If your husband has been missing that long, I'm sorry, but he's probably dead."

"Not according to your camera."

I hung up on her. The next day Andy found me in my carrel in the library. "I'll go with you," he said.

Hannah paid for our airplane tickets. When she picked us up in her Jeep, she was already dressed in climbing gear. Andy changed at the ranger station, where three rangers, all armed, joined our team.

Marcus, the head ranger, pointed to a photo hanging on the station wall. "This was taken at a fundraiser Sean threw for the park about a month before he was lost on the mountain." In the photo were five men. I quickly recognized Marcus. All the men were dressed in tuxes, all had their arms draped around each other's shoulders. Marcus pointed to the man in the middle. "That's Sean Wilcox." He was about thirty-five, short, slender, bangs falling into his laughing eyes, a broad grin on his face. Just from that one picture, I liked him.

"Practical joker?" I asked.

Marcus grinned. "Oh, yeah."

We took two Jeeps back to the place where, a week ago, Andy's Land Rover had been parked.

Marcus passed around canteens. "Better pack in some extra water; it's a scorcher."

"Julie, do you want something to eat before we start out?" Andy asked.

I shook my head no, trying not to shiver. I wasn't cold, I told myself. I wasn't cold.

"Look," he whispered, "I'll be right beside you the whole time. I'm not going anywhere, okay?"

"You're not going to climb?"

"I was, but I think I'll stick with you. I'm sure the four of them can find this guy."

The rangers, Hannah, Andy, and I hiked together to the base of the mountain. There Hannah handed me a pair of high-tech binoculars. Hannah's plan revolved around me being able to, once again, find the two men scaling the peak. It was ludicrous, of course. Why would they be on the mountain again today, exactly where they were a week ago? But . . .

At first, my hands trembled. I was barely able to hold the binoculars. After an hour of fruitless searching, I began to calm down. I had a sandwich and Cheetos, and an Almond Joy.

About five in the afternoon, Marcus, the head ranger, put a gentle hand on Hannah's arm, "Perhaps we should head back," he said, nudging her, like any friend would, to give up, to accept her husband's death.

She turned to me, her voice shaking, "You took that video after dark, right?"

"Yes."

"Well, maybe . . ." She was openly crying now. "We just need to wait . . . to wait a little longer. Please."

I didn't feel sorry for her. I felt respect, overwhelming respect. She'd gotten five people to follow her out into the middle of nowhere to search for a man who was probably dead. Surely, she'd only thought that was him on the video. I had no idea how far it was from here to the point on the mountain where I'd seen them—and there had clearly been two men, not one. The chances of the unknown man I'd recorded being her husband, were so remote, yet, here she was, still hoping. That's when everything changed for me, when the fear briefly faded. She loved him, and a love that rich called to me, compelled me to continue searching. I tried to remember, where had the fellows been, and where exactly had I seen the other two men?

Several hours passed, and Marcus again said we should consider leaving. This time I objected. "No. We're here; we're staying." About seven, I saw movement. The sun was still up, but the side of the mountain was now coming into shadow. It was difficult, but I saw them again—two men.

"There!"

Five pairs of binoculars followed the clues I gave. "About halfway up, find the large outcropping of rock. Go left along a line parallel to the top of that outcropping."

"Sean! Sean!" Hannah shouted. Somehow, he heard her, and turned. She wept. Then the other man, the one crawling like a spider, the Beast, also turned. Through the binoculars, I saw him look straight at me. He took a hand from the side of the mountain, like it was nothing to hang there holding on with only one hand, and pointed at me.

Instantly, the rangers sprang into motion. "Somehow that guy has Sean trapped."

With quick words, "We'll take the eastern service road to the peak, and rappel down," the rangers left. Hannah went with them, over the rangers' objections, but they knew, as I knew, that nothing would stop her. She left Andy and me the keys to her Jeep.

As the shadow of the mountain covered us, cold dripped into my bones.

"Let's go back to Hannah's Jeep," I said.

Andy was watching the progress of the rangers now beginning to rappel. "I can see them."

"Please, Andy, let's go back."

He took a step forward, moving the binoculars left, then right. "I don't understand," he said. "Where's the second man?"

"Andy, let's go."

"He's disappeared."

"Andy, please. Please, Andy. I want to go now."

"Where is he? He was there, and then . . ."

He came upon us like wind rather than flesh. He blew in. He stood over Andy, grinning, while Andy looked through his binoculars. I couldn't move, couldn't speak, couldn't warn him. I was frozen. The Beast moved so swiftly. With two hands, one on the front of Andy's neck, one on the back, he picked up my friend, by the neck, strangling him in mid-air. Andy was dying in front of my eyes.

*Do something!*

I trembled out the words, "You'll . . . never . . . catch me."

The Beast turned, still strangling my frantically twitching friend. I forced my ice-cold fingers to move. I reached for the Jeep keys in my pocket, held them up, and jingled the Beast a challenge. The Beast dropped Andy.

*Oh, please, God. Help me.*

I ran full out through the undergrowth, navigating ruts, hurdling nature's garbage of fallen branches. The Beast ran beside me, un-winded, un-taxed, keeping pace. I threw myself into the Jeep and started her up as the Beast calmly sat down beside me. I could see his teeth, pointed, and growing longer like claws he extended as he prepared for a meal. I put a look of pity on my face. "Not fast enough to hoof it?" I asked.

He grinned, chilling my heart. I gasped as it skipped a beat. He got out; I floored it, and he ran beside the car. My fingers ached from the cold, my hands turning purple as I clutched the steering wheel. With the switchbacks dead ahead and the Beast on the cliff-side of the car, I downshifted and turned. Two wheels off the road, two wheels on. I hoped he'd go over the side, but the Beast jumped like a monkey, up onto the roll bar.

Another switchback. I was going way too fast; the Jeep's center of gravity shifted . . .

I made my decision in an instant. It was a no-brainer. I turned the steering wheel and headed her straight over the side, straight down the mountain, knowing the swerve would knock him off the roll bar and onto the hood. He hit the hood with a thump.

We fell: The Beast, the Jeep, and me.

As he gathered himself to jump, I grabbed my backpack and threw it, high above the Jeep, into his path. Whack! It caught him, mid-jump, in the gut. His feet furiously scrambled, like he was some stupid Wile E. Coyote, but with nothing to push against, he fell with me.

The first time the Jeep hit solid ground I was thrown . . . I hadn't bothered with the seatbelt . . .

~

When I woke, Andy stood beside me, purple bruises ringing his neck. He held up a piece of paper. "Can't talk." Then another. "Push this button for pain medicine."

"Where's the Beast?" I whispered. "Is he dead?"

Andy warily glanced behind him, toward the open door. Through it, I could see the nurses' station. He scribbled and held up the paper. "I don't know."

"Maybe he thought I was dead," I said.

More scribbling. "I called 911. The police called in search and rescue. They found the rangers and Hannah—dead. They also found Sean's body. J, he'd been dead a while. I think we saw a dead man climbing up that mountain."

The creeping cold returned. Andy, seeing me shiver, got a blanket from the closet and covered me.

"I want to go home," I said.

Andy scribbled some more. "You have to stay for a few days."

I couldn't stop the tears. "Andy," I asked, "Will you sleep here?"

He nodded and climbed in beside me.

~

Weeks later, when I could think about it without shivering, I sat down at my computer and sent an email to my undergraduate American Lit prof.

"Have you ever considered that the story might be true? Maybe there really was a waitress and a Circle K and a man with fangs for teeth. Maybe there are Beasts in this world. Maybe most of the time, they stay hidden, hunting only the isolated person, so we never know to look for them. Maybe the reason we tell this tale is to warn each other. There's something out there, something you can't outrun, and it's coming for you."

# UNINTENDED CONSEQUENCES

*Stanley W. McFarland*

"Here, raise your head," he said as he held a bundle of long grass to support my neck.

"We should call . . ."

"Your phone was in the truck."

I looked over at the flaming wreck that was once my F-150.

"You don't know how much freedom your mortality gives you."

I took a few moments to let those words soak in. I'd just seen this . . . person pull me out of a fire that had engulfed my truck. I was almost certainly dead if not for him. I was lying in prairie grass by the side of Highway 2 in northern Montana. He was squatting there and staring at me. I was in surprisingly little pain though barely modest, as much of my clothing had burned away.

He wasn't hurt at all. His clothes were untouched. He didn't even smell like smoke. He looked and seemed the same as he had when I had picked him up hitchhiking outside of Cheyenne.

"You need medical assistance," he said. "You're about to go into shock. Nobody's likely to come down the road this late at night."

"Maybe you could carry me?" I asked.

"The last town was what, ten miles back?" he asked. "I have no idea how far the next one is. I don't think you'd survive that."

"Oh," I said, unable to think of anything else to say.

"You see," he told me, "the problem is the law of unintended consequences. Rescuing you from the fire was instinct. They rarely blame you for that as long as your reaction is benign in nature. Now I have time to make choices, to think things through. That makes everything more complicated."

"Maybe somebody will come by," I said.

"Maybe," he agreed, "but unlikely. I can't base my choices on unfounded hope."

I couldn't think of anything to say, or rather I had too many thoughts to pick one. I wanted to plead with him for my life. I wanted to ask him what kind of person isn't touched by fire. Was he an alien, a superhero, a mutant, a god? Were there more like him hitchhiking the prairies and foothills?

He stood, knuckling his back as he straightened just like any sixtyish human man might. Whatever his powers might be, they didn't include super-dry-cleaning. His jacket and pants were rumpled. He had what looked like a coffee stain on one sleeve. Then again, maybe he did have dry-cleaning power, but using it might lead to his unintended consequences.

"No," he said, as if I'd asked him a question, and I wondered if he'd read my mind. "No lights that I can see, no houses. Left alone, you'll be dead in a couple hours or less."

"Bad luck," I said, thinking it was an incredibly stupid thing to say, but the only thing that would come out.

"Yeah," he agreed.

"So . . . ," I asked, "you can heal me?"

"Yup."

"But you're afraid to?"

He dropped back down to sit on the verge, hugging his knees in front of him. "I'm not afraid, exactly. It's not like anyone will do anything to me if I do."

"Well, I'm for it," I said.

He laughed. "Good to know."

"Maybe it would help if we talked it out."

He reached into his pocket and pulled out a pack of gum. "You want a piece?" he asked. "The chewing might help you stay with it."

I nodded my head weakly, and he unwrapped a piece of perfectly normal Wrigley's—also undamaged by the fire—and put it in my mouth for me. I wondered why he didn't just hand it to me; then realized that one of my hands was clenched like a claw, while the other was red and swollen. I could only feel the swollen one, which throbbed horribly.

"The thing is," he said, "that even talking it out is a choice that leads to unintended consequences." I must have grimaced, because he paused and looked at me.

"A lotta pain?" he asked.

"Yeah," I said.

"I can do something about that." He laid a finger on my forehead. It reminded me of the movie ET, only his finger didn't glow or anything; the pain just stopped.

"Better?" he asked.

"Thanks."

"It'll come back," he warned me. "Just let me know."

"So stopping pain doesn't have unintended consequences?"

"I suppose it does," he said, "but they're rarely worse than letting somebody suffer."

"Oh," I said, stupidly.

"You see," he told me, "the way you're wired, the pain is supposed to tell you that you've got a problem and where it is. You're not likely to forget that even when the pain stops, so it's not like I'm stopping your body from doing its job."

"Makes sense," I replied. "What about keeping me from going into shock?"

"That's more complicated. Giving you gum, making you comfortable, and elevating your head are all things that any of your people might do, but beyond that . . ." He shook his head.

"I see," I said, and contemplated the choice between dying now versus surviving horribly disfigured and probably one-armed. How much of what I did with my life would have to change?

"What if I promised never to tell?" I asked.

He smiled and shook his head. "I'll never understand you people and your promises. You know that they're worse than useless, don't you? A bad person's not going to change his behavior just because he makes a promise; a good person won't either, but the weight of that promise is going to bog him down."

"I don't understand."

"A good person," he explained, "is going to break his promise if he has a good reason to do it, but he'll carry a load of guilt for it. If he's forced to do it enough times, the load of guilt will get so heavy that he'll either get depressed . . ."

"Or sear his conscience?"

"Exactly," he said. "You see, you people know how destructive your promises are, but you still make them. Please don't make me any promises. That's one consequence I want nothing to do with."

Though it was a warm night, my teeth started chattering. I spit out my gum, so I didn't swallow it.

"Forgive me," he said. "I wasn't thinking." He took off his jacket and laid it over me, tucking it under my arms."

"Better?" he asked.

"A little," I manage to say.

"It's going to have to do," he said. "There's nothing left in the truck."

"I'm going into shock, aren't I?"

"'fraid so."

"So, what have you decided to do?"

"Ease your pain," he said, and he reached his finger over to touch my forehead.

~

I woke up in a hospital bed. A deputy sheriff was staring down at me.

"There you are," he said, smiling.

"Huh?" was all I could answer.

"It's the drugs," said the deputy. "You'll be a little stupid the next few days, but I gotta tell you, you are the damned luckiest son-of-a-bitch I ever did see!"

"Wha'?"

"You'll have a few scars to remember it, but you're gonna be fine."

"Oh."

"But I oughta cite you," said the deputy.

"Wha'?"

"We got a seatbelt law in Montana. No way you got out in time if you was buckled."

I knew I'd buckled my seatbelt, but I wasn't going to argue.

"One thing I can't figure," said the deputy.

"Huh?"

"Your jacket. How'd your jacket come out of it like that? It ain't even scorched."

I looked where he was pointing and saw my rescuer's jacket hanging from the back of a chair.

"Oh, I helped myself to a stick of gum," said the deputy. "I hope you don't mind."

"No consequence," I mumbled.

# HELL OF A DEAL

*DT Krippene*

For an upscale real estate advert, the slogan "Hell of a Deal" should not appear as a headliner, Frank thought. "The Wall Street Journal should know better," he muttered. He carefully folded the Mansion supplement of the Friday paper in triplicate and dropped it in his mahogany waste bin.

All he wanted was a good place to semi-retire. Didn't have to be a big place, just have enough acreage to pad himself from other humans, but large enough for a custom library to house his book collection. And trees—had to have trees. His penthouse view of Central Park was the only thing he liked about the damned city.

Charlotte Baskins, his dealer in antique collectibles, strolled into his office with an artist's sketch of his new gallery advert and placed it on the desk. "I know what you're going to say. The name is not prominent enough."

He held the sketch to the light to study the gallery name, "Hawthorne's—Purveyor of Antique Books and Artifacts of Writing History."

"Maybe if you shorten the gallery's name, it might fit the template," she added. "How about 'Hawthorne's'? You're practically a common brand name, like Lloyd's."

"Just because I'm turning the day-to-day business over to Ted, doesn't mean I'm going to change anything."

Charlotte hiked up the hem of her body-hugging skirt and sat on the corner of his desk, her ebony skin lustrous against the cherry-red dress.

Frank squinted over the rim of his reading glasses. "Let me guess, your appointment this evening is with a Russian."

"Qatar," she smiled. "Member of the royal family. He's interested in the Gutenberg Bible we acquired last month. I want to be sure we turn that interest into a sale."

Frank scowled at her reference to an extremely rare, nearly complete volume of a first edition printed Bible. "What's he going to do, burn it?"

"He hasn't balked yet at our thirty-five million dollar asking price."

"And you think I shouldn't care," Frank fired back.

Charlotte rolled her eyes. "You heading out of town this weekend to look for that perfect retirement place?"

Frank removed his reading glasses to polish them. "Everything is either too gaudy or too close to neighbors."

Charlotte extracted a gold lipstick tube from a Lana Marks purse. "I suppose you've completely given up on a custom build."

Frank remembered the vacation place he built on Lake Winnipesaukee, where the slipshod contractor used subpar materials, yet continued squeezing him for cost overruns. Sold at a loss two years later; *never again,* he thought.

Charlotte smacked her lips, snapped a compact mirror shut, and slid off the desk. "Gotta go. I'll tell Fitz to lock up and brief the night guards."

"If you're going to sell the Gutenberg to a heathen, nothing less than asking price," he said.

Certain she didn't wear panties by the jiggle of her sashay from his office, he might once have been tempted to secure Charlotte's future with a dalliance, not that she needed a career boost at the gallery. She had a way of finding discreet collectors who didn't ask questions.

Unmarried at fifty-six, he'd tinkered with lovers of both genders, but grew tired of the rollercoaster emotional displays and always having to compromise. *No, he thought, I'm in love with my work of collecting relics of humanity's written word, my books, and my solitude.*

Frank methodically tucked his glasses in a leather case and locked the activity log of private collectors in his safe. He passed one of several display rooms on the way to his private garage when he heard a noise in one of them.

He found a man studying a third-millennium B.C.E. cuneiform clay tablet in a Plexiglas case. Entering the private section of the gallery was by invitation only, through a locked door.

"Excuse me," Frank said. "It's after closing."

A man with coifed black hair turned around. "I'm sorry; must have lost track of the hour."

With a prominent nose of someone with deep Mediterranean roots, his voice had the timbre of a well-educated person. Frank's interest piqued at the man's stylish, upscale attire, pegging him as well off.

Frank stuck out his hand. "Frank Hawthorne."

"Short for Franklin." The man smiled. "Of the Hampton Hawthornes, if I'm not mistaken."

Frank pinched his lips without answering. Last thing he wanted was to acknowledge the murder-suicide of his parents, leaving him with no relatives and a mansion full of bad memories. Forty-six years since and people still dragged it up.

"Whitaker Leffingfield," he said, shaking Frank's hand. "How fortunate to stumble on the purveyor himself."

"Were you referred to us, Mr. Leffingfield?"

"I was perusing your amazing rare book gallery and just happened to wander in here."

The hairs on Frank's neck bristled. "Which—is a referral-only section." *With a large sign stating, "'Employees Only." Where are Fitz and his security Neanderthals?*

"Oh dear, I am frightfully sorry if trespassing. The door was open, and curiosity drew me inside for a look-see."

*Or to case the joint.* "As you can see, we don't keep much here, only lesser-valued items that have yet to sell. Aside from our collection of rare books, our antiquity deals are handled privately."

"Lesser value?" A look of amused shock creased Leffingfield's face. "My dear man, this Sumerian cuneiform tablet is priceless."

Obviously, the man didn't know much about it. Cuneiform tablets from the Mesopotamian age were not that rare and available for low-to mid-four figures. The real money was in ancient stone bas-reliefs that came with them. This tablet came with an estate sale containing an exquisite 5,800-year-old early relief of Anu, the winged supreme god of Mesopotamia, and other artifacts worth millions.

Last offer for the tablet he kept for display purposes was only $1,600, even though it was valued at twice that. "Well sir, there is a price for it, and it's available for forty-eight hundred."

"Whitaker, please," he said. "Has it been translated?"

"It's in the file," Frank lied. Despite efforts by the Cuneiform Digital Library Initiative, nobody seemed to know anything about the tablet, which smelled of counterfeit and might explain why no serious collector wanted it.

Leffingfield pointed to the fourth line of cuneiform characters. "It mentions the Sumerian deity, Nergal, god of darkness and death. Very few tablets mention him."

Frank wondered if Leffingfield made it up, maybe as a dodge to cover his true intent. Anything considered unusually rare would surely be recognized in the antiquities business. Still, unless Leffingfield had prior knowledge, ability to read cuneiform characters was a rarity in itself.

Frank offered Charlotte's business card and looked at his watch. "Mr. Leffingfield—Whitaker. I'll be happy to schedule an appointment with one of our agents, that is, if you're interested in the piece. I think we have a little wiggle room on the price." *It's a hell of a deal.* "Do you have a card?"

"Oh goodness, Franklin, I'm not much for passing out paper badges that get tossed in the trash after cleaning one's desk. I'm staying at the Mandarin Oriental. I'll be there until Thursday."

Slightly irked at the continued use of his formal first name, Frank ushered Leffingfield out through the book section to the front door. He locked the door and mused for a moment. Had to admit, if the man is staying at the Mandarin, he's not cheap. *And if anyone can squeeze an extra two-grand on the sale, it's Charlotte.*

Frank left a voice message for Charlotte and headed to the garage, thinking somebody's ass in security was going to be in his briefcase by noon tomorrow.

~

Frank nearly gagged on his 25-year-old Cragganmore single malt when a message popped up on his laptop. It was from Whitaker Leffingfield. *How did he get my email address?*

> *My dear Franklin:*
>
> *Please forgive my intrusion, but I had the most delightful conversation with Ms. Charlotte Baskins, an enchanting lady whose ancestor could be the mysterious Queen Nefertiti.*

Frank blinked in confusion, wondering how Charlotte had time to meet with Leffingfield on the eve of a big sale.

> *In our discussion of the Sumerian tablet, she mentioned in passing your interest in finding a quiet country abode. I just happen to know of an estate that will soon be up for sale. The owner recently passed away and had no known relatives. I have done business with the agent in the past, and he graciously gave me the link to the draft listing, as it has yet to be posted on the real estate network. It is not the usual McMansion, as cynics oft quote, but a converted former eighteenth-century rectory of a religious cloister on 230 acres of natural woods.*

*What makes the house unique is one-quarter of its square footage comprises a two-story library of exquisite architectural design. Of course, I thought of you immediately.*

*I understand the agent is motivated to sell quickly, as the property is less contemporary than most customers seek, and might be had for less than market value, especially if sold before investing in expensive adverts and time intensive showings. The website access password is "Enliltened."*

*Be a shame to see such a jewel razed for its land value only. I would buy it myself, but extensive traveling is not conducive to setting roots in a remote setting of such natural loveliness.*

*Well, it is off to Asia for me. Forgive me if I have intruded upon your privacy, but I felt this might be an opportunity for you to investigate.*

*Best regards,*
*Whitaker Leffingfield*

Frank closed the laptop and downed his scotch. "Surprised he didn't say it's a hell of a deal."

ᔕ

Frank marched into Téodoro "Ted" Osorio's office with murder on his mind. "Where is Ms. Baskins?"

Ted looked up from his antique desk of ancient Spanish wood from the forests of Sagua La Grande. "She's off for a few days, said something about a spa," he said warily without a hint of an accent. He beamed a toothy smile to disarm Frank. "By the way, she sold the Gutenberg for thirty-eight mil."

Frank's anger dissipated with the news. "Well then, I guess it can wait."

Settled in his office, Frank opened his laptop. "That's my girl," he chuckled.

The display still had the email chain from last night's session. He gave it a moment's thought and selected the real estate link Leffingfield had given him. On the market for $3.4 million somewhere in Pennsylvania, he typed 'Enlightened' for the password. Nothing happened. He checked the email again, noted the misspelled 'Enliltened', and gave it a shot. The site took him right to the photo gallery.

"Mother of God," he uttered when the first picture popped up. Wasn't sure what he expected, but it wasn't the stone architecture of the vergeboard-gabled, two-story structure or witch hat turret that stilled his breath. He zoomed-in on the columned stone archway, where two bearded, human-headed winged lions known as Lamassu from ancient Assyria bookended immense medieval-like, dark wood double front doors. *What is this, a Babylonian temple disguised as a Gothic Revival?*

About to hit delete, his eye caught a particular thumbnail shot of the two-story private library. The description claimed the walls and bookshelves of the open two-level, 1,600-square-foot space had been constructed of old-growth Italian walnut. A wrought-iron staircase spiraled from the lower level to an upper mezzanine, each floor furnished with reading tables and timeworn-buffed, cushiony leather chairs. Books filled the custom built-in cases spanning the walls of both levels.

He scanned the list of assets in the deal. *Oh, my Lord.* The price was inclusive of all seen. He tried expanding the picture to read some of the book titles, but poor resolution blurred the image. With a quick scribble of the address and agent's name, he tapped the screen closed and dialed the number listed.

~

Keys jangled in the palsied, liver-spotted hands of the real estate agent fumbling to find the right one. The man had to be a hundred years old or close to it, Frank thought with a headshake. He took the opportunity to examine the quality of the home's stonework. Several of the stones had the powdery signs of weathered efflorescence, expected for a place originally constructed in 1792, but the human-headed Lamassu sculptures flanking the front door looked practically new.

"How long have these been here?"

"They're nearly as old as the house," the agent replied in a breathy, graveled voice of someone near death. He pushed open one of the eight-foot, six-inch-thick oak doors. "Here we go."

Frank tested the swing of the door while the agent flipped switches. For the ponderous thing it was, it moved as effortlessly as a screen door.

Light flooded the entrance foyer of a great stair hall of marble flooring and dark wood paneling. Frank marveled with admiration at an exquisite chandelier a dozen feet above his head, illuminating a pair of opposing, geometric, quarter-turn stairs with filigree, wrought-iron balusters that met at the second story landing.

"This was a religious cloister?" Frank asked.

The agent hobbled through Romanesque columns to an open great room toward the back. "Extensive changes have been made over the years."

Frank whistled. "No kidding." He ambled into the great room and perused expensive European couches, chairs, and tables. "Is—all this included in the sale price?"

"Everything you see," the old man rasped as he flung curtains open.

Frank ran a finger along a dust-free table he recognized as made by Francesco Molon. *Damn, this furniture alone is worth a fortune.* He went to the bay windows extending the length of the great room and stared at seven statues of women in hooded robes, circumscribing a fountain inside a manicured garden at the edge of an old growth forest.

"Yet another aficionado of post-Renaissance crap," Frank muttered aloud.

The agent swiped a lock of wispy white hair from his face. "Memorials of the last seven sisters who lived here, actually. They died in a terrible fire, and the original owner who bought it from the cloister in 1823 had them commissioned in memoriam."

Must have been a fire somewhere else if the house hadn't been rebuilt, Frank thought to himself. Though discolored from bird droppings, the century-and-a-half-old statues lacked signs of weathering. Frank let it go, convinced the old man likely had dementia.

"The grounds and house are still maintained by a contract service," the agent added. "You have an option to renew the contract, something you should seriously consider if living alone."

Frank squinted with suspicion. *Did Leffingfield share that little ditty?* "Are there conditions on the sale?"

"Yes. The property is not to be sub-divided or carved up in any way. The estate wishes to find the *right* buyer, one who will appreciate its uniqueness."

"Sounds a trifle—discriminatory."

"Which is why the estate is not publicly listed." The old codger looked at Frank with rheumy eyes. "I'm surprised you weren't informed before coming. It was assumed someone of your familiarity with the gray areas of legality wouldn't question it."

Frank's neck hairs bristled at his blatant insinuation. "What is that supposed to mean?"

"Would you like to see the library?" the agent asked instead.

Frank debated leaving immediately but decided to follow the agent down a long hallway lined with closed, dark wood doors hung with wrought-iron hinges impressionistic of an old castle.

"Guest bedrooms," the old man said as if reading Frank's mind. He shook out the right key on the first try. "The master suites are on the second level, south wing."

Frank wondered if he meant to say "suites" in plural as they approached another set of arched double doors similar in design to the front entrance. His jaw dropped in amazement when he stepped inside the library. Fairy-like dust particles danced in beaming daylight from the domed, second-story, stained-glass-ceiling window. The listing photo didn't do justice to the real thing. It was like a smaller version of the Linderman Library at Lehigh University.

He went to the bookshelf and scanned the titles of reference books and world literature. He froze with excitement when his eyes fell on a brownish-red book cover typical of 16th-century calf hide. His breath hitched upon reading the title, *Romanarum Historiarum–Ex Bibliotheca Regia*, by Appian of Alexandria [c95 – c165]. He carefully opened the cover to find a publishing mark dated 1551, which he recognized as an authentic Charles Estienne device. Conscious of handling it without gloves, Frank gently re-shelved it, and circled the stacks with growing excitement, settling his sights on the mezzanine. He hopped every other riser of the spiral staircase like an impatient child. Glass cases, which he guessed to be hermetically sealed, immediately drew his attention. His hands shook to discover papyrus and parchments going back thousands of years.

"My dear Lord," he murmured to himself. Did the estate lawyers even know what this library held?

"Would you like to inspect the other rooms?" the agent asked from the lower floor.

"No need," Frank answered, trying to contain himself. "I'll accept the seller's offer."

ॱ

Hawthorne's exclusive lawyer since the day a shingle went up above the gallery door, Brendan Shaw, attempted one last plea. "Frank, this place has more conditions than a dockworkers union."

"Do any of the conditions address the contents of the house specifically? I mean, did you see the listing pictures?"

"Didn't get a chance, the site was taken down when you signed the Letter of Intent." Shaw sat back in his chair. "It's this *trust*, whatever it is, that I don't like. A city-block apartment has fewer backdoors. We can't find who or what really manages it."

"If I buy it, do I own it lock, stock, and barrel, or not?" Frank asked insistently.

"The conditions are specific not to make exterior changes to the house and not sell any part of the property, defined as the land. If you want to sell the place as a whole, it must go back to the trust at the price paid plus annual interest rate of eight-percent after a minimum ownership time of five years. Interior contents of the house are not mentioned."

"Which means I can redecorate the inside any way I desire, sell the old furniture—get rid of a few garden ornaments . . ."

"Nothing in the deal that prohibits it," Shaw answered. "You sure the place isn't haunted?"

"We deal in antiquities and rare books, Brendan." Frank laughed. "Hell, half the stuff we handle is loaded with curses and the like. If there were ghosts, I'd have seen them by now. What I do believe in is an ironclad contract of sale, which gives me indisputable ownership of the contents inside that house. Unless you have any tangible concerns, I want this property."

∾

Frank closed his eyes and breathed in the distinctive aroma of old book leather and polished wood. Still amazed how quickly his lawyer consummated the deal, Frank patted the briefcase containing a ring of keys and his copy of the deed. His things wouldn't arrive for several days, but he wanted to immediately begin the process of sorting through his windfall housed in the library.

He fitted cotton museum gloves on his hands and ambled along the lower level stacks. *Where to begin.* He pulled out a first edition of *Bleak House* by Charles Dickens.

"Excellent condition—better than my copy," he whispered to the air. "I'm going to make a fortune."

A distant clank of pots and pans drew his attention. *Must be the cleaning service still on contract.* He pulled off the gloves, grabbed his briefcase and made toward the kitchen. A woman dressed in a pewter-gray nun's habit and head covering tended the stove.

Frank set his briefcase on the counter. "Excuse me."

A gauzy shroud concealed her face. Frank zoomed in on the burn-scarred hand clutching a metal spoon. He opened his mouth to inquire as to who she was when the sound of a door slam echoed from the front of the house.

He flashed an insincere smile. "Be right back."

A rolling suitcase and old-fashioned steamer trunk sat by the front door. "Hello," Frank shouted.

He spotted a man with charcoal slacks and cinnamon waistcoat inside the great room, staring out the bay windows that overlooked the garden and statues. Frank approached him and froze when Whitaker Leffingfield turned around.

"My dear Franklin," Leffingfield smiled. "Can't tell you how thrilled I am to see you've bought the place."

Out of habit, Frank's evaluative fashion eye scanned Leffingfield's elegant button-down cream shirt, flint-gray merino wool vest, and small-dotted gunmetal silk tie with matching pocket-handkerchief, practically smelling the polish of his laced Italian brogues. He accepted Leffingfield's hand with caution. "Thank you?"

Leffingfield returned to pondering the statues in the garden. "You've likely had intentions of having those removed."

"It crossed my mind. I'm not overly fond of cheap lawn statuary . . ." *Wait a minute.* Two of the statues were missing. "It would appear as if someone has beaten me to it."

"Little known lost fact, the sisters who cloistered here were not your garden variety devotees. It was rumored at the time that their piety was in pretense of a real devotion to the dark forces." Leffingfield turned to Frank with a chuckle. "Bet you couldn't wait to spend time in the library. That collection took centuries to amass."

Frank decided it was time to cut it off. "Is there—something I can do for you Mr. Leffingfield?"

"Please, address me as Whitaker, now that we're associates of a sort. I canceled my Asia trip, and decided a few days at home might do me some good—give us time to get to know each other."

Frank's belly squeezed. "Home? I'm sorry—Whitaker, I don't recall the purchase including a housemate. Nothing personal, but I'm a very private person and not interested in *getting to know you*."

"Come, have a seat. Best we get rules settled as it relates to the trust."

"I don't wish to sit." Then it dawned on Frank in a flash. "Are you—a representative of the trust that sold the place to me?"

"My dear fellow, I *am* the trust."

*I should've listened to Brendan.* "Look, whatever it is you're referring to, I purchased this property free and clear, and agreed if I wished to sell the place after five years, I must sell it back to—you, I guess. Aside from that, if you have issues with a bona fide contract of sale, you'll have to take it up with my lawyer."

Leffingfield grinned. "You mean the contract in that briefcase?"

Frank's skin electrified with pins and needles to discover his briefcase was not on the kitchen counter where he left it, but on an end table near his hand. He opened the case, withdrew the document, and went slack-jawed when typewritten legalese metamorphosed to cuneiform characters.

"It's the first true written language of humanity," Leffingfield said. "Assyrian—dates back to . . ."

"I know what it is," Frank said with a titter in his voice. "This isn't the real estate contract I signed."

Leffingfield pinched the last page between thumb and forefinger to reveal the signature. "It's right there, Franklin. Surely you remember signing it."

"What are you, some sort of a magician? Bravo. Just for the record, my lawyer has a copy in his office, along with a signature and stamp of the notary public who witnessed it. Now, you've had your fun, and I must ask you to leave."

Leffingfield gently shook his head. "I was truly hoping for a more civilized introduction."

Leffingfield's eyes transformed to blazing orbs of purple. An invisible force gripped Frank's body, dragged him backward, and planted him in a plush leather chair. Choking in shock, Frank struggled but found himself pinned. Leffingfield translocated a matching chair with a waggle of his finger, unbuttoned his waistcoat, and sat opposite.

"I should have known," Leffingfield sighed. "All your predecessors have reacted as you did. Thought perhaps as fellow devotees of humanities linguistic history, we might have connected. The error is mine."

Caught in waves of anger and fear, Frank struggled to catch his breath, unable to look away from Leffingfield's fiery purple eyes. "Who are you supposed to be? Satan?"

Leffingfield grimaced as he sucked in a breath, his orbs of purple fire intensifying. A halo of darkness engulfed the room, and his voice thundered like that of an angry demon on a public-address system. "I am not that *thing*," he roared.

The click of hard nails against marble sprinted toward them from the direction of the front door. Frank's eyes goggled when a bearded, human-headed lion entered the circle of darkness with eyeballs of glowing amaranthine. Baring spiked teeth, it pressed within inches of Frank's face.

Leffingfield held up a hand to halt the lion's advance. "Easy, La'am," he said in a normal voice.

The lion-man sat on its haunches alongside Leffingfield, still thrumming the air with a throaty *gnarr*.

"Leave it to the cursed Zoroaster cult to plant that seed, as if I would allow myself to be villainized as a beast with horns and pitchfork." Leffingfield hand-slicked mussed hair to compose himself. "Very rude of me, Franklin, I humbly apologize. Father always said my temper is the reason behind my fall from grace."

Frank's mouth dried up. *Father—fall from grace . . .*

The silver of Leffingfield's irises returned, though his eyeballs still radiated a violet tinge. He patted Frank's hand and smiled at the Lamassu. "My manners. This is my loyal companion and protector, La'am."

"Where's—the other one?" Frank squeaked.

"La'am is a—how shall I describe it—an embodiment of one inside the manifestation of two." The Lamassu lowered its head with a high-pitched whine. "He was once one of us until father severed his ability to speak and cast him out with an exact clone to guard temples like a dog. When father grew tired of him, of course, I took in both of them." Leffingfield stroked the lion's hair. "You've no doubt wondered why I don't have a security system in place. Who needs one when my two La'ams are around?"

The room's dark halo disappeared with a casual flick of his finger. "Now, if I release you, will you behave?"

Frank glanced at the Lamassu's sinister glower and nodded with frightened enthusiasm.

"Allow me to clarify something. I am not . . ." Leffingfield cleared his throat as if unable to utter the word. ". . . that devil thing, or any rendition of a myth perpetuated by desert dwellers through time. I understand why as a follower of the Nazarene, you would immediately think you signed your *soul* to me."

"Then who are . . ." Staring at the Lamassu, Frank went into panic overload. An ancient Babylonian deity—protector—Leffingfield's interest in the cuneiform tablet in the display room—or rather, what inscribed it. "You're—*Nergal?*"

Frank's bladder nearly released when Leffingfield inhaled sharply and the room's edges blackened. The darkness quickly dissipated when Leffingfield slowly exhaled. "I prefer the name Father gave me before he exiled me and rescinded my position at his side."

Frank's thoughts scrambled through chaotic memories of Mesopotamian mythology. "The supreme god of light—was Anu, right? And Nergal—given the power of destruction, fires of hell—wait—Nergal was third-generation—progeny of" . . ."

Then it dawned on him. *That misspelled password, Enliltened.* "The son of Anu—Enlil."

"Excellent deduction." Leffingfield beamed. "Or I was Enlil until I angered my father, a story I will share with you in its entirety someday when you have had time to adjust to our new relationship. You think *I* have a temper. When you humans decided to abandon the light, he *bestowed* upon me the power of death, destruction, and everlasting darkness with instructions to wreak havoc among the masses of humanity in retribution."

Frank turned to the shuffling of the kitchen woman bearing a silver teapot and coffee urn on a gold-plated tray. As she poured a cup, Frank's skin crawled when the veil slipped, revealing a burn-disfigured face and bulbous milky eyeballs.

"Thank you, Abigail." Leffingfield took a sip. "Ah, marvelous, Pu-erh blended with handpicked Taiwanese white tea." Abigail clasped her scarred hands and waited patiently. "You drink Ospina Columbian, correct?" Leffingfield asked. "Had it specially ordered for you."

Frank shook his head, certain he didn't want anything touched by those hands.

Leffingfield waved the woman away. "As I was saying, it wasn't long before I realized how good I was at manipulating the worst of humanity, *buuutt,* leave it to eons of egocentric human misinterpretation through a slave baby to rewrite our legacy." Leffingfield looked past Frank. His brow darkened. "Should have drowned that misguided malcontent when I had a chance before he went off and rewrote the covenant."

Leffingfield quipped in a mocking child's voice. "Thou shalt not covet thy neighbor's wife." He sniffed. "What a kill-joy."

Leffingfield set his cup down. "But enough of the sordid past. We have much in common, you and I."

"How so?" Frank managed to squeak.

"We are—both the result of abusive, narcissistic fathers who spurned us. We walk in the shadows to accomplish the things we desire, care little for others, and prefer privacy in the manner in which we exist. You have an affinity for the relics of civilization lost, and I play a major role in *guiding* those civilizations to—become lost."

Somewhere in his fast-fading hold on reality, Frank desperately hoped it was all just a technically well-orchestrated prank by someone with an ax to grind, but he decided to embrace the latter option of a boat charter's trope, fish or cut bait.

"Mr. Leffingfield, Whitaker, with all respect, I wish to be very honest with you. Though I initially considered the residence as a place to retire, I confess I was motivated primarily to profit from the contents of the library. I now know that was foolish of me and regret those intentions. You can keep the money I paid for the place. I'll give the place back to you for a dollar to make it legal if we can go our separate ways." In the fright-inveigled ruins of Frank's mental state, he resisted the urge to say it was a *hell of a deal.*

Leffingfield roared with laughter. The Lamassu sneeringly hissed like the dog from Hanna-Barbera's 1970 cartoon series, *Dastardly and Muttley.* "What is it with you modern spiritual types," Leffingfield chuckled. "Always embracing true confessions as a way out, like it had anything to do with—anything."

"I'll sweeten the deal if you like," Frank said with a jitter in his voice.

"Franklin, Franklin, Franklin, such a doomsdayer. Had this very same conversation with your predecessor, but he came around eventually, like all my associates before you. I'm sure you've heard of him. Threw him a few juicy tidbits about some of my escapades, and he became the world's bestselling author of horror novels."

Leffingfield stroked the Lamassu when it let loose a mournful cry. "Yes, I know you miss him, La'am. He was a jewel, a mind frame to rival my own, and probably scaring the bejesus out of those who made it to the next dimension."

Frank pressed against the chair back with a surge of fear when Leffingfield levitated the cuneiform document in midair. "Now, about the rules. Let us review a few things that don't translate well in the English language—or any modern language for that matter."

Leffingfield's form transmuted to the elderly real estate agent. "As my associate, you are charged with the care of this home and property. You may decorate to your heart's content, but no book or artifact is to be sold, given away, or any variation thereof. Oh, and don't move the statuary of the sisters in the garden. They are the contracted workers who keep the place neat as a pin."

His body transformed into a living effigy of Nergal with a flowing, curly beard flecked with gold. "Stay out of my affairs, and speak to no one about who I am. Trust me, I will know if you do. I travel extensively, so you'll likely not see much of me. Times I do come home, we can open a vintage bottle or two from the cellar, share in Cornelia's amazing culinary skill—oh, she's the one with a hex sign on her left hand. I will introduce you to the sisters later. They'll be attending to your needs while I'm gone."

Frank pulled on what tiny shred of fortitude remained. "And if I decline your—generous offer—you'll what—turn me to a stone slave—send me to burn in hell?"

Gorge burbled up Frank's esophagus when Nergal morphed into Frank's dead mother. She wore the same dress when he discovered her body that terrifying day after school, a half-inch bloody hole above her left eye, the gore of the exit wound from the back of her head dripping on her shoulder. "Oh, Franklin, leave it to the macabre human imagination to conjure the excruciating pain of everlasting fire and brimstone, but I blame the current dogma, where you're taught to pray, bully, or buy your way into paradise with good deeds. Such silly creatures, as if floating in the clouds with wings had any semblance of reality. Talk about mythology."

The next visage morphed to Frank's dead father, the left side of his face a ragged bloody mess from inaccurately shooting himself in the head after killing Frank's mother. "You see, Franklin, there is only one aspect of importance in the universe. 'In the beginning, there was darkness.' Recognize it? It's been plagiarized so many times, I've lost count, but the essence of it is valid."

Frank squinted when the body transformed to a blinding light in the form of a winged Assyrian god. "In between the realm of my father, and mine is that most unique of all gifts— sentience and free will. But after ancient humans scoffed at the gift given them, my father decided he was done with it all, and sentenced humanity with a stain of darkness."

The light went out when the old agent reappeared. "Think of it as when you're born, you already have a stamped ticket to eternal darkness when you die. Only the few and special get a reprieve and move to the next plane of existence."

Frank sighed in relief when Leffingfield reverted to his normal form. "As young people are fond of saying, 'It really sucks,' but there you have it." He reached over and pushed a perspiration moistened lock of hair from Frank's face. "I know what you're thinking. If you're already condemned to darkness, what's in it for me?" The room dissolved to where only Frank and Leffingfield were visible. "Perhaps a glimpse of what darkness really is when your consciousness leaves its corporeal form."

Everything went pitch black.

Blind in a total cave-like darkness, Frank tried to speak, but no sound came out. An attempt to wave his arm came up empty, for he had no limbs, or body for that matter. No sensations of hot or cold. Where he had sat in a chair bathed in fear sweat, no smell either. Nothing—except his thoughts, which scrambled for any flicker of stimulus.

*Okay, I get it,* hoping his thought was heard by Leffingfield, *point made.* No answer. *Fine, I can deal with it. I'm an educated fellow. It'll be like Stephen Hawking, trapped by a disease in the company of his own thoughts. Much more palatable than burning forever after.*

Moments turned to minutes, which turned to hours, and led to days, weeks, months; it was impossible to know. In a void of complete senselessness, Frank's consciousness slowly unraveled. His mind began to betray him and refused to recall pleasurable things remembered or imagined. The darkness enticed instead; repeated loops of his past, the bad parts, the horrifying scene of discovering his parents' violent end, the lovers he jilted, the people he screwed in business dealings— the regrets of a life wasted on self-indulgence. He wanted to weep in remorse but had no physical means to shed tears. Time had no meaning or end. At some point in the unrelenting void, he wished for deliverance from his sensory dispossessed consciousness by praying for the death of it, over, and over, and over again.

∾

In a blinding flash, Frank awakened in the chair. After endless deprivation, the flood of instantaneous sensation overwhelmed his body. Frank leaned over the chair to vomit into a waste bin conveniently placed there. Tears spilled from his face. Mewling in anguish from the ordeal, he dry heaved until nothing was left but viscous strings of mucus dangling from his lips.

When the shock of it lessened, and his mind and body reached equilibrium, Frank leaned back in the chair to regain a semblance of normal breathing, his shirt soaked in sweat. He drank in the feel of his butt in a chair with the scent of good leather, the taste of bile coating his tongue, the glory of sunlight streaming through the windows, and the sound of the Lamassu nearby, scratching an itch in boredom. A chill swelled on his crotch, and he realized he'd pissed his pants.

His tormenter sat across from him as if the centuries of time lost in the darkness had been restored. Frank swallowed to moisten his throat. "How long did you leave me there?"

Leffingfield looked at his Patek Phillipe watch and gave it a shake. "Little over two minutes." He pushed the fouled waste bin toward the Lamassu with his toe. "Be a good lad, would you." La'am rumbled with a gripe, clenched the bin with his teeth and took it away.

"Felt longer, though, didn't it," Leffingfield said. "Imagine a true forever without the relief of unconscious bliss, never able to sleep, your mind trapped in a place where—what did your predecessor say when he first experienced it—'having to read the same crappy novel that lacked any reference of the five senses'—for an eternity."

"If I agree to be your associate, you're offering to prevent my consciousness from ever going there again?"

"Ah, now you've grasped the big picture," Leffingfield smiled. "Here's the deal. As I've said, most people never live up to my father's ideals required to move to the next dimension. However, dear old Dad gave me carte blanche in the realm of darkness he so lovingly bequeathed me, to include a 'get-out-of-jail' right of refusal of any consciousness I feel doesn't belong there." He adjusted his tie. "Actually, I think Mother made him do that when he booted me out of the light. I don't do it very often, practically never when I think about it, but I do make exceptions for those I grow fond of."

"Like me?"

"Exactly, oh and certain despots who embrace the sort of chaos I sow—like that twentieth-century German fellow who waged war on the world. Did you know his lovely wife did the deed by killing him in that bunker before she turned the gun on herself? Historical revisionism, it is a beautiful thing when woven correctly."

Leffingfield erupted into a fit of sniffing chuckles. "I can still feel my father's ire when I kicked that blighted soul to the light." He quickly recovered himself. "Anyway, yes, follow the rules, be here on my infrequent trips home—I really hate coming home to an empty house—and when your time comes, and I do hope you live a long and fruitful life, it's so hard to find a compatible spirit these days—I will send you to the next plane of existence, dimension, universe, whatever. Oh, don't be stupid and kill yourself in hopes it might help your cause. There is an exclusionary clause with such things. Being the *enlightened* spirit of the family, pun very much intended, Father is a little closed-minded when it comes to willfully wasting the gift of sentience."

Frank nodded in acquiescence, his heart heavy with anguish and defeat.

Leffingfield's manner softened. "Don't be so glum, Franklin. You'll be fine, you'll see. You have this marvelous mansion practically to yourself, a collection of artifacts to hold and admire to your heart's content, and seven ladies to administer to anything you need."

As if on cue, Abigail appeared with another tray bearing a bottle of Frank's favorite scotch and a glass with one ice cube. He didn't bother to let the cube "temper" the scotch and downed it in one, choking gulp.

"They're very quiet by the way," Leffingfield said as Abigail poured another. "First thing I did when I agreed to spare them the darkness if they served me was to remove their vocal chords, so I wouldn't have to listen to them constantly chatter."

Against his better judgment, Frank had to ask. "Why did you make them stone garden ornaments?"

Leffingfield's mouth twisted to keep from smiling. "I like my privacy, as *you* do, and didn't want them padding about the place when not working." The effort to contain his mirth failed, and he exploded in laughter. "I have to be truthful, though," he guffawed. "I just thought it was funny."

A tear escaped the pool in Frank's eye and dripped off his chin.

Leffingfield regained composure and sighed. "Allow me to build on your earlier suggestion and sweeten the deal for you. What's your net worth, somewhere in the neighborhood of forty, fifty million? I'll make sure your account never drops below a hundred. Go travel, buy things, and indulge in your wildest fantasies. I promise with solemn sincerity you will move to the next existence in the light. Just remember old chap, no revealing my identity or meddling in my affairs. I'm just an old acquaintance who stops by on occasion to share our mutual love for human antiquities."

Leffingfield patted Frank's cheek. "When you think about where your consciousness was bound before we met, you won't find a better situation of its like anywhere."

Frank sucked in a breath. *Oh God, don't say it.*

Leffingfield smiled, and his eyes flashed purple. "It's a hell of a deal."

# CASTING OFF

Suzanne Purvis
*Winner*
*2017 Bethlehem Writers Roundtable Short Story Award*

The cold reaches down, rips the air from my lungs. An arctic jolt, like a lightning strike, if lightning was dark and wet and frigid. I sink, my ice skates slicing their way toward the bottom of Whalen Pond.

I kick. I flail. I want up, but go down, down, down.

I gape at the shattered ice above me, and Keri, my twin sister, thrashes. Her skate blades honed, quicksilver. If I reached for her, I'd lose a hand. And I know better than to battle Keri, especially for something as vital as air.

My suede midi coat and jeans act like sandbags dragging me deeper. Every inch of me numbs like I've been doused in novocaine. I know enough not to scream. I hold my breath. A whispering trail of colorless bubbles floats up, and I fall soundlessly into my watery grave.

I imagine Connor Barnes, wide-eyed and heartbroken, peering over the edge of the broken ice, reaching for his sophomore sweetheart. Not me. Keri. No one reaches for me. But I'm used to it. At our birth, Keri was pulled from Mom's C-section incision. She wailed and kicked and cried. Probably a lot like she is now, minus the skates. The surgeon called for sutures then realized—another baby, a much tinier baby, still waited. Me, forever second, smaller, quieter, less developed in all ways that matter.

Dad tries to tell me otherwise, but at fifteen, Keri has a 36DD chest, which explains Connor Barnes and every other boy in our small charter high school tripping all over her. Me? 32A. Like I said smaller, less developed where it matters most.

Connor Barnes's tripping is why I'm sinking, freezing, dying. Showing off for Keri, performing some hockey stunt, he face-planted so hard the ice cracked, cracked some more, and then more. It happened so fast. But it didn't. It happened slow-motion instant replay speed. Connor flat on his stomach, wiggling snake-like backward, managing to stay safe and dry. Spiderweb zig-zag fractures, shifting ice, and I'm marooned on an island. But balance, inertia, maybe the tipping of karmic scales, and I splashed into Whalen Pond.

My skates land on the squishy, muddy bottom, only it's not the bottom; a faded rose couch sits in the silt. I'd heard the pond held tons of garbage. Mom even organized a clean-up drive last spring. I drop onto the couch, thankful she hasn't raised enough money.

Wisps of my hair float in front of my face. I pretend I'm a mermaid in my undersea living room. I conjure up my merman, but instead, Gran appears, beside me, knitting.

Her watery blue eyes shimmer.

God, I miss her.

"Hold on, dear." She holds up a finger wrapped in purple yarn. "I've got to cast off the last stitches." Her knitting needles slide in and out devoid of their usual, productive click, click, click. "There now. What do you think?" She stretches out the purple striped scarf she'd been working on for years.

I don't expect to be able to talk, but my voice sounds clear, not a gurgle or a bubble. "You finished?"

"Don't sound so surprised."

I want to tell her the surprise is her sitting at the bottom of Whalen Pond, and that since she's dead—

*Am I dead?*

Maybe this is the afterlife, the garbage-filled bottom of Whalen Pond.

"I see Keri made it out." Gran points a knitting needle up toward the surface. "Why are you still here?"

Above us, the water is dead calm.

I consider a joke, or saying I want to spend more time with her, which is true, but the truth leaks out. "I don't have what Keri has . . . I'm not enough."

"Why would you say such a thing?"

"Because every single second of every single day Keri is there to show me how I don't measure up." I slap the couch, and a rush of bubbles escapes.

"Measure up?" Gran ties a knot and bites the wool between her teeth, severing the scarf from the ball of yarn. "Who's measuring?"

"Everyone." I stomp my skate. Murky silt rises in a bluish gray cloud.

"Really?" She winds the loose end of yarn around the ball, leans over, and wraps the scarf around my neck. "Nevertheless, I'm glad you've come. I needed to give you this. Purple still your favorite color?"

I nod, look down, and finger the tails of the scarf. Gran taught me to knit when she lay in her hospital bed waiting for her lungs to fill with fluid one time too many. I'd twist yarn around my fingers, fumble with the needles. She'd started this scarf for me. We worked the purple yarn together until . . .

Since her death, I've knit scarves, hats, fingerless mittens, even socks. But the unfinished purple scarf stayed untouched in my bottom dresser drawer.

I caress the scarf riddled with holes from dropped and mismatched stitches, too tight and too loose binding. Far from perfect, but somehow perfectly warm and comforting. Like Gran, and her simple words. Who's measuring?

I twist her purple wisdom around my wrists, and turn, searching for more. But she's gone, evaporated. On the couch, the ball of purple wool, the loose end floats free, stretches upward.

## CASTING OFF

I cast off the stitches of self-doubt, reach out, grab the end. And hand-over-hand, pull myself up, up, up.

# THE BREAST LAID PLANS

*A. E. Decker*

Mark regarded me thoughtfully. "You know what, Connie? You'd be an absolute ten with breast enhancements."

I choked on the *arancini* I'd been blissfully masticating. The moment a guy mentions cosmetic surgery is the moment a right-thinking gal considers introducing him to Mr. Curb. But Mark . . . he looked like someone had sliced off the best bits of Paul Newman and Robert Redford in their heyday and melded them together. And those *arancini* I mentioned? Mark cooked them. I knew all the best trattorias in New York, but if Mark ever decided to turn professional chef, half of them would close in despair of surviving the competition.

A sip of Lambrusco bought me time to think up a response. "Sure," I said, laughing airily. "And let's upgrade your package to the Godzilla deluxe while we're at it."

Smiling, he dipped a fork into his *parmigiana*. I hid my triumphant grin behind my wineglass. The "surely you're joking" ploy rarely disappoints.

∿

But the next day, out walking through Prospect Park, Mark grabbed my arm, nearly spilling my macchiato. "Doesn't she look fantastic?" he asked.

I looked. An obviously enhanced redhead jogged past, assets bobbing in her halter top.

My jaw clenched. A fresh vision of Mr. Curb appeared, spreading welcoming arms.

But Mark was my first steady boyfriend in years. My thirty-*cough-cough* birthday was rapidly approaching, and I had no ring on my finger. Soon, people would start shaking their heads sadly around me. At the very least, cats would be mentioned.

So, okay, the "joking" ploy hadn't worked. I had other weapons in my arsenal. "She does," I said, nodding my enthusiastic agreement. "I wonder what salon she visits?"

Frowning, Mark dropped my arm. I surreptitiously pumped a fist. Let's hear it for the "missing-the-point" ploy.

~

Two days later, Mark left an ad for a plastic surgeon beside my morning coffee. I found a convenient spider to grab up with it. Over the next week, I kept finding magazines lying about the apartment, opened to centerfolds. Finally, on my birthday, Mark abandoned the "passive-aggressive" ploy in favor of an all-out assault.

At first, my heart leaped at the sight of the wad of bills that confronted me when I opened my present. Then I noticed the sweet, sweet green stuff was wrapped around yet another printed-out ad and my heart plopped back into its usual position.

"What's this?" I asked, contemplating the "bitch" ploy. Sometimes, if you hit the right tone, a guy will never mention a certain subject again. The danger with the "bitch" ploy is it also sometimes sends the guy shooting out the door, never to be seen again. And only yesterday, Belinda from work asked if I wanted to visit the Flatbush Animal Shelter. I just knew she was longing to connect me with my first Mr. Fluffles.

"Dr. Worple is a first-rate plastic surgeon," said Mark. You should've seen his expression. Anxious, yet proud, like he'd just presented me with a cure for irritable bowel syndrome but didn't want me to realize he'd noticed me farting up the apartment for the past few weeks. (That's just an analogy, by the way.)

I stared at the ad. It featured a bunch of blonde women with their heads tossed way back and their boobs thrust way out and their lips parted in that way men find way inviting.

Mark stroked his hands down my arms. "It's not for me, darling. I think cosmetic surgery would enhance your career."

I couldn't guess how he figured that. I worked at an art brokerage. You'd think the last thing I'd want was people ogling my goods while I was trying to convince them to buy someone else's. Then again, I've known men who'd buy crap-flavored toothpaste if it came with a pair of knockers attached.

"Just consider it," said Mark, still arm-stroking. "Imagine how gorgeous you'd look in a little black dress." He paused. "Or, perhaps a white one."

A white dress? Was he implying what I thought? The image of my mother that lives in my head certainly thought so. She clapped her hands and raced to call all her friends before remembering that she was only a figment of my imagination.

What the hell. *Considering* isn't the same as *doing*, right? "Okay," I said.

Mark smiled hugely. His stroking hands went around my back, and soon after, to even more interesting places. I happily submitted, visions of cannoli cream-filled wedding cake wafting through my brain.

∾

But the very next day, I blew most of the green stuff on a Victorian necklace. My brokerage deals in antiques as well as art, and I'd lusted after this particular sparkly the instant I clapped eyes on it, with its big clusters of garnets dangling from a thick gold chain that twisted like a grapevine.

# THE BREAST LAID PLANS

*The money was a gift*, I reminded myself, stroking the box. You can't tell someone how to spend gift money. That's practically a law.

Still, I felt a twinge of guilt as I sat down to work. It mixed with something else entirely when Belinda pulled a picture from her wallet. "This is Nicky," she said proudly. "Isn't he handsome?"

I looked. Any hopes I had of Nicky being six-foot-something and tanned were dashed when I saw the orange tabby stripes.

*Belinda's only two years older than me*, I thought, contemplating my chest. So, okay, they weren't much larger than two halves of a hardboiled egg. No man had complained before.

Belinda set Nicky's picture on her desk, alongside those of Snowy, Miss Pickles, and Moxie.

Then again, no man had mentioned white dresses before.

"Mr. Teller of Queens Zoo wants to sell some paintings to raise funds," announced Janet. Her turtleneck clung lovingly to her assets. A gold Rolex gleamed around her left wrist. She'd gotten a good settlement from her divorce.

My gaze shifted from Janet to Belinda. Don't tell me there's no real difference between "spinster" and "divorcee." You know which description gets the pitying looks —looks I was already starting to see on the faces of my younger, married sisters when we met for family dinners.

"Connie, can you take Mr. Teller's case?" Janet asked me.

"Sure, send me the file," I said on autopilot. Other thoughts occupied my mind.

If bigger boobs were my ticket out of cat lady-hood, I'd pay it. One snag, however: Unless I returned my Victorian necklace, I could no longer afford Dr. Worple. And if even if I received a diamond ring in exchange for my beautiful, gold-and-garnet sacrifice, I'd end up resenting Mark, and then we'd be lucky to last until the wedding, let alone the honeymoon.

Don't be stupid, I chided myself. *There are other plastic surgeons in Brooklyn.* Surely one could double my boobs for half Dr. Worple's fee. A quick Google search spat up a dozen names. One halfway down the list jumped out at me: *Dr. P.*

**63**

*Manky, Cosmetic Wizard. Spectacular results, guaranteed painless.*

Painless, huh? Well, he'd hooked my interest. I clicked the link and was instantly greeted with pictures of his clients. These looked nothing like the teenage nymphets featured in Dr. Worple's brochure. I don't know if you've heard of the artist Boris Vallejo, but he paints warrior chicks in bronze bikinis, often posing on the backs of panthers. The type of woman who eats cobras for breakfast and cracks Macadamia nuts in the crook of her elbow. A quick perusal of Dr. Manky's site got me thinking he was the one who supplied ol' Boris with his models.

*So?* I asked myself. *Would you rather go under the knife of a surgeon who wants to turn you into a Playboy bunny or one who envisions you as an Amazon?*

Put like that, the choice seemed obvious. And wonder of wonders, Manky's fee was half what Dr. Worple charged.

There had to be a catch. But for now, I was willing to overlook it. Pulling out my cell phone, I dialed.

~

"Just relax," said Dr. Manky.

Everything had happened so fast. I'd expected weeks of prepping, but after a single consultation, Dr. Manky booked me for a Monday appointment, barely two weeks after my birthday. The speed of it worried me some, but that consideration came second to giving Mark time to pull the "I-forgot-I-mentioned-a-white-dress" ploy.

Dr. Manky made some adjustments to this big stick-like instrument wrapped with wires he carried. He wasn't what I'd expected in a plastic surgeon. If I'd seen him walking along Maple Street, I'd have taken him for a hippie academic type, with his sandals, beard, and white hair tied back in a ponytail.

"Is this place sterile?" I asked, lying back on the chaise lounge I'd been provided with. The room didn't resemble any operating theater I'd ever seen on TV. They're not usually carpeted, are they? Or have walls lined with shelves of crystals?

And no one's invented smell-o-vision yet, but I'm pretty sure patchouli isn't industry standard.

"Sterile?" Dr. Manky's brow furrowed as if the word didn't fit into his mind.

"I believe she's concerned about the possibility of infection, Master," said the male nurse. At least I hoped he was a nurse. He looked awfully young and pimply.

Nurses don't usually call the surgeon "master," do they?

Dr. Manky's face cleared. "Ah. No, no worry of infection. My appren—*assistant*, Pip, purifies the energy fields daily. Don't you, my boy?"

"Yes, Master," replied the nurse.

Energy fields? Sparks flew from Dr. Manky's staff-thing, and my misgivings grew. Oh, crap, Dr. Manky was one of those New Age-y sort of doctors, wasn't he? I'd probably be lucky if he just chanted a mantra before cutting into me.

If I were unlucky. . . .

"Now, Ms. Fettulopi." Dr. Manky bent over me. "Here are a few instructions for when you awaken from the procedure. Do not allow yourself to become agitated."

So many things can go wrong on the operating table. I know; I've watched *Code Black* and *Chicago Med*. Those doctors always wore scrubs, not long, spangled robes, like Dr. Manky's.

"Move slowly and carefully," he continued.

Nurse Pip started chanting. I started contemplating making a run for the door.

"And, whatever you do, avoid jewelry," Dr. Manky concluded.

Were the walls beginning to glow pale blue?

"Here we go," said Dr. Manky. I reoriented on him just in time to see him aim an atomizer at my face.

"Wait," I said. But he'd already pressed the button. A cool mist blasted over me, smelling of dried lavender, oregano, and sage. I fell into blackness.

ﬁ

A friend who'd gotten breast implants told me it felt like someone had inserted two full soda cans under your chest muscles. Despite Dr. Manky's ad's guarantee, I'd resigned myself to feeling like someone had shoved two broken beer bottles with rusty caps under mine.

I woke up sore. Not the cut-open-and-sewn-back-together kind of pain I'd expected. More of an ache, centered in my biceps, belly, and thighs, like I'd spent too long at the gym the day before.

*Odd,* I thought, blinking grit out of my eyes. My surroundings cleared. The recovery room was odd, too. It resembled a study, with weird, twisty symbols painted on the walls. Dribbly candles burned on the table beside me. I lay on a sofa, covered with a fur blanket. My clothes sat in a folded pile on a wooden chest.

I sat up cautiously, meeting with only small flares of stiffness from my muscles. The blanket slid off, revealing the simple blue robe I'd worn for the surgery. Parting its folds, I looked down at my new anatomy, braced for the sight of swelling and redness.

A pair of boobs, round and firm as two shaved coconuts, stared defiantly back at me. "What the hell you looking at me like that for?" I snapped at them.

Then I noticed what lurked beneath them. Washboard abs, half-hidden under the overhang of my new rack. And wasn't my skin more tanned than it should be this late in October?

A knock sounded at the door. "Just a minute," I called, swinging my feet to the floor. Halfway to my pile of clothes, I realized I'd broken Dr. Manky's admonition about moving too quickly. I cringed, waiting for the dark beast of pain to pounce out of the dark corners of my flesh and eat me whole.

Then, just as suddenly, I uncurled. Pah, so what if it did? I could take a little pain. Hell, I could take a lot of pain. Bring it on. I'd kick pain's ass. I stomped the rest of the way to the chest. The floor trembled beneath my steps, making me smile.

The smile died when I started putting on my clothes and my left arm got stuck halfway through the sleeve. "Dammit," I muttered, tugging futilely.

Another knock, harder than the first. "Give me a minute!" I shouted, eight inches of empty fabric flapping ridiculously off my arm. In a burst of pique, I ripped it off.

Oops. Wasn't "avoiding agitation" another of Dr. Manky's directives?

Ah, the hell with it. The shirt looked better without the sleeves anyway. I tore the right one off, too, and pulled the sweatshirt on. My new rack strained its soft cotton. I forced my legs into the yoga pants. A few stitches around my thighs popped. When I bent down to pick up my sneakers, I noticed something lying between them. The wooden box, containing my Victorian necklace. A curl of paper tucked into its lid bore Belinda's handwriting. *Stopped by to see how you were doing,* it read.

How thoughtful of her. I kept the necklace at work because I wasn't yet ready to explain to Mark where I'd gotten the money to pay for it. I'd never worn it, and it certainly didn't match the hobo gear I had on.

*Oh yeah?* The thought flared up suddenly. *I'll wear whatever I damn well like.* I opened the box and hooked the chain around my neck. Garnets sparkled.

Oh, that was *good.* I held the chain under the candlelight just to enhance the gleam. Shiny, glittery gems and metal—

A fresh knock interrupted my reverie. Scowling, I let the necklace settle onto my chest. "All right, I'm coming," I shouted, stomping over. The door tore off its hinges when I opened it, revealing Dr. Manky standing in a wood-paneled corridor, his sparking staff in hand.

"Crappy construction," I commented, handing him the door. "I'd have words with my carpenter if I were you."

He staggered under the door's weight. Wimp. But, he managed to lean it against the wall before turning to me. "Splendid," he said, looking me up and down. "My most magnificent work yet, I believe."

I grunted. Just like a man, taking credit for a woman's appearance. I considered thumping him, but it seemed unsporting. Might break him in two. "Yeah, you did great work, Doc."

But his eyes suddenly widened. "Ms. Fettulopi, you're wearing a gold necklace." He backed up a step.

Oh, right. No jewelry; that was another of his recovery rules, wasn't it? Sounded stupid then, and even more so now. Gold was great. I *loved* gems. *Shiny, shiny, shiny. . . .*

*Maybe the brokerage hasn't sold all the jewelry from that estate auction,* I thought. The impulse to go see was harder to resist than a slice of tiramisu, so I didn't even try. Brushing past Dr. Manky, I stomped down the corridor.

"Wait, Ms. Fettulopi." Dr. Manky threw out a hand. "It would be wiser for you to remain here."

Pah. I felt fine. Moving eased the lingering stiffness in my muscles. "Relax, Doc," I called back. "I'm just going to see a gal about some gold."

The outer door also tore off when I opened it. I crammed it back in place before I left, but the doc really needed to speak with his contractor. And possibly give him a thumping.

∾

"Connie!"

Eyes bulged when I walked into the office. Jaws dropped. I shrugged, and my new assets did a one-two punch inside my sweatshirt.

"Yeah, huge, aren't they?" I said. "Did we sell all the other jewelry from that estate auction?" I flicked my necklace.

Janet swallowed. "I believe so. Belinda has the details."

I glanced around the office. Rows of heads quickly bent over monitors. One scrubby, ash-blond head was missing, however. "Where is Belinda?" I asked.

"At Queens Zoo, appraising Mr. Teller's pictures." Janet gulped again. "I thought, well . . . you were off for the week. To recover."

"Recover?" I snorted, and Janet shrank in on herself. "I'm perfectly fine. Actually, a trip to the zoo sounds great."

"Shouldn't you be resting?" asked Janet. I looked at her sharply, and her throat bobbed. She shrieked when I reached for her. Drama queen. All I did was snatch her Rolex off her wrist and clap it around my own.

*Shiny, shiny, shiny,* I thought. It flashed nicely in the sunlight as I stomped back out the door.

~

By the time I reached Queens Zoo, I'd acquired three necklaces, two bangle bracelets, and this curving gold snake ring that was practically a knuckle-duster. I was also wearing steel-toed leather boots with four-inch heels, although I didn't remember buying them. They proved useful when I had to drop-kick a pair of men who ogled me while I was waiting for the subway.

Belinda stood in front of the zoo's administration building, her thumbs flying over her smartphone's screen. She looked up as I approached. "Connie," she said. Her voice squeaked. "I thought you were off for a week."

I rolled my eyes, privately vowing to thump the next person who said those words. "What, lie on a sofa for a week watching television? Boring!"

*Wasn't that exactly what I'd planned to do?* I vaguely recalled loading my Netflix queue for an *Outlander* binge.

I brushed the nagging thought aside. "Did you speak to Mr. Teller yet?"

Belinda took a breath. "Connie, Janet texted me—"

But I was already striding into Mr. Teller's office. His door came off at the hinges, too. And splintered. The carpenters' union needed to be lined up and shot. Letting the fragments drop, I trampled them under my steel-toed boots. Inside the office, Mr. Teller, a thin man with a receding hairline, huddled in his swivel chair.

"Good afternoon," I greeted him, my voice booming off the walls. "I'm Constance Fettulopi. Where's this art you want us to hawk?"

"Ms. Fettulopi," he said. An audible swallow. "I heard you were off for a week."

I thumped him. Belinda, watching from the doorway, shrieked. Her cry sent up an instant commotion. You'd think the security guards had already been put on high alert from the way they reacted. Men in uniforms—green polyester uniforms with the insignia of a befuddled gorilla, but uniforms nevertheless—rushed into the room.

I'd never gotten into so much as a slapping fight in grade school. So, the delighted whoop that came boiling up out of my chest shocked me. While I was being shocked, my right hand snatched a brass letter opener off Mr. Teller's desk, and my legs catapulted me towards the guards.

A lot of things happened then. Fast, violent things. I understand now why they slow down the action sequences in movies because I moved too quickly for thought. My brain, seeing it wasn't needed, stepped out for beer and popcorn, only tuning back in a few minutes later when things had quieted down.

*Hmm*, it said, looking around, *I seem to be jogging along a dirt trail lined with wooden railings and overgrown greenery.* My breasts led the way, jutting out beneath my sweatshirt's fabric like a pair of proud torpedoes. Gold clinked with every step. The air smelled of exotic dung.

*What the hell just happened?* asked my brain. Unfortunately, my body hadn't been taking notes. It shrugged.

A wooden shelter came into view ahead, a kind of rustic awning made out of logs with a wire grid across the back to allow a view of the animal inside the enclosure. It seemed as good a place as any to stop and try to unknot the crazy tangle my life had suddenly become.

Inadvertently, I'd made a good choice. Under the shadow of the awning, the gold didn't shine so brightly. Slowly, my mind cleared. The jewelry; Dr. Manky had warned me to keep away from it, and I'd certainly gone a bit . . . bizarre . . . ever since putting my necklace on.

My body protested, but my brain forced it to strip off every gleaming piece and lay them in a dark corner of the observation hut.

"Mrr?" A large cat with tufted ears brushed against the wire grid. A Canadian lynx, according to the placard on the hut's wall.

"Hi there," I said, welcoming the distraction. "No visitors today, huh?"

Most likely, the polyester uniforms had cleared the visitors out of the park due to the crazy lady with the letter opener running wild. I hoped they didn't send a riot squad after me. Mostly because part of me hoped they *did* send a riot squad after me.

"Connie!"

Spoke too soon about visitors. Three figures jogged down the red dirt path. Only I gathered they weren't actually here to visit the animals. I recognized the front-runner by his artfully disheveled blond hair. Mark. Janet must've texted him, too. Belinda followed a few feet behind with Dr. Manky and his crackling staff.

"Connie," said Mark, coming to a stop before me. His eyes bugged when they focused on my new chest. But as they wandered further afield, taking in my washboard abs and the biceps rolling like grapefruit beneath my bronzed skin, his glazed expression hardened into a frown. "My poor darling," he said. Taking my hand, he caressed it softly. "What did this quack do to you?" He glared at Dr. Manky.

Dr. Manky raised an eyebrow. "Exactly as my ad promised."

"You don't like it?" I asked Mark. Maybe it was only my boots, but he seemed smaller. Instead of making me feel all melting and tingly, his hand-rubbing reminded me of a toddler begging Mommy for sweets.

"He did a good job on your breasts," Mark allowed. "But the rest of you . . ." He shook his head. "Well, we'll get another doctor to reverse all of that after we sue him."

"Are you certain that's what she wants?" asked Dr. Manky.

"Of course," snapped Mark, petting my hand and glowering at the doc. "She only wanted breast implants, not to be turned into some muscled freak."

Whipping my hand from his grasp, I slammed it on my hip. Behind me, the lynx growled. "Freak?" I said, and this time I didn't stint on the "bitch tone."

Smiling, Dr. Manky stroked his staff.

"Oh, darling, I didn't mean it like that," said Mark, all instant contrition. "But this isn't what you wanted. You know it isn't."

Wasn't it? I *had* chosen to be an Amazon rather than a nymphet. Only . . . I hadn't thought it would be quite so literal.

When I didn't instantly agree, Mark began fidgeting. "Well." He licked his lips. "I meant to wait until you healed to do this, but . . ." He pulled a small, velvet-covered box from his pocket and held it out. Belinda gasped softly and clasped her hands.

I looked at the box a long time. The ring. Now I remembered. That's why I'd gotten these boobs I hadn't wanted, which led to this body I hadn't asked for, in the first place. Well, here it was. My plan had worked perfectly. All I had to do was say "yes," and the specter of single cat lady-hood would vanish forever.

"Well, darling?" Mark asked.

While staring at my boobs.

I took the box gently and opened it. A simple gold band with a very nice diamond rested inside. *Shiny, shiny, shiny.* I slipped it onto my finger.

"So that's 'yes' then?" Mark asked, beginning to grin.

I looked up. "What do you mean?"

He blinked. "You accepted the ring. That means you'll marry me, right?"

"Oh, I'm sorry," I said sweetly. "You didn't ask *me* to marry you," I pointed at my face. "You asked *them*." My finger lowered to point at my boobs. Mark's eyes, as if helpless to resist, followed. "And *here's* their reply."

I rammed him with my chest. Mark staggered back three feet and fell on his ass. Reaching behind me, I ripped the wire grid from its mooring. With a happy snarl, the lynx leaped at Mark and hooked its claws into his leg.

Oh, Mark's terribly allergic to cats. Did I mention that? Howling and sneezing all at the same time, he kicked the lynx off and bolted. It chased him all the way up the path.

Maybe I wasn't sure who I was any longer. But I sure as hell refused to be a boob-delivery system.

"Well done, Ms. Fettulopi." Tucking his staff under his arm, Dr. Manky applauded.

"Connie." Belinda seized my hand, her voice low and urgent. "Mr. Teller called the police. Dr. Manky says he'll fix things, but don't trust him. You wouldn't believe what I saw when I came to visit you. He was talking to this round, black mirror, and I swear, it spoke back."

"I see." I turned to Dr. Manky. "Cosmetic wizard. Very funny. That wasn't just a catchy advertisement, was it?"

His smile was faintly patronizing. "More than you know," he replied. "Only women who will respond favorably to my spells can see the advertisement. You're wondering why I do it."

Actually, I was wondering if he'd turn me into a frog if I thumped him. I managed a stiff-necked nod, and he returned an even more condescending smile.

"Gornkash, the world I come from, is under the attack by the Dread Queen Emodahlia," he said. "Any male warrior who opposes her ends up in her thrall, so—"

"So, you need a constant supply of Amazons to fight her," I finished. Sirens wailed in the distance.

"Exactly," he said with another smile worthy of being hit with a dead trout. "You will earn a fine living, fighting for Gornkash. You even get to keep your spoils."

No wonder Dr. Manky charged so little for his services. He undoubtedly got paid a handsome sum for every Amazon he procured for Gornkash's army. But the word "spoils" lit up a small, greedily glowing flame inside my head. Besides, the sirens were growing louder. What were my options?

"What are your options?" asked Dr. Manky, as if reading my mind. "Stay in this world, and you'll be arrested for certain."

A "yes" hovered at the back of my throat, oddly reluctant to emerge into the sunlight.

"You're not going to do it, are you, Connie?" asked Belinda, twisting her hands together. "Go away to another world? They might not even have proper sewage or—or gelato!"

The "yes" curled up in my throat and died. Belinda was right. Gold was great. I *loved* gems. But neither compared to gelato, particularly creamy *stracciatella* gelato, the kind layered with enough flaky chocolate shavings to make it crunch in your mouth.

No way was I going to risk going to a world without gelato. But how to stay in this one without getting incarcerated? I pondered. As I did, I noticed Dr. Manky's staff idly spitting green sparks. They lit a bonfire of inspiration inside my head.

I forced myself to wilt. "What else can I do, Bee?" I said in a whispery, wee voice. "If I stay in Brooklyn, I'm sure to be arrested."

"That's right, my dear," said Dr. Manky. "Come with me to Gornkash."

All masculine smugness, he stepped up to me and put a hand on my shoulder. Spinning around, I snatched his staff away.

Men. They always fall for the "damsel in distress" ploy, even when the damsel in question could snap them over their knee.

Holding the staff over my head, I laughed as Dr. Manky danced about, trying to grab it back. "What happens if I break it?" I asked, bending it.

"Don't! You wouldn't like the results!" he cried, still dancing.

"I'm guessing you'd like them even less." I bent the staff until it creaked.

Dr. Manky stopped dancing. "What's your price?" he snapped.

I gave the staff a twirl. "You're a wizard. A real one. So, fix this. Get the police off my back and then get out of Brooklyn. Go on. I'll have this delivered to your office when I'm sure I'm in the clear."

He kept glaring, so I snapped one of the spikes off his staff just to prove I meant business. "You win, you win!" he howled, taking off up the path. I gave his rump a kick to get him moving faster.

While I was in the hut, retrieving my jewelry, the lynx returned and rubbed against my leg. "Hi, there," I said, scratching its tufted ears.

Belinda beamed. "What a cute kitty."

~

I returned home that evening to discover Mark had already fled into the arms of Mr. Curb. It was all right. As I pointed out to Mama, I had the ring, and if you think about it, that's what I'd really been scheming to get all along.

I still work at the brokerage, only in security now. Janet gives me first pick of all the jewelry they acquire. I'm not mentioning any names, but I also do some modeling on the side.

And the lynx? He came home with me. I call him Mr. Fluffles. He doesn't cook Italian, but he's also never complained about my boobs. I consider that a trade up. In fact, I'm thinking of returning to Queens Zoo to collect their puma. Then maybe the snow leopard from Central Park.

Hey, I might be doomed to single cat lady-hood now, but there's no reason I can't do it in *style*.

# A LATE AFTERNOON VISITOR

*Carol L. Wright*

My grandmother clears her throat with determination. I didn't notice her come in, but looking up from my book, I see her sitting in her favorite rocker across from me. She's wearing a hippie-style floral shirt, olive-green bell-bottoms, orange flip-flops, and a vintage Phillies baseball cap. I'm surprised I didn't hear her outfit enter the room.

"Whoa, Grams," I say, my heart flipping over. "It's so good to see you." I know I'm wearing the same broad smile her visits always evoke. "You surprised me."

"You were reading, as usual," she says, a mock rebuke in her voice. "No wonder you didn't hear me come in. You know, you'll ruin your eyes reading without a light on."

"My eyes are already ruined," I tell her, taking off my reading glasses and turning on the lamp to dispel the October dusk. "Besides, if I read too much it's your fault. You're the one who always read to me and took me to the library."

She clicks her tongue and gathers her lips in a tuffet of wrinkles.

I smile, remembering summer days spent at Grams and Granddad's house. She was the thinker; he was the doer. Granddad was always puttering around, fixing stuff, tending his garden, and keeping their old Victorian house in prime condition. Grams was the philosopher. We'd sit together on the porch swing, sipping homemade lemonade, and discussing the important minutiae of life. She'd tell me to be true to myself and not worry about what the other kids thought. She and I always had a special connection. We understood each other as well as any two people on Earth. Every kid should have such a childhood.

"So, what are you reading today?" she asks, nodding at my book.

"*Persuasion*," I say, pulling on my cardigan.

"Ah. Jane Austen."

"It's my favorite." I know my smile is a bit sheepish.

"I seem to remember that the first time you read it you didn't like it. You said Anne Elliot was mopey and moony and you didn't care if she lived happily ever after." We both laugh at the child I once was. We always laugh when we're together. "But the book seems to have—"

"—grown on me? Yes, it has." I know this pleases her. *Persuasion* is her favorite Austen, too. "I think reading Jane Austen with you is one of the reasons I decided on an English major in college."

"Good choice. I know some people think you should choose a major that will lead to a career, but I think you go to college to get an education, not a job. And what better major than English?"

"Well, it certainly isn't a vocational degree."

"Don't you worry. With your brains, you'll do fine."

I sigh, thinking about my "career" working at an indie bookstore for little more than minimum wage, supplemented by teaching a few English as a Second Language courses at the local community college.

"Speaking of Austen, have you ever noticed that all of her heroines get married at the end of the books?" Gram's eyes twinkle with mischief.

Okay—we're on that topic. "True," I say, "but we don't know whether they all lived—"

"—happily ever after?" She shakes a finger at me as she finishes my sentence. "I'm confident she wouldn't create those wonderful characters and not give them happy marriages in the chapters left unwritten," she says, cocking her head.

"Maybe," I say. "Jane Austen was once engaged, but she never married. Maybe that's why those books all stop at the engagement. Maybe she didn't know how to write about happily married people."

Grams shrugs, then locks her eyes on me. She is not to be deterred. "So, is there a special young man in your life these days?"

"Sadly, no." I'm not really sad about it; I'm just sorry to disappoint her.

"Well, you're not getting any younger, you know."

*You have no idea, Grams.* I reach up and pull my graying hair into a knot.

"While books can be good company," she continues, "there's no substitute for a life mate." She sits back and knits her fingers together across her tummy. "Look at Granddad and me."

I let out an involuntary sigh. "Not everyone is as lucky as you and Granddad," is all I can think of to reply. "Tell me, how is Granddad?" I say, trying to change the subject.

She looks confused for a moment. "He's happy." She looks upward past her wrinkled brow. "He sends his love," she says at last.

"Thanks for that." I smile, thinking of the black-and-white wedding photo that now sits on top of my dresser. Grams in a long white dress—Granddad, with a full head of hair, standing tall in his Navy uniform. They got married just as World War II began. My dad was on the way before Granddad shipped out. "Give him my love, too. I miss him."

Grams nods. "Then why don't you come to visit?" It isn't an accusation; she seems genuinely confused.

Her question pulls at my heart. "You two . . . moved so far away," I say. "But I think of you *every* day, and I'm always thrilled when you come back for a visit."

"Florida isn't the dark side of the moon, you know," she says, raising one eyebrow.

She's right. It isn't, but . . .

"Have you seen Lucy lately?" I say, hoping she's visited my little sister.

"Oh, that Lucy!" she says, slapping her knee. "She said the funniest thing the other day. What was it now? . . . Oh, I forget, but she's such a little card."

Yep—that's Lucy. If she's a card, she's the Queen of Diamonds. Gorgeous, funny, talented. She married a zillionaire high-tech geek who sold it all and "retired" at thirty-eight. They moved to Bimini with their two kids and priceless designer dogs. She's certainly living happily ever after. But I know she misses Grams as much as I do and would love a visit. For some reason, though, Grams never goes there. Maybe she just doesn't know how to get to Bimini.

Despite Lucy's good fortune, I know I'm the lucky one. By the time Lucy was old enough to spend time at Grams and Granddad's house, they'd moved to a retirement community in Florida. She never got to help Granddad weed his garden or harvest the sunflower seeds he grew to feed the birds. She never got to spend days in the library or read with Grams on the porch swing.

"You've always been special to me," Grams says, winking. "And I love our little chats."

I sense she's getting ready to go. My eyes fill, and there's a lump in my throat. "And you've always been special to me." We grin at each other like a pair of carved pumpkins. I look at my grandmother's sparkling eyes and crazy clothes. To her, I'm still nineteen, still that college sophomore deciding to major in English, still with a lifetime of possibilities ahead of me.

"And all I want is for you to be happy, dear." Her voice cracks just the tiniest bit.

I consider my life. My marriage fell apart before the first anniversary, and my only other serious relationship ended in a lot of heartache instead of the life-long happiness she had with Granddad. But I remain true to myself, and at forty-nine and single, I have a great circle of friends. I'm using my English degree doing work I love. I live in a ground-floor apartment in their old Victorian house, tend Granddad's garden growing sunflowers to feed the birds, and sit on our porch swing to consider the minutiae of my life.

Then I look at Grams. She looks just as she did on that terrible day in 1988 when she and Granddad were driving along Highway 19 and were T-boned in an intersection by a truck driver blinded by the setting Florida sun. As bad as that time was, I soon discovered that I didn't really lose both of them. Grams still comes by every now and then—just to reassure me with her smile and remind me that I'm special to someone who is special to me.

"Don't worry about me, Grams," I say as I watch her fade from view. "I am happy. . . . Happy ever after."

# Un-Familiar Spirit

*Christopher D. Ochs*

I gawked at the impressive line of photographs along the mantelpiece in the Credere mansion. The row of photographs, their paper browned with age, were set in silver and gold frames that reeked of antiquity.

Each picture portrayed my Aunt Victoria, by herself or with Uncle Ambrose, hobnobbing with high society and ne'er-do-wells alike, and even a few minor royalty of long-gone days. They stood in chronological array, bookended between two ovoid vases. Etched with hieroglyphs, one was capped with a ceramic jackal's head, the other with a hawk's.

Uncle Ambrose, bedecked in his favorite smoking jacket, forsook his other guests when he spied how low my jaw was hanging.

"Is that who I think it is?" I pointed at the last picture—a snapshot of Aunt Vic I had never seen before, set in a platinum frame. She stood between two men, one sporting a fez who looked like he had slept in his sand-encrusted, three-piece suit, the other a rather dapper but unassuming man with an impish grin.

"Yes, that's Professor Johann Jakob Hess," he replied with a chuckle.

"C'mon, Uncle. I know Dr. Hess," I said with a touch of impatience. "You and Aunt Vic introduced me when I visited your excavations near Tanis and Giza. Who's the gent in the tux?"

"Oh, him," Ambrose responded with mischief thinly veiled under a veneer of nonchalance. "That's Harry Houdini." He took an unhurried sip from his snifter of eighty-year-old brandy to hide his poorly-feigned indifference.

I chuckled with fond admiration. "I knew you and Aunt Vic rubbed elbows with countless notables, but one so far removed from academic circles? How in the world did you two make Houdini's acquaintance?"

One of the other invitees brushed past me and picked up a frame and held it close as he squinted to examine it. "Goodness, that's Sir Arthur Conan Doyle kissing Dr. Credere's hand," he sputtered in a Danish accent.

"Quite so," Ambrose said, as he coaxed the photograph from the man's hand, returning it reverently to its place on the mantelpiece. "Dr. Plevny, may I introduce my nephew, Ernest Credere, who is quite the engineer. We were unable to pry him away from his all-consuming project for last night's experiments, though I'm pleased he could join us tonight. Ernest, have you finally succeeded in breaking the sound barrier?"

"No," I replied with a shrug. "This week's trial run shivered itself to bits at Mach 0.9."

"If anyone can crack it, I'm sure it will be you." Ambrose wheeled in place, his drink swirling in his snifter. "And this, my boy, is Dr. Sigurd Plevny, who studied under no less than Niels Bohr and Albert Einstein, and is a remarkable physicist in his own right."

Plevny took my hand in a forthright manner, nearly wrenching my arm out of its socket with a strength surprising for a desk-bound scientist. By the time the series of handshakes was completed, I was surrounded by all the evening's guests, inundated by a bewildering string of introductions and small talk. In addition to Plevny the scientist, Uncle Ambrose hastily walked me through the gauntlet that included

Mme. Marnier the physician, Gundsman the philosopher and *avant-garde* photographer, and Mme. Anders the spiritualist.

"Spiritualist?"

"A physical medium, if you please," she corrected.

"You missed quite a productive session last night, Ernest," Ambrose said, beaming with serene satisfaction. "Mme. Anders exhibited some unique phenomena, under the scientific scrutiny of our guests. I feared Dr. Marnier would be so absorbed by her microscope studies of the ectoplasm samples collected, and Dr. Plevny in his spectroscopy data, that they both would miss tonight's event."

"Wouldn't miss it for the world, Dr. Credere," beamed Marnier.

I nodded my head politely, holding my questions until I got Uncle Ambrose to myself, corralling him into a conversation nook. The two of us settled in two crushed-velvet wing-back chairs, facing each other on either side of a centuries-old grandfather clock.

"Getting back to your original question, my boy," he harrumphed, "we met Mr. Houdini during his long-running sequence of debunking spiritualists. Like him, Victoria had a deep suspicion of the lot, and was more than willing to expose charlatans when the opportunity presented itself."

"I recall Aunt Vic was an ardent agnostic," I said through a frown, "but that's beside the point. In fact, it's quite the opposite. I don't understand why you have . . ." I surveyed our immediate vicinity to ensure I wasn't about to plunge myself into another awkward situation. ". . . why there's a spiritualist, a medium here. Aunt Vic would box your ears before letting one in her house."

"Ah, that's where you're wrong, my boy. But then, we haven't kept abreast of each other's lives all that well. Family relations were never the Crederes' strong suit. In fact, I must confess that your invitation was not strictly due to any familial tie. Rather, I required your engineer's eye for detail. Your presence was sorely missed at last night's experiments." Ambrose wagged his finger at me, accompanied by that mischievous smirk. He drained the last of his snifter and smacked his lips with satisfaction.

"Correcting your misapprehension, Victoria was *not* an agnostic. Rather, she had never decided which of the world's faiths—if any—as the true path. Granted, most Egyptologists tend to run the gamut from agnostic to pure atheist, but not my Victoria. She was quite interested in the spirit realm, though as an archaeologist, she approached it with scientific curiosity rather than a deep-seated need for purpose or spiritual fulfillment.

"As for Houdini, they found a kindred spirit in each other. He plied her treasure trove of expertise in Egyptology. In exchange, she learned all his pointers for detecting fraudulent spiritualists. They communicated often, sharing results to avoid duplication of effort." He chuckled with a wistful look in his eye as he pointed a thumb at the picture Plevny had admired. "You should've been there when Victoria and Houdini gave Sir Arthur Conan Doyle a good thrashing over his belief in fairies. Victoria loved a good argument and hated to lose."

"But if Aunt Vic was so dead set against spiritualists, why did you invite one here? And what is this cockamamie experiment you keep harping about?"

Ambrose raised the empty snifter, and his grin melted into a theatrical pout of disappointment.

"To settle a long-standing argument, your Aunt Vic and I made a pact. On the anniversary of either of our passings, the survivor would attempt to contact the other. Much like Houdini's wife attempted every year after his death, we resolved to validate whether any portion of identity or spirit lingered after the body failed. If anyone could be called a true agnostic, it was I. Your Aunt Victoria's leanings, however, were more along those of the Bible."

"You mean tonight's experiment is . . ."

"A séance. Yes."

I stifled a guffaw into a polite cough. "You're kidding."

"On the contrary, I'm quite sincere. As far as the subject of departed spirits went, Victoria espoused the philosophies found in Job, Ecclesiastes, Isaiah, II Corinth—"

"I simply can't wrap my head around Aunt Vic swallowing anything from the Bible."

"From her viewpoint, the Bible was as valid as any other religion's treatise. 'A text's validity stands or falls on its pedigree, its self-consistency, and its ability to withstand rigorous examination.'"

"She rattled off the same admonition more than once when she tried to teach me basic Aramaic. Even more so, when my interests turned to the physical sciences."

The grandfather clock chimed, declaring the quarter hour before midnight.

"To cut to the chase, my boy, Victoria was adamant in her opinion that ghosts, departed *human* spirits, did not exist. When one dies, they immediately go to their reward—Heaven or Hell, Valhalla or Jahannam—whatever Great Beyond your ethos may hold dear. Rather, Victoria maintained the things we mortals perceive as ghosts are in fact familiar spirits—angelic or more probably demonic—taking on the identity of the deceased with the intent of deception."

He rose out of his chair and pointed me toward the mahogany sliding panel doors into the adjoining room. "Which brings us to this weekend's enterprise. Out of all the mediums that Aunt Victoria examined, Madame Anders was the only one that she could not prove as fraudulent. Last night's experiments likewise vetted Madame Anders' abilities to our guests' satisfaction. But I'm afraid the hour is upon us, Ernest, and we have preparations to make."

The other guests were already following Anders through the doorway into the darkened room beyond. Ambrose paused in front of the mantelpiece to collect two photographs of young Aunt Victoria in her bridal gown and one of the curious ceramic containers.

Ambrose placed the photographs in the center of a circular table draped with black satin. Anders set three candles on the table, equally spaced between each pair of chairs. She lit each taper, then placed a tall, open, glass cylinder around it while mumbling a repetitive phrase. I gave up trying to understand her words once I recognized a few syllables of Aramaic.

Gundsman hobbled after her, extinguishing a series of mismatched oil lamps as he went along. As he passed by, I directed his attention to the unused light fixtures on the walls.

"Did the room blow a fuse?"

"Not at all. Alternating current in the vicinity would have invalidated last night's measurements." Gundsman pointed at a pile of equipment stored in one corner. Under a drape of sheer netting dotted with sleigh bells sat boxes of chemistry lab glassware, a series of cameras with lens caps firmly in place, and an army of electrical apparatus standing next to a disconnected array of large dry cells. One of the few machines I recognized was a Geiger counter.

"In addition, electrical current of any type is a particularly disruptive influence on séances. For tonight's experiment, Madame Anders required the room to be free of all electrical emanations for an entire day," Gundsman continued. "It was a terrible distraction for her yesterday, having to deal with the isolation chamber net your uncle devised, my cameras with film sensitive to infrared and ultraviolet, Marnier's collection apparatus and Plevny's devices. But Madame Anders soldiered on, providing us with rather remarkable results."

"I would've thought alcohol was not conducive to this type of enterprise, either," I carped in a whispered aside to Uncle Ambrose.

"Only for the medium, my boy." He uncorked a second bottle of cognac from a corner table, placing a glassful of the liquor between the outward facing photographs.

The grandfather clock in the outer hall began its dirge of twelve.

The six of us took our places at the table, with Plevny and Ambrose on either side of me. Anders closed her eyes, and in the steady, warm candlelight took several deep breaths. "Take your neighbor's hand, let the circle be not broken."

Several of us exchanged embarrassed glances before clasping each other's hands on top of the table.

"Focus on the images of Victoria Credere before you," she said. "Let all your thoughts be on her, and your desire for her to be among us."

I expected a melodramatic diatribe to follow—a string of corny phrases about the veil between the worlds, and hackneyed admonishments against disbelievers. Instead, every square inch of skin over my spine squirmed when Anders' voice descended into a deep contralto, uttering undecipherable phrases in Aramaic. Her intonations must have similarly affected my neighbors, as Ambrose's palm became slick with sweat, and Plevny's quivering hand threatened to crush my own.

Anders' voice was hypnotic, repeating the same cycle of Aramaic, though each time it ended on a different word. Occasionally a repetition would end with "Victoria." At the end of other iterations, there was a twitch of recognition in Gundsman's eyes, then in Marnier's, and lastly in Uncle Ambrose's—I wondered what other hidden or mystical names Anders might be invoking at the end of each cycle.

Without warning, her voice rose in pitch, and her words in speed. Her head swayed from side to side, and I detected the waft of a faint breeze in the shuttered room.

The candles guttered and might have expired had it not been for the glass cylinders shielding them. Their top edges blackened with soot. A column of steam rose from the cognac that swirled together with the three rising trails of smoke. They combined into a vortex of misty vapor above the photographs, pulsing with an unearthly green luminescence as it twisted and whirled with greater velocity.

Plevny's deathgrip on my hand shook violently, and sweat covered his brow. A nervous titter escaped his lips.

Anders' fervent cries reached an ear-splitting crescendo before commanding in English, "Victoria, speak, I implore! We await."

Breathless moments passed, all of us transfixed by the ghastly whirlpool. Every one of us save Anders shivered when a voice, small and timorous, emanated from the vaporous cyclone.

"I . . ." it began as if unsure or fearful. ". . . am Victoria Credere."

Uncle Ambrose and I both gasped. It had been years since I had heard that voice. Though small and uncharacteristically meek, it was unmistakably my Aunt Victoria's.

"My . . . dearest Ambrose. Is . . . that you?"

"It is, my love."

His voice shook terribly, though I could not discern if it was from fear or hope.

I stared at him in utter confusion as he blurted out a sentence in Egyptian. I wanted desperately to ask him what he was doing, but I held my peace.

Victoria's disembodied voice responded in that ancient tongue as well. It grew in firmness, though sounding as if it originated from the depths of some forbidding well.

Anders' eyes were squeezed shut, and her teeth clenched in a death's-head rictus. Her head sank low, bobbing like a conductor's baton with each heavy breath. Plevny whimpered a small cry as Ambrose continued in German.

Again, Victoria responded in kind from the green whirlwind. I could only guess at what Ambrose and she were saying. It then occurred to me that this might be some agreed-upon ritual, a prearranged set of passwords and responses. Such a detail could easily be the product of my aunt's and uncle's ingenuity.

Ambrose cleared his throat and continued with increased authority in his demeanor. He straightened his back and clasped my hand firmer. In clear tones, free of all dismay, he called a third challenge—this time in French.

And again, the whirling emerald serpentine of smoke and steam responded, the mellifluous words of that provincial tongue rolling out with a newfound strength and affection. In the corner of my eye, I spied Marnier in the flickering light, smiling with relief at Victoria's response.

"It *is* her," she sighed.

Ambrose heaved his own sigh, though it seemed laden with apprehension. "And now my love, the final test—one I'm afraid we never discussed."

He let go of Marnier's hand to his right and leaned to his side. From beneath the table, he produced the clay container from the mantelpiece, setting it on the table directly in front of himself. He uttered a few words in Egyptian and popped off the ceramic Anubis head from the container, like a cork from a champagne bottle. He reached into his jacket pocket and sprinkled a smattering of colored powder into the vase.

"Ambrose, my love, what are you doing?" cried the voice from the whirling green well. "I forbid—"

A puff of smoke and a flash of red flame erupted from the glyph-covered container. A coil of red smoke rose and arched, turning in opposition around the emerald vapors spinning above the table. A voice, shivering with rage, emanated from the clay container.

"What . . . is this?" it demanded with an authority that shook the entire room. Plevny gibbered softly, as a mischievous grin spread across Ambrose's face.

It was . . . *Aunt Victoria*?

"Ambrose, who is this impostor?" demanded the cavernous voice from the bilious whirlpool.

"Imposter! What . . .?" echoed the febrile smoke as it transformed from a pastel magenta into an angry crimson. It reared like a cobra above the vase, ready to strike. The head of the vibrant red serpentine of charnel vapors loomed over my uncle's head. "What have you *done*, Ambrose? Put *me* in a canopic jar?"

"Just your brain, my dearest. Extracted and prepared precisely as the Egyptian Book of the Dead prescribes. Though you and I concocted our array of verbal tests in confidence, a familiar spirit would be privy to every secret you had while you lived. Who's to say it could not pass any test we devised? You have to agree—this was the only way at my disposal to be sure, my love."

"Heretics—unbelievers—infidels! You all shall pay," roared the voice from the vomitous green whirlwind, all pretense of Victoria's humanity disintegrating into rumbling hatred.

"Harm my Ambrose? Not before I send *you* back to the hell from which you came," Victoria screamed, her blood-hued smoke pulsing with neon vehemence.

With a cry of naked ferocity, the writhing red smoke dove at the whirlpool. They entwined, two great ethereal serpents locked in combat, each searching for an advantage in hopes to envelop and crush their adversary. The Gordian knot of red and green smoke gyrated above the table with increasing speed, as the walls of the room began to tremble. The windows flew open, and their shutters blasted out into the night air.

With a scream of utter terror, Plevny stood bolt upright, tumbling back his chair end over end. He reached under the table with both hands and upended the whole affair. The pictures of Victoria, the glass tumbler of cognac and tapered cylinders all shattered against the opposite wall. Gundsman and Marnier bailed out of their seats in the nick of time to avoid the sudden outburst. Anders, still oblivious to the physical world and the ensuing melee, was knocked unconscious to the floor.

The squirming ball of smoke erupted in a noisome flash of green and red, spiraling and collapsing into nothingness. Plevny galloped into the hall, his unhinged screams fading into directionless echoes.

Gundsman and I carried the unconscious Anders from the wreckage of the séance room into the main hall, gently arranging her on the nearest wingback chair, so that Dr. Marnier could tend to her injuries. When I returned to the séance room, I was surprised to find Uncle Ambrose pacing about the debris, staring lovingly into the bridal photographs extracted from their broken frames. His body twitched, stifling the alternating urges to break down in crying despair and boisterous laughter.

"C'mon, Uncle Ambrose," I said, hugging him close. "Pull yourself together. Help Gundsman and me in a search party for Plevny. Make sure he hasn't injured himself as well."

"Be with you in a minute," he sobbed.

Gundsman excused himself, informing us he would check upstairs while Ambrose composed himself.

"An unforgettable experiment, Uncle. But Aunt Victoria sounded . . . displeased, to put it mildly. You may have proven ghosts indeed exist to the satisfaction of everyone involved in tonight's escapade, but it seems to me that you may be in a bit of a pickle. Aren't you afraid Aunt Victoria will return to haunt you to your grave?"

"Not at all, my boy." Ambrose's casual easiness made a sudden comeback, as he took a healthy gulp from the undamaged decanter of cognac. "Though I probably would deserve it."

"What's to stop her?"

"My dear Victoria loved a good argument but hated to lose. If she were to haunt me, her very presence would be a continual reminder that ghosts indeed exist and that she was wrong."

# DOPPELGANGERS

*Paul Weidknecht*
*first published in EveryWritersResource.com*

These weird, double-people Melody observed from time to time around the house never hurt her, but the moment she realized they were imitations and not real people, a chill would run through her that made her scalp tingle. They were always silent, and seemed sad, or at least like something bothered them.

The first one—a copy of Uncle Trey—appeared last year just before she started second grade. Melody had come in from playing outside to get a snack in the kitchen, and as she passed him sitting in his recliner watching the NASCAR race, asked if his driver was winning. The fake Uncle Trey said nothing, its dull eyes straight ahead, its hands gripping the armrests like a man strapped into an electric chair. She thought he hadn't heard her, when a second later the real Uncle Trey came trudging up from the cellar, wiping his hands on a rag, saying her dad would be happy now that the water heater was finally fixed. When she snapped a look back into the living room, all she saw was an empty chair facing a black television.

Since then she had seen doubles of her dad, and the nice old lady next door, Mrs. Wilson. Thankfully, she'd never seen a double of her step-mother; one of her was one too many. Melody couldn't imagine dodging two Helens, each trying to wash out her mouth with hot sauce or locking her in the attic for hours at a time, a true torture in summer or winter, with threats of worse if she ever told her father.

But now she woke with a start, strands of hair pasted to her face with sweat, her pillow damp. The night air was thick and charged around her, like something was prowling the house. Melody glanced at the glowing red numbers of her digital clock, 2:08 a.m. Slipping from bed, she padded down the hallway toward the bathroom, passing her father and Helen's open bedroom door. They lay side by side, two mounds covered in white sheets, the moonlight stenciling them with the shadow of the window's framework. She reached the bathroom and filled a glass with water. In the corner of her eye something moved, and she turned toward the steps leading downstairs. Melody gasped and flinched, the glass shattering on the floor.

A fake Helen ascended the stairs, wild-eyed and breathing heavily, its hands balled into fists.

"Girl, what did I tell you about wandering around at night? Well, you're gonna learn now."

Melody shuddered, understanding immediately: This was the real Helen. "No. Please."

Then she peered into the dark bottom of the stairwell behind Helen. The black-hooded figure showed no face, but she could see it glided quickly upward with purpose. And as it reached out with its pale bony hands toward Helen, Melody knew she'd never again have to stare out that attic window wishing she were somewhere else.

# THE ROMAN COIN

*Marianne H. Donley*

Duncan Pryor took one look at his wife as she walked into the kitchen and knew he was in trouble. Imogene had her you-are-a-bug-and-I'm-going-to-squish-you face in place. He racked his brain trying to figure out just what he had done wrong. This time.

He sighed. Not that Imogene's unhappiness was a new revelation, or that he, and only he, were to blame for her lack of bliss.

"I can't find my gray blouse," she said.

She didn't ask a question, so he didn't mention that he forgot to bring dry cleaning in from the car last night. Maybe he could sneak it in after she went to work.

He moved back to the stove and continued stirring the oatmeal for the boys' breakfast. He heard Imogene suck in a big breath of air, and then her toe tap-tap on the kitchen floor. He didn't think she was sampling the spicy scent of the cinnamon and bacon and becoming impatient for breakfast. She never ate breakfast with them.

"Duncan, are you listening to me?"

"Yep," he said. He sprinkled in a bit of cinnamon, added Craisins and dried cherries.

"Well, I can't find my gray silk blouse. Did you pick up my dry cleaning?"

*Just tell her the dry cleaning's in the car,* he thought, but said, "What's wrong with the one you're wearing?"

"You forgot, didn't you?"

"No," he said louder and more sharply than he intended. The timer dinged, so he switched off the oven, pulled out the pan of bacon, and placed it on the trivet next to the stove. The fat sizzled and spat at him when he reached for the plate lined with paper towels. He looked up and spotted Howie, Robb, and Barret, just inside the kitchen doorway, wide-eyed and frightened. Behind the boys, two big labs, Fergus and Jones, poked their heads under legs and around bodies, trying to get past.

Duncan attempted to smile at the boys, but could see from the fear on their faces, he failed. "Guys, your mom and I have some big people stuff to talk about. Why don't you take the dogs out for a walk? I'll join you in a few minutes."

"No," Imogene snapped. "There isn't time. If they go out, they'll miss the bus."

"Outside, boys." Duncan nodded toward the back door. "Grab your coats. It's cold this morning."

For a few seconds, the room was awash with a whirlwind of boys and dogs, getting coats, getting leads, getting outside. Once the door slammed shut, he turned back to Imogene. Her arms were folded tight across her chest, her mouth a thin straight line.

She dropped her arms and walked closer to Duncan. "You always do that. I tell the boys one thing. You tell them another." She punctuated her words with a finger jab in the air. "Don't you care that they'll miss the bus?"

"Today's late start, Imogene."

"Oh god." She rubbed her forehead. "How am I supposed to keep track of all this stuff? It's hopeless. Did you pick up my dry cleaning like I asked? "

"You don't ask," he said. "You issue orders."

"What's that's supposed to mean?" She turned away from him and marched over to the table where the ingredients for the boys' lunch boxes were spread out. She grabbed the pea-nut butter. "See? I told you to buy Jif. You bought Skippy."

"When was the last time you ate peanut butter?" He strug-gled to keep his voice low, reasonable. Why did she challenge every tiny decision he made?

"What?"

"When was the last time you had a PB&J or peanut butter on toast or an English muffin, or celery, or apples?"

"What does that have to do with anything?"

"The boys like Skippy, so I buy Skippy. They're the ones eating it."

"But . . ."

He put up his hand to stop her. "I'm damn tired of this, Imogene."

"Of what?" She bit the words out.

"You. You finding fault with everything I do, everything the boys do. Like we're employees, not your family. When you're home, we're afraid to breathe wrong."

"That's not true."

"We did all of your chores from the list you created. The ones you said you would do. We dusted, we vacuumed, we did the laundry. Because we wanted to help *you*. Did you say thank you? Did you smile? Did it make you happy?"

"I didn't ask you or the boys to do any of those chores, now did I?" She threw up her hands and stomped her foot. "All I asked is that you pick up the dry cleaning."

"Is it too much to ask for you to say thank you when we try to help?"

"Okay. Why do I have to thank you? You live here, too. Why do I have to ask you to do stuff before it gets done? Why do you expect me to come up with lists of chores that you then ignore? So, thanks for doing stuff I didn't ask you to do. Did you pick up my dry cleaning?"

Duncan turned his back on her and checked the oatmeal. The quick stir he gave it released a burst of cinnamon, and he breathed in the calming scent.

"Duncan, answer me."

"Did you make Howie's concert?"

"Howie's concert? What does that . . ." She paused. Duncan could almost hear the gears in her head whirling. "Wait. Is that why you didn't pick up the dry cleaning? Are you trying to get back at me for missing the concert?"

"Seriously?" He glanced over his shoulder. Her face was tight with anger. He shook his head. "Why would I do that? Why would I try to make you unhappier than you already are?"

"Admit it, you were angry that I missed a dumb school concert."

"It wasn't dumb. Howie had a solo. But it's not like we expected you. Since your new job, you haven't attended a single school function. Not one. We're used to it. Heck, the boys didn't even ask if you would be there." He went back to stirring the oatmeal.

"We agreed that I would take that job, right?"

"Yes."

"I want to make sure I have this straight. We agreed that I would take the job and that you would do more here at home. Right? You said I didn't need to worry because you and the boys had my back. Right?"

"Yes." He bit out the word.

"So why are you punishing me for it?"

"I hate to tell you this, Imogene, but not everything is about you." He lowered the heat on the burner and put the spoon on the counter.

"Oh. My. God."

Duncan faced her. "What?"

"You're sorry that you turned down your promotion."

"No, I'm not. I don't want to work those hours. I want to be here for the boys. You might have gotten the fancy title and that fancy salary, but everyone knows I'm the better parent. Why can't you see that?"

"You're the better parent? That's what you think?"

"You can't remember school functions. You can't remember the boys' schedules. You don't even know the babysitter's name. When you come home, all you do is complain about chores. It's like you wish we didn't exist. Like we should just disappear from your life."

Her cell phone rang, and her face relaxed. She patted her skirt pocket and then moved toward her home office. Duncan could see that she was already at work, the argument with him all but forgotten. He put a hand on her arm. She shrugged him off, so he stepped in front of her. She looked up at him as if she were surprised to see him. "Duncan, I have to get that."

"No, you don't," he said. "What you have to do is decide whether or not you want to be part of this family. That doesn't mean just sleeping here and complaining about everything. That means really being engaged with the boys and me. You can start by coming to parent conferences this afternoon. Our first one is at three-fifteen."

The phone ringing ceased. She stared at him.

"And if I don't . . ." She stopped talking and looked at the floor. Her skin was pale, the vein in her neck pounding.

"You'll get your wish." He turned the stove off and pushed the pan of oatmeal onto a cold burner, then picked up his coat from the hook by the back door and walked out to be with his boys.

~

*I'd get my wish.* Imogene watched Duncan storm out of the kitchen and wondered how asking about her gray blouse had turned into a fight. Another in a long line of arguments. She rubbed her forehead and sat on the edge of a kitchen chair. The smell of peanut butter made her stomach roil, so she whipped through finishing the sandwiches, capped the peanut butter jar and put the supplies away in the pantry.

She glanced around the kitchen and spotted Duncan's morning coffee cup on the counter by the phone. The warmth of the mug seeped into her almost like a hug, and she blinked back tears. She would not cry. At work, she managed a staff of fifty with less stress and strife in a month than she faced at home in a day.

She didn't know how to fix it. She didn't even know what was wrong. She was a rising star at work and a crashing failure at home. Nothing she did helped.

The household chores weren't getting done, so she sat down with Duncan and the boys and made a schedule. She'd insisted they pick their tasks, figuring they would be more likely to do the ones they wanted to do.

Wrong.

Duncan was supposed to do the laundry, but instead, he vacuumed the house. Barrett was supposed to take out the trash, but instead, he picked up after the dogs. Howie was supposed to load the dishwasher, but instead, he made all the beds every morning. Robb was supposed to dust, but he decided cleaning the bathroom counters was more critical.

And they all acted like they were doing chores for her—not just because they lived in the house, too.

She was supposed to remember everything, the dentist appointments, the haircuts, the laundry. She looked at the dumb calendar—another of her ideas that didn't work. Writing things down on the kitchen calendar wasn't good enough; she had to tell Duncan, or he wouldn't remember. Yet, he didn't feel the need to tell her anything. Did he remind her about last night's concert? *No.*

And there it was in dark red ink on the blasted calendar.

*Parent conferences.*

How she hated them. The teachers all squealed with delight when Duncan walked through the door. They all knew his name because he volunteered to be room parent and attended PTA meetings and did fundraisers. If they noticed her . . . what had Barrett's teacher said last June? "Oh, the mother? For some reason, I thought you had died or something."

She looked at the closed kitchen door and shut her eyes. Duncan had no idea. She didn't wish that he and the boys would disappear from her life. She wished Duncan would find out how it felt to do your best and have it thrown back in your face.

~

Duncan's backyard was surrounded by maples and oaks and white pines and hemlocks. In between the trees, a narrow path twisted back and forth until it stopped in a small clearing, also part of his yard but a bit more wild and uncultivated.

Here, he watched his sons and their dogs run through the fallen leaves. An early-morning mist hovered low along the base of the trees and muffled the sounds of play. Someone, somewhere, burned dry yard clippings and the sharp scent wound its way around with the mist.

He snapped a few pictures with his cell, posting them to Facebook for his parents to enjoy. He puffed out a quick breath and tagged his in-laws as well. They weren't to blame for his problems with Imogene. He slipped his phone back into his pocket when the dogs loped to him and dropped two slobbery wet tennis balls at his feet. The dogs sat tense and alert at his side, waiting for his command. He pitched the balls one at a time.

"Fetch," he said, and they took off with soft woofs, leaping over pine needles and logs, dodging tree trunks and kids, in their eagerness to comply.

Howie and Robb gathered piles of crunchy autumn leaves with the strategy of Alexander the Great. They glanced his way and grinned, so he knew he was the intended target of a leaf bomb attack. They'd be fine, no matter what happened, he thought, but Barret worried him.

Instead of playing king-of-the-leaf-hill with his brothers, Barret walked toward Duncan while half-heartedly kicking a rock back and forth as if it were a soccer ball. "Are we getting a divorce?"

"What?"

"Mommy is mad all the time. Gordon said when his mommy and daddy got mad that they got a divorce."

"I see. And who is Gordon?"

"He's my new-guy buddy. He moved to a new house with his mom. He's new at school. When you're new at school, you get a buddy to help you make friends. He doesn't know anyone but me." Barret refocused on rolling the rock around. "Will we have to move with Mom? I don't want to."

"Try not to worry." Duncan rubbed his son's shoulder, unwilling to lie to him but wanting to comfort him just the same. He didn't want a divorce, but he also didn't want to go on living like this—always wondering what bombshells Imogene planned to lob his way just because she could. Yet, deep down, he relished Barret's wish to stay with him.

"I don't want to move," Barret said again. He sounded more like a nap-needing toddler than an eight-year-old. "I don't want a new school. I don't want to have a new-guy buddy. I don't want new friends. I like my old ones."

*Friends. Right.* Duncan gave himself a mental slap in the head. "We'll work things out, Barret."

"Hey, Dad," Howie shouted. "Look at what Fergus and Jones found."

The dogs paced about a hollow at the base of a maple tree, whining and pawing at a mound of wet leaves. The boys joined them poking the pile with sticks.

Last week's storm had blown all sorts of junk around. So, Duncan hurried over to investigate, expecting a rotting carcass or a trash bag of decaying garbage, hoping to intervene before baths would be necessary. Instead of storm-tossed trash, he spotted an old brown leather bag cinched with a red-tasseled drawstring. It reminded him of a larger version of the fancy dice bag his older brother carried about when *Dungeons and Dragons* raged, but ancient, even mysterious. "Where in the world did this come from?"

Howie reached out to grab it, but Duncan stopped him and picked it up himself. This was no dice bag; it was much bigger, much more substantial, more the size of one of Imogene's handbags. Its contents clinked when he shook it to test its weight. *At least twenty pounds.*

The suppleness of the leather surprised him, as did the elaborately tooled owl with words scrolled around it. He looked closer, not fake gaming runes but . . . he traced the letters . . . Latin. He was sure it was Latin, and suddenly wished he had paid more attention in that Latin class he had been required to take for grad school. The bag warmed in his hand.

He blinked and laughed when the translation popped into his brain, *Wish with Wisdom.*

"What is it, Dad?" Robb tugged Duncan's arm to get a better look. "A treasure?"

Not to be outdone, Howie tried to push his brother out of the way. "I bet it's magic beans, and we can grow a beanstalk."

"Is it a bomb?" Barret's eyes were wide with anticipation. "We should throw it and see how big a hole it makes."

"It's not a bomb or beans. But it might be a treasure." Duncan untangled the cord and looked inside. Gold. Dozens and tens of dozens. Okay, maybe hundreds of gold coins. He pulled out a few—five-dollar pieces, and ten-dollar pieces and twenty-dollar pieces.

Duncan's father collected old coins. So his hands shook when he read the dates on these coins. 1885,1882,1877. Yet, they looked brand new as if no one had touched them before. They clinked and flashed in the morning light, save one, which was smaller, more worn looking than the others, and had a distinct green cast to its face.

The boys oohed and crowded in, hopping from foot to foot trying to see the coins. The dogs nosed in as well, tails wagging, eyes bright with excitement.

"We found pirate treasure." Howie took the small coin, held it in the air and danced around, singing. "We're rich. We're rich. We're rich."

"We're so rich." Robb's eyes narrowed in little boy avarice as he took the small coin from his brother. "Can we buy the new Nintendo? Mom said we don't have the money, but now we do. I wish we had a new Nintendo with all the games." He flipped the coin in the air and then caught it with both hands. "Hey, this coin is hot."

"Not so fast, boys." Duncan jiggled the coins in his hands before pouring them back into the bag. "They might belong to someone. Like a museum or a coin collector. We have to figure out where they came from."

"Finders. Keepers. Dad," Robb said frowning at the small coin in his hand. "Everyone knows pirate treasure is finders keepers."

"It's not pirate treasure, Robb. We have an obligation to find out if someone lost it and return it to them. How would you feel if you lost something . . . say your bike, and someone else kept it?"

Barret snagged the coin from Robb. "It's not hot, Robb. You said it was hot. It feels cold to me." He turned the coin back and forth. "Look, guys, it matches the design on the bag."

Duncan held out his hand for the coin. Barret tossed it to him. He held up the coin. The sun didn't glint across the surface as it did with the others. On one side he thought he could make out the name Caesar around the circumference, so maybe the picture was some old Roman emperor. The other side was stamped with the same design that was on the bag; an owl surrounded by the Latin words *Wish with Wisdom*.

"Finders. Keepers." Robb folded his arms across his chest and frowned. Duncan had a sudden vision of Imogene insisting—no demanding—the very same thing. If she didn't have to support the family would she stick around?

He thought about their fight this morning, and one last night, and the one the morning before. *What the heck am I going to do?*

He shook his head. Even though he was angry right this second, he wanted her to be happy. But was it too much to ask that he and the boys be happy as well? Couldn't she just leave him and the boys alone, stop the constant fussing and stop the drama. If she couldn't do that, he wished she'd get her wish.

He felt a sudden warmth in his hand, and he almost dropped the coin. He caught it between his thumb and index finger before it hit the ground. He opened the bag to slip it back inside with the others, but Howie stopped him.

"What do the words say?"

"I bet it says, 'finders keepers,'" Robb added, his lower lip a fraction of an inch from a full-on pout.

"Sorry, Robb, it doesn't. It's Latin," Duncan said. "It says to wish with wisdom."

"A wish. We get a wish?" Robb's eyes lit up. "I wished for a Nintendo. Does that count?"

"I don't think so. Come on." Duncan laughed. He held the bag in his hand, but he put the weird little coin in his jacket pocket. "Let's head inside. We haven't even had breakfast yet, and it's almost time for the bus."

~

Imogene opened her eyes when her cell rang again. Her vision blurred, and her breath caught in her throat as if she were riding a roller coaster. The room tilted and spun around her. A desk. A door. A bookcase. She held on to the arms of her chair until her vision cleared.

*What in the world?*

She sat in her office at work but had no memory of how she got there. Her efficient assistant stood in the doorway with a slight frown on her face. Behind her Imogene noticed staff bustling about busy as cartoon bees. She glanced at her watch. Just after seven in the morning. *What is everyone doing here so early?*

"Your cell phone is ringing, Ms. Osbourne. Should I answer it for you?" asked Audry, that efficient assistant.

The last thing Imogene remembered was fighting with Duncan in the kitchen. The phone stopped ringing, and she shut her eyes and then opened them again.

She was still in her office, but not her office. Her desk was free of pictures of Duncan and the boys. The coffee cup that Robb made last year at summer camp had been replaced by a store-bought one with the words *World's Best Boss* on the side. Instead of the boys' artwork on her wall, she had two huge, framed, modern-art paintings, all texture and color. She hated modern art. She asked her assistant, "Do you know what happened to my coffee mug?"

"What's wrong with it?"

"It's missing. So are the pictures of my husband and kids. And the boys' school paintings."

"Ms. Osbourne, your usual coffee cup is right on your desk." Audry tucked a pencil behind her ear and bit her lip. Imogene knew she only did that when she was worried about something.

"No," she waved her hand at the mug. "The one Robb made me. It's blue and lumpy and has a heart on the side."

"Robb?" Audry asked.

"My son." Surely Audry remembered his name?

"Ms. Osbourne, are you all right?" Audry looked at Imogene as if she were losing her mind.

"Wait. Why are you calling me Ms. Osbourne?"

"What else would I call you?"

"Imogene." She snapped out her name. Was her staff going to start acting like Duncan? Was Audry mad at her, too?

Audry straightened her shoulders. "I'm sorry, Ms. Osbourne, I wouldn't feel comfortable calling you by your first name."

Imogene rubbed her temples. The beginning of a nasty headache throbbed in time with her heartbeat. *What the hell is going on?* "Then you should at least call me Mrs. Pryor."

"What?" Audry asked.

"Mrs. Pryor. It's my name." She spoke slowly and carefully as if talking to someone slow and confused.

"Your . . ." Audry swallowed whatever words she had been planning to say. She stepped into the room and closed the door with a quiet snick. "Ms. Osbourne, I've worked as your assistant for four years. This is the first time you mentioned being married or having a son."

After dropping her hands, Imogene fixed a cold look on her assistant. Time to take control of this situation, whatever it was. "You know very well I have three sons."

Audrey shrugged and bit her lip.

Determined to make her point, she added, "All three boys were here last Saturday when we were finishing up the Johnson project. Duncan brought us pizza for lunch . . ." Imogene stopped talking when Audry's eyes went wide with concern or fear or a bit of both.

"Ms. Osborne, maybe you've been working too hard. Maybe you should take the day off. I can cover your ten o'clock appointment . . ."

"This isn't funny." Imogene grabbed her phone and clicked on her photos. She would show Audry pictures of her boys, and this foolishness would stop. She scrolled through her photos with shot after shot of the products her firm advertised, but gone were the images of the boys, the dogs, and Duncan.

When she realized her hands were shaking, she placed the phone on her desk. She swiveled her chair around and cleared her throat. "Give me a few minutes, Audry."

"Yes, ma'am," Audry said.

Imogene heard the door snick shut behind her. She took several deep breaths and then turned back around to pick up her phone. She scrolled through her recent calls—all business. Her favorite numbers—all business. Duncan wasn't on the list, and neither was her mother.

With a massive knot low in her stomach, she checked her contacts and found her mother. She hit the call button. "Mom, I . . . I need some help."

~

"Dad! Dad! Dad!" All three boys shouted at once. He dropped the bag of coins on the desk in Imogene's office and ran into the kitchen expecting to see spilled milk or dog barf or some other morning complication. But, instead of sitting at the table the boys stood just inside in the family room looking at the TV cabinet as if it had come to life and was dancing around on its stubby wooden feet.

Duncan didn't notice anything different, but as the dogs were sniffing around, he figured something was up. Robb found his voice first. "I wished for a new Nintendo. And there it is."

Howie walked, slow and steady, toward the cabinet and opened the door. Out spilled stacks of Nintendo games. "And all the games. You wished for all the games."

"Is that two wishes?" Barrett asked. "Do we get three? All the stories have guys getting three wishes. It's not fair that Robb got two wishes, and Howie and I didn't get any."

"You can't just wish for things. There has to be a logical explanation," Duncan said in his most official dad voice.

The boys looked at him, then looked at the Nintendo and then looked at him. Jeeze. Even the dogs were staring at him with a get-a-clue expression on their faces. The back of Duncan's neck prickled, and he swallowed hard as he thought about the coin warming in his hand. "Maybe Mommy got the Nintendo as a surprise for all of you."

Now the boys' expressions turned incredulous as if he had suddenly sprouted an extra head. He had to admit, if only to himself, that his reasoning was weak. Imogene hated video games and regulated the time the boys were allowed to play to the second.

Then Barret said, "We don't have a mommy."

"Of course, you do," Duncan said.

"No, we don't," the boys said together, still studying him oddly.

"Boys, look at the pictures." Duncan gestured to the family pictures on the wall. They shrugged. He walked over toward them. Imogene wasn't in the photo from the beach from last summer. She wasn't in the one from last Halloween when they all dressed up as Minions. She wasn't in any of the Christmas ones. Hell, she wasn't in any of them.

It was like she had vanished.

Disappeared.

And just like that, he could feel the coin burning through his jacket pocket just like it had heated in his hand this morning.

He glanced at the boys.

"See, no mom," the boys said together, then they turned back to the video game.

"Can we play?" Robb asked. "Can we stay home from school and play?"

"Yeah, that's my wish," Howie said. "We get to stay home from school and play Nintendo."

"I want a unicorn and a flying carpet," said Barret. "I should get two wishes because Robb got two. That's fair. Right?"

Duncan barely heard the boys over the questions scream-ing in his head. What was happening? How was it possible? Had he lost his mind?

He didn't want to scare the boys, and said, "Go on and play one game. I have something to do." He tried to laugh, but it came out strangled and forced.

He took a deep breath and ran to their bedroom. Imo-gene's jewelry box was missing, and so was that ugly green chair she loved so much. He yanked open random drawers in Imogene's dresser. They were filled with his clothes. In their closet, there were none of her shoes or handbags, and it was cleared of her dresses, skirts, and the damn silk blouses they fought over this morning.

He went into the bathroom. No bottles of lotion on the counter, no perfume or makeup in the top drawer. Her towel wasn't even on the rack, and the silly picture made from sea shells she had picked up at a flea market right after they were married was gone, too.

Imogene hadn't just left him; she had vanished.

He sat on the edge of the tub. The boys didn't even re-member her; it was like she never existed. How could that be possible?

This was his fault. He had wished she would get her wish to disappear from their lives, and she had.

Duncan shook his head; there should be some evidence somewhere that he had a wife. The boys' delighted shouts from the family room sent him to the file cabinet in the office.

He put the family file folder on his desk and sat down in his chair. The boys' birth certificates were in the folder right where they belonged. He let out a quick breath as he turned them over one by one. Imogene Pryor was listed on each of them. Beneath the boys' papers was their marriage certificate. He picked it up and spotted the divorce decree dated a few months after Barret's birth.

*Eight years. We've been divorced for eight years.*

He scanned the papers. He had full custody of the boys, and there didn't seem to be any record of visitation or child support.

*She got her wish. No wonder the boys thought they didn't have a mother.*

His hand shook as he pulled the old coin out of his pocket. It felt cold to the touch, like any other coin. He flipped it in the air and watched it spin. He caught it and held it in his hand.

*Should I wish for her to come back home?*

Duncan thought about that for a good long time. A good long time. He rubbed the letters on the coin. *Wish with wisdom.* He could use a giant dose of wisdom. Maybe he should wish *for* wisdom.

~

Imogene sat at her mom's kitchen table sipping hot tea laced with lemons and honey. Her mom put a plate of oatmeal raisin cookies in front of her. "Eat something."

"I can't." She folded her hands in her lap, willing them to stop shaking. "I . . ."

Her mom took her hands. "What's wrong?"

"I think I've lost my mind."

"Oh, honey."

"Mom, this morning I had a huge fight with Duncan . . ."

"Duncan? Honey, why would you have a fight with Duncan. You've been divorced eight years."

"See," Imogene snapped. She pulled her hands out of her mother grasp. "That's just it. This morning Duncan and I were fighting about the dry cleaning. In our kitchen, while he's making breakfast. I shut my eyes. Poof. I'm at work, and everyone's calling me Ms. Osborne. I don't have the coffee cup that Robb made in summer camp. Or the pictures Barett and Howie painted for my office."

"You've been divorced for eight years," her mom said again.

"This doesn't make any sense." *Divorced?* She would remember that. Of course, she would.

"Divorce rarely makes sense." Her mom patted her hand and then poured more tea. "Come on, honey, eat a cookie. You'll feel better."

Imogene looked at her mother. "I don't even have pictures of the boys on my phone. Don't I get to see the boys? Don't I have visitation?"

Her mother shook her head.

"Why not?" She couldn't have just given up her sons.

"You said Duncan was a better parent. You said it was better for the boys if you just left them. That they would be happier without you."

Imogene rubbed her head, which pounded with a fierce and steady beat. "Was the divorce all my fault?"

"No," her mother said, but Imogene heard the hesitation in her voice.

"What?" She was afraid to look at her mother.

"It wasn't *all* your fault. You treated Duncan as if you were the CEO and he worked in the mailroom. You had lists of chores and schedules for everything from meals to nap time to books he could check out of the library for the boys. Yet, you managed to find fault with just about everything he did."

Imogene remembered the chore chart hanging on the kitchen wall and the peanut butter that Duncan said the boys didn't even like. She swallowed. "I . . . oh my god." A nightmare. She sat straighter. That was it; she was having a horrible dream. Her mom patted her hand. She could feel the soft touches that were meant to comfort. *Do you feel things in your dreams? No, no you don't—hence the pinch. Nope, I'm awake, divorced, and have actually given up custody of my boys.* "So. My fault?"

"No, of course not, I said *not all*. There was plenty of blame to shovel around. Duncan acted like everything was your responsibility, and he was just *helping out*. If you didn't tell him to do something, it didn't get done. Yet, he resented you telling him what to do. He wasn't the least bit subtle about claiming he was the better parent as if it were a competition and not a partnership."

Imogene put her face in her hands. She felt her mom stroking her hair like she did when she was a little girl. "What am I going to do?"

"What do you want?"

"My family back."

∾

"I want to play another game," Barret whined. "I don't want to go to school." He had his coat on, but he stood in the doorway with his arms folded and his face in full pout mode. Howie and Robb were at least on the sidewalk, but both matched Barret's sour expression. Jeeze, even the dogs were whining and pulling at their leashes.

"If you ever want to play that video game again, you will knock off the attitude."

"Nag. Nag. Nag." All three boys shouted together.

*What is wrong with all of them? When did my kids start acting like little monsters? Heck, when did the dogs?*

Oscar, a neighbor kid, hollered as he ran up the street ahead of his dad. His boys turned their backs on Duncan and crowded around Oscar, chattering about the Nintendo and the wishing coin and the other coins. Oscar's dad raised an eyebrow, "You found a bunch of old coins in the backyard and got the kids a Nintendo? Wow. No new car? No new fence? No new clothes for the kids."

"I didn't buy . . ." Duncan just stopped talking. Goosebumps crawled up his arms as he thought about the coins just sitting on the desk in his den. He thought about the wishing coin still in his pocket.

More parents and kids joined the boys and Duncan as they walked to the bus stop. Everyone buzzed with the news of the gold coins. Duncan heard "pirate treasure" and "finders keepers." Someone suggested he could get a wife now that he was rich. Someone else suggested he could get his old one back. And finally, someone said, "Hey, maybe you could paint your house."

It the middle of all the laugher, Duncan glanced back at his home. *Hell.* Not only did the whole place need painting, the trees needed trimming, and the fence needed pickets replaced. *Of course. How could I afford the upkeep on just my salary?*

"I'm doing the best I can," he said.

"Right," said Oscar's dad. "Did you make it to the band concert last night?"

"He had to work," Robb said. "He always has to work."

"Parent of the year," someone shouted.

Duncan shifted his shoulders. He watched the boys trudging up the street. All three of them looked unkempt, and he knew without Imogene around he forgot to get the boys to comb their hair, heck, wash their hair. He bet their beds were unmade. From the looks of Barret's too-short jeans and mismatched socks, he hadn't remembered the laundry, either.

Imogene hadn't been complaining just to drive them all nuts; she'd been trying to keep everything running smoothly, or at least as smoothly as possible given three little boys and two big dogs. And how had he acted? Like a kid not wanting to do his chores.

*Damn.* He could have handled this morning's argument better. He could have handled his whole life better. Dear god, how he wished he had handled it better. He felt the heat of the coin in his pocket.

The world went blindingly white.

~

Duncan took one look at his wife as she walked into the kitchen and knew he was in trouble. Imogene had her you-are-a-bug . . . he stopped, slipping his hand in his pocket for a second, brushed the coin with the tip of his fingers, and repeated his last wish. *Let me do this better.*

He looked back up at Imogene. Crap. What was he thinking? She didn't look mad at all. She looked exhausted. How had he not noticed how tired she was?

He turned the oatmeal off and pushed it to the back burner. He walked over and put his arms around her. "Didn't you sleep well?"

She put her head on his shoulder and said, "I had an awful dream."

"About?"

"We were divorced. All I did was work all the time. You weren't there. And I never saw the kids. It was . . ."

"A nightmare?" Duncan brushed a kiss on the top of her head.

"Yes. A nightmare," Imogene said.

"Are you sure you wouldn't be happier without . . ."

"Yes, I'm sure." Then she pushed away. "Wait. Is that what you want?"

"No," he said, pulling her back. "I don't."

"Are you sure?" Her voice was muffled, but Duncan detected an odd hesitation in her speech as if she were uncertain of his answer.

"I'm positive, Imogene. I don't want to imagine this family without you. We're a team."

"A team?"

"Yes, team. I have your back, and you have mine. Right?"

"Right." She didn't move away as he expected her to do.

"Imogene?"

"I have that big meeting today, and I can't find my silk blouses."

"Sorry. They're still in my car," he said. "I had to carry Barret in the house last night after Howie's concert, and I forgot to go back and get them."

"Howie's concert. Oh god, I missed it."

"It's okay. We recorded it. You can watch it later."

"But . . ."

The anxiety in her voice grabbed his attention. "Hey, don't worry about it. We'll all watch it together tonight. We'll make popcorn. It'll be fun." He looked up. The boys were in the doorway making kissy faces at him, and the dogs were trying their hardest to get around them. He laughed. "All right, you clowns. Late start today, so, you have time to take the dogs for a walk. And Howie bring in Mommy's dry cleaning."

For a few minutes, the kitchen was awash in little boys and big dogs. When the door finally slammed, Duncan said, "Do you have time for breakfast?"

"I hate oatmeal."

"I know." The timer dinged. He let go of Imogene and pulled the pan of bacon out of the oven and set it on a trivet. "But, I figured you might like a bacon bagel with your coffee.

We have a few moments of quiet while the boys are out running off some steam with the dogs. If you don't have time, I can wrap it up for you to take with."

"I have time." She smiled at him. She smiled!

He couldn't remember the last time Imogene smiled at him. She got coffee cups out of the cupboard while he piled the bacon on two bagels. They met in front of the kitchen table. He leaned down and kissed her.

He could hear the kitchen door squeaking open.

"Oh, gross," Howie shouted. "They're kissing."

Imogene looked at their son and, laughing, said, "Better hurry and hang the cleaning in the hall closet, Howie. Because I'm pretty sure I'm going to kiss your dad again."

"Eeeewwww." Feet pounded. The closet doors opened and slammed shut. Ditto for the kitchen door.

Duncan put the breakfast sandwiches on the table and tugged a chair out for Imogene. She put the cups down, and they both sat.

"The boys are watching us through the windows," she said.

Duncan leaned in and kissed her again. A choir of fake gagging and wild barking competed with receding footsteps. He lifted his head to see Imogene smiling at him. He smiled back. "That should keep them outside until the bus comes. Now, eat. You don't want to be late for work."

When Imogene took a bite of her bagel, Duncan pulled the coin out of his pocket. He fingered the owl and the Latin words, *wish with wisdom.*

The coin flashed blindingly white in his hand. Then hot. So very hot, he dropped it. Before the coin hit the floor, it vanished.

He blinked, but when Imogene put her hand on his cheek, he decided he didn't care. Hell, he didn't give a rip if the whole stupid bag of coins disappeared.

# THEY

*Jerome W. McFadden*

I am mad. Irrevocably insane. Everyone says so. Because I see strange things in the cornfield behind our house in the late evening.

They are not ghosts. But their bodies are pale, transparent, shimmering, never firm. Their movements blend between a flickering dance and an erratic darting around like water bugs on a stagnant pond. And I hear their voices. Nothing verbal. More like musical tones. High pitches mixed with low notes. Like chimes. The sounds do not sound menacing, but they do cause unease, a foreboding.

My husband, Earl, laughed at me in the beginning. He would watch me standing out on the patio, staring at the cornfield as the sun went down, waiting for them, and he would mock me. "Are you seeing your cornfield people again, Sweetie?" I would point at them, when they finally came, but he could never see them. I would motion for him to be quiet, but he could never hear them, either. But I could see them, and I could hear them, and there were more and more of them every week.

Earl finally got angry. He put on his hunting clothes, hiking boots, pulled out his shotgun and loaded it, took his good flashlight, the kind the police use, saying, "If there is something out there, by God, I'll find them and chase them away. Are you gonna come along or not?" I backed away. No way was I going out there and I didn't want him to go. But he slammed the back door and left.

He came back empty handed and even angrier. "There is nothing out there," he said. "Nothing. So stop your damn nonsense now."

But more of them came. A few more each evening. I saw them weaving in and out of the rows of corn and through the far trees, singing to each other, whistling to get each other's attention, as if they were exploring a new world around them. I dared not stop watching. I couldn't take the time to cook supper for Earl anymore, and I no longer had the time to come inside to watch television. Earl had to come out to steer me back into the house to go to bed. Some nights I'd slip back out to watch, but he always caught me and got really upset.

He took me into the city to see the doctor. I was physically fine, the doc said. Blood pressure a little high, but nothing to be worried about yet. A small pill of Diovan every day would take care of that. I was in great shape, for a woman my age, yes, indeed, he said. But he added two more prescriptions for Earl to take to the drugstore. Xanax and Prozac. If one didn't work, we could try the other.

The first one made me drowsy for most of the day. Not getting anything done. Didn't really care either. A nuclear bomb coming down our chimney wasn't going to bother me much. But they were still out there. Coming closer. I could tell.

We moved on to the second prescription. But we must have overdone the dose because I was now lost in my own head. Dreams. Memories. Long periods of nothing. Earl had to feed me and take me back to my bed. Then come back to take me to the toilet, if it weren't already too late. In the afternoons I'd lie on the sofa and watch the ceiling while he cleaned the sheets and did the laundry.

But I could still hear them. Late at night. Their songs penetrated the gray fog of the pills. They were coming closer. Now almost to the edge of the backyard. Fully awake for the first time in days I slipped out of bed trying not to wake Earl, to stand on the patio in my nightgown. They were looking at me now, pointing. Talking at me. I could tell. It was a warm summer evening but I felt a chill and needed to hug my arms around my body to keep warm.

Earl came busting out of the sliding glass doors, mad as hell, saying I am goddamn crazy standing out there in the middle of the night in my bare feet and half nude. He hit me. For the first time in our married life, he hit me. In the morning I had a huge black eye, but I couldn't remember where it came from. But Earl was crying and hugging me and saying he was sorry and he will never do it again and I gotta forgive him. I didn't know what he was talking about. Didn't care.

We went into the city to see another doctor. But this one didn't give me any pills. At least not then. Just talked to me. And talked and talked and talked. Asked me stupid questions about my family and about my father and about how I felt about Earl and if we were still having sex and did I feel like going somewhere for a rest?

I told him I didn't want to go nowhere. I didn't need to rest. I needed to stay home. To watch them. They were getting closer.

He and Earl had a long talk afterwards. More pills. No big surprise to that. But then a woman came into the house to watch after me while Earl was off at work. I didn't remember her name but she was pleasant enough. Fed me well. Made sure I made it to the toilet. Let me sleep. Earl came home after work to take over. Gave me a lot more pills at bed time.

But they didn't work. I could still hear them out there. But I couldn't get up to see them now as Earl had strapped me down in a cot in the spare bedroom. I couldn't move my wrists or ankles. But they were talking to me, now just outside the windows.

Earl had to go on a trip for work, so the woman came to stay day and night. It was going to work out. She put together a schedule for me, for when to eat and when to pee and when to do the other things I needed to do. She dressed me and fit on my shoes for me. It was nice, I thought.

One night she saw me listening and trying to look out the window. Asked what I was hearing. I told her. She nodded and smiled to herself. Then untied me to walk me out to the back patio.

They were there. Excited at seeing someone new. But she didn't see them. Or hear them, just like Earl. I took her hand and pulled her past the patio into the yard so she could be closer to them. Surrounded by them. But she put her hands on her hips and stared around the yard and out into the cornfields and into the trees and said she didn't see or hear a thing. That made me so mad I picked up the rake Earl had left in the yard and hit her with it. Again and again. Damn her. Damn her. Damn her. Broke the handle but I kept hitting her with the rake head.

They took her away. That surprised me. They took her by the arms and legs and pulled her into the forest.

Earl came home two days later and asked me why the woman wasn't here. He was really angry. The house was disheveled and my clothes were soiled and the toilets were backed up. I told him. I told him. They took her. Out into the trees. Which made Earl even angrier. He hit me again. Said I'm lying. Said I drove the woman away. Said I'm a crazy bitch and he couldn't take it anymore. I said she was out there in the trees. With them.

He looked at me funny. Then went out the back door, telling me to stay here, he'd be right back.

I watched him go and I knew what I needed to do.

Took him a long time but he came storming back, even angrier than before. I was waiting for him at the back door. I blasted him with the shotgun. The first barrel stopped him—straight up. The second barrel blew him past the patio table, right out into the yard.

I sat down on the patio chair to wait. They came in the evening, really excited to snatch another body. They dragged Earl away, singing and whistling just as I thought they would.

So now I'm waiting here at the house with the shotgun to see if anyone else will show up. They'd like that.

# BAILEY'S MOUNTAIN

### Jeff Baird

*W*here is he now?
I could see the black lead of his thirty-foot, retractable leash rising over the boulders in the creek bed of Glen Onoko Waterfall Trail, but where was Bailey?

My hiking companion was a rescued German Shorthaired Pointer who was fearless as he darted in and out of the dark-green rhododendrons that lined the creek bed.

*There he is.* I saw him as he poked his head over the top of the humongous boulders that were scattered around the beautiful, but dangerous, trail. He appeared confused as to why I was down at the bottom of the run when he was ready to assault the next series of adventures.

Bailey barked as if to say, "C'mon, Dad, hurry up! What's taking you so long?"

A GSP, as his breed is commonly called, is a hunting dog, but our hikes in the mountains were as close as he got to the chase. That didn't stop him from seeking out bear scat and rolling around in it from head to toe. Thank goodness for the waterfalls. Not only were they beautiful, but they also served as a doggie car wash. He instinctively ran onto any ledge where he could drench himself in the cascading falls that plunged into the rapids, fifty to one-hundred feet below. The water danced off his brown- and liver-spotted fur. Once thoroughly soaked, he rushed toward me, only to stop at my feet and "shake, shake, shake his booty," showering me until I was as wet as he was.

After a half-day of hiking, we reached the top of the falls. It would be hard not to be inspired by the beautiful vista before us. The scenic overlook resembled a Norman Rockwell landscape with its red, green, and yellow foliage. The majestic backdrop of the Poconos only added to the beauty, and it took my breath away. This, coupled with the soothing sound of the gurgling water as it flowed off the cliff to the next series of runoffs below, brought Mother Nature alive.

After chasing waterfalls up and down and around the creek beds of Glen Onoko, Bailey used the car ride home to nap. Once he was in the car, he draped his torso over the front seat and rested his head in my lap.

He had been sleeping at least a half an hour when we happened to pass a mountain that we sometimes explored near our home. I liked to call it "Bailey's Mountain," because he loved our romps there and invariably woke up at the exact moment of passing by his mountain trail.

"Zzzzzzzzzzzzzzzz."

There was a palpable electricity in the air as we drove past. I looked around, checking my rearview mirror, but the road was clear. The disconcerting rumble persisted when, all of a sudden, Bailey bolted upright and stared at the mountain. As he froze in place, I began to feel a strange tingling sensation all over, as if I had lost circulation throughout my body. The numbness waned the farther away from the mountain we went. I puzzled over what could have caused the sensation. Driven by curiosity, I decided our next hike would be to explore that very same mountainous trail.

We got home to our family and Bailey's older sister, a 20-year-old Terrier Poodle named Casey. Because of her age, Casey could no longer join us on our hikes, but I couldn't help but think of the days when they hiked together, with Bailey on the outside of the trail and Casey a few feet behind him on the inside. Casey's little legs made several strides to Bailey's one, but she was a trouper. Watching Casey's stubby little tail wagging back and forth as she trotted along to catch up to her bigger little brother was comical, and I missed those days.

~

Our next hiking day, we made our way to the base of "Bailey's Mountain." I knew from previous climbs that it was one of the pathways to the Appalachian Trail and had multiple trailheads throughout the area that we had never explored.

I donned my thermal skull cap, gloves, and hiking backpack and did a quick check for necessary survival supplies.

"Wait, where is it?" I ask myself when I couldn't find my emergency flashlight. "I know I had it the last time I went hiking." I turned to ask Bailey if he knew where it was. He was always hiding things from me. You guessed it. There it was cradled in his mouth. He was just teasing me, like always.

When we reached the beginning of the trail, I found myself staring across a gorge with the Lehigh River rushing through it. I looked up at the opposite mountain to what I called the "House on the Hill." It seemed to have once been a stately home that had a great view of the surrounding valley. However, the house sat on a mountainous landscape that resembled a scene from the planet Mars. Judging from the appearance of the multiple turrets at the corners of the roof and the gables trimming the large windows, it struck me to be of Victorian architecture, but it was in such disrepair as to give it an eerie appearance and had all the makings of a set from an Alfred Hitchcock movie.

I had never scaled this particular mountain, despite repeated attempts. "I think I can," became my new motto, as I slowly but surely crept up a little bit higher each time, often times letting Bailey act as my personal sled dog and pull me up the trail.

After many failed attempts, I was determined that this early autumn morning was going to be the day that I conquered "Bailey's Mountain." I told myself, "Self: Today is the day. I don't *think* I can; I *know* I can!"

After pushing hard, I had the summit in sight, and I was elated to see a leveling off of the elevated trails. My heart was pounding, and I could sense that Bailey was excited as well, judging by the wag of his tail. Our excitement did not last long, though, as each of us saw a foreboding darkness drifting toward us. The wondrous view that moments ago was inspiring was now a blackened haze that was becoming harder and harder to see through. Unfortunately, it was not as if we could get into the car and drive to safety. When you are over three thousand feet high and must walk several miles to find shelter, you have limited options. It's also not like you can stay in place and withstand the approaching storm. Bailey's tail was rapidly waving side to side, and his ears were flapping nervously about. I believed we both had the same idea, which was, as they say, "It's time to get out of Dodge."

We started to head down the gradual switchback trails that lined the mountainside. The darkness that enveloped us was growing uglier by the minute. A fog wafted across the Lehigh River Gap and, as strange as it sounds, seemed to be searching for us. The river below got choppy, and the leaves on the trees lost their grip on the quivering branches.

I became overwhelmed by the idea that someone or something was trying to warn us. It was time to react and not think. It was critical to take the express route to the bottom. The gradual elevation switchback trails that were our upwards guide were too slow. There was only one choice now. I called Bailey, and we took the lesser of two evils. We headed straight down. I turned my body sideways and sidestepped down the mountainside. This was working fine, but when my front leg, that was taking the brunt of the stress, complained, I decided to do a 180, letting my other leg take the lead. As I transitioned to the other leg, I tripped over a rock hidden by a pile of fall foliage.

I lost my balance and began to tumble down the hill, rolling down about thirty to forty feet. I have no idea how I hung onto Bailey's leash. Unbelievably, while I had multiple bumps and bruises and some open wounds, it appeared that I had not broken anything. Adrenalin was kicking into high gear, and the storm kept coming for us. I knew that this was still the way to get down the mountain despite previous evidence to the contrary, so I started my sidestepping action again. This time when I needed to change lead legs, I slowed down at the transition to the other leg and made it safely down the mountain.

Once at the base, my adrenalin began to wear off, and I felt woozy. Strange, mixed-up images flashed through my consciousness. This was just plain scary, but it seemed to be more of a warning than an actual danger. Thoughts that were playing dodgeball in my mind became increasingly coherent. Suddenly it became all too clear to me!

"Casey. Casey. Casey!"

Panic filled me. I had to get home. Something was terribly wrong with Casey.

By the time Bailey and I reached the bottom of the trail and raced to the car, a dread chilled me to the bone. "Bailey's Mountain" is not very far from home, but even so, it seemed to take an eternity to get there.

I pulled into the driveway, and Bailey and I ran into the garage, where I would typically have seen Casey hopping up and down to peer out the kitchen door window. She wasn't there.

When I opened the door, she was usually standing there with a sad look on her face, as if to say, "Daddy, why didn't you take me with you?" But she wasn't there, either.

A few moments later we learned the reason for the foreboding that had gripped me ever since we began our trek down "Bailey's Mountain." Sadly, we found our beautiful Casey lying on the living room floor. Her whole body was twitching, and her eyes had a disoriented faraway look to them. She had apparently suffered a stroke.

I went to her side, tears in my eyes. "Who's a pretty girl? That's right, you're a pretty girl."

We mournfully repeated this mantra all night long as our family stayed awake, hugging and petting our beloved family member. Her body shook uncontrollably, but her joints were rigid at the same time. Her tongue that used to lick us for hours was hanging out and flapping about as her body continued to spasm. Emotions overwhelmed us as we reached the sad conclusion that Casey would shortly pass over the "rainbow bridge" to be in doggie heaven. We braced ourselves for the inevitable. I took a small measure of comfort knowing that we were able to spend her last hours with her because we took the express route down the mountainside.

It was such a helpless feeling lying next to her, hoping she was not in great pain. Granted she was twenty years old, and we had seen the tell-tale signs of her deterioration. But as everyone who shares their life with a pet knows, you keep praying that they will stay with you forever. When you come to the sad realization of what must be done, you pray that you have the strength to put them out of their misery with as much love and tenderness as you can find within yourself.

We wrapped her up in her favorite blankie. We each took turns through the night holding and petting her and telling her what a pretty girl she was, hoping against hope that she would show us signs that this was a temporary ailment. Seeing the look on our son's and daughter's faces, as they said goodbye to their childhood friend, broke our hearts. Sadly, our fondest hope was that she would pass away in the night being surrounded by her loved ones.

Unfortunately, this was not to be the case. We made the decision to call the vet and arrange for an appointment to humanely put her to sleep. The rainbow bridge was calling. There she would return to the Pretty Girl that we had known all her life.

Casey crossed over, and we buried her in our yard, next to her brother Murphy, sister Cody, and our other beloved pets who had previously passed on.

I was grateful for whatever force had told me to hurry home from our hike that day, and I vowed to make a return trip to that mysterious peak so that I could pay my proper respects to the spirit of "Bailey's Mountain" and revel in the loving memory that was our Pretty Girl, Casey.

∿

As we arrived at the base of Bailey's namesake, I peered up the mountain four thousand feet above. Even with the predicted perfect hiking weather, I mumbled to myself, "Damn, that's high. Am I really ready to attempt this hike?"

That thought was immediately followed by, "I think I can, I think I can." Eventually, I heard an echo in my head that simply repeated over and over, "Casey."

*Okay, here we go!*

Five hundred feet: "Ain't nothing but a thing!"

One thousand feet: "No problem, I got this."

Two thousand feet: I was hanging in there, but I had to admit that my mind was drifting in and out about Casey and all of my past furry friends that had made the journey across the rainbow bridge. A swirl of fall leaves brought me back to reality.

Three thousand feet: Despite the forecast, ominous, dark-gray, clouds laced with surrealistic lightning bolts rolled in. Oh no. The tingling sensation I felt the last time I was here was returning. It was getting difficult to see around me, and I could barely make out the "House on the Hill" across the river. I stopped to get my bearings and attempted to restore a sense of calm. I had to keep in mind why I was here. I looked up to see how far I had to go, but the haze, the wind, and the rain that had begun made it hard to judge the distance. I grabbed my GPS device, but there was no signal.

Thirty-four hundred feet: The storm was raging all around us, and I was in full-blown panic. I knew I couldn't navigate us down the mountain in this weather and state of mind. Our only option was to complete the climb and look for cover.

Thirty-six hundred feet: I wasn't sure how or why, but Bailey seemed relatively undisturbed by the events unfolding around him, which helped me to maintain a semblance of calm.

Four thousand feet: We reached the apparent top of "Bailey's Mountain," but don't ask me how, considering my disoriented state of mind. The sky was black, and the wind blew in all directions, pelting us with heavy raindrops that stung as they struck my exposed skin. I spun around, looking for some kind of shelter from the torrential storm.

I took out my flashlight to help penetrate the near-zero visibility. While my light was intense, I caught only vague impressions of my surroundings. However, off in the distance, I glimpsed something shiny going in and out of my field of view. I focused my light in that direction, trying to locate whatever it was. *Wait—there it is—I see it!*

I urged Bailey forward toward the unknown glistening. As we approached, it took shape. It appeared to be a part of the mountain that I couldn't remember passing by before. Atop the summit was a smallish hill about seventy-five feet high. I spied a waterfall cascading over a rock bed strewn with fallen tree trunks. The mist from the waterfall blended with the maelstrom surrounding us, making visibility even worse. But as the storm raged around us, I tugged on Bailey's lead, heading toward the base of the waterfall toward that semblance of cover. I clung to Bailey, as much for his safety as mine, while trying to control my trembling body. I looked around, seeking any other shelter, when I noticed a small cave at the top of the falls. From that angle, I couldn't see into the opening, but my instincts told me that was where I should go.

Carefully, we inched our way up the hill and into the cave. The raging tempest grew stronger behind us, leaving us with only one direction to go. Bailey pulled me forward, his tail whapping at the walls of what now appeared to be a tunnel. The sounds of the waterfall gushing and the storm blended together to an almost deafening level. Suddenly Bailey pulled on his leash and barked frantically. *Is there some wild animal ahead that has also taken shelter here?* It was getting harder and harder to keep control of my hiking partner, and of my rising panic.

I knew I couldn't possibly go back into the storm, so staying put or going forward were my only options. Bailey made the choice for me. I prayed his barking had scared off whatever might lay ahead of us. After moving forward a few feet, Bailey went into his pointer stance and stood there stock still. I shone my flashlight beam into the tunnel, but it just bounced off bare rock walls, creating bizarre shadows. In the surreal whirl of wind and storm and light, Bailey broke his frozen stance, yelped, and bolted away from me.

He caught me off guard, and as the whirling of the thirty-foot retractable leash made its telltale *whoooossssshing* sound, I tried to calculate how long the leash would play out before it came to its inevitable end. I braced myself, knowing that keeping hold of a seventy-pound dog with a full head of steam would require all my remaining strength. In my muddled state, I must have miscalculated, because before I could react, Bailey wrenched the lead from my hand and broke free. He took off to who knew where before I could get out his recall command.

"Oh my God, Bailey, come! Come here, boy." My voice was swallowed by the echoing storm. "Please come, Bailey. Come here, boy."

But he was gone. Desperation and tears overwhelmed me as I charged forward, hoping he was okay. I ran at top speed, stumbling over rocks, searching and praying to find my best friend. Somewhere along the way, I lost my hiking stick, but that paled in comparison to my real loss. Panic-stricken, I found my way deep into the tunnel and paused, not knowing whether I was following Bailey or if he had wandered down to explore a different branch. I took a step forward, and my foot struck an object. I shone my light down onto the ground, and I stood there half relieved, half frozen in fear. It was Bailey's retractable leash and collar. At least I knew I had taken the right path, but where was Bailey?

"Please, God. I can't lose another dog. Not my Bailey! Please help me."

"Bailey, here, boy," I called again. "Come, Bail-Bail. Where are you, Bailey?"

I realized that the storm and haze that drove us into this passageway were quickly clearing, and I could see a bit of light ahead. *I must be coming out of the tunnel.* I called again for my best friend and listened for his friendly bark. I heard faint noises but couldn't quite make out what they were. At least they weren't the sound of the storm.

I followed the tunnel a few more yards and discovered the exit, dead ahead. The clouds and fog and darkness had dissipated. I stuck my head out and felt the warmth of the sun on my skin. But what I saw was not what I expected the view to be from the top of "Bailey's Mountain."

I emerged from the darkness and saw light and sunshine magically appear. A rainbow arched overhead from one end of the deep gap to the other. Dumbfounded, I tried to get oriented. *Isn't that where the "House on the Hill" should be?*

"What's going on here?" I said aloud. "More importantly, where is Bailey?" These questions and those strange noises continued to draw me forward. I felt I was in a trance, compelled to move toward the gap between "Bailey's Mountain" and the hill where the old house was supposed to be. As I approached the beginning of the rainbow, my prayers were answered. There at the opposite end of the rainbow was Bailey, in his classic pointer pose. He was not looking at me, but rather toward where the House on the Hill should have been. *How the heck did he get over there?* There was no apparent alternative trail to get to the other side of the ravine that separated us. *Could he have crossed on the rainbow?* How was I going to get to him? He was still ignoring all of my commands.

Meanwhile, all those whimpering sounds became clearer and sounded strangely familiar. Somehow, I had to cross over the ravine, and the rainbow was the only option available.

If there was ever a leap of faith, this was it. The rainbow was almost transparent and did not appear to have substance. Nonetheless, I tentatively put my foot onto the glowing surface as if I were putting my big toe into a tub of water to test the temperature. It held. Satisfied I placed my whole foot down. It felt kind of squishy, but relatively solid.

*Okay, here goes.* I pushed off with my other leg, and I stood on the rainbow. The colors began to glisten, and the surface pulsated, but I felt strangely comforted. I inched forward toward the other end of the rainbow—toward who knew what. All I knew was that Bailey was there and I had no choice. I had to rescue my best friend.

I continued to cross the divide and was near the other side when I began to hear the noises again. *Bark, Bark, Yelp, Howl, Squeal.* As I stepped back onto solid ground, everything came into focus. Tears stung my eyes when I realized why those noises were so familiar. I looked past Bailey and saw her.

"Oh my God! Casey! But how?"

There she was, in a beautiful meadow that looked like it came out of a Thomas Kinkade painting, filled with lovely, pastoral colors. After a moment of hesitation, I ran toward Casey and found myself in the middle of the meadow with my dog built on springs jumping up and down on me. I collapsed to the ground as she smothered me with licks and kisses. Tears of joy streamed down my cheeks, and I bawled like a baby.

I was soon overwhelmed by the memories of the many years of loving and playing with Casey. Like the time we were out in our backyard, and a blizzard had dropped two feet of snow onto the ground. All you could see was the top of her head for a brief second as she bounded up and down, up and down through the drifting mounds. I was laughing so hard watching her play in the snow almost like a dolphin suddenly surfacing and then immediately going underwater.

Wiping the tears of joy from my eyes, I sensed something more profound. Like the little boy in an old Coca-Cola commercial, I was soon lying on the ground while all my lifelong canine companions came romping in the meadow, covering me with kisses. "How? How is this happening?"

Murphy, my beloved Golden Retriever, ran toward me, despite two knee operations that he had later in his life. I flashed back on the time that we heard muffled cries coming from him, and feared he was in pain. We finally discovered the noises were not coming from Murphy himself, but from a baby bunny he was guarding inside of his jowls. He was carrying the baby bunny around all afternoon and was protecting it from cats that used to roam in our backyard. What a proud and majestic father he was, such a kindly spirit.

My other dogs from over the years joined us, romping and playing with me and one another, sharing unconditional love. My first dog, Fritz, our beautiful Weimaraner had protected me from a backyard bully by biting him in the butt. Next was Shannon, our Irish Setter with epilepsy and who I had carried out of the forest for several miles, thinking she was having a heart attack when she was in the throes of her first grand mal seizure. Then there was Cody, our beautiful Siberian Husky, who saved a woman's life from a serial killer by scaring him away.

Next were Zoey and Bandit, who would serenade my dad in a chorus of howls and tail wagging as they all lay together on our living room floor, singing and teasing each other. Then Stoney, our gentle giant English Setter, who was six feet tall when standing on his hind legs. My father would go to McDonald's every Sunday morning to get Stoney an order of pancakes and bacon for breakfast. When we lost Stoney, we lost our last canine link to my dad.

I stroked and caressed all my beloved companions. Lance, Mimi, Drew, Harper, Ladybug, Nikki, and Holly. Each was special in their own way, and each looked strong and healthy and happy in this idyllic setting.

I have no idea how long I was there playing fetch and stroking my past furry friends, but after some time, I finally noticed my treasured Bailey sitting off to the side of the rainbow bridge, and lying next to him was my precious hiking stick. I had found my lucky pot of gold at the end of this magical rainbow.

Bailey had such a loving and devoted expression on his face. He was not jealous of the attention that my older dogs were lavishing on me. He sat there confident in our love for each other. Bailey had helped me cross the rainbow bridge for the briefest of moments to again share the lifelong love, however fleeting, of all my former man's best friends.

We played and teased each other for what seemed like hours. With sadness, I noticed the intensity of the rainbow slowly fading. As if on cue, Bailey wandered over to me and began nudging me down the mountain. We realized it was time to let go and say goodbye. The air slowly turned into a haze drifting toward us. The trail that we came up on did not exist anymore. The rainbow bridge now led all the way down the mountain like a yellow-brick road.

All my dogs began the trek down to the valley below, but as we descended, I noticed that, one by one, my former canine buddies faded out of view. They lovingly wagged their tails and gave me a final look of unconditional love as they disappeared into the mist.

When we came to the end of the trail, all that were left were Casey and my best friend, Bailey. At first, Casey came over to her brother, and they rubbed noses and said goodbye to each other. Then my little Pretty Girl came over to me, and I bent down and gave her a final caress and hug. With that, she faded into the haze, and I was left with my Bailey, who had made all this possible.

As we approached the bottom of the gorge, the bridge evaporated from sight and the haze cleared to reveal the House on the Hill, right where it should be. At the base of "Bailey's Mountain," my best friend assumed his pointer stance toward the house—a kind of salute to his brothers and sisters on the other side of the rainbow bridge.

Even with the bittersweetness, realizing that my beloved furry companions were once again beyond my reach, I held onto the joy and contentment of being with my rescued GSP. It was obvious to me who rescued whom.

# Paying the Night Differential

*Paul Weidknecht*
*first published in EveryWritersResource.com*

The East River's dark surface rippled in blurry color from the reflections of the anonymous apartment towers and the light-crowned Chrysler Building straight ahead, its spire bright under the chilly spring night. Though no tourist, Pasquale thought Midtown looked just fine. What wasn't fine was standing on this pier waiting for Johnny, late as usual, panicking about something he wouldn't discuss over the phone. But Johnny was right about not talking on the phone; friends of theirs were doing decades for that sin.

Pasquale heard footsteps down the pier and saw Johnny's thin form moving briskly toward him, hands buried in his front jeans pockets, shoulders up around his ears in mystery. His tough guy strut was exaggerated, almost fierce; a sure cover for his anxiety.

"Whatcha got?" Pasquale asked.

"A problem. On the new construction site. Remember how we set up a no-show job there a while back?"

"Yeah. What about it?"

"The guy is showing up to work."

A flicker of confusion passed through Pasquale. "Huh?"

"He is *on-site* for his midnight shift."

"Not possible, Johnny. You know that."

"Of course. I forget, was it Pelham Bay or the Meadowlands?"

"We dumped him over in Jersey."

"I'm telling you, Pas, workers are seeing him wandering around the main building, wearing a hardhat and work belt, and then he'll just disappear through a wall. The foreman's complaining he's starting to get call-offs on midnights."

"Kinda gives new meaning to the phrase 'ghost worker.'"

"Tell me about it. There's more. I went there the other night, you know, to check out the place. Afterwards, while I'm sittin' in my car ready to leave, I look into the rearview and he's in the backseat," Johnny said.

Pas knew Johnny was a street guy, certainly no fool, and he wasn't a junkie or fall-down drunk, so this story didn't materialize out of some meth-clouded hallucination or Saturday night bender.

"Did he have piano wire in his hands?" Pas asked.

"No, but a length of insulated copper #10 will do the same."

"Was it an electrician's job we set up?"

Johnny nodded solemnly.

"What happened then?"

"He just faded away. I think he was trying to scare me. And guess what? It worked."

Again, Pas looked over at Manhattan. If every lighted window represented a person, or sort of, then that was a whole lot of people. He couldn't imagine that any of them were thinking of how to get rid of a potentially profit-wrecking, revenge-seeking ghost. But this was New York, and anything was possible.

"Okay," said Pasquale. "I'll speak to someone tomorrow about changing that no-show from electrical to something clerical. Maybe this will keep him on day shift. No ghost is gonna make a move on anybody with a paperclip."

"And if that doesn't work?"

"I got a nephew who's a priest. We can all take a daytrip to Jersey."

**133**

# THE MAN FROM HOOVERVILLE

*Carol L. Wright*

Mother always had something to give the men who came to the back door. Their threadbare clothing and careworn countenance told her all she needed to know. They never had to tell her their story of losing a job or a home or a family. She just put a finger to her lips and invited them to have a seat on the bench on the back porch. Moments later, she brought them a bit of whatever leftovers we might have, or what she was preparing for our dinner. The Depression had hit everyone hard, she said, and they deserved to have their dignity. "There but for the grace of God . . ."

So, one warm Monday in late April, when a young-looking man rapped on our back door while Mother was at work, I didn't hesitate to follow her example. This gentleman was different from the rest. His suit looked new, and his shirt was bright white. He was clean-shaven, not scruffy like some who came to our door. And, instead of a woebegone expression, he had a quick, friendly smile. He hadn't been on the road long, I guessed. He still had hope.

"Hi there," he said, tipping his hat when I answered his shave-and-a-haircut knock. At first, I thought he might be a salesman, but they usually came to the front.

"I'll get you something to eat," I answered, keeping the closed screen door between us. "Just sit over there."

"Actually," he said, arching one brow, "I was wondering if you folks have any work you need to have done around here. I see your lawn could use a mowing, and I'd be happy to fix that loose railing on the porch here. I could even add a coat of paint on your shed. Looks like it could use it."

I scowled, realizing he was right. Even though we lived in Minnesota, the lawn already had a shaggy spring growth. And I had to admit the porch railing was a bit loose and the shed looked pretty neglected. But did he really need to point out all the ways Mother and I hadn't managed to maintain our home the way Daddy would have?

He came closer to the door and looked directly into my eyes. "I'd be happy to help you get started with some of the work around here."

I wasn't stupid. I understood that young ladies needed to be cautious, and knew better than to give him a reason to hang around. He seemed nice, but you could never tell.

"I'd be happy to give you something to eat, but I don't think we need any work done. We have it under control."

"Under control" was Mother's favorite phrase these days. It seemed to me that since Daddy died, we couldn't control anything anymore. But she pretended we could, and I went along.

While Daddy was alive, the three of us made out okay. Mother stayed at home, I went to school, and Daddy worked as an accountant at whatever jobs he could piece together. We were never rich, but we did okay.

After cancer took Daddy late last winter, Mother found office work and, at fourteen, I was able to chip in babysitting money. We could stay in our little house—for the present, at least. We were so much better off than many. Certainly better off than this man, and all the others who lived in the Hooverville shanty town down by the railroad tracks. It was named in honor of President Hoover who got us into this Not-So-Great Depression. I never thought I would talk to someone who lived there. Everyone said they were all hoboes and thieves.

The man looked disappointed, so I hurried to add, "I think we have some bread, and maybe a bit of left-over chicken in the icebox."

He smiled again. Suddenly, that didn't seem like enough of a meal. "And maybe part of an orange," I added.

"That's more than generous, Miss," he said, reaching for the screen door handle. "And, if it's not too much trouble, maybe a glass of cold water?"

I hooked the screen door lock, and he took a step back. "Have a seat on the bench," I said, following Mother's routine. "I'll be right back."

I sliced some bread and checked the icebox. I knew Mother was counting on the chicken for tonight's casserole but was sure she would want me to share with the less fortunate. I hesitated as I approached the screen door. What if this man . . .? No—he didn't seem scary. In fact, something about him seemed . . . familiar.

I undid the hook with one knuckle and opened the screen door with my hip as I balanced the food and water glass. He stood at one end of the bench as I brought it out.

"Thank you most kindly, Miss," he said. "Won't you join me, perhaps for a little conversation?" He patted the other end of the bench.

"No," I said, "I was in the middle of something. Just leave the dishes there when you're done." I opened the screen door and stepped inside. "And good luck to you," I said as I hooked the lock and closed the inner door.

I watched for a moment from the kitchen window, my heart pounding, not sure what to think of this man. But remembering Mother's insistence on allowing such men their dignity, I left the kitchen and settled on the davenport in the living room to start my homework. *Doing well in school is your most important job.* Mother's voice ran through my head. I had to work hard to get the diploma Mother missed out on.

The city sounds of cars and children and distant sirens wafted into the room, but I focused on my mathematics, nearly forgetting the man on the porch. As the room began to darken I got up to turn on the light. Mother would be home soon; it was time to start preparing dinner. My culinary skills were modest, but I was learning.

Crossing the kitchen, I opened the back door. The plate, flatware, and water glass were stacked neatly on the bench, but there was no sign of the man. I stepped outside to retrieve the dishes, but just as I was about to pick them up, a thought struck me. I went over to the porch steps and wiggled the railing. It was looser than I realized.

∿

When Mother came home, she was exhausted. Riding the streetcar to and from work, and making two transfers each way, made her work day very long. I served her the casserole I had made with what was left of the chicken.

"Seems kind of light on meat," she said, poking it with her fork. "I'm sorry, Patty."

"Oh—it's my fault. A man came to the back porch, and I gave him the leg."

Mother stopped eating. "While you were here alone?"

I nodded.

"I'm not sure that was a good idea, sweetie," she said, shaking her head and fixing me with a stern gaze. "Perhaps you shouldn't open the door when you're home alone."

We hadn't yet worked out all the rules for our new life without Daddy, but I could feel irritation rise within me. I was careful, and everything turned out all right.

I took a deep breath before responding,. "I did just as you always do," I said. "I had him sit on the bench while I put together a plate of bread and chicken and some orange segments. Oh—and I gave him a glass of water from the pitcher in the icebox. Then I left him alone while he ate."

"Well, I think it's better if you keep the doors locked when you're in the house alone from now on," she said.

My jaw was set, which made it harder for me to chew—or to swallow her lack of confidence in my ability to handle things in her absence. I had to be able to handle things. She was taking as many hours at work as she could get, so I was alone at home every day after school and part of every Saturday. She would just have to get used to the fact that I wasn't a child.

But I decided she was right about locking the screen door.

~

The next day after school, I heard whistling outside. I went to the kitchen door, and there was the same man, dressed exactly the same, except that he had removed his hat and jacket. He stayed at the bottom of the porch steps and spread some tools on a cloth on the ground.

I hoped he didn't want more food. Our kitchen looked like Old Mother Hubbard's. All I could offer him was a thin slice of bread and a glass of water. Wasn't that what they gave prisoners?

I was supposed to go down to the market after I finished my homework. I had helped Mother make the shopping list: a pound of ground beef, a dozen eggs, a box of macaroni, a pound of cheese, a loaf of bread, some vegetables, and a pint of milk. We had saved nearly a whole dollar in the money jar, which should cover it, but it wouldn't help me feed the man now.

He looked up and saw me watching him. I waved half-heartedly through the screen. He smiled and bowed, before going to work on our loose railing. He narrated as he went.

"First thing we do is drill a hole on the bottom of the post into the stair below. . . ." I watched everything he did and took notes. We had a loose banister inside the house, too. I used to like watching Daddy work with his tools, but he had never shown me how to use them. This man seemed happy to teach me.

As he finished and started putting his tools away, I realized I still hadn't come up with any ideas about how to feed him. I stuck my head in the icebox, wondering if adding pickles would make bread and water more of a meal. Then I heard his distinctive knock.

"Hi there," he said. "You're all fixed now." He smiled and gave a ta-da flourish. "Come and see what quality work I do. You can recommend me to your friends."

I hesitated, but it wasn't like I hadn't been outside with him before.

I opened the screen door and walked across the porch.

"Try it. It won't bite."

I tried to wiggle the railing, but it was solid.

"Wow," I said. "Great work."

He looked me in the eye and said, "Once you learn how to use tools like this, there is nothing you can't fix."

I blushed a little. "I don't know how to thank you." I really didn't. I couldn't pay him, and I couldn't really feed him.

"You just did," he said. "This is my way of thanking you for your generosity yesterday."

"I'm sorry, but I don't have any food in the house except some bread . . . and water."

He laughed. "Isn't that what they give prisoners?"

I could feel my face get warm and knew I was turning bright red. I hated blushing. I tried to laugh in a poised, movie-star fashion, but felt like a ninny. I had to change the subject.

"Where did you get the tools?" I asked, hoping he might not be homeless after all.

"Some nice fella where I'm staying loaned them to me. He was once quite a carpenter."

"Oh, well, thank your friend for me, too, okay?" I backed up toward the door.

"I certainly will," he said, putting on his jacket and tipping his hat before placing it on his head. "It's been a pleasure, Miss . . . ?

He wanted to know my name. Well, what was the harm? He already knew where I lived.

"Shephard." There. I'd said it. But I wouldn't tell him my first name.

"Well then, it's been a pleasure, Miss Shephard."

He gathered the tools and strode away, whistling a song I almost recognized. I guessed he didn't want bread and water after all.

As he walked toward the street, I called after him. "Wait! What's your name?"

Without turning, he called back, "Just call me Joe." Then he whistled his way down the street.

~

After school on Wednesday, I hoped Joe might return, but even after I finished my homework, there was still no sign of him. It was too soon to start dinner, but the grass still needed mowing. Mother did it last fall after Daddy got sick, but she hadn't pulled the mower out yet this spring. These days, she came home so tired. She wouldn't be able to get to it until Saturday, and by then it would have grown even longer.

Daddy's old mower was in the shed. I had watched him oil it around the rubber wheels and sharpen the curved blades, but he never showed me how. It wasn't women's work, he said. Except now it was.

I pulled the mower out of the shed and hoped it would work without having to oil it or sharpen it. But it had been many months since we last used it.

I tilted the mower and rolled it over to the grass, lined it up, and pushed. It didn't budge. I stepped back and leaned with all my might against the handle. The mower crept forward, slowly at first, then more easily. Soon the familiar rattle of the blades reminded me of summer. I could almost close my eyes and imagine Daddy mowing, and me making lemonade for him to drink when he was done.

I mowed a long, wobbly swath from the shed to the house. Daddy always said, when you have a big job to do, don't look at how much is left to finish—look at all the progress you've made so far. So, I turned back to see what I'd accomplished.

I could clearly see where I had passed the mower over the grass—not because it was neatly clipped, but because the long grass just lay on the ground, bent flat by the mower. Only a bit of grass had made it to the blades and left their shorn tops on my shoes and socks. I wanted to cry. How did Mother do it? Why hadn't Daddy shown me how?

I heard a familiar whistle coming from up the street. I left the mower and scrambled into the house, locking the screen door. I was still in the kitchen when I heard his knock.

I smoothed my hair before I answered the door.

"Hi there, Miss Shephard. I see you agree with me that the lawn could use a mowing," he said. "Shall I help you?" He rolled up his white sleeves revealing tanned arms. "Your roller is probably set at the wrong height, and your mower might need a bit of sharpening. I'd be happy to help."

"No need," I said. I'm not sure why, but I didn't want him in Daddy's shed.

"It's no trouble at all," he said, striding over to the mower. I opened the door and followed him.

He brushed off the grass clippings, and checked the blades, just as I'd seen Daddy do. "Here. Let me show you how."

I almost said no. I almost told him to leave Daddy's things alone. But this man had already been helpful, and if he could teach me how to use the mower, it would make things easier for Mother.

"You see," he began, "here's how you adjust the roller. . . ."

Before I knew it, I had helped him sharpen the mower blades, and cut some of the grass.

"I'll take it from here," he said. "Why don't you go get dinner started for your mother."

I glanced at my watch. He was right; I needed to start dinner. When I set the table, I almost pulled out a third plate, like I always did when Daddy was with us. The memory made me choke up, but I didn't want to cry. Not with the man just outside.

I heard the mowing stop. I didn't have any lemons to make lemonade, but the least I could do was offer him a glass of water. I chipped some ice from the shrinking block in the icebox into a glass. It wasn't lemonade, but it would have to do.

"Ice water," he said. "Thank you kindly, Miss Shephard." He turned to sit on the bench.

"The ice man will come tomorrow, so . . ."

"It's a luxury, and I am grateful," he said, finishing the glass and standing to go.

"Oh, uh, dinner will be ready in about half an hour if you can wait."

He looked up at the sky and shook his head. "Thank you, but your mother will be home soon, and you'll be able to show her all you've done today. I would only be in the way." He tipped his hat, descended the steps, and whistled his way down the road.

~

Mother was impressed with the cut grass and ready dinner. She seemed in a better mood than usual, so I didn't let on that I had gone outside and let Joe show me how to mow the lawn. After dinner, we played cribbage and listened to *One Man's Family* on the radio before I had to go to bed.

That night, I dreamt that Daddy was alive. He looked like he did before he got so thin and sickly. His shiny head with a fringe of graying hair reflected light from a bright sun, and his mustachioed face held its usual broad grin. I ran to him, saying, "I'm so glad you're alive. I thought you were supposed to be dead."

Behind his glasses, he arched one eyebrow higher than the other. When I was younger, I spent a lot of time teaching myself to copy that. Then he said, "I know I'm supposed to be dead, but that doesn't mean I can't come back to visit you, Patty-girl." I leaned into him and felt the warmth of his hug. "I'm just sorry I didn't prepare you better—"

I awoke in the darkness. Daddy was gone. The hole he left in my heart ached, and I cried myself back to sleep.

~

It rained all day Thursday. Before I left for school, I remembered to put the cardboard IC

E sign in the front window. I only felt a *little* guilty about chipping some of the last of our ice block into Joe's water glass the day before. Mother probably would have wanted ice today anyway.

I grabbed my umbrella and left for school, knowing the ice man could get the new block of ice into the icebox through the little door on the porch.

The gray weather matched my mood. I was really missing Daddy, especially during math. He was always so good with numbers. I used to watch him run his finger down a long string of digits, adding them in his head. Being an accountant, he had an adding machine, but he said his head was faster and more accurate because he never hit the wrong button in his brain. "Max," people used to say, using his first name, "you're a numbers whiz." I wished my brain could do that.

It was still raining when I walked home from school. I avoided puddles and dodged waves of dirty water splashed up by passing cars, but my feet got wet despite my best efforts, turning the white toes of my saddle shoes dark. I would have to polish them when they dried.

As I approached our house, I looked for Joe. He wasn't in the yard or on the back porch, and I couldn't hear him whistling down the street. The rain probably kept him back at the Hooverville, where I'd heard they burned fires in old metal drums to keep the chill off. I couldn't blame him.

I curled up on the davenport, threw Mother's knitted afghan over my knees, and started on my homework, but I just couldn't concentrate.

I knew Daddy kept his tools in a metal box in the shed, so I went out through the rain and brought it inside. Opening it, I looked at each tool. Daddy's hands were the last ones to touch the drill, but now I had to. Could I really use it by myself?

I got out the notes I took when Joe was fixing the porch rail and found everything I needed. Putting aside my doubts, I went to work.

I loved turning the drill handle and seeing the curls of wood spin out. But I remembered to keep it straight, just as

Joe said. Slowly, I mimicked what I remembered Joe doing on Tuesday.

It took me a lot longer than it took him, but when I was done, the banister didn't wobble anymore. I'd done it! All by myself. I wished Daddy were there to see it—or even Joe.

Instead of putting the toolkit back in the shed, I stowed it under my bed. They were my tools now, and thanks to Joe, I knew how to use them. I couldn't wait for him to show me more—if he ever came back. I'd heard most Hooverville folks moved around a lot. When there was no work for them in one place, they'd get on a train and go someplace else.

When Mother came home, I hadn't even started working on getting dinner ready. She didn't scold me, but I could see the disappointment in her eyes.

"Did your homework take you all afternoon to finish?" she asked, putting down her purse and pulling out her hat pin.

"Well . . ." I tried hard to conceal my smile. "I didn't get it done yet."

"They really shouldn't assign so much that you can't finish it before dinner." She went into the kitchen and pulled out a saucepan to make her famous macaroni and cheese. I set the table and settled down with my homework to await dinner. I knew Mother wouldn't notice the banister until she was ready to go upstairs, but I couldn't wait for bedtime.

"Wait," I said before she could even boil the macaroni. "Come and see what I did."

I brought her over to the banister. "Wiggle it," I said. She reached out and took hold of the newel post. Despite her effort, it stood stock-still.

"What did you do?" she asked, looking surprised. "This used to be so loose."

"I fixed it," I said, beaming, "using Daddy's tools. The man from Hooverville fixed the one on the back porch, and I watched him as he worked. Then I did this one myself."

"Patty, are you sure you didn't let the man into the house to do it for you?"

I was hurt. Not only did Mother think I couldn't do the work on my own, but worse, she didn't trust me to tell her the truth.

∿

By Friday afternoon, the rain had dried up and the sun was warm, promising the coming days of summer. As I walked home from school, I remembered Mother's accusation. I had shown her my notes, and Daddy's tools under my bed. I think she finally believed me, but I still felt bad about the whole thing.

Then I thought about how much Joe had taught me. He was like a big brother, and I wished, not for the first time, that I wasn't an only child.

No sooner had I formed the thought than I heard footsteps and turned to see Joe striding up next to me.

"Where did you come from?" I was so startled; I hadn't been aware of his approach.

"Where I always come from," he said. I guessed he didn't want to admit he lived in the Hooverville, so I let it go at that.

His clothes were still clean. I was surprised because I got grass stains on my socks on Tuesday, and working on the banister made me perspire. Did he have changes of clothes in his Hooverville shanty? I didn't think hoboes had extra clothes.

"Where are you headed?" I asked, shifting my books in my arms. He reached out, offering to carry them for me, and I was happy to relinquish them.

"I thought perhaps we could start work on that shed of yours this afternoon." He looked up at the clear sky. "The wood won't be dry enough for paint until tomorrow, but today, we can get everything ready. Do you know if you have any spare paint in the shed?"

"I think so," I said, hurrying my pace to keep up with his long strides. "We can check when we get there."

As we arrived at the house, Joe dropped my books on the back porch and went straight to the shed.

"I have to change my clothes," I said, going inside . . . and locking the door. By the time I emerged, he was using a stiff brush to scrub the clapboard shed walls. "You have to get all the loose dirt and paint off first," he said, narrating as he went along. "And scuff up the shiny surface of the last coat of paint so the new paint will stick." We tied back the early stalks of Mother's peonies so they wouldn't touch the newly painted surface. Joe showed me how to nail in a couple of loose boards, and cover the hardware with tape to keep it from getting painted over. Together we checked Daddy's paint cans and brushes to see if we had what we needed.

"Looks good," he said after we finished. "I'll be back tomorrow. Now you'd better get dinner started." He left, whistling his usual tune before I could even suggest warming up some leftovers.

*Tomorrow.* I worried what Mother would think when she saw Joe there. She wasn't happy that I was letting him help us out around the yard—and she didn't yet know I was outside with him. Would she be angry? I knew she would. But since Mother would meet him, wouldn't she be certain to realize he was helpful, and not a threat at all? I hoped so.

～

Mother worked on Saturday morning, and soon after she left, Joe appeared. We worked together, painting with long, overlapping strokes along the wood grain until we completed the back and the far side of the shed. We finished in just over an hour, and were about to start the front—where Mother would see it—when Joe said, "That's enough for me today."

"Why?" I asked. "Can't we finish it up and surprise my mother?"

Joe just shook his head. "Got to be on my way. Besides," he said, looking me straight in the eye, "you can take it from here." Then he winked.

Before he left, he showed me how to clean the brushes, then tipped his hat, and strode away, whistling that tune.

As I watched him go, I decided that I didn't want to wait until he returned to finish the shed, so instead of cleaning my brushes, I got back to work. It took a lot longer without Joe's help, but I finished half of the near side of the shed before

Mother returned. As I'd hoped, she was very pleasantly surprised.

"What a wonderful thing for you to do," she exclaimed. "Whatever made you think of it?"

"That man from Hooverville mentioned that it needed painting the first time he came."

Mother's smile froze. "Was he back today?"

I looked at my shoes. "Yes, Mother, but he's really nice. He knows how to fix things, and I've learned so much from him. Without him, I couldn't have mown the lawn or fixed the banister, or painted the shed."

Mother gave me a scowl that was almost half a smile. I knew she wasn't quite angry, but not quite happy, either. "Well, let me get changed, and I'll help you finish," she said, removing her hat.

"Okay. I'll keep going until you get back." I thought about Joe not changing his clothes, yet he didn't seem to get a spot of paint on his trousers. Despite the heat, he didn't seem to sweat, and his shirt was still the bright white it had been on the first day I saw him. How did he manage that? I wondered.

When Mother returned, I was just finishing work around the door—having masked the hinges with tape, just as Joe showed me. Mother picked up Joe's paintbrush and gave me a smile.

As we painted side by side, I started whistling. It wasn't something I did often. Mother used to say, "Whistling girls and cackling hens, always come to some bad ends." But I was happy, and whistling felt right.

Mother stopped painting and, in a scolding manner, asked, "What's that you're whistling?"

"It's just a tune the man from Hooverville whistles. I don't know what it is."

"Well I do," Mother said, obviously a little unhappy.

I wondered if it was a song not appropriate for girls my age. *Some bad ends,* indeed. "What is it?" I asked, almost afraid to find out.

"It's an old song. Something from the Navy, I believe. Your father used to whistle it when I first met him."

"Daddy was in the Navy, wasn't he?"

"Yes. In the Great War."

"I don't remember Daddy ever whistling," I said. Then I realized, he probably stopped because Mother didn't like it. I stroked more paint on the wood and wondered if Joe were in the Navy. I was sure he was too young to have been in the Great War. "Sorry, I won't whistle it anymore," I said.

"It's okay," Mother mumbled. "I like hearing that song again after all these years."

I hummed a bit, thinking of Daddy. When I pictured him, I still thought of how he looked when he was sick, thin, and weak. I wished I remember him as he was before, with his mustache, wearing his glasses and a mischievous smile, and his bald head that I would kiss every night before going to bed. I wondered what he looked like when Mother first met him. In my mind's eye, I tried to imagine him young, with a full head of hair and clean shaven, whistling a tune, arching one brow. As his image came into focus, a shiver ran down my spine.

"Mother," I said, almost afraid of the answer. "Did people ever call Daddy any other name besides 'Max'?"

"Silly girl," Mother answered. "He's always been called 'Max.'"

I breathed a sigh.

Then, after a moment's hesitation, Mother continued. "Except in the Navy, when there were several people with that name. Then they made up different names for each of them. They called one 'Uncle,' and another one 'Sam.'" She chuckled at the memory. "But since they knew he was born in St. Joseph's, they just called your daddy 'Joe.'"

# TOMMY

*Dianna Sinovic*

*Video time stamp: 1 June, 19:39*

Weeja lit the tall patchouli candle, turned the table lamp to low, and set her cell phone on record. Then she laid her hands on the brocade tablecloth and took a deep breath. She spoke softly to the candle flame and the emptiness of the small kitchen.

"Tommy, listen up, darlin'. We need to talk. I know it's been ten years, but this time it's really important."

How many times had she lit the damn candle, waiting for an answer? In the last decade, maybe once a month at first, then once or twice a year. And she'd never had a tap on the shoulder or felt a cold breeze flow through the room. Hell, most people would think she was crazy to believe, but still, she persisted.

"I'm begging you, please, Tommy. I need your advice. I'm even recording this session—on my phone; we can do that now. Just in case you do decide to respond, I'll know I wasn't dreaming."

She paused. No sound except the faint ticking of the bird clock on the wall and the sigh of the refrigerator cycling. The candle flame was still. The musky scent of the patchouli embraced her. But no Tommy.

"So here's the issue," she spoke again. Another pause to drink from her mug of lemon tea. "Wes Nichols and I want to get married, but Sunny is dead set against my settling down with him."

Sunny specifically had threatened to hijack the ceremony, but her daughter had always been a bit of a drama queen.

"I know you won't mind about Wes and me. You and I had our good times, but your good times are long over—for here, anyway. I hope you've made peace, wherever you ended up."

Weeja shook her head. This time was no better than any of her other attempts to reach over. If Tommy was anywhere, he was not loitering near the world of the living. And yet she really did want his opinion, as she had for so many things after he died.

After a long stretch with no one in her life, Wes had rekindled her desire. He would never replace Tommy, but his interest in her made her feel special again. Yes, they had met at rehab—she as a volunteer, he as an attendee—but he was clean now, with a steady job and a fondness for her chicken pot pie. And he wasn't bad looking, with his green eyes and neatly trimmed beard.

"I'll take your silence as your acceptance," Weeja said. "We'll agree that it's fine for me to remarry. Wes has asked me, and I've said yes. And—hey!—

The patchouli candle flared brightly in the sudden breeze that swept through the kitchen and knocked over Weeja's phone.

*Video time stamp: 5 June, 19:03*

"Mom, this is just weird," Sunny said. "I really don't want to be here."

At twenty-five, Sunny Washburn looked enough like her mother that people sometimes mistook them for sisters—sisters who constantly argued. Her belief in the hereafter had waned in adulthood as Weeja's had grown stronger.

She and Weeja sat at the small kitchen table, the same one the family had dined around since she and Cassidy were little.

"You saw the video," Weeja said. "Your dad is trying to send us a message. So just hang tight, and we can discuss this together—with him."

Sunny snorted. "What I saw was you dropping your phone, and then the recording stopped."

"I distinctly remember the phone being knocked over by the wind that came through the kitchen. And all of the windows were closed tight. I tell you, Daddy was here. He made his presence known when I started talking about Wes and me getting married."

"Then Daddy was agreeing with me. Wes is a creep. He just wants your money."

"Sunny—"

Sunny frowned. "Don't call me Sunny. I'm not using that name anymore."

"But Sundance is your name." Weeja sighed. This argument had been raging for the last few years. "Remember when you and your brother built that lean-to in the yard and pretended you were outlaws? You spent practically the entire summer holed up there."

"That was when I was eight, Mom."

Weeja and Tommy were in full agreement on the names for their children, even if the rest of the extended family was not. Butch Cassidy was Tommy's favorite movie character, and Weeja thought Sundance a fine girl's name. It reminded her of her lush flower garden, the source of the dried arrangements that adorned every room in the Northeast Philly bungalow and the tinctures she sold on the side to a customer base that believed in the power of naturopathy.

"I don't know why you don't like Sundance."

Predictably, Sunny rolled her eyes. "Because I don't rob trains, and I'm tired of the endless questions about that film festival. Besides, *you* don't use your real name, so why should I?"

Weeja conceded the point. She hated the name Chastity and had discarded it as soon as she reached high school. Her mother seemed to think it would somehow keep her celibate when her hormones kicked in. Instead, she adopted the nickname bestowed on her by friends after a memorably spooky slumber party.

"But look at Cass." Weeja made one last plea, standing up to bring two mugs of lemon tea from the stove. "Your brother's not running down to the courthouse to change *his* name."

"Cassidy is not me," Sunny said. "And he's at the courthouse often enough, remember? He's a cop."

Weeja turned off the overhead light in the kitchen and lit the candle. "Okay, let's get down to business." She reached across the table for Sunny's hands.

"Stop it—"Sunny pushed her mother's hands away. "I'm not going to hold your hand while we pretend to see ghosts. Anyway, I need to get going soon."

"Tommy, honey," Weeja began, "Sunny—er—your daughter and I are here tonight to talk a little bit more about Wes. Your daughter doesn't believe me, but he's really turned his life around."

"Yeah, he talks a good line. He's nice to you because of your trust fund."

Weeja smiled. "No, honey. He's making a decent salary at the warehouse now. He doesn't need to tap into my little fund—if he even knows about it." She waved off Sunny's protest. "Oh, I know he used to be a bad boy." The stories she had heard had spooked her at first—drugs, guns, knives. He had sworn off all of that, he told her. She believed him, or wanted to. "But he's found Jesus. He's as straight as—"

The candle flame went out with a flash, and the pillar fell to one side, knocking the phone once again off its stand.

"Mom!— " Sunny screamed in the darkness.

*Video time stamp: 12 June, 20:53*

With shaking hands, Weeja lit the candle on the kitchen table and sat down to face it. She had waited a week before trying to reach Tommy again.

"Tommy," she said to the candle flame, "I know you're upset. I figured maybe a few days' break might cool you off, although when you're facing eternity, a few days might not even register on your cosmic calendar."

It was just Weeja at the table this time, even though Sunny—Emily now—had warned her not to try another séance without her. Weeja didn't tell her what she was doing. Tommy had been her soul mate; she was sure he meant her no harm. Still, for fortitude, she had spiked her tea with a bit of bourbon.

"I *do* miss you, darlin'. The night you OD'd I felt like a chunk of my heart was ripped from my chest. I blame myself." If only she had gone with him that night, she might have been able to stop him from using that needle. But she wasn't a user, and Tommy had sworn he was only going out to meet a friend. He had been clean for five years.

"When the police called to tell me you were in the Jefferson ER, I was crazy with worry. Cassidy met me at the hospital, but it was too late. They said the dope had been cut with something lethal. You'd already crossed over, and they couldn't bring you back.

"Cass cried like a baby. He was eighteen, Tommy. His anger hit after the tears dried. He vowed to find the son of a bitch who sold you the bag that killed you. Of course, I didn't let him. I didn't want to lose him, too."

Tears welled. "Damn! I didn't mean to go all blubbery on you." She wiped her eyes on her arm and blew her nose on a paper napkin.

The candle flame slowly elongated, stretching up and up, until it was at least a foot high. Weeja marveled at the sense of peace she felt, where she had been bitterly sad only a moment before. And she knew it wasn't just because of the bourbon in her tea. "Is that you, Tommy?" The flame did not answer with movement but continued to burn straight and tall. "You always did have a way of cheering me up even when the world was going to shit around us. I'm just going to savor this moment."

*Video time stamp: 15 June, 23:40*
Determined, once and for all, to have Tommy's blessing, Weeja again placed the candle on the kitchen table, but this time, at minutes before midnight, Wes was there, next to Sun-

ny. Cassidy was due at the door any minute; his shift had ended at eleven.

Sunny and Wes were already sniping at each other. "I see you didn't waste any time mixing a drink," Sunny said, her mouth a grim line. "I thought you Baptists avoided alcohol."

"Not Baptist—Fellowship Biblical. We enjoy our spirits, both big S and little S," Wes said, swirling his glass of Bacardi and pineapple juice. "You mom offered me a drink. It's been a long day, and the evening's just begun." He took a sip.

Weeja clapped her hands and said brightly, in an attempt to ease the tension in the room, "What can I get you, Sunny?" When her daughter glared at her, she quickly amended. "Emily, that is. Honey, a Sprite? Or hot tea? I have a pot already made."

"Jack Daniels," Sunny said, a defiant edge to her words. "No ice."

Weeja raised her eyebrows at the request but poured the whiskey into a glass and set it on the table. She lit the candle with her Zippo and switched off the kitchen light, immediately shrinking the room to the soft bubble of golden glow cast by the flame. The light glinted off a Tarot deck that Weeja had stacked on top of her namesake Ouija board.

Sunny slugged back her whiskey in one gulp. "Another one, please. And don't forget to record this, Mom. I can't wait to see what Dad does this time."

Wes picked up the Tarot deck and hesitantly looked through the cards. "So, this is a real séance? Ectoplasm and mysterious tapping and all that—all for your ex-husband?"

Weeja was just about to remind him that she was a widow, not an ex-wife, when there was a knock at the kitchen door. Cassidy let himself in, still dressed in his uniform, hat in hand, gun in his holster.

"Sorry I'm late." He saluted Sunny and nodded briefly at Wes. "I had a call over on Oxford that took longer than I thought it would."

"Grab a beer from the fridge and sit down," Weeja said. "We were just getting started."

Cassidy drew another chair up to the table and hung his jacket over the back.

They sat briefly in silence in the dark room, their faces reflecting the flicker of the flame. Then the candle went out.

"Damn!" Weeja said, reaching for the lighter.

Sunny looked around the room. "Mom, is a window open?"

"I shut them earlier this evening," Weeja said, lighting the candle, "before you and Wes got here."

The candle went out again. Wes pulled out his lighter this time and caught the wick.

"Thanks, Wes," Weeja said, flustered. "I can't figure why it keeps going out."

"It must be Dad," Cassidy offered.

Wes laughed. "Yeah, and I'm Saint Teresa." He sobered suddenly and frowned. "It may be a sign that we are delving into matters best left alone."

A third time the candle went out.

"That's it," Wes said, standing up. "It's the devil's work—the Tarot, the Ouija."

"Stop, Wes," Weeja said. "Sit down. We are going to do this." She lit the candle once more and spoke to the flame. "Tommy, if you're extinguishing it, please just let it be. If you're trying to talk, let's use the Ouija. Cass, hand me the planchette. It's behind you on the counter."

Cassidy cradled the pointer gently, then gave it to Weeja. "We talked with the Ouija every Friday night when Sunny and I were little. I remember Dad asking complicated questions to try to trip up Grandpa Pete, but Grandpa always had the right answer."

Even in the dimmed light, a thin sheen of sweat could be seen on Wes's brow. "Was your grandfather dead or alive at that time?"

"Dead," Weeja said. "Peter died of a heart attack when the kids were little. Oh, we talked not only with Peter, but also Great Aunt Sue and my Granny, and some others.

"And George Washington," Sunny added.

Weeja laughed. "I'm not so sure about that one. But he was a convincing soul." She placed the pointer in the center of the board. "Two of us put our fingers lightly on the planchette, Wes. Let's start with you and me. The spirit energy flows through us and onto the board. Don't press down; just let it move as it will." She spoke to the flame. "Tommy, we're ready. This is our favorite old board. Are you there?"

The pointer slowly began to move to the upper left corner, where Yes was marked.

Wes jerked his hands away from the pointer as though it were scorching.

"No!" Sunny said savagely. "Keep your hands on it. So he can feel you."

Wes shook his head. "This isn't right. I sense evil in the room."

Sunny quickly put her hands on the pointer, sharing it with her mother. It moved a short distance away from the corner, and then returned to the Yes.

"Tommy, is everything okay?" Weeja asked. All four of them stared intently as the pointer moved smoothly to the opposite corner of the board, where the No was marked.

"Is the problem on *your* side, Tommy?" Weeja asked. The pointer stayed on the No.

Wes laughed nervously. "Yeah, if this *is* your ex-husband, maybe the heat's up a little too high."

"I don't like what you're implying," Cassidy said.

"Hush, Cass," Weeja said. "All right, that was a No, Tommy. It's something over here?—" The pointer almost flew back to the Yes corner. This time Weeja pulled her hands away and sat back. "Jesus, that was fast."

"So, what's next?" Wes said. "I saw the Exorcist years ago. It was Satan giving the answers through this kind of board. How do you know this is really your ex?"

"Daddy died!" Sunny said. "Mom's a *widow*. And the Exorcist was made up to scare the pants off people."

Cassidy nodded and took Weeja's place on the pointer. "This *is* Dad. I can feel it. Mom will ask him to spell out the problem, letter by letter."

"That's right," Weeja agreed. "Tommy, we're ready. What's the first letter?"

"W," Cassidy read.

"Keep going," Weeja said to the candle flame.

Cassidy continued to read out the letters as the pointer moved beneath his and Sunny's fingers. "E-S-L—"

"Stop!" Wes ordered. "You're spelling my name." He slammed his hands on the table, causing the candle flame to flicker wildly. "You roped me into doing this trick so your kids could let me know how much they hate me."

"It's not us," Sunny and Cassidy said, almost in unison. "It's Dad."

Weeja shook her head. "They don't hate you, Wes. Like I said earlier, the spirit flows through us to the board. Put your fingers back on the planchette, and you'll see."

Cautiously, Wes placed his fingers on the narrow pointer, and Weeja's fingers joined his.

Weeja spoke to the flame. "Tommy, I'm thinking you might be jealous, but let's face it, honey, you're dead. No need to resent Wes. You're in the spirit world now."

"He's moving it again," Sunny said. "D-E-"

Weeja addressed the candle. "*This* is why Wes is the problem?"

"A-L-E-R." Sunny paused to put the letters together. "Dealer? Gambler? Drug dealer?" She looked at her brother and then at Wes.

Wes was silent.

"Wes?" Weeja said. "You deal?" Her voice was shaking slightly at the revelation.

Slowly, Wes nodded. "Not now. A long time ago. Distant past."

Sunny gasped as the pointer moved again. "More letters— B-A-G."

"Bag?" Weeja said, puzzled.

"I guess so," Cassidy said, taking over the litany from Sunny. "And now—O-D."

"Tommy, we know you OD'd," Weeja said. "What does that have to do with Wes?"

"Nothing," Wes said, breaking his hold on the pointer to take a gulp from his glass.

Sunny took Wes's place on the pointer.

"He's moving it again," Cassidy said. "H-E-S-O-L-D."

"Hesold? What's that mean, Tommy?" Weeja said.

"It was *you!*" Cassidy stood up from the table, his hand resting on his gun. "You sold him the bag that killed him. That's what he means."

"Bullshit," Wes said, standing up as well to face down Cassidy. "How would he know that? You're blaming me for your father's death because you don't want me to be with your mother."

"Sit down," Cassidy ordered. "Dad wasn't the only one who died from that supply you sold. I looked the case up once I got on the force."

Weeja moaned and covered her face with her hands.

"First of all, I was the just the middle man," Wes said. "I didn't cut it with any shit. That came from farther upstream. And second, the statute has run out. You can't touch me."

With a growl of anger, Sunny threw her drink at Wes, dousing his shirt front and beard. At that same moment, the candle skidded across the table and tipped over onto Wes, and the flame from the ignited alcohol set his shirt and beard on fire. Screaming with pain, he stumbled back from the table and knocked over his chair. Cassidy grabbed his jacket and tackled him, smothering the fire. Sunny ran to turn on the kitchen light. For a long moment, the two men lay together on the kitchen floor, both breathing heavily. The scent of patchouli was replaced by the smell of burning flesh and hair.

The hot wax from the candle had spilled onto the Ouija board. It settled and congealed near the bottom, precisely over the words *Good bye*.

# THE SISTERS IN THE MUSEUM

*Christine Eskilson*
*Winner*
*2018 Bethlehem Writers Roundtable Short Story Award*

Julia visited the museum daily, even in the worst Boston winter, to perch on the long, padded leather bench in front of the picture. It was virtually all she had left of her family—this large oil painting of her and her sisters in the front hall of the sprawling Paris apartment they intermittently called home. Although she never spoke to them, the museum guards must have sensed how much the picture meant to her because they always maintained a respectful distance.

She was the last born of the four sisters, but their father's bearded young friend, who liked to paint children, chose her for the foreground. There she sat on the blue carpet, clutching a pink-faced doll, staring out of the ornate gold frame with a solemnity not seen in many four-year-olds. *What happened to that doll?* She had a vague memory of crying on one of the family trips home to Boston because the doll had been left behind.

Julia always preferred to be alone as she sat before the picture, but today a couple shared her bench. At least they had the decency to sit at the far end away from her.

The man cleared his throat. "It's been a subject of continuing commentary as to why the littlest girl is the one you see most clearly," he pronounced in a voice Julia suspected was intended to impress. She'd seen his kind linger at the painting before.

"It might be very simple," his companion suggested, brushing back her long dark hair. "Maybe she was the cutest one. Or maybe she was the favorite."

Julia suppressed a smile. Her sisters were not as prominently featured in the painting; a fact that couldn't help but please Julia each time she visited. Not that she didn't love her sisters, but as the last member of the family, it seemed fitting now that she alone was posed in the clear and even light. Florence, the oldest at fourteen, was sideways, leaning carelessly against one of their father's massive Japanese porcelain vases, while twelve-year-old Jane stood in the shadows at the back of the room. Even Mary Louisa, who at eight had insisted on wearing a red dress underneath her white jumper, stood off-kilter at the far left.

"Art is never simple," the man replied. He stroked his small goatee, staring at the picture. "It's also said to be a riff on Velazquez's *Las Meninas*."

"Are you going to show me that one, too?" the woman asked, crossing her legs. Julia thought her black wool skirt was far too short, even though it was paired with tall black boots.

The man laughed. "Not today, my dear. That painting is in the Prado in Madrid."

The woman pointed to the two giant blue and white vases decorated with birds and flowers that stood on oval pedestals, flanking the painting. "Are those the same ones that are in the picture? They must be at least six feet tall!"

"Those are indeed the actual vases," the man agreed. "The family used to ship them back and forth between Boston and Paris. They were a great acquisition for the museum. They really provide texture for the painting."

"I wonder where the parents of these girls are," the dark-haired woman mused. "I mean, if you're going to paint a picture this big, why not capture the whole family?"

The man gave the woman's hand a squeeze. "You clearly neglected to take art history at Brown," he said fondly. "This is a very famous picture about four stages of childhood, not just some family of plutocrats. Besides, I think there's a separate portrait of the mother somewhere in the museum."

Julia wasn't entirely certain what a plutocrat was but thinking about her mother made her sad. Although her mother had been so boisterous and full of life, she died suddenly when Julia was only sixteen. Julia didn't like the picture the bearded man had painted of her mother; it showed her seated with her head thrown back to reveal a slight double chin and the red spots on her cheeks that appeared after a few too many glasses of champagne. Julia never visited that painting.

"There's also a theory that there's some kind of sexual power play going on with the father," the man continued. "Like you don't see him in the picture, but he's actually there, omnipresent in the room, staring at his daughters and controlling them from afar as they move through adolescence."

Julia's back stiffened and her pale hands, which had been resting in her lap, clenched into fists. Their handsome father had done his best; to twist his love and care into something unseemly was an outrage. She considered leaving the bench right then and there, but she was determined not to permit yet another nonsense-spouting fool ruin her morning visit.

The man kept on talking. "The father's second marriage somewhat confirmed that theory. Picture this guy in his late fifties marrying a twenty-something who was a friend of one of his daughters. And he marries her only a few years after his first wife dies. Plus, the new wife is Florence—the same name as the oldest girl!"

Julia's first instinct was to cover her ears, but she didn't want to give the man any satisfaction. Besides, she thought bitterly, for once he was speaking the truth. The new Florence had been a shock to all of them.

"That must have been weird for the girls," the woman agreed. "So what happened? Did they live happily ever after?"

The man shook his head. "The father finally got healthy boys, two of them in fact, but the young wife died shortly after having the second one."

"And what about the daughters? You know so much about the background of this picture—what happened to them?"

Before answering, the man got up from the bench and walked to the painting, careful not to cross the sensors on the floor. The woman joined him. The museum guard, who had been hovering in the doorway to the next gallery, edged farther into the room. After a moment's hesitation, Julia rose to take her place in front of the picture.

"They spent most of their time traveling between here and Europe. They didn't need to worry about supporting themselves because they were all trust fund kids from their mother's side of the family. None of them ever got married."

*And what was so wrong with that?* Julia thought, turning her head to give the man a disdainful look. He ignored her, but at her age, of course, she was used to being invisible to the young.

"Seems a little sad," the woman commented. "To have four daughters and none of them ever married."

The man moved to the side of the painting to stand closer to one of the giant vases. Julia was gratified to note that he was a small man; much shorter than her father. The top of his head didn't quite reach the vase's scalloped blue and white lip.

"There actually was a son, too, but he's not in the picture," the man said. He waved his hand at the vase. "They took these huge pots to Paris and never bothered to take him. When he was six, he suddenly stopped talking, so they shut him up in an institution. He died there alone, still without uttering a word."

*No!* Julia wanted to shout, but she couldn't find the words. She had never known her older brother, but this man had Neddie's story all wrong. Neddie hadn't been shut away; her parents had sent him to the best boarding school in Massachusetts in the hopes he could be cured. They did everything they could; it wasn't their fault that it wasn't enough.

"And the oldest girl, Florence, the one standing against the vase? She only lived to about fifty. She died in a mental hospital outside of Paris. The second daughter, Jane, wasn't much better. She was so obsessed with playing the piano that she refused to eat. They took her to all sorts of doctors, but she was never able to live on her own."

"Maybe it was for the best none of them married," the man concluded. "Mental illness must have run in the family—probably inherited from the mother. I told you how the son stopped talking; well, when the mother was in her forties, she stopped walking. After she lost the use of her legs, she couldn't use her arms, and the next thing you know she's completely paralyzed. She was dead within a few months."

Julia couldn't bear to listen any longer. How dare this man speak so cavalierly and cruelly about her family? Rummaging through people's lives and picking out the saddest parts to trumpet to the world, with no regard for how they really lived. He was more than just another insufferable art critic; he was a monster.

Finding a strength she didn't know she had, Julia reached out to her father's massive vase and pushed it over on the man, knocking him to the floor. Alarms blared as the vase shattered into blue and white pieces, mingling with the blood that pooled around the man's head. His companion screamed, and the museum guard rushed past Julia to kneel beside the motionless body. He shouted something into his walkie-talkie, and heavy footsteps sounded from the adjoining galleries.

Ignoring the cacophony, Julia closed her eyes and floated up to the John Singer Sargent plaque on the wall. Then, with all the dignity she could muster, she stepped into the painting to nestle in the shadows with her sisters, where, after all, she had always belonged.

# SHADKA

*Ralph Hieb*

Three men sat around a low campfire in a rustic camp-site in the northern section of Maine's dense woods.

"What do you think is killing all the animals?" Dave asked, looking around at the dark forest.

"Don't know and don't care," John answered with a shrug. "We're getting paid to find it and kill it before hunting season starts."

"I don't know, but I've heard stories about this area," George said, a gleam in his eye. "A bunch of locals believe it's some kind of demon."

"Well, I don't believe in demons or spirits or any of that nonsense," John said, "but I do believe in the money we are going to get paid when we get whatever is bothering all those hunting clubs."

"That brings a question to mind," Dave said. "They are all hunters, so why did they hire us to find whatever it is?"

"Because they are all weekend warriors," George said, pride in his voice. "And we're the real deal."

"I think that sums it up nicely," John said. "I think I'll have another beer, then turn in."

"Oh my God," Dave said to his two camping buddies, dropping his can of beer. "Did you hear that scream?"

"Hear what?" John answered. In his usual way, he ignored almost anything that did not directly involve him.

"That screech," Dave said.

John looked at George. "Oh, that sound? It was probably just some animal that got caught by a bigger animal. Sit down and grab another beer and enjoy air without the smell of diesel in it. You know—not looking at what you're breathing. Besides, it's probably just a bear, or whatever it is we're looking for, making a fresh kill. We'll track it in the morning."

"It's not just the scream," George said. "There aren't any sounds from night creatures or insects."

"I'm not so sure this job is going to be as easy as we thought," Dave said. "Hunting for something we know nothing about isn't the greatest of ideas." Dave's gaze darted around the dark woods surrounding them. "There is a river aways over there." He pointed toward the distant sound of rushing water—the direction opposite from where the scream originated. "Whatever it is, I'm guessing it will need to drink. We can kill it there and leave."

Again a high-pitched shriek pierced the stillness of the night.

The men looked in the direction the sound came from. None of them moved for a moment.

"Something is in a lot of pain," George said, pushing his glasses up the bridge of his nose. "I don't know what can make an animal cry out like that." Squinting, he looked at the silent woods. "I don't see anything." He fidgeted with his collar. "I think I'll sleep in the SUV tonight."

"Do you think we should check it out?" John asked. He popped the top of his beer can, apparently unshaken by the sound. "You know, so that we can sleep peacefully."

"No." George's response was quick and given with a tone of certainty. He picked up a revolver and checked to make sure five chambers were loaded, with the hammer resting on the empty one. The weapon shook in his hands.

"Why not?" John asked, squinting at George's strange reaction. "And put that thing down before it goes off and hits one of us."

"Because that's Shadka causing all that screaming," George answered, the gleam in his eye replaced with a wariness. "And don't worry. I only hit what I aim at." He laid the gun on a rock beside him.

"You're not gonna start that again." John took a sip of his beer. Keeping a tight grip on the can with both hands, he shook his head. Speaking toward the ground, he added, "This story is getting old; try something new."

"Locals swear it's true." George wiped his hands on the leg of his pants, never taking his eyes from the forest.

Helping himself to a beer, but not opening it, Dave asked, "What's a Shadka?"

John groaned, and took a long draw from his beer.

George answered. "They say it's a creature that looks like a moose. And kills for the fun of it."

"And you know all this *how*?" John took another swallow and then picked up a stick to poke the fire. "You've been talking about this mythical creature as long as I've known you. And you never said how you *know* about it." John made air quotes around the word "know."

"It's an old Indian legend. . . . And there's a guy at the hardware store in town who's one of the few to see it and live." George answered.

"*Claims* to be, you mean," John parried.

Dave moved a bit closer to the fire. "Where did it come from?" he asked.

"It was created by the devil." George warmed to his story. "Legend has it that a medicine man who couldn't conquer his enemies summoned a demon to help him. Only the demon decided that there would be a price for his help—a really high price. He made the medicine man into an immortal creature that kills randomly and absorbs the spirits of his kill. And when the conditions are right, it appears and starts to killing."

Dave looked up at the full moon. "Is this one of those times?"

George nodded and looked away. He started to talk again. "A full moon and something to do with the position of those stars." He pointed at some bright stars near the moon.

"Then what are we doing here?" Dave asked.

"Oh, c'mon. You're not buying this are you?" John said, throwing Dave an incredulous scowl. "Sounds like the souvenir vendors get more out this tale than any demon ever got."

"What more does it need besides your soul?" Dave asked.

"I don't know. Only that it's not anything I want to mess with," said George.

Dave looked at George, then John. Both of them had smiles on their faces.

"Got ya." George doubled over with laughter.

John burst out laughing also. "You should have seen your face. You looked scared witless."

"You don't think we believe that old story," George said. "It really is just a tourist come-on."

"Very funny. All of those old stories have some basis in truth." Dave answered, and took a long drink of his beer.

"It's too dark to find out anything now. We better wait till morning, to find out what did the screaming," John said. "Maybe then we can quit talking about this story."

The men arranged their sleeping bags in the SUV. Dave kept waking at every sound coming from the woods. Only John and George slept peacefully.

~

"Rise and shine," John said in a loud voice. "I made breakfast."

"John making breakfast is less likely than hitting the lottery," George said, helping himself to a large serving of sausage and eggs. "Smells mighty good."

Dave just stared at the food sizzling in the cast-iron pan.

"Dave, aren't you hungry?" John looked at his friend. "You look a bit pale. You need some food in you. You'll feel better."

"I feel okay. Just no appetite," Dave answered. "Besides, didn't sleep well last night, thinking of that screaming."

"Don't worry about Dave," John said to George. "That leaves more for us."

John and George finished everything from the frying pan.

"Now that we've had a good meal, let's look for whatever made that screaming sound last night," John said, picking up his rifle. "I think you'll find some tracks from a *real* mountain lion instead of some fictional moose."

"I believe the sounds came from that direction," George said, pointing. John walked into the woods, with the others trailing behind.

~

After an hour of tromping through the brush, Dave stopped. "You think we should head back? We're not going to find anything." Then he mumbled to himself, "And it's damp and muddy. Didn't even rain and it's like sloshing through a bog."

"Damn bugs." John swatted insects hovering around his head. "I'm hot and thirsty, and this place smells worse than a cesspool.

"I guess Dave's right," John hollered to George who had taken the lead. "I think we should take a different way back to camp."

"Good idea," George answered.

"Oh my God!" Dave said. The crack of a gunshot followed his shout.

John and George ran to where Dave was standing and looking at the ground. In front of him were the remains of a black bear.

"What are you shooting at?" George demanded.

"Nothing. I just wanted to make sure you heard me." Dave stood pointing at the ground.

"Yeah, we heard you," George said, attempting to catch his breath.

"Whatever did this tore the critter apart pretty bad." John was looking at the carcass that had been ripped to nearly un-identifiable pieces. Entrails and bone were strewn about the trampled area covered with paw and hoof prints. "This happened recently. Hasn't even had a chance to stink yet."

"Bears don't scream," Dave whispered, keeping his eyes on the remains.

"I guess if it's in enough pain, it will," John answered.

"I've spent years hunting. And listening to legends. Dave is right, they have some truth to them," George said in a low voice. "And I only know of one thing that can make an animal scream like we heard."

"Yeah, we know," John said, with a tone of irritation. "Shadka. I thought we agreed it is a tourist come-on. Don't tell me you really believe it."

"Mock me if you want," George insisted. "But just look at the mess that's left of that bear. And the smell of blood is still so thick you can damn near taste it."

"Yeah," John said sniffing the air. "Whatever it is, we should probably track it and kill it for our own safety, if nothing else."

An ear-piercing scream from deeper in the woods interrupted their conversation.

"Come on," John said. "We need to find and kill it before it finds us."

The men headed in the direction of the sound; more ear-splitting screeches followed. Guns at the ready, they crept on.

Arriving at the edge of a cliff, they looked down at a distant scene across a river on the other side of a deep ravine. Through binoculars and rifle scopes the three watched the drama unfolding about a mile away.

"I thought you said it was just a moose," Dave said.

"You ever see one that is gray with black antlers?" George asked.

"I swear it's eating the thing alive," Dave added.

"Focus on the mouth," John said. "It has fangs." Then he added in a low voice, "Okay, I'm a believer."

George looked at his friends and whispered. "Keep your voices down. I think it knows we're here."

"It can't," Dave observed. "We're lying in the brush, sheltered by overgrowth."

"So why is it staring at us?" George questioned.

Suddenly Shadka started to run in their direction. The men watched agape as it forded the river and scaled the gorge as if it were nothing more than a slight hill.

The men stood and fired their weapons, emptying all three rifles, at the charging creature.

"Bullets don't affect it. Let's get outta here," George yelled.

The three ran in the direction of their camp.

"It's gaining on us fast." Dave puffed the words out.

"Just keep running," George yelled. "Maybe we'll find some way of hiding from it."

Running through the brush, they ignored branches and thorns scratching and cutting them.

"Here's a tree we can climb. Maybe we can lose it," John said, reaching for a branch. They climbed up and found perches on high limbs.

Shadka slowed to a walk as he neared the men's hiding place, sniffing the air for signs of them. His own scent of heavy musk, sweat, and blood oozed from his body, clinging to the air as he walked. Swinging its head from left to right, he sliced through the vegetation with his razor-sharp antlers.

The men held their collective breaths while the beast walked under them before continuing on the trail. Letting his breath out, Dave whispered, "Do you think it's gone?"

"No," George said. "I can see its antlers moving in those bushes. It's lying down, hidden by the foliage."

John whispered, "We can't stay in this tree forever. It has to move, and when it does, so do we."

George whispered, "Quiet, it's moving."

As he said the words, Shadka got up and walked to the base of the tree.

"Move up, guys," Dave shouted. It's on its hind legs, trying to grab me."

Sharp fangs snapped the air below Dave's feet as he scrambled for a safer height. Jerking his legs and almost losing his balance, Dave grabbed the tree in a tight bear hug.

Looking down at the open maw with red-tinted fangs at least two inches in length snapping at him, Dave clung tighter to the tree. The gleaming teeth, with rotted flesh and bits of fur still sticking to them, were only three feet below the limb he stood on. The stench of death rose from his mouth.

"It has red eyes, and I can swear there's fire coming from its nostrils," Dave yelled as he tried to climb farther up in the tree, before slipping.

Catching himself, his arms in a tight grip around the tree trunk, he stopped his fall only a few inches from the snapping jaws.

"Dave, don't move," George shouted. "Just plant yourself there."

"George, give me your gun," Dave said, his voice shaky.

"You have a rifle," John answered.

"Your pistol," Dave shouted.

George passed the sidearm to Dave.

Taking aim, Dave fired at the open mouth of Shadka. The creature became frantic in its desire to tear Dave from the tree limb. Its eyes bulged as a deadly antler sliced into a branch and sheared it off. A second swipe of the antler cut some more of the tree.

"You shot it in the mouth, and it only seemed to really piss it off," John said. "I don't think it can be hurt."

The furious snapping of the monster suddenly stopped, as it panted heavily. Every exhale sent a spray of blood from its mouth. Falling back to all fours, Shadka quickly ran toward the water running at the bottom of the ravine, where they had first seen it. Its bellows sounded of pain.

"It's hurt. Now's our chance," John said. "Get a move on, before it recovers and comes back."

"John's right," George added. "We need to get to the SUV before it returns."

As the men scrambled from the safety of the tree, they hit the ground running, only stopping to retrieve the guns dropped before their jump.

"I think I landed wrong," George said grabbing his arm.

"Just keep running," John shouted. "We can't wait for anything."

George kept moving, ignoring the pain in his elbow.

Approaching the SUV, they heard the sound of branches breaking, and the beat of hooves pounding the earth. An angry bellow from the beast sounded louder than a semi's air horn.

"I think my heart is going to explode," Dave yelled as he climbed into the back of their SUV.

Firing up the engine, George turned the vehicle around and started back toward civilization.

"Hang on," George yelled, flooring the vehicle. They bounced over the rough, unpaved, logging road.

"Slow down! You'll break an axle," Dave hollered.

"Look behind us," John said, as he stared out the back window.

Turning, Dave saw Shadka charging after them, its head outstretched in front of it, the weight of the enormous antlers seeming to pull it along faster.

"I can see fire coming from its nostrils," Dave yelled.

"Hurry up," John shouted. "It's gaining on us."

Dirt and stones spitting from the tires and striking the beast did nothing to hinder the pace of the monster as it continued to close the gap separating it from the fleeing vehicle.

The SUV took a high bounce, and a cracking sound came from the front, as metal groaned and squealed.

"I've got an idea," Dave shouted over the roar of the engine. "Head down that old road off to the side, just before we reach the open area."

"I'll have to turn, and it can get closer," George protested. "I'm having a hard time just keeping it at this distance."

"It's a slight decline," Dave shouted.

Yelling, George ordered, "Hold on." He cut the steering wheel a hard left.

Shadka had closed another car length on them. They picked up speed, heading down the seldom-used trail, gaining a little more distance.

"I don't believe this," Dave shouted. "It doesn't seem to be tiring."

Using the butt of his rifle, John broke the rear window out. It hung for a few bounces then fell. Shadka's hooves never slowed from the shattered glass cutting their bottoms. Leveling his rifle out the back of the SUV, John fired. "I can't hit it with all this bouncing around."

"I ain't gonna stop for you to get a shot." George tried to mash down harder on the accelerator, using the steering wheel to brace himself for extra pressure. Everything in their vehicle bounced on the uneven road, making it difficult for John to reload.

Twisting his body, Dave turned and shot at their pursuer. The smell of gunpowder filled the SUV, their ears rang from the sound of shots fired in the confined space.

"I think we're wasting ammo," John shouted over the noise of the straining engine.

Dave turned back to watch where they were heading. "Turn there," he said, pointing.

George looked to his left and saw that they had merged onto a service road running parallel to railroad tracks. In the distance, he saw a light centered on the tracks. Cutting the wheel, George put their SUV with one tire between the rails and headed straight toward an oncoming train. As they approached, the train's horn blasted a continuous warning to clear the track. Still, George held straight, racing toward inevitable destruction.

"Get us off the track!" John screamed.

"There's a crossing up there," George yelled. "I need to make it so I can get the wheel free."

In a moment the train would be upon them, but Shadka was directly behind them, closing the distance. With only a few feet until the crossing, George cut the wheel hard. They sailed right over the crossing, freeing the trapped wheel. The SUV bounced, and metal snapped; he used all of his strength to control the skidding vehicle. The train's horn faded as it moved past them. George braked, and they spun sideways as tires tore loose from their rims.

George and John never watched the drama on the tracks. They didn't hear the screeching sound of steel wheels skidding on steel rails, forcing the train to slow and stop.

"That was close," Dave said, shaking as if in an earth-quake.

"Hurry up and get us outta here," John said.

"I think we have time," Dave answered, as he stared down the tracks.

His voice shaking, George said. "I think we broke this thing pretty bad." He looked around the now lopsided interior of the SUV. Turning to look behind them, George and John saw no sign of Shadka.

"I saw it start to get off the tracks," Dave said. "It was only a car length from us, and got only part-way off before the engine caught him. I think if we walk a few hundred yards down the tracks, we'll find parts of it." Dave sat back, leaning against the car seat, and took a deep breath to calm his nerves.

John got out of the SUV, grabbing his rifle and a fresh box of ammo. "I'm going to make sure that it's good and dead."

George and Dave joined him, each taking their firearms and extra bullets. Dave grabbed their camp ax and carried it over his shoulder. They turned to take a quick look at the remains of the SUV. The smell of gas and steam came from under it. Nothing other than a flatbed wrecker would be able to move it.

They walked for a half mile before coming upon the front half of Shadka. The train had caught its midsection, rending the body in half. As they looked at the head, the eyelids opened, and the head turned toward them. Even with one front leg and the back half of its body missing, the creature tried to attack. George and John started to shoot the head; as it kept trying to reach them, using its only hoof to desperately attempt to pull the monster to its prey.

"Stop shooting and stand back," Dave said.

The two looked at Dave as if he'd lost his mind, but they stood back, leaving their weapons aimed at the creature.

Then hefting the axe with both hands, Dave stepped forward and swung hard, severing one of the glossy black antlers. He kept swinging and chopping the head as the beast bellowed in rage. Finally, Shadka stopped moving.

Down the track, a couple of men from the train ran toward them.

George bent over and picked up the antler with both hands.

"What do you think you're doing?" one of the men shouted.

"You're never going to believe it," George said. He used the antler to point at the ground, as he started to explain. Looking down, he was stunned.

Staring at what George was looking at, Dave asked, "What the? . . ."

All that was left was a dark, blood-stained section of earth and the shiny black antler in George's hands.

# THE BASEMENT

*Jerome W. McFadden*

The dots did not connect. There had to be a catch. The size and location of the basement apartment was exceptional: The building was on Lexington Avenue and 46th, in walking distance to Bryan's office at Rockefeller Center—for only $800 per month? There had to be something the super wasn't telling him, something he was hiding. Radon gas? Constant leaks? A major rat infestation? A cockroach resort? Faulty or dangerous wiring? Something even more disastrous? What could be worse than any of those?

The entry was beneath the front steps of the building, hidden under the stoop. No hint of a garden or any greenery, or even a hint of a place for greenery; very few plants or even vines grow in total shade. Inside the apartment, the narrow windows were high on the front wall, giving limited light. The only view was the ankles of people walking past. But the room was spacious and recently refurbished to make it livable. They had managed to squeeze a small kitchenette into one corner, a minuscule bathroom in another.

The super walked around the room, giving the hard sell. "You could call it a loft, you know what I mean? Just look at this space. Look at the iron beams on the ceiling. The open brick walls."

"Lofts are on upper floors," Bryan said. "This is a basement."

The super didn't even blink, "So call it a basement loft. The start of a new category. You could be the leader of a new trend. In on the ground floor, so to speak."

"This is not the ground floor. It's a basement."

"But a beautiful basement."

"What's wrong with it?" Bryan asked. Enough with the sales dance, already. "What are you hiding?" In spite of being in the basement, with poor lighting and no view, the apartment was still a steal. But Bryan wasn't about to come right out and say it.

"Ain't nothing wrong with it. What kind of question is that? Is that the way you wanna begin our relationship?"

Bryan gestured at the size of the room, imitating the way the super talked with his hands. "An apartment this size, in mid-town Manhattan, going for $800 a month?"

"You wanna pay more?"

Bryan sighed. He did not want to pay more. He could barely pay the $800. Recently divorced, with two kids in college, carrying a lease on a car he couldn't afford, which, by the way, was now parked in a garage here in the city that was more expensive than the mortgage payments on his old house in New Jersey. His wife now had the house, but he still had the mortgage. His "cash flow," if you could call it that, looked like a dry river bed populated with large rocks.

"So, you gonna tell me what's wrong with this place, or are you going to BS me all afternoon?"

The super held up both hands in surrender, "Okay, Okay. I can't keep the place rented. No one stays for more than a week. They break their lease and walk out, telling me to sue them, they don't give a damn."

"Why?"

"It's haunted."

"It's haunted?"

The super glanced around the basement, then quipped, "I didn't know we had an echo in here."

"Why don't you explain it to me, rather than trying to be a comedian?"

The man shrugged. "It's an old building. It comes with a ghost."

"The whole building?"

The super nodded his head at the walls around him. "Just the basement."

Bryan stared at him in disbelief., "And you can explain it? Right? There's a story that goes with it? Right?"

"No. I don't have a clue. Nobody ever explained it to me. Anybody who lived here who might know has moved out or left long ago, died, or sold the building. I don't know. It is what it is."

"And you yourself have seen this ghost or whatever it is?"

"It's a she. And, no, I haven't seen it. But everybody who has seen it said it's a she. But I ain't coming down to see it, or to see her, or whatever the hell it is. I take their word for it. They all come in, happy as a clam that they are stealing a great apartment from me with a cheapo rent, just like you, as if I don't know it, then they move out in a few days, madder than hell at me."

"Scared or mad?" Bryan asked. The use of the word mad rather than scared seemed unusual in this situation.

The landlord smiled, appreciating that Bryan had picked up on the word mad. "Yeah, that puzzles me, too. They go away mad, not scared."

Bryan shrugged, and took the apartment. For $800 he could risk getting mad at the super, and/or the ghost. He moved in later that week with the few pieces of furniture that his ex-wife had generously left him, mainly an ancient fold-out bed with broken springs, a wobbly wooden table with a short leg, three canvas field chairs, and a chest of drawers that once belonged to his great-aunt Emma. He went to the Goodwill shop to purchase cooking utensils, plates, glasses, and silverware, plus a black-and-white TV that appeared to be built in the 1950s. It was big, bulky, and cheap, but it still worked.

The ghost came into the basement the very first night, just as he was turning off *Monday Night Football*.

"So, we can't afford colored television?" it asked.

Bryan spun around, nearly tipping out of his canvas chair, to see a whispery, grayish, female form standing in the center of the room. She was fat, in a drab, ankle-length dress, at least as far as he could tell. The hairs on his arms and neck stood straight up as if reacting to static electricity. "Oh, my god, my god, my god, it's true," he said, more to himself than her.

"What's true? That we can't afford a color television?"

"N-No. T-That you're here!"

"Where the hell should I be?" the ghost replied, then added, "Ah, actually I shouldn't be saying things like that."

"Y-You're really here."

"You're not much of a conversationalist, are you?"

Bryan blushed, lost for words. "It's just that—"

"What were those blurry white lines on the TV? They seemed to trail the football players whenever they made a move?"

Bryan looked from the ghost to the set, then slowly understood what she was talking about. He was almost embarrassed to explain it. "Oh, They-They're called ghosts. That's because the reception down here is really, really, bad. I can't afford cable, so I ran an antenna out the window against the outside wall, but it's too low with all the buildings around here, so the reception sucks."

"Lord, can you imagine that? Being stuck inside a TV? It's bad enough being stuck down here in this stupid basement."

"You-You're stuck down here?"

"Your conversation is not getting any better. And you stutter. With a little luck on my side, you ain't going to last too long, like all the others." She fluttered her transparent hands in front of her transparent face, fanning herself. "Don't you find it hot in here?"

Bryan wondered if translucent hand flapping could really create a breeze, but said, "No. In fact it's a bit chilly. I was gonna talk to the landlord about that."

"I think I'm having hot flashes. And my feet hurt. I think they're swollen. I feel bloated, too."

Bryan looked down at her feet, at least where he thought her feet should be, but couldn't see anything distinct. "Do you want me to run you some warm water so you can soak them?" That was a little weak, but it was all he could think of to say.

"No foot massage, huh? Thanks for the sympathy."

"What do you want from me? I've never met a ghost before."

The woman/ghost sighed. "Lucky me."

"I thought ghosts were supposed to be scary?"

"Wrong basement."

"So, instead, I get a ghost with an attitude?"

She walked, or rather floated across the room, to sit in one of the folding chairs. "I'm in a bad mood. But then, I am always in a bad mood."

"W-Why are you here?"

"Why am I here? What kind of stupid question is that? I'm here because I'm here. Where else am I gonna be?"

"I mean . . . why are you ghosting up this basement apartment? Is there a reason why you're stuck down here? Something bad happen to you or—"

"'Ghosting up this basement apartment?' What kind of phrase is that? 'Ghosting up?' You just make that up? I never heard that kind of shit before."

Bryan was about to reply when she interrupted him. "You know, we ought to rearrange this furniture. It just doesn't look right in here."

"Rearrange the furniture? I have three chairs, a rickety table, an old TV sitting on an orange crate, and a chest of drawers, and you want to rearrange the furniture?" Bryan stared at her for a long moment. This all sounded too familiar. Then he burst out laughing. Before he could stop himself he said, "Jesus, I'm living with a menopausal ghost!"

"Hey, you think this is funny? I didn't ask to be stuck down here in this stupid basement at my age. It just happened. You shoulda seen me when I was young. I was a looker."

"You couldn't tell it now, could you?" Bryan said, surprised at his own rudeness.

"You have a problem with the way I look?"

"You trying to pick a fight with me?" Bryan replied.

"Don't take that tone with me!"

Bryan sighed, then pulled himself up from his canvas chair. "I've been through this before and I don't need a repeat. Hang around and ghost up this place, or whatever the hell it is that you do, but I'm going out to a bar to have a drink and then coming back to go to bed. Don't bother to wait up!"

There was no response as he went out the door but he heard the banging of pots and pans, deep sighs, and the shuffle of feet walking around the apartment. That, too, was a repeat of what he had before. But she was gone by the time he came back to the apartment and went to bed.

All the next day while at work he thought about the basement and the ghost, trying to decide what to do. Should he leave? Give up the great location with the great low rent? Go to a church to see if he could call in an exorcist? Or just put up with it?

He made his decision that evening on his way home. He put a small bag of groceries on the kitchenette shelf and yelled out to the empty room, "Hi, honey, I'm home," pleased, in spite of himself, to have company in this dismal basement; someone who was going to hang around, no matter what, even if she was annoying as hell. Maybe, just maybe, if he could learn how to massage her non-existent feet, she might even do some house cleaning.

# Ride of His Life

*Christopher D. Ochs*

I was twelve years old when we saw a ghost—at least, we all thought it was a ghost at the time. Twenty years later, I'm not so sure what it was.

Me and a few other kids who lived between Maxwell and Nelson Streets made up the Canal Crew. We were a rough-'n-tumble gang of brats who managed to find trouble most every day of summer vacation.

Nothing dastardly or criminal, you understand. Just the usual tomfoolery that filled boys' idle hours during those carefree days before Hitler and Stalin came along: diving in the quarry pool, stinking up people's homes by burning cattails and pussy willows next to their open windows, poling up and down the canal on makeshift rafts made from plundered lumber, skinny-dipping and getting old ladies' girdles in a bunch when we flaunted our privates at passing canal-side trolleys.

The high point of each summer came two days before the annual carnival opened in East Side Park. Jim, Frank, Slappy, and I would slip through the fence and nab all the free rides we could stomach until dark.

The carnies didn't mind, as long as we didn't wreck anything or draw the attention of the carnival dick. They needed to load-test their machines before opening to the public, and we were more convenient than lugging piles of sandbags back and forth on a hot summer day.

But the real treat, the "piece of resistance" (as Jim would mispronounce it), was getting free rides on the Vortex.

By modern standards, that roller-coaster wouldn't be much to look at. Nor would its climbs and drops compare to those of today's computer-engineered metal dreadnoughts.

But consider this—there were no seat belts, no safety bars, no padding or restraints of any kind. The cars were bare metal and wood, with a single leather grip for each seat. And constructed with pallet-grade lumber, slap-dash pipe and girder, the track was a rickety nightmare that made a Wild Mouse ride seem safe as houses. Mind you, this was decades before anything like the amusement ride safety laws came along.

But was the Canal Crew satisfied with the challenge of riding a mere deathtrap like the Vortex? Not in the slightest—so we did it one better.

And this day, we were breaking in our newest member.

"I gotta *what*?" exclaimed Mort, pleading with his eyes. He jerked a thumb at Slappy. "Is he nuts, Stan?"

"You heard me," said Slappy, poking his finger into Mort's chest. "You wanna be in the Canal Crew? Then here's whatcha do. Get in the last car. By the time the Vortex returns to the station, you gotta be in the *first* car."

Jim and Frank busted out laughing, between taunts of "Easy-peasy," "Scaredy-cat," and "Don't be a Mama's Boy."

Mort was about to whine again when I clapped him on the back. "C'mon, Mort—it's fun. I've been waitin' all year for this. Watch me, I'll show ya how it's done."

I signaled the carnie leaning against the brake lever with its handle carved in the shape of a tornado and jumped into the last car. He took a swig from his hip flask, spraying out a few drops of Old Panther-Piss as he barked, "Hang on, kiddo." He heaved the lever back, and the train lurched forward as the chain dogs caught the clanking conveyor loop.

I climbed two cars forward by the time the coaster reached the top of the hill. Holding on for dear life to the ratty leather strap while the cars zoomed down the hill, I swung into the next car as the Vortex bottomed out.

Ya hafta time that maneuver just right—early enough so that momentum forces you down safe into the next car before the next climb, but not too late or you'll bust your nose against the wooden seats. For most of the ride, you hang tight with everything you got. The last opportunity to get in the front car is just before the corkscrew leading into the station. That last short stretch of straightaway is just long enough to clamber into the catbird seat. Let me tell ya, taking that corkscrew leaning headfirst out of the front car is a rush.

The cars sped around the final hairpin turn into the station. The ride jerked to a stop, as the carnie leaned on the brake lever. I vaulted out, panting like a racehorse and damp with sweat. But I think Mort was drenched even worse, just from watching me. The carnie laughed so hard, he hacked up two days' worth of cigar smoke.

Slappy stood by the next-to-last car and pointed at Mort.

"Yer next, small fry," he bellowed. "Move it or get lost." He twitched his head toward the last car and swiped his blond bangs out of his eyes.

With a dread-filled frown, and his eyes hollowed out like those of the condemned heading toward the hangman's noose, Mort reluctantly plopped himself in the last seat. Slappy gave the thumbs up to the carnie, who took another gulp from his flask and with a lopsided grin yanked the tornado handle.

"Ya cain't start afore the hill," Jim called out, with his hands cupped like a megaphone. "Or ya gotta do it agin."

Frank was less helpful, sending him off with one last, "Nice knowin' ya, Mortimer!"

The chain grabbed the cars and up went Mort. The poor guy was so scared, he cringed at every clatter of the conveyor chain. He scarcely made it over a single car by the time the coaster disappeared over the crest of the hill. Jim and Frank ran alongside the tracks until the first turn, teasing Mort with their never-ending jibes. I leaned against the exit gate, watching the coaster as it turned and dipped. I had to crane my neck, but I spotted Mort still in the next-to-last car by the time he reached the corkscrew.

I shook my head in disappointment and called over to Slappy in a singsong taunt, "I don't think he's gonna make i-i-it."

"Then it's too bad for him," said Slappy.

He took up his traditional position near the beginning of the platform and extended his right arm. Holding his open palm in the path of the oncoming cars, it was at the perfect height to connect with the passenger's head.

Yeah, you got it right—that's how Slappy got his nickname.

"Aw c'mon," I protested. "Cut Mort some slack. He's having a hard enough time as it is."

"Eh, shaddap," he tossed at me over his shoulder.

That's our Slappy—he never listened to no one.

Around the corner, the cars whipped. I stepped toward the platform edge and leaned over past Slappy, to see how far Mort had managed. I stopped in my tracks when I spotted what sat in the next-to-last car.

A dirty, ragged and burnt man wearing a dirty, ragged and burnt uniform sat where Mort should have been.

As the train careened forward, the carnie shouted a string of words that even the Canal Crew had never heard before. He dropped his flask as he fumbled for the brake. The lever flexed under the strain of his weight, and the cars shuddered, squealing against the brake calipers.

The raggedy man leaned out of his car. He stretched out his right arm caked with mud. Wisps of gray smoke snaked upward from the tattered edges of his charred uniform. What was left of it looked military, but nothing like any doughboy's getup I had ever seen.

The burnt man grabbed Slappy's collar, pulling it tight around his scrawny neck. His unearthly strength knocked Slappy off balance, dragging him the length of the platform before the train finally screeched to a dead stop. Slappy tried to wriggle out of the man's grip, but to no avail.

Then the stranger stood up, lifting Slappy up to his tippy-toes with him.

The thing that once had been a man was missing his left arm and the bottom half of his left leg. Shreds of his burnt uniform sleeve and pants leg hung from bloody stumps that ended in raw meat and bone. Viscous gel oozed out of the socket where his left eye had been, and half his scalp was scorched off. What was left of his blond crew cut smoked like a cigarette. The stench of burnt hair filled the air.

The carnie pissed himself and ran screaming from the platform.

The burnt wreck of a human being yanked Slappy close and stared him straight in the face with his remaining eye. Slappy's face contorted into a silent scream.

"Listen, ya little turd," grated the raggedy man, "and listen *good* for once in your worthless life. When Mort tells you to follow him, you *follow*. Otherwise, Jerry will getcha." The living corpse stretched out his arm again, dangling Slappy by his neck in mid-air. "So listen up to Mort—when he sez 'jump,' you say 'how high.'" His voice lowered to a growl I could barely make out. "Ya got it, 'Diaper Dan'?"

The living corpse pivoted in the car, still hefting Slappy at arm's length. The stub of a broken rib poked out of his left side, tearing a fresh hole in his burnt shirt. His eye fixed on the speechless boy, not seeing me or anything else in this world. With a guttural yowl, the shattered half-a-man flung Slappy against the brake lever. The car rolled forward and caught in the conveyor chain.

My feet nailed to the floor, I stared at the dead man as he calmly sat down in his car and disappeared over the peak of the coaster drop-off. It wasn't until he plummeted out of sight that I spotted Jim and Frank cowering at the Vortex's entrance gate.

They stumbled onto the platform and knelt next to Slappy's slumped body.

He was out cold. We patted his hands and cheeks until he snuffled and coughed his way back to consciousness. I grasped him by the forearm and levered him up to a sitting position. The three of us scooped him up, planting him on his shaky legs.

He stared through us, his eyes not quite aligned, while the lot of us peppered him with a flurry of questions trampling over each other. "Wuzzat a ghost?" "Didja ever see the like?" "What the heck happened to that guy?" "Who's Jerry?"

Snapping to full alertness, Slappy screamed, "What the hell *was* that?" His hands became a blur of panic as he scraped at his neck, chest, and forearms, trying to remove any trace of the creature that touched him. "Didja see that? I wasn't imagining that . . . that *thing*?"

"No, we all saw him," I said. Jim and Frank nodded silently, their lips pursed into taut frowns. "He was warning you about somethin'."

"Yeah, whadidee say?" said Jim, rubbing the sweat off his forehead.

"You were supposed to listen," said Frank. "Listen . . . to Mort?"

"Yeah—*that'll* be the day," chuckled Jim, rolling his eyes. "Slappy don' listen to no one."

"And what was that crack about 'Diaper Dan'?" I asked.

Utter shock was painted on Slappy's face. "Sunovabitch," he whispered as tears welled up. "You heard . . .?"

He knocked me aside and dashed off the platform, crying like a little schoolgirl. The three of us stood aghast, staring dumbfounded at Slappy's back as he ran away, disappearing through our hole in the fence.

"Umm," Frank started after an awkward silence, "that's something his boozer of a Mom calls him when he doesn't pay her no mind."

"That thing didn't look nuttin' like Slappy's Mom," said Jim. "Looked more like his Dad."

"Kinda—if he was run over by a burning trolley," said Frank. "Besides, it couldn't have been him—he's as bald as Daddy Warbucks."

"I never heard anyone call Slappy *that* name before. What's it supposed to mean?" I said, scratching the back of my head.

Frank's cheeks flushed as he pouted at his feet. "I think that's 'cause he's a member of the rubber bedsheet brigade."

The platform began to shake, and the rumble of heavy wheels rounded the corner behind us. Mort's scream sounded like an ambulance siren as he hurtled around the bend.

"Holy Toledo—we forgot all about . . ." I blurted before I dove for the brake lever.

Sparks flew as the air filled with burnt rust and asbestos until the train bucked to a halt. Mort tumbled headfirst like a sack of turnips into the second car. Without missing a beat, he scrambled over the car's side door. He scuttled like a crab to the center of the platform and planted a wet kiss on its wooden planks.

We hefted Mort up to his feet. It took us a minute or two to calm him down and get him to talk without sobbing. The only sensical thing we could wrest out of him before the carnival dick chased us outta there, was that as far as he was concerned, he rode the Vortex once and was never *ever* gonna ride it again.

The Canal Crew broke up soon after that escapade. Slappy's bed-wetter secret was out, and he couldn't bear showing his face, let alone pal around with us anymore. He forever after denied anything remotely resembling the events of that weird summer afternoon.

The rest of the gang wandered away over the years. Though I tried to keep tabs with most of the Maxwell-Nelson Street kids after graduation, the draft started, and the whole world went to war again. I say "tried," because I lost touch with my old friends as they all got married, had kids, got work in another state, or passed away.

That's what happened to Jim and Frank. I attended Jim's hometown memorial after he went down with the USS Arizona at Pearl, and Frank's wake after he bought it at the Battle of Salerno.

The memories of that strange day at East Side Park were buried deep and almost lost, until I attended Slappy's—I mean Harold's—memorial service at his family's old church. It took several long months after the war for his remains to return home.

As I often did, I shook the hands of servicemen and women who paid their respects, thanking them for their service. They did what I couldn't do with my 4-F, due to a punctured eardrum from infected canal water.

I greeted one of them—an army sergeant—when he surprised me with a cheer of laughter and a bear hug.

"Stan, you old sunovagun!" he roared. I clasped him back in return, although with far less enthusiasm. Once I held him at arm's length, I recognized the boyish mug grinning from ear to ear, attached to a grown-up body.

"Mort? Holy cow, look at you!" I shook his hand—and cringed. His right hand was scarred with the discolored ridges and gullies indicative of deep tissue damage left by fourth-degree burns. It was then that I spotted the Purple Heart on his chest, surrounded by a battalion of other insignia and medals.

Standing outside the church's front doors, we dove into a long string of happy reminiscences and small talk. When we couldn't think of anything else to yammer about, we circled around to the topic of the day.

"What brings you here, Mort? Last time I saw Slap . . . I mean, Harold . . . he wasn't too keen on hanging around with any of the old gang."

Mort shook his head, his face a mask of confused introspection. "Yeah—no one ever *did* tell me what happened there at East Side, and why Harold left the Canal Crew."

"Er, it's a long story." I scuffed my heel on the cement like a recalcitrant kid. "Maybe I'll tell you over a beer after the service. Getting back to my question, what brings you back to this dump?"

"Harold and I were at the Battle of the Bulge. That's where I got these trinkets." He flicked his Purple Heart with a flippant chuckle. "I was leading two squads to take a strategic hill. Only thing was, Army Intelligence had screwed up our little patch of heaven, and they sent us over the wrong hill. Germans to one side, and a minefield to the other. We got hammered."

Mort looked me in the eye, peered through the open church doors, then up at the sky. The boyish grin was replaced with a somber sigh. "Harold was in the other squad. Things got really rough, and he must've lost his head. He headed straight into the minefield. I tried to stop him, ordered him to back out. I ran to the edge of the road and tried to guide him back, help him retrace his steps—but he wouldn't listen."

He held up his burnt hand and grimaced. His forearm trembled with effort as he squeezed his hand into a fist. "I got sidelined when a mortar from Jerry tore into the gas tank of a nearby Jeep. The last thing I remember seeing was Harold getting thrown into the air by a landmine blast."

Swells of organ music flowed out of the church doors. Mort let out a whisper of a sob, followed by a squaring of his shoulders and nodding his head toward the narthex. "All right, that's enough outta me. C'mon, they're ready to start."

We walked in, ambling down the aisle toward the closed casket draped with Old Glory. Wreaths hanging on easels stood vigil at opposite ends of Harold's coffin. A photograph graced with a black diagonal sash rested on the center of the lid—a portrait of Harold. He stood at half-profile in dress uniform, complete with the long blond bangs of his youth bobbed to a crew cut.

That's when it hit me, like a haymaker to the gut.

Staring back at me was the raggedy man who grabbed Harold at the Vortex.

Poor ol' Slappy. He never did listen to no one. Not even himself.

# THE DREAM

*Carol L. Wright*

"I dreamt about Edward last night," Father said at breakfast. My little brother, Joey, and I were much more interested in the fact that it was Christmas Eve than in any old dream, but Mama reacted sharply.

"Edward? Why ever did you dream of him?" she asked. "He's been gone now, well, I suppose it's been about five years."

"Five exactly." Father nodded. "It was such a real dream. He was out in our old rowboat in the middle of the lake, and when he saw me, he raised his arm and beckoned for me to join him," he said with an uncomfortable laugh. Then he waved his arm to imitate what he saw in his dream, a tear appearing in the corner of his eye. "It's left me quite melancholy for him, I'm afraid."

"Why?" I said. "What happened to him?"

Father looked at me as if he hadn't noticed I was there. Then he glanced at Mama, who shook her head. "She's too young," she said. I knew that meant that she didn't want him to tell me whatever it was. But Father's eyes told me he thought I was old enough to know.

"You were just a sapling, little one," he said. "Not much more than a baby then."

"I'm not a baby now," I said, remembering not to whine. Father looked at Joey, who was focused on running his fork along the table and making rumbling sounds with his mouth, pretending his fork was a truck.

Father sighed. "I guess you're old enough to know." He folded his napkin and put his face close to mine.

"Just after you were born, your Uncle Edward moved to California."

I had heard of California. I had some cousins there that I never expected to meet because it was over a thousand miles from our home in Kansas.

"Before that, we used to go fishing together a lot," Father continued. "We would sit in the boat with our lines in the water, and your uncle would tell me the biggest tall tales you ever did hear. I used to say the only reason we ever caught any fish was because all them big ones swam up to our boat, so they could hear what Edward would say next." Father laughed, like he was halfway back in that old boat with Uncle Edward, hearing him tell a tall tale.

"Then what happened?" I said, not wanting Father to forget he was telling a story of his own.

"Well, then, we got a telegram on Christmas Day, five years ago. It said that Edward was getting ready to go to church on Christmas Eve. It was the first snowy Christmas Eve they'd had since moving to California. He was wearing his best clothes, and had just finished slicking down his hair, when he dropped his comb on the floor. Next thing they knew . . ." Father snapped his fingers close to my nose and I blinked. "He keeled over dead. Just like that." He shook his head. "I just wish I'd known our last fishing trip was to be our last one ever." I could hear regret in his voice, and it made me feel sad.

"That's enough of that," Mama said. It's Christmas Eve, and I need these children to help with the baking instead of lollygagging with you all day, old man. She shooed Father out of the kitchen, and, as soon as she finished washing the dishes and I dried them all, we got to work on our cookies.

We spent the whole day with Mama. I don't remember what Father did. He might have gone to work. All I remember is that by the time Mama was making supper, he came into the kitchen. He still looked sad, and I wanted to cheer him up.

"Look at all the sugar cookies we made," I said, waving my arm at the piles of cookies cooling on brown paper on the table. It was my job to package them up, so we could take them to church to hand out to our friends and neighbors. "We've got enough for the whole world."

Father barely looked at the pile. I asked Mama if he could have one. Joey had already taken a piece of a broken cookie and was licking the crumbs off his fingers.

"No cookies for me," Father said. I could tell he was still thinking about Uncle Edward. I didn't know how to make him feel better.

I wrapped bundles of cookies, and then set the table, still trying to figure out how to make Father feel better. It was Christmas Eve. Shouldn't he be happy?

Father was quiet at dinner, but Joey was a chatterbox. He talked about Santa Claus and whether he would get the toy truck he asked for. He didn't understand about Father feeling sad.

After supper and washing up, Mama sent us to our rooms to get gussied up for church. Joey could pretty well dress himself, but sometimes it was hard to get him to wear the stuff Mama had put out for him. I got my dress on all right, but I couldn't do up the buttons on the back, so I went into Mama and Father's room for help.

"Come here, child," Mama said. "Now pull your hair up while I button those buttons."

I turned my back to Mama and pulled up my hair. It smelled like cookies. I looked over at Father, who winked at me as he buttoned his own shirt. I laughed. Maybe he was starting to feel better. "Oh look," he said, pointing to the window. "It's snowing."

I looked out and saw big, fluffy flakes drifting by the street lamp.

"I hope it doesn't pile up too fast," Mama said. "It might be hard to drive home after church."

"I wouldn't worry," Father said, pulling up his bright red suspenders. Then he picked up his comb to neaten up his hair. He was halfway through, when he turned back to me with a look of surprise on his face. Then he dropped his comb and fell down on the floor. He didn't move.

At first, I laughed. I thought he was making a joke, and I was glad he was in a better mood. But then Mama rushed over to him and called out his name. She felt his neck. Then she let out a wail I'll never forget.

Christmas was never the same after that. Mama, Joey, and I stopped going to church. "I'm not fit company on Christmas Eve," Mama said, and we never questioned it. We didn't feel like celebrating, either. Even Joey, who only had a few patchy memories about Father, knew better than to talk about Santa Claus or presents.

Years passed, and we grew up. I got married and moved to Nebraska. Joey became some kind of scientist and got a job with an oil company in Oklahoma. Mama lived alone in our old house. My husband and I would come to visit with our children a couple of times a year. Joey made it back about once a year, but could never seem to make it when we were there. We'd always plan to all get together sometime soon, but never did. Then, one day in early December, Mama joined Father.

We all gathered for her funeral, and I stayed on at the old house, going through stuff and settling Mama's affairs. Joey took time off from work to help.

"Stay for Christmas," I said to him. "It will take me at least that long to get everything settled. Besides, since I got married, I've found joy in Christmas again. Hugh and the kids are coming, and I'd like to share it all with you."

Joey looked doubtful. "I can't stay that long," he said. "But maybe I can return."

I held him to his word, and, since Christmas was on a Monday, I invited him to come on Saturday and bake with me on Christmas Eve as we did all those years ago.

We sat across from each other, in the mid-afternoon of Christmas Eve, packing up homemade cookies for him to take back home. Hugh and the kids had gone off to a matinee at the old theater in town. I couldn't shake a certain sadness, knowing it was our last time together in Mama's house. Joey seemed sad, too.

"There is something about being back in this house," Joey said, biting a broken sugar cookie. "I even dreamt about Father last night."

I stopped sorting the cookies and looked up at him. "Wow. It's been so long." I counted in my head. "Twenty-five years. What did you dream?" I asked.

"It was the oddest thing," he said, licking the last crumbs from his fingers. "I don't remember ever going fishing with him, but I saw him out in a boat with some fishing rods, and he was waving for me to join him. It was so real."

"That *is* strange," I said, hoping my face wasn't as white as it felt. Was it poor insulation that caused a sudden chill in the old kitchen?

For the rest of the day, I couldn't shake the sense of foreboding. I worried that something would happen to Joey if he stayed in the house that night. I told myself it was irrational, but I'd seen it happen before.

"You don't have to stay tonight," I said. "You probably want to get home for Christmas."

"That's okay. I said I'd stay," he said. "I don't want you to be left alone with all the work to do."

"I can handle it," I said. Joey was a scientist. I couldn't tell him the real reason I wanted him to go. He would just laugh.

"Besides, it's started snowing," he said, drawing back the curtain from the window. "The traffic will be terrible."

I looked outside. Sure enough, fat flakes drifted by and settled on the brown grass.

"Anyway," he said, scratching his head, "I'd rather be here with you for one last Christmas together."

"That's the problem," I blurted out. He gave me a quizzical look, but I felt compelled to go on. "It *will* be our last Christmas if you stay."

"What do you mean?"

I broke down as I told him the story about Father's Christmas Eve dream. "And you had that dream, too. If you stay . . ."

His look said, "You're nuts," but his words were more charitable. "C'mon, Sis. There's nothing to worry about. It's just a coincidence." He sounded so certain. "I must have heard that story somewhere along the line, so being back in the house just brought it back to me. The subconscious is capable of all kinds of tricks."

"I hope you're right," I said, looking down. "I guess it does sound a little silly, but it's just such an odd thing to dream—especially here—and on Christmas Eve."

"Of course," he said. "But there's nothing in the world to worry about."

As I turned toward him, I saw him pull out his comb and raise his arm to straighten his hair.

# Four Quarters of the Apocalypse

*Walter Bego*

~

T he world is my oyster, and I'm not sure how I feel about that. What to do—what to do? Maybe I should flip a coin.

~

In 1981 I arrived for my first day of orientation with Gentab. I was just out of college and pretty surprised to have landed a job so quickly. It wasn't that Gentab was so special; they were much the same as a dozen software companies dotting Boston's I-95 beltway. Then again, I wasn't so special myself. A 2.7 GPA doesn't turn a lot of heads, and changing my major from business management to liberal arts my junior year didn't look good either. I think Loretta Sims in human resources hired me on a hunch. After all, she was hiring for her own department. She could use more subjective criteria than she could if I were applying for an engineering position.

The training room had four rows of half-desks, much like a college classroom except for the row of data entry terminals along the far wall. I was greeted and handed a folder as I walked in. I checked my greeter's name tag. "Stephanie Harding, Human Resources," would be one of my co-workers. I got a handshake and a half-smile as she told me to take any seat in the first three rows. She didn't show much interest in getting to know me, but she did seem busy. There were already several nervous new hires seated. The room smelled of new clothes and dry-cleaning. I found three empty seats in a row, sat in the middle one and attempted to appear fascinated by the welcoming letter in my orientation packet.

Fellow neophytes filed in. A guy about my age, in what appeared to be a particularly uncomfortable suit, apologetically took the seat to my right. I decided to schmooze.

"Hey, I'm Ernie."

"How do you do, Ernie," he replied with a heavy accent. "My name Li Sin Teh."

"Hey Li, I take it you weren't born in South Boston."

Li laughed politely, "No, I have come from Malaysia. I have just finished my bachelor's degree at MIT."

"UMass—Boston," I replied. I knew that was maybe two levels above getting a degree off the back of a Honeycomb box, but Li smiled and nodded the same as if I'd said Oxford.

I liked Li.

Something had interrupted the perfunctory rhythm of greeting at the door.

"Yes, Mr. Granger. It's wonderful to finally meet you! If I can be of any assistance, please don't hesitate to call me at extension 5523." Stephanie Harding, Human Resources, was like a different person and she wasn't alone.

"Mr. Granger!"

"Call me Fry."

"Fry, I'm Headly Rhodes. I'm department head for R&D. I can't tell you how thrilled we are to have you with us. Of course, we'll be seeing quite a bit of each other."

"Not too much, I hope, Headly. I work best if I'm left alone."

"Of course! I understand completely."

Who was this guy? I turned to see what kind of person tells his boss to leave him alone on his first day. A kid, no older than I, in patched blue jeans, hiking boots, and flannel shirt grabbed the seat on my left, dragged it a foot or so closer to the wall and sat down. He placed his orientation packet beneath his seat without giving it a glance and plopped a quarter on the attached half-desk in front of him.

"Hey, I'm Ernie." I got a raised eyebrow in response.

"That your lucky coin there, Fry?" This time I got a grunt that might have been an affirmative.

There was something odd about the coin. It was fully silver. I leaned over to check the date, and it was a 1962. There was also something about Washington's head. Granger didn't seem to care that I was looking, so I got closer and saw that the coin had been double-struck.

"That's neat; where'd you get it?"

"Found it," he said, "on the road when I was little."

I suppose there's something to be said for a person who can hold onto a lucky coin so long, but I still didn't have a warm feeling for Fry Granger.

"Yes, I have known who Fry Granger is," Li told me at lunch, "and he is knowing who I am. We were both going to MIT, but we are not friends."

"Competition's tough at a school like that."

"Yes, you are right that competition is fierce, but I was not a worry to Fry Granger. He was the very best and had no one to fear from. He also had no one as friends."

ᴎ

There are advantages to working in Human Resources. After my first week, I looked up Li's file and saw that he graduated twelfth in his class. He had quite a few honors and accomplishments for someone so young. It made me wonder why he felt himself no threat to Granger. It took another month before Granger's file made it to the common drawers, and as expected, he finished first in his class and had easily twice the honors Li had. Additionally, there were notations of unspecified contributions to efforts with McDonnell Douglas, Honeywell, and several lesser known government contractors. The fact that they were unspecified almost certainly implied "classified."

No wonder people were falling all over themselves around him. Granger was a lodestone, the kind of guy that can make a little company like Gentab competitive.

Granger had an impact quickly. Gentab had a top ten software product within the year and three more hot titles over the next two years. That's how we came to the attention of Hudson Pierce.

Gentab's financial gains and cash position made it an attractive takeover target. Hudson Pierce, known in the papers as "the liquidator," was one of two major players seeking to acquire Gentab. You could tell which employees had taken advantage of the stock purchase plan. Those of us who hadn't been so farsighted felt like chickens invited to a Frank Purdue dinner party.

Monday morning, we got the word. Pierce had bought us out and would address the employees on Wednesday. The classifieds were in high demand over the next couple of days. It was a rude awakening for me to realize that no one out there was panting to hire a twenty-something personnel clerk with less than two years' experience. Come Wednesday afternoon, Hudson Pierce had our full attention.

If I hadn't watched him so closely, I might not have noticed it. Before he spoke, Pierce laid a few items on the table by the podium. On top of the stack was a 1962 double-struck quarter: a dead ringer for Fry Granger's lucky coin. I glanced across the room at Granger. He was staring off into space while randomly rearranging his Rubik's Cube. On the half-desk sat his coin.

Was 1962 a bad year at the mint? Other than Pierce's and Granger's, I couldn't recall seeing any other double-struck quarters from that year, or any other year for that matter. Eccentricities like lucky coins fit the profile of a flake like Fry, but not an all-business corporate raider. Granger and Pierce were about as different as two people could be. How odd that they'd both keep the same coin as a good luck piece.

There was one area where the two men were very much alike. They were both successful in their different venues. Could there be something to lucky coins?

In thinking about coins, I missed most of what Hudson Pierce had to say, but the relieved look on the faces of my co-workers assured me I still had a job. With two such lucky coins, I figured it might be time to buy some company stock.

∿

Ten years at Gentab Human Resources isn't the most glamorous way to spend your twenties, but by hitching my star to Loretta Sims, I found myself as the number two honcho in the department. Buying company stock had been a good idea as well. Gentab stock split nine times in the late eighties and early nineties as the company made a mint on unused "Star Wars" technology, expanded into the growing personal computer market, and created a very lucrative information technology division. New wunderkinds came to challenge "seasoned" veterans like Li Sin Teh. Fry Granger remained top dog.

Thankfully, thirty-two was not considered over the hill in the jungle which is upper middle management. My job was to seek out those wunderkinds, and that's what brought me to Stanford in the spring of 1992.

Rosa Rodriguez was only a sophomore undergraduate student, but that wasn't stopping Microsoft, Apple, or IBM from courting her, and it certainly wasn't going to stop us.

Pierce himself called me into his office, showed me her file, and stressed the importance of bringing the rather mousy-looking marketing student "into the fold." As it seemed so important to him, I felt justified swiping his lucky quarter. I wasn't trying to steal his mojo. I just figured that if Ms. Rodriguez was so important, I needed all the luck I could get.

From that moment, things started going my way. Without even asking, I was upgraded on the flight out to first class. The University gave me no problems about interviewing an underclassman when they had so many seniors to shop. Even my meals at the campus cafeteria were complimentary.

I wasn't very surprised that Rosa carried a double-struck 1962 quarter with her. Not wanting to tip my hand, I kept

Pierce's in my pocket. I don't remember ever being so charming. My job was schmoozing, and I was on top of my form. Rosa spoke of such incoherent subjects as the importance of domain control and ISP integrators, and I pretended to understand.

Rosa signed a contract that afternoon, and we made a date for dinner in Boston on her arrival.

~

Pierce never mentioned the quarter, and I didn't see any comfortable way of returning it. The corporate vice presidency in charge of marketing development was a nice surprise. I was getting used to nice surprises.

I became very active trading stocks and futures. I could do no wrong. Always a portion of my profits went to buying Gentab. I was gathering a nice little nest egg.

~

Rosa was making a habit of "dropping by" several evenings a week and staying till morning. I had told her that we should see other people, but her unscheduled visits made that difficult, which, I was certain, was her intent. She was the most valuable asset in my division, but she was getting to be annoying.

Most troubling was that she always left for work an hour after I wanted to be in the office. Rosa loved me, I suppose, but I still couldn't get her to do things my way. She'd lie in bed late or insist on a big breakfast. When I'd tell her I needed to go, she'd just smile and tell me to go ahead, and she'd lock up on her way out.

I wasn't going to give her a key.

One such morning, Rosa was running exceptionally late. I'd already canceled the morning staff meeting and was now running late for an appointment, and she was still in the shower. She had left her things haphazardly on the kitchen counter (her apartment had to be a pigsty). Several items had spilled from her purse, including her '62 quarter.

What would happen if I took the coin?

I hadn't noticed an immediate change in Pierce except that he seemed friendlier, almost deferential towards me. Last week, Kirk Tellurand from Info-systems had commented on how my boss "lost his edge," but that didn't really concern me.

If Rosa lost her edge, my whole division would suffer. But if I held the coin, would I suffer? Whatever Hudson Pierce's recent failings, I was doing better each day.

From the shower, Rosa was singing "I feel pretty" as she did every morning.

I took the coin, wrote her a note to lock up and left the note and key on the kitchen table.

Later that afternoon, the super let the locksmith in to change the locks.

ᴎ

It was a nice picture on *Barron's* cover: "New President for Technology Giant, Gentab." It wasn't the *Rolling Stone* cover I'd always wanted, but I still bought five copies for my mother.

The article stated that Hudson Pierce retired to enjoy the good life. Pierce may have wanted the good life someday, but it was the board of directors that said that day was today.

Though Fry and the guys in product development were still going great guns, my marketing division was now the star. If Rosa had lost her edge, several new go-getters took up the slack. My division alone was bigger than all but five of the Fortune 500. The fact that this was attributable to a strong team of developers instead a single star like Rosa convinced the board that despite my youth (still only thirty-six), I was the man for the job.

Unfortunately, the job didn't come with a seat on the board. Instead of Hudson's CEO, the board named me Chief Operating Officer: a slight, well noted by those in the know.

I began to wonder how a board that lacked the strength to oppose Pierce could turn around and oppose me. For the good of the company, I needed to acquire more leverage.

I already knew that taking the coin from Pierce and Rosa may have depressed their individual talents but had nothing but positive effects for me personally. I knew there was at least one other coin and I knew where to find it.

~

My secretary arranged a very generous fruit and flower arrangement to be forwarded to County Hospital for Fry Granger. The cretins had managed to acquire the quarter, but Granger had put up a considerable fight. I felt a strong desire, almost a compulsion, to over-pay the thugs for their trouble. Once I had the coin in my hand, I came to my senses. I paid them a fair amount—enough to keep their mouths shut, anyway.

My problem with the board turned out to be quite simple. I had less than two percent of the company stock. The key to acquiring power with the board was as simple as acquiring more stock. From my position at the head of the world's largest high-tech corporation, such an enterprise should be a piece of cake.

Daily, my secretary was inundated with calls from pseudo-journalists trying to get the inside scoop on what was going on at Gentab. Their goal, of course, was to get an information edge to help them win on Wall Street. Sure, these guys had their websites and newsletters, but they were no more journalists than I was. I informed Ms. Pellatier that I would take one of those calls each day but never twice from the same lowlife in the same week. I wouldn't be surprised if the old hag made a few bucks deciding who got to speak to me each day.

With each phone call, I let slip "unintentional" hints about who Gentab might be contracting with in the near future. Sometimes the leads were true, sometimes not. It didn't matter. I knew who to buy and who to sell short and the value of my portfolio advanced handsomely. The profits went to buying Gentab stock, and my share in the company grew.

~

The call from Marshall Turlinger wasn't unexpected but was gratifying nonetheless. In four years, my share of Gentab stock had risen from two percent to sixteen. As the corporation's second largest individual stockholder, the seat at the head of the table was mine at last. While Hudson still owned twenty-eight percent, he was off building houses with Jimmy Carter and didn't even bother sending in his proxies anymore. It angered me that my hard work was making that shirker so rich.

What really bothered me was that my own success was making acquisition of stock so difficult. Hudson, for all his power, still served at the pleasure of the board, and the board forced him to retire. I didn't want any such thing to happen to me.

Through our corporate interest in the world's less fortunate, I had discovered that Gentab growth opportunities in the third world went far beyond cheap labor. For tiny sums of money, we cornered markets, regulated the flow of commodities, manipulated bond rates, and even maintained limited control of the International Monetary Fund. In a couple dozen nations around the world, we had not only the ruling party in our back pocket, but the opposition leaders as well. The entire project was immensely profitable and with far less risk than it had been before the fall of the Soviet Union. As it gobbled the planet, Gentab retained a four hundred percent rate of growth, splitting for the fifteenth time since I'd taken the reins.

No matter how much money I put together, Gentab stock rose in price and became harder to buy. Would you want to part with a stock that showed a rate of growth that could turn a hundred dollars into a Lexus in four years?

I had to bring the price down.

Now it may be true that I had crossed a few lines on my way to the top—seventy-five cents in petty theft comes to mind—but I couldn't bring myself to do company sabotage. I had to find a way to keep the company strong and well run while bringing the stock price down. It seemed an impossible task, but, as luck would have it, I met exactly the right person in a chance encounter at Starbucks.

I don't usually go for these fancy coffee bars. They're far too crowded and trendy, and I prefer my coffee without an inch of whipped cream gumming up my mustache. But I've also learned to trust my instincts, so when I felt the urge, I pulled the car over.

Like the twenty other Yuppies in line before me, I checked my email on my PalmPilot while waiting, all the while keeping an eye out for a table to come available.

It was strange that I finished second in the table race. I hadn't finished second in anything for quite some time. The other guy was nice, though, and offered to share.

He went first in the "what do you do for a living" ritual, and he captured my interest when he said he brokered stocks and specialized in the technology sector.

"The whole market is overvalued," he told me. "All we need is one good scare, and all the NASDAQ stocks will lose half their paper value, maybe more."

"Even the more solid stocks?" I asked. "The ones that are actually making money?"

"They'll do better," he agreed. "Microsoft, Gentab, eBay, Intel all have a good basis for their value, but the common investor's just betting on the sector, and when the dot-coms start to topple, everyone will suffer."

"Half their value," he had said. Yet half wasn't good enough. I needed the price to drop two-thirds or more and to have the sort of panic that would convince more seasoned investors to sell. One of the big companies had to show weakness so that investors of all levels of sophistication would question the entire sector.

Gentab had stayed out of the operating system business. It wouldn't surprise me if Gates had a quarter of his own, and it was much easier to pick our fights elsewhere. Periodically, some minor software player would try to enlist Gentab in a crusade against Microsoft. My policy was always to listen politely, gather the facts, and do nothing.

There were ideologues in the Justice Department who knew nothing of macroeconomics. A lot of Theodore Roosevelt wannabes who salivated at the thought of bringing down the big kill. The administration also had some pesky scandal issues that they wanted out of the spotlight. Bringing down a corporate giant would distract reporters from reporting on ill-advised sexual encounters.

This wasn't going to be hard at all.

~

"Just deny the charges," my attorney advised.

Did he think he was talking to a child? Surely, at the prices I was paying, I deserved something more original than that. I never would have hired the simpleton, had he not been the son of a senator.

It's true that both Gentab and I had divested of other tech stocks before the crash. I even sold most of my Gentab stock, but the gamble paid off weeks later when I bought back more than three times as much for the same money.

The board of directors was now *my* board of directors. Gentab was one of only a handful of technology sector companies to make a full rebound.

The House investigative committee was hearing testimony about a possible conspiracy to crash the market. There was no danger of them uncovering anything because there was no conspiracy. The only people I involved were the press and Justice Department, and they cooperated "innocently."

"Idiotically," might be a better term.

What do I care if people lost money with "internetgeekoftheweek.com"? Gentab investors who held their stock did just fine, and that was my *only* responsibility.

Just to play it safe, I asked a Massachusetts congressman serving on the committee to come for a consultation. The kid was only twenty-six, but he was already making waves in Washington. No need to be college graduate if you manage to win Tip O'Neill's old seat in the House.

~

"I can't say much about the Senate, but I wouldn't worry about the House committee. Besides, everybody's paying too much attention to Enron right now." It wasn't what he said, but the way he said it that captured my attention.

H. Joseph Riordan was a handsome, clean-cut kid from Arlington, a working-class suburb of Boston. He reminded me of Andy Garcia. His dad and uncle owned a butcher shop, and his grandfather on his mother's side had served in the Kevin White political machine in the 70s.

I could see that, unlike his granddad, H. Joseph was no party plow horse. He was dressed down but with impeccable taste. Canvas pants, chamois shirt, and a Red Sox warm-up jacket gave him the air of the typical working man but without the sloppy, rumpled look. The material was common, but I could tell the cut was tailored. This man looked better in his "work" clothes than most guys did in their best suit.

It was his eyes and his tone of voice that really grabbed me. The kid had a presence that was both friendly and imposing. People wonder how Germany ever followed a loony like Hitler. If the old paperhanger was anything like H. Joseph, the mystery is solved.

"There's a Senate seat open this November," I reminded him. "I'd like to contribute to your campaign."

He laughed and shook his head. "Sounds too much like a quid pro quo, but I might need your help in the future." He reached into his pocket, pulled out a coin, flipping it casually.

Of course. How else does a working stiff from Arlington rise so quickly? I grabbed the coin out of the air and stuffed it in my pocket.

The expression on his face was comical. The kid still had a presence, but now I knew I was in control. So did he.

∿

"Ms. Pellatier, would you please send Jefferson in?"

"Yes, sir."

So, here I am, without a peer in the world of technology, finance, and marketing. I control forty percent of the planet's population through corrupt third world regimes, and now I have a perfect demagogue to set up as a figurehead here in this country. All, thanks to half a handful of imperfectly stamped silver. The president may be able to scare a few terrorists, but his power is hardly a shadow of mine.

"You called for me, sir?"

"Yeah, Jefferson. You know, I like you. You're young, but I think you have a big future here at Gentab."

"Thank you, sir."

"Of course, for the time being, I'm still the boss around here so . . ." I handed him some coins. ". . . here's a buck. Go get me a Pepsi from the machine, will you?"

"Okay."

I don't know. I guess it's no fun taking over the world once you're sure you can do it. Hudson seemed to enjoy his life building houses with Jimmy Carter.

Maybe I'll look into what Bill and Melinda are up to.

# OLD MAN OMAR

*Jodi Bogert*

New graffiti spread across the scratched Plexiglas walls of the bus stop. It was hard to read, but I thought it said the word "sweeze" or "swaaze." Right next to the "e" was a red circle with an X in the center. My cheeks stung as I scratched at an itch. Wasn't exactly steady with the razor and I nicked myself twice.

A frizzy-haired woman I never saw before sat to my left. Stuffed into a raincoat, luminous flowery leggings, and teal rain boots, she looked like she would burst at the seams. Even her eyes bulged. Her tattooed knuckles on her right hand spelled out the name "Lady."

The only thing that wasn't new at the bus stop that morning was a homeless guy, sitting at the far end of the bench. I always saw him there. He was part of my morning routine. Ever present with his faded windbreaker, scuffed sneakers, stained sweat suit, and gray hairs sprinkled across his beard. In his gnarled hands, he held a dented steel cane.

"Bus . . . which one you waiting for?" he asked me. His voice was deep and slow, like the thoughts he had couldn't come out fast enough.

At first, I thought I imagined him talking because he never said anything. People treated him like any other homeless person, as in they ignored him.

"Uh . . . the number six. Where the heck is it?" I replied. I had finally obtained an entry-level position as a copywriter after a year and a half of interning, and I couldn't afford to screw up in any way. Feeling friendly, I asked him which bus was his, and felt immediately bad. Where would he have to go?

"Don't have a number," he stated.

The bag lady tapped me on the shoulder. "Don't pay Omar mind, son. He's crazy!" she whispered. "Tells the same story, over and over. Best to give him some space."

Taking her advice, I pulled the newspaper out of my backpack and pretended to read, trying to diffuse the tension. My palms felt warm, even though it was a crisp, wet morning. I'd lived in inner-city Philly my whole life, but there was something about the homeless that made me a little nervous. Something in me believed that they could turn at any moment, like a rabid dog.

"I am waiting for my friend, Sam. He got a birthday today," Omar added.

The newspaper wasn't deterring him, so I put it on my lap, trying to be a man for once. Maybe I was ridiculous. It wasn't like Omar was carrying a gun instead of a cane.

"Sam got on the bus . . . forty year ago. Satan was the driver, and it dragged him to hell. Never seen since." His bloodshot eyes stared back at me, all serious like he had wanted to say that for a very long time.

The newspaper slid from my hands and fell to the ground, soaking up rainwater. The bag lady shook her head, wheezed as she got up and waddled away. She turned to me and gave me a look that said, "I told you so!"

"You look at me straight in the eye, give me the time of day. I knew there was some good inside you."

Now I knew I had made a mistake. Too late to turn back now.

"Sam was one of the toughest kids in school. Ma didn't want me hanging with him, but at 17, that advice went through one ear and out the other. Maybe if I'd listened, wouldn't be here now. But Sam, he was cool. Create a rumble in five minutes and take out a gang . . . twice as many guys. One half of the senior class worship him, other half scared of him. Make anyone feel important if someone mattered 'nuff."

Omar slipped his hand inside his pocket and pulled out a yellowed photo, shoved it in front of my face. A boy on the cusp of manhood stared back at me. His Afro almost touched the edges, and he wore a scowl, a cigarette perched in between his lips. I imagined he would probably lean against banged-up lockers with his arm slinked around a young girl in a miniskirt and platforms. He wouldn't be paying attention to her; he was too busy being the king of the world.

Omar continued. "The day he disappeared, we were running like we never had before in our lives. Trying to get away from the owner of Jay's. Eleventh and Penn. Sam stole some booze and a nudie mag. My hamstrings were straining, couldn't feel my legs. Sam pumped his arms, and the soles of his shoes slammed against the sidewalk." Omar smiled and hacked out a laugh. "Sam never let go of that bottle or that magazine. Farrah Fawcett was on the cover, had to see more of her."

Philly might be a big city, but I remembered Jay's, especially the owner. He was around when I was a kid. That man probably never exercised in his whole life. The only time he would ever run in a race would probably be if someone yelled out, "Thief!" instead of shooting the starting pistol.

"The next few minutes went by in a flash. Bus pulled up just ahead of Sam. Swerving to the left, he jumped on. The doors slammed closed before I reached. When I finally made it to the front of the bus, couldn't see a damn thing inside. Light from a match flickered inside, and I saw the driver. Drawing the match up to his face, he lit a cigar held in his grimy teeth. Smoke billowed out from a hole in his neck, like a chimney. Like a skeleton covered in skin, with sunken, reddened eyes. He stared straight at me and smiled, beckoning me with his finger! There were horns, too, small and sharp, sticking out of his forehead."

This story was going too far, and I was wasting my time. I protested to Omar that I couldn't stay, but he held out his hand, begging for me to listen to the rest.

"It killin' me . . . keeping this story deep inside. Please listen!"

Glancing at my phone in my pocket, I saw that I had some time to kill if I walked to work instead of taking the bus. It was best to let Omar finish, get him off my back.

"Sam's hands and face slammed against the front seat window. His eyes were wide open, raising his eyebrows up to his forehead. Scabbed and bruised hands wrapped around his neck, pulling him away. I couldn't hear anything, only my heart beating in my ears. Shut my eyes. When I opened them, bus was gone."

I had to hand it to Omar. He might have been crazy, no doubt about it, but he could tell a great story. I looked at my phone again, and the clock told me it was time to leave Omar alone with his disturbed thoughts. "Nice story, Omar. I'll see you later, okay?" I grabbed my backpack and got up to start walking the five long blocks to work.

"You don't believe me, do you?" Omar shouted. I turned around and went at him, miffed that he just gave me heck even after I just listened to his cock-and-bull story. It is one thing for a homeless person to be mean. It is another for them to be cruel even after someone goes out of their way to help them out. I'll admit it; I am not so good with difficult people.

"No! I am sane and going to be late for work!" I snapped.

Omar hung his head. "I knew you would say that. The store owner finally caught up with me and slammed me to the ground, pinning my arms behind my back. I tried to speak, say Sam's name.

"When I later told the cops, laughed at me . . . richest story they heard. The cops don't believe you, then your folks . . . not even your friends. Many counselors talked to me . . . saying that Sam probably skipped town, leaving me behind. Told me I was better off without him."

I secretly agreed with the counselor's advice. Sam was a thug who gave Omar the run-around, and maybe a helping of drugs that can make any dumb kid see Satan in the flesh. "Hell, Omar, he probably wasn't even real!" I said.

Omar turned his face up towards me, tears streaming down speckled cheeks. "Don't ever say that again! He is real and still out there, 17 and alone. Began to believe that I was crazy. But I couldn't stop thinking about his face. Every time his birthday roll around, I hoped to find him getting off that damned bus. Was going to turn 18 that year . . . 'fore all this happened, the beginning of a person's life. Everyone moved on, but I at least stayed behind for him."

Omar buried his face in his hands, shuddering through quiet sobs. Even if Sam wasn't real, there must be a horrible story behind it all. I sat down and patted him on the back, pulling out tissues from my backpack. I bet no one ever showed him that much kindness. Omar blew his nose and continued.

"Few weeks before he disappeared, Sam and I were walking home late at night. Wasn't his usual self, all cocky and full of it. This time, he looked down. I asked him what was up. He confessed that he wondered if cheap thrills were what life was all about—booze, bars, and fights. He loved the buzz of a good broad or beer, but I think he was starting to get bored.

"'Now don't go thinking I am turning over a new leaf in school or anything,' he told me. 'I just wish that something would take me away, at least for a while. And hey, I'll be legal soon. Then I can go anywhere, and no one can stop me!' He asked if I would come with him, wherever he go. I said sure, didn't even think twice. I would've gone anywhere with him, but I didn't get on the bus with him. I shut my eyes and let him slip away."

That must be one of the most profound regrets someone ever had over anything. The only thing I ever regretted was not going with Susan Telesco to the Days Inn on prom night.

"Listen, I am sorry I yelled and said I didn't believe you. I've got to get to work, though," I said. Omar nodded, staring at his hands. "But maybe I'll see you tomorrow?"

Omar looked over at me and nodded, smiling. He sniffed and rubbed his eyes. "You do believe me, though, just a bit?" he asked.

I shrugged and said I did. I let Omar have this one. After what he told me, he looked miserable, tired, and old.

All through the rest of the day, I couldn't get the story out of my head. I did say I believed him, but not because I thought what he said was true. Sometimes I experienced things like déjà vu or seeing someone on the street who bore a strong resemblance to a person pictured in the obituaries. I wasn't about to explain those occurrences, and Omar's story was no different.

That night, I couldn't sleep. I pictured Omar still sitting on that bench, looking out into the street, waiting for something that would never come. I got out of bed and went for a walk, try to burn some pent-up energy.

The city was oddly quiet and still, not one star in the sky. A bus passed me. I couldn't have been sure but thought I saw a flicker of light shining from inside. Smoke flew out, thick as exhaust, from the driver's open window. I practically ran to the bus stop. It would be the only way to know if what I saw was all in my head or not. When I got there, the bus stop was empty. I went to Omar's usual bench, but what I found was an empty bottle of beer perched on top of an old, ripped magazine. Farrah Fawcett was on the cover, showing off a broad, sparkling smile.

# THE DRAGON WITHIN

*Courtney Annicchiarico*

Once upon a time, there was a kind and gentle prince who was so mistreated and unloved as a child that he grew into a harsh and angry king who never approved of anything his subjects did. His cooks made food he deemed either too bland or too spicy; his musicians played music he said was too mournful or too jolly. He even complained that his horses trotted either too fast or too slowly. The people of the kingdom knew him to be a monster and were terrified of displeasing him. But no one was more fearful of the king than his young daughter, Kora.

The only one who did not fear the king was the sorceress, Astrea, who had known the king since he was a boy.

Time and time again, Astrea tried to appeal to the king's old nature, and the goodness she hoped was still there. But try as Astrea might, the king rarely granted her an audience with him and did not listen to her when he did. Discouraged, Astrea found solace in looking after Princess Kora and trying to protect the girl, who wanted nothing more than her father's love. When the king had servants come and take away Kora's toys because the child was messy, Astrea held her as she sobbed. When he instructed servants to no longer give her sweets because he said she was not taking enough pride in her appearance, Astrea snuck her treats. Stoically, the princess bore her hurt and refused to show her fear, until, at the age of six, the princess began to ask the sorceress for help only she could give.

"Astrea," asked Princess Kora, "can you make me a potion that will make me less clumsy?" A quick spell later, and the princess no longer stumbled on the stairs.

Another day, on the verge of tears, she asked, "Astrea, what about a charm, so I always know the right thing to say?" A quick spell later, and the princess spoke far more eloquently than her years.

On and on, Astrea helped the princess each time she begged for a different bit of magic. But it was never enough, because there was always another perceived failing for the king to point out.

"Princess, it is almost your seventh birthday, and I see you have a new stallion in your stable," Astrea said, pulling Kora aside. Astrea's smile died as she looked more closely at Kora. "What happened, child?"

Astrea listened as Kora whispered her tale. The king, she said, scared away her kitten because she played with it too much and did not work hard enough to make him or the kingdom proud. The sorceress hugged the girl, but the child was inconsolable.

"Child," the witch said after the child quieted, "come to me tomorrow. Come find me in my garden." Astrea smiled at Kora's reaction. The child was all wide eyes, flushed cheeks, and wringing little hands. Astrea paused for a moment and then nodded. "I'm going to try to help you."

The next day, Astrea watched as Kora tiptoed through the gate and gazed around. The princess peered through the rows of hyssop, anise, and chamomile. *No doubt*, Astrea thought, *the child is looking for spirits.* "I'm over here, child."

Kora swallowed a scream and spun around. "You startled me."

Astrea beamed and held up the basket she was holding. "Come here, Princess. You may help me collect flowers. This herb is called clary sage."

"What is it used for?" Kora asked while picking more of the herb.

"It is used to help people's eyes heal after an injury. Some say it can restore sight." Astrea cast a quick levitation spell on the basket, so it hovered next to the princess. The old woman sat on a nearby bench as Kora continued to fill the basket.

Slowly, the girl's enthusiasm waned, and she became sullen.

"Kora, what's troubling you?" Astrea asked, although she could guess the answer. "Are you thinking about your kitten?"

"I am wondering why my father is angry all the time," Kora responded.

"I've known the king all his life," Astrea said. "I bet you didn't know that. He was not happy or loved as a child, and he was often ill-treated and in need of my ointments." Astrea sighed before continuing. "I should have protected him. But I was young and not brave enough to fight a king, especially your grandfather. So, I am ashamed to admit, I did very little other than heal his physical hurts . . . and try to be his friend."

"Father had friends?" Kora said.

"Of course, your father had friends. But," Astrea paused before continuing, "he changed as he grew into a man. He became sullen and quick to anger. Your mother had a calming influence on him and brought him some peace, but her death destroyed the last of his joy, and it became clear that the little I had done in his youth hadn't been nearly enough. Rage is like a living thing with claws and teeth, Princess, that can harden even the best and purest hearts. By the time your father assumed the throne, people called him, 'The Dragon.'"

Astrea's heart sank as Kora swiped at her tears, puffed her chest forward, and said, "Maybe Father doesn't know that he is like a dragon. Astrea, can you please perform a spell that would make the king see himself the way that others see him?"

"Princess, I believe he knows." But the child's hope was so pure that Astrea found herself clinging to the possibility that the simple spell could make a difference. *Maybe he just needs to see more clearly.*

A quick time later, Astrea and Kora set off to distribute the clary sage that would bewitch the king's sight. The bright purple flowers adorned every bedroom and common area in the castle.

But something went wrong.

Instead of changing how the king saw himself, the charmed clary sage changed how the king looked to everyone else. The people had already feared their king, but from that day on, anyone unfortunate to be in the castle reported seeing flashes of red scale and fevered yellow eyes whenever the king lost his temper. Suddenly, servants spilled wine, cooks burned food, and craftsmen fumbled their tools. Children screamed in his presence, and the citizens cowered until, finally, the people saw that there was very little of the man left.

～

One day, Astrea was in the Great Hall, and one of Kora's servants begged her to help the princess. When she arrived at the girl's bedroom on the heels of her maid, Astrea found the child sobbing and clutching the pieces of a broken tiara. Kora explained how the king had overturned the furniture in her bedroom and snarled as he pulled all her gowns from her closet in an effort to find the tiny crown.

The old woman stared at Kora for several moments. Then she simply opened her arms, and Kora ran into them, whimpering and crying against her chest.

"All I did was lose my tiara, but then I found it! He hates me!"

"No, child," the old woman said. "No." Together, they walked to the Great Hall and sat at a trestle table far from the dais and prying eyes. Astrea sighed before continuing, her brow knitted in thought. "He loves you. I know it! It would shatter his heart if he saw . . ." Astrea paused, her eyes twinkling. *Maybe it's not himself that he needs to see clearly, she thought.*

"Do you trust me, child?"

Kora nodded.

~

In the witch's chamber, the old woman held Kora's hand, and, together, they stood in front of a large mirror. Astrea closed her eyes, her lips moving slightly. An aura of light emanated from the mirror and pulsated in tempo with the spoken enchantment. Finally, the witch's gaze fell upon the girl, and she kissed the princess, lightly on the top of her head.

"Don't be afraid, child. I want you to think of all the times your father has hurt you. Try to recall every insult, every time you were afraid, every time he ignored you and made you feel worthless. Every time you made a mistake, and he destroyed you with his words."

Kora closed her eyes. "No, no, no, Sweetheart," Astrea said. "I need your eyes to be open so that, in turn, so will the king's."

The light that had been surrounding the mirror swirled above Kora's head and slowly began to descend, coiling around the girl. As it enveloped the princess, the girl's reflection gradually changed. Kora recalled how she had felt when her father broke her tiara, and her cheek turned purple and red. When she thought about her kitten, another bruise appeared, this time around her eye. Pretty soon, consumed by memories from her past, Kora's face and body were covered by cuts and welts.

"What have you done to me? I look hideous."

"Anyone who looks at you, Princess, will only see you as you are—with one tiny bruise marring your knee—until I complete the spell. Once I do, your father will see what the mirror has shown: You look like a scared little girl who has been very hurt for a long time."

"My father has never struck me. This is a lie," Kora yelled.

"Your father never hit you, that is true. But look at yourself, Kora. Is this how you feel inside?"

Astrea hugged Kora as the girl stared at her reflection. Slowly, as the anger drained from Kora's face and was replaced by shame, Astrea released the child. "Then, let's go see your father."

They walked along in silence, at last arriving at the entrance to the throne room. A knight of the king's guard announced their arrival. Letting out a slow breath, the witch whispered, "Be brave and know that I will be there with you."

Upon seeing Kora, the king ran forward, outraged by the girl's bruise on her knee. "You are always falling." The brave knights instinctively grabbed the hilts of their swords as they saw fingers of fire shoot from between the king's razor teeth.

With that, Astrea stepped forward and threw a small vial at the king's feet. The glass broke, and a red smoke filled the room. Gagging, many of those gathered fled the room.

When the smoke cleared, the king started screaming. The completed spell revealed to him what the mirror had shown.

Astrea stood between her king and the child she loved. Quietly, so only the king could hear, the sorceress whispered, "It is only an illusion, but it is showing you a truth you have not allowed yourself to see." The king's anger, which had been his most faithful and constant companion for countless years, suddenly deserted him. In its place, terror bloomed. Throughout his youth, he had looked as his daughter did now, but without the use of a sorceress's trick. Astrea touched the king's face. "I know you never meant to be a monster."

The king covered his face and wept. "Break the charm, please. I can't bear to see her like that."

Astrea smiled and touched the side of the king's face to quiet him. "You have a choice. After the effects of the spell wear off and you see only your princess, physically whole, you can either dismiss what you have seen, or you can earn back the trust and faith of your daughter and, therefore, your people." Astrea kissed the king's hand. "I still see the boy you were when I gaze at you, my Lord. You bore so many scars, and I, ashamedly, did not help you as you needed. I am sorry I failed you then, but I do not plan to fail you or her now. You have a choice."

Astrea moved aside as the king stared at his daughter. The witch gasped and held Kora as he turned and left the throne room.

~

Spring matured into summer, and the king's shame kept him mostly isolated from his people. No one saw glimpses of red scale, claws, or fire anymore when they beheld their king, but neither did they see much of a ruler. Little Kora suffered most of all, convinced her father's absence was her fault.

Astrea was not surprised when Kora appeared in her garden and asked for a final charm. "Astrea," the little princess barked, "give me a spell that stops me from caring." The princess had been crying, but after a few poetic words and a wave of Astrea's hand, Kora's small features twisted, and her eyes flashed. Kora's whimpering faded. "I never should have come to you." Kora dashed away her tears and yelled, "You made everything so much worse!" The princess turned from the sorceress and began stomping and pulling plants from the soil. Astrea sat on her bench and allowed the destruction to happen. Kora ran from row to row, leaving trampled and torn herbs in her wake.

Rumors of Kora's rage and Astrea's spell reached the king. He summoned Astrea at once and demanded she break the spell.

"There was no spell, my Lord." When the king started to protest, Astrea held up her hand. "Your majesty," the witch began, "Kora has always been generous and kind, but is it truly hard for you to believe that her sweet nature could change? She is frightened and confused by your silence, probably believing that I was wrong and that she has deserved your criticism all along. Now, she is becoming prey to the same beast that has threatened to devour you all these years. I promised your daughter that you would repent, that your love for her would allow no alternative, but you have shown her no proof."

Astrea turned to leave the king's chamber. At the door, Astrea heard the king say, "This is my fault," and since Astrea could not argue otherwise, she allowed the door to close behind her.

Over a period of many weeks, Astrea watched as the king struggled to find ways to heal the princess's heart. Astrea longed to advise him, but never did. *He has to find a way on his own, but I will remain close,* she thought. He ordered the servants to fill the child's room with new toys. The princess refused to play with a single doll. He ordered the minstrels to play her favorite songs. Kora didn't even smile. The cooks were ordered to bake towering cakes. Kora would not take a single bite. Astrea felt helpless because nothing the king did reached his daughter's heart.

Until one night, the king went to Astrea with a plan and a request for her help.

The two worked tirelessly until morning. Astrea beamed as the king knocked on Kora's door. When the princess's maid answered, there was only a white kitten standing where the king had stood. Tied around its neck was an invitation to that night's banquet.

For much of that day, as Astrea suspected, Kora's poor servants struggled to keep the girl still and away from the kitten long enough to style her hair and dress her. She wanted to bring her kitten with her to the dinner, but Astrea insisted that the king would not approve.

When the princess arrived, the dining hall was empty. Hovering above trays of Kora's favorite food, cookies, and cakes were an enchanted teapot and utensils, all ready to serve. Pink and purple flowers draped the walls and the backs of chairs. A crown of white roses rested on the table, clearly designating where the princess was meant to sit. Astrea stepped out from the shadows and discreetly asked the girl's attendants to leave. The king's banquet was for him and his daughter alone.

Once Kora took her seat, the king entered the room. He was dressed in his finest attire, and, with only a shy smile, he embraced Astrea. "I'll be right outside this room if you need me," Astrea whispered in his ear. "No doubt straining to listen along with Kora's attendants." The king laughed as Astrea left the room.

"Do you like your new kitten, Kora?" The king's voice trembled as he took his seat. He cleared his throat.

"She is lovely, Father. Thank you," Kora answered without intonation. The king's smile faded as he nodded.

Suddenly, tears were running down her cheeks, but her shoulders were pushed back, and her trembling hands were fists at her side. She stood as tall as she could as she faced her father. "I know I am a disappointment to you. I am clumsy, lazy, and careless, and I don't try hard enough to make you proud. But do you love me at all?"

From the hallway, Astrea's breath caught in her throat as she waited to hear the king's reply. *Please be the man I know you can be,* she silently pleaded.

The king gathered Kora's hands in his own. "I love you without measure." The king sighed. "In fact, there has never been a day that you haven't made me proud."

Astrea let her breath out, spying from outside the room, satisfied that her faith had not been unfounded.

"As your father," the king continued, "I haven't tried enough to make you proud or make you feel loved."

Kora shook her head. "That isn't true."

The king kissed the top of Kora's head and stroked her hair. *They called her "the little dragon,"* Astrea thought, *but perhaps they will tame their dragons together.*

"You have a kind and forgiving heart, little one," the king said. "It is true that I have not tried hard enough. It was true," he corrected, "but it will not be true from now on."

Kora looked down and was silent. Again, the king's smile disappeared.

"Ah, you are also wise," the king continued, "to not take me simply at my word. It will take time for me to repair the damage. I'm exceedingly grateful to Astrea for giving me that time." The king cupped Kora's chin and tilted it up so he could look into her eyes. "I assure you that I do not need a charm to see clearly anymore. I have always seen that you are more than I deserve."

Momentarily forgetting herself, Astrea stepped into the room, clapped her hands and quickly pushed them down to her sides. She watched through her tears as the king pulled his daughter to him, encircling her small frame and peppering

her face with kisses. Astrea joyfully rejoined the other wom-
en assembled outside the room. "And now," she said, "I think,
both their scars can begin to heal."

# POINT OF VIEW

*Dianna Sinovic*

J ack decided to buy the painting within a minute of seeing it. Done in thick layers of oils, it wasn't the typical Bucks County pastoral landscape that cluttered so many gallery walls in New Hope. No covered bridge or bank barn, but a solid mass of greenery, a thicket of vines. The Amazon rainforest? He could even imagine that the paint gave off a whiff of rich, wet earth. Whatever the setting, Jack liked it. Eleanor would love it.

He was wrong.

"You still don't get it," she fumed. "Twenty-five years of marriage and you still give me gifts that suit *you*." She pointed to the ornate wooden coffee table, the Chinese table lamp, the painting he'd given her last year, for their 24th anniversary. "You, you, and you." She handed the newest painting back to him. "Thanks, but no thanks."

And with that, she was gone. She took nothing with her but a suitcase full of clothes and a few pieces of jewelry. The rest of the house, so lovingly decorated by Jack, was his to have and to hold. She'd had enough of doing things his way, she said.

*What did she mean,* he wondered.

At first, Jack was stunned by the sudden shift in his personal life. Eleanor had been a fixture for so long, the house seemed echo-y and empty without her. And he felt slapped by her rejection of all he had done for her. The Chinese table lamp alone had set him back $1,500. The workmanship was exquisite, the inlay of pearl; how could she not like it?

And then he realized how much more peaceful his days were now. He got up, went to work, came home, ate dinner, watched what he wanted on TV—all without having to defend his choices or preferences.

He kept the new painting and hung it in the master bedroom. The artwork was small, only about a foot square, with a thin silver frame—silver for their twenty-fifth year, but that was no longer relevant. Jack would see it each morning when he woke, and that pleased him. It would represent a watershed in his life: before Eleanor left and after.

He centered the painting on its hanger and stopped to study it more closely. A rough-hewn hut of tan and walnut peaked through the foliage, but the focus was the mass of vines, turning and twisting, looping and curling. Even the kudzu he'd seen on vacation in Pine Mountain, Georgia, seemed anemic compared with the vibrancy of this painted forest.

Maybe next year, he thought, he would sign up for a trip to the Amazon basin. He might find this same patch of ground, see that thatched hut, meet a few natives.

Jack didn't socialize much with his work colleagues, but he had a close circle of friends that he hiked with on the weekends. The local chapter of the Appalachian Mountain Club organized events throughout Eastern Pennsylvania and central New Jersey. He hiked at least several times a month, enjoying both the challenge of a tough terrain and the easy camaraderie of the trail.

Just after Eleanor left, Jack noticed a sudden fall-off in attendance on the hikes. He phoned Paul, the club president, after the third hike in a row consisted of himself and only two or three other people.

"Frankly, Jack, I think people don't know what to say."

"They don't have to say anything. I didn't do anything wrong."

"Of course not. It's just that . . ." Paul paused.

"What?"

"Everyone liked Eleanor."

"But she hated hiking. That was one of the litany of things she blamed on me when she walked out."

About that same time, Jack took another look at the vine painting. He missed hearing the alarm one morning and was running late for work, but something made him stop with his shirt half-buttoned. The picture had changed—or had it? The vines still writhed, but where was the hut? He tried to think back to the day he'd hung the painting, but presented with the scene as it now was, he just wasn't sure.

"Must have been a trick of the light," he murmured and went back to buttoning his shirt. A dab or two of white paint, the enhanced shadows, maybe even his assumption about a scene set along the Amazon River. Hut or no hut, he still admired the painting.

Eleanor's lawyer phoned Jack about a divorce. It seemed the logical next step, of course. She had been out of his house, his life for three months now. Numbly, Jack agreed. His own lawyer clapped him on the back over drinks at the Piper Tavern.

"You are one lucky man," Andrew said. Andrew, the lawyer, a friend from his college days, met him at the bar the Friday after the divorce papers were finalized. "I've been handling breakups for most of my career, and I can count on one hand—maybe two—the cases where the ex-husband walks away with just about everything. I don't know what you did, but it worked."

Jack nodded. He had done nothing but be the jerk Eleanor made him out to be. Swept with a sudden sadness, he didn't feel lucky. "Am I a jerk, Andy?"

Andrew laughed. "Even if you were, does it matter?"

With Eleanor officially out of Jack's life, one day slipped into the next, and the weeks rolled by. Work ramped up, with new sales quotas. His territory expanded, but he won the quarter's commission target. The AMC members returned to the hikes and said nothing to him about Eleanor, which suited him just fine. But the hikes had lost their appeal. Even TV no longer held his interest.

Instead, it was the Amazon painting that kept his attention. He moved it into the living room, where he could view it from the couch, with his feet up on the coffee table. Night after night, even on the weekends, he would rouse himself from his reverie to realize several hours had passed. He had been staring nonstop at the picture.

The painting itself presented no new surprises. The hut—if it had ever been there—did not reappear.

One evening after work, his next-door neighbor Matt walked over as Jack was pulling his briefcase from the back seat of the car.

"Sarah wanted me to check on you," Matt said. He seemed embarrassed. "She says since Eleanor left you've become a hermit of sorts." He scuffed his shoe on the cement of the driveway. "You—you're always welcome to drop over for dinner. Anytime."

Surprised and touched, Jack nodded. "Thanks."

Matt lingered for a moment or two longer. "Say," he added, "you might want to pay attention to that vine." He pointed to the far corner of Jack's house. "I've heard it's pretty invasive."

As Matt strode away, Jack scrutinized the leafy vine crawling up the gray siding. How long had it been there? From the thickness and height, it might have been years, but that didn't make sense. He'd never noticed it before today.

Settled on the couch that night, he opened his laptop and booked a spot on an Amazon River barge tour. Why not, he thought. The divorce had made such a small dent in his savings that on a whim, he decided to go.

A week before his trip, he noticed another change in the painting. No hut, but now peeking through the thick mat of vines were the colorful feathers of a macaw. Jack peered more closely. He heard the ruffle of feathers and the faint scream of a bird. Startled, he searched for the sound and was relieved to see a living room window opened slightly.

Returning to the painting, he blinked several times. The parrot was there, and then it wasn't, and then it was. Curious, he removed the painting from the wall and turned it around, looking for any information from the artist. Was it some kind of 3-D paint?

He saw only the title, a cryptic Self Portrait #3, in block letters. No name. He turned the painting back around. There was a signature in the lower right corner of the canvas, but the tiny brush strokes were indecipherable.

Disappointed and sure that the artwork was now worth far less than the $325 he paid for it, Jack vowed to sell it back to the gallery once he returned from his trip.

The weather cooled the day before Jack's flight out. He skipped out of work early to hike along the Lehigh River. The leaves were turning on the sugar maples and red oaks, and the air was crisp—so different, he imagined, from the sultry equator where he was headed.

With growing excitement, Jack finished packing that evening. He opened a bottle of pale ale and from his perch on the couch toasted his good fortune to be setting off on the biggest adventure of his life.

"*Salud*," he said to the painting. Tomorrow or maybe the next he would be immersed in a jungle very much like the one depicted in oils.

He stood close to it, then closer. One more step forward, and he felt the plants press in on him from all sides. The air was thick and heavy, rich with the aroma of wet earth. Long, verdant tendrils caressed his arms and his face. They shifted and moved, looping him with surprising speed into a tight embrace.

Jack cried out, but his yells were muffled by the drone of insects and the screams of a band of howler monkeys. Above his head, he saw the brilliant red and blue feathers of a macaw.

# OUT OF PHASE

*Ralph Hieb*

"So glad you could come over for coffee," Wendy said, offering her new neighbor, Darla, cream and sugar.

"We're happy to welcome you to the neighborhood," Darla said. "I suspect the welcome wagon will be here within a few days. They like to let new people settle in before they show up. I figured what the heck, I'd show up, anyway."

Darla had a genuine smile that warmed Wendy's heart. *Perhaps,* Wendy thought, *we've finally found a home where we can all be happy.*

"What is your little girl doing out there? She keeps calling someone." Darla said, staring at Wendy's young daughter playfully running along the edge of the woods. Her light-blonde hair shimmered in the warm spring day, streaming behind her as she ran. It was in perfect contrast to her mother's long raven locks.

"Oh, she's just calling for Casper, our, uh, dog." Wendy held up the coffee pot, offering to freshen Darla's cup. "You have exceptional hearing to have heard Susan through the door."

"You don't need good hearing. She is yelling loud enough that they can hear her two blocks away." Darla laughed.

Suddenly Darla stood up and screamed. "You need to get her back in the house now!"

"Why? What's wrong?" Wendy ran to the door fearing for her daughter.

Stuttering, "L-look at the size of that thing in your yard." Darla pointed to the edge of the woods. "It just trotted out of the woods."

Putting her hand on her chest to help slow her racing heart, Wendy looked around the yard. "It's okay. That's just Casper. He and Susan are playing."

"You let her play with that ferocious animal?" Darla was horrified.

"Casper would rather die than let something happen to Susie." Wendy relaxed and sat down, taking a sip of her coffee.

With a stunned look, Darla watched from the safety of the house for a minute. "I need to leave. I just remembered I left the stove on." She almost ran for the front door.

*It's always the same thing,* Wendy thought as Darla departed through the front door. *Devon said it would be different here, but no such luck.*

Finishing her coffee, Wendy picked up the dishes from the kitchen table and then watched the playful pair in the backyard.

A short time later, Wendy saw a sheriff's car pull in front of her home. Stepping out of the patrol car was Devon, her husband's best friend. The officer put his hat on, then looked around the yard. Settling his gaze on the front of the neat little house, he gave a sigh, then walked toward the home.

Wendy answered the door as soon as the sheriff knocked. "Good afternoon, Devon. Or should I say, Sheriff Wolfe," she added exasperated. "It's happening again, isn't it? People run when Casper shows up." She looked at the floor, grinding her teeth.

"Now, Wendy, don't get your fur up." He looked past the doorway. "Can I come in?"

"Yes, of course." Wendy stepped to the side, allowing the officer to enter. "Have a seat in the kitchen. Want some coffee? I baked some cake for later tonight."

"Yes, please," Devon said, taking off his hat and placing it on the table as he sat. "No thanks on the cake, but the coffee smells good. Fresh pot?"

"About fifteen minutes ago. Sugar and milk?"

"I take it black, remember?"

Wendy nodded, pouring a cup of coffee. "I suppose Darla called to express her concerns about Casper."

"No matter where you go, there's always one of them busybodies around," Devon said, shaking his head. "Any suggestions on how I can handle her?"

"None." Wendy looked out the window as Susie threw a ball. Casper ran to fetch it like a big happy dog.

"Full moon in a week. What're you gonna do?" He took a sip and scratched behind his ear.

"Like always. My husband will be back for a few days, we'll try to catch up on things, and then he'll go away again until the next full moon."

"I wish we had an explanation of how this happened." Again, he scratched behind the ear.

Tears formed at the corners of Wendy's eyes. "Yeah. One minute he is a normal man, and the next he's a wolf, without the benefit of the moon."

The sheriff took a sip of coffee. "I have the rest of the pack trying to figure it out. One of my guys suggested this witch a few towns over, so I looked her up. She said she'll look into it."

Putting her hands over her face, Wendy leaned forward, her elbows on the table. "I wish I knew what to do. We can't go on like this."

"I know." Devon stood and placed a hand on Wendy's shoulder. "I'll make sure some of the pack is standing guard during the moon."

"I'm not afraid of wolves."

"That's not what I'm talking about," he said. Picking up his hat, he walked to the door. "We'll figure this out."

Wendy watched as he walked to his patrol car. He hesitated, looking up and down the street. Then he got in and drove off.

"Susie, Casper, come in for lunch," Wendy yelled out the back door.

As the pair entered the house, Wendy stopped them. "Susie, wipe your feet." Then, looking at Casper, she added, "You, too." Wrinkling her nose, she bent down to get a good whiff of the large white wolf. "What have you been doing? I swear you are turning into more of an animal every day. You need a bath."

Holding back tears, Wendy made a sandwich for Susie and opened a couple cans of dog food for Casper.

Casper walked over to Wendy and nuzzled her. Then stopped and sniffed the air.

"I know," Wendy said. "They wouldn't hurt Susie . . . would they?"

A short nodding of the wolf's head gave her an answer that sent chills up her spine.

~

Several days later, Wendy adjusted her daughter's clothing. "It's dark—almost time for Daddy to come home."

"Will Daddy like my new dress?" Susie asked.

"I'm sure he'll love it."

"Mommy, how come you get scared when the wolves howl? Casper howls and it doesn't bother you."

Giving a final brushing to Susie's long blond hair, Wendy said, "Well, there are good wolves and bad ones. Sometimes the howls sound like they are from the friendly wolves, and other times like they come from the ones not so friendly."

The sound of the back door breaking caused both Susie and her mother to scream. Turning, they saw a large sandy-colored wolf. Wendy put herself between the creature and the frightened six-year-old.

"You need to leave us alone," Wendy demanded. "The sheriff and his men are watching this house."

It was almost a laugh that came from the animal as it approached, carefully putting one paw in front of the next, creeping toward Wendy and Susie.

234

Another loud crash, and two more wolves entered the room, snarling at the first and baring their teeth. The sandy-colored wolf gave a quick growl, turned, and leaped through a window, shattering the glass, before disappearing into the night. Their defenders walked over to either side of Wendy and stood at alert.

Reaching over, Wendy stroked the neck of a sizable dark-brown wolf. "Thank you, Devon. Jacques is starting to get pretty bold."

Shaking her hand away, the dark-brown wolf walked to the door and gave a long, demanding howl. Within minutes other howls could be heard throughout the neighborhood and into the surrounding woods. He looked directly at the other wolf, who nodded as if to acknowledge unspoken commands. He left the remaining wolf to stand sentry, keeping an eye on both the door and the broken window.

As the darkness faded, the sheriff's wolves stayed until daylight, then retreated into the woods adjacent to Wendy's backyard.

"Come on, Susie." Wendy took the child's hand and led her to the garage. "We need to leave."

"Daddy never saw my new dress," Susie protested.

"He will, honey," Wendy answered. "But right now we need to leave."

As Wendy grabbed the remote to open the garage door, a sheriff's car pulled in front of the driveway.

"I think I've brought you some help," Devon said while exiting his vehicle. He beckoned to a woman who was seated in the front.

"I don't know what to do about all the mess," Wendy said, indicating the broken window while ushering Susie back into the house. "Stay inside, sweetie," she said to her daughter, then turned her attention to their visitors.

The woman exited the patrol car and walked up to Wendy as Devon introduced them. "This is Sharlett. She's the witch I told you about."

"I understand your dilemma, and will do whatever I can," the woman said, extending her hand.

Darla came running up to the sheriff. "Did you come because of all the wolves? I called last night, but the deputy said you were busy with them already. What are you going to do to stop this infestation?" She paused to catch her breath. Before she could start again, the sheriff held up his hand.

Leading the woman away from the garage, Sheriff Wolfe addressed her. "Darla, I am doing everything in my power to deal with the situation. If you would wait a minute, I need to get Wendy's statement about what happened last night." He turned and faced Wendy, before rolling his eyes.

"Yes, Sheriff. If you would follow me, I'll show you the damage." She led the way into her home.

"I almost lost it when Jacques broke in last night."

"He is becoming a major problem," Devon agreed. "If Casper isn't cured soon, I'll have to challenge him myself."

"Maybe I can be of some help." The two turned and looked at Sharlett. Both had forgotten the witch. Looking around the living room, she commented, "I see you have some repair work that needs to be done." Lifting a section of torn curtains, she held it to her nose. "Smells a bit like a rabid animal, but I would say it's an over-aggressive werewolf."

"That isn't the reason we asked you here," the sheriff spoke softly, unusual for him. "We have a wolf that only turns human during a full moon, then reverts back to wolf the rest of the time."

Sharlett walked to the remains of the kitchen door at the rear of the house, as a group of men appeared. "I see you have some of the local pack coming over. At least I hope they are the local pack."

"They are my pack," Devon said. "Is there anything you can do?"

The witch walked around the room, sniffing the air. She stopped and stared out at the backyard. A large white wolf paced back and forth along the tree line.

"I take it that's the wolf I need to cure," Sharlett said.

Wendy's words choked out as her eyes filled with tears, "Please, can you help him?"

"He will need to come with me. This needs to be done before the moon rises tonight, or we will have to wait until the next full moon. Tonight, we should still have enough of its light to do what needs to be done." She turned and looked at Wendy. "I believe I know who is responsible."

"It's getting that we can't tell when he will be human or when he will be wolf," Devon explained. "It used to be the day before and the day after a full moon he would be human. Now he turns human only at night. And it keeps getting to be longer times that he's a wolf."

"Then time is of the essence," Sharlett said. "The curse is getting stronger."

Wendy ran to the window and shouted. "Casper, come on in now." Even she heard the desperation in her voice.

"Mommy is something wrong with Casper?" Susie asked.

Wendy knelt in front of her daughter. "Yes, honey. But this nice lady is going to try to cure him." She looked up at Sharlett.

"What is your name?" Sharlett asked, a tear at her eye.

"Susie," the child replied.

"My name is Sharlett. And I will do my best for Casper."

"Why don't you go to your room and play with your stuffed animals," Wendy said as she gently ushered Susie toward the hallway.

"I saw you tear up when talking to Susie. What's wrong?" Wendy asked.

"It's a long story," Sharlett said, wiping her eyes. "I believe Casper is at the door."

The white wolf entered and sat directly in front of the witch.

"Is there a room we can use? And Sheriff, would you fetch my bag from your car?"

Devon winced at the word fetch, but nodded and went to retrieve the bag.

~

Casper walked into the guest bedroom, behind Sharlett.

"Stay in the center until I tell you to move," Sharlett ordered.

Sitting in the center, he watched as the witch first drew a pentagram, in blue chalk. Then within it a circle of black chalk. Finally, she drew a circle around the outside of the pentagram making sure the line touched all five tips, using white chalk.

He watched with interest as she looked around and then placed scented candles at the four compass points, east, south, west, and finally north.

"I know the smell is not something that you find agreeable, but I assure you the stench of this incense will help with the purification that needs to be done. It was black magic that did this to you, and black magic is needed to undo it."

Taking a book from her bag, Sharlett read a verse at the east point, then at the south point and west, then north. She continued this routine for a total of thirteen trips around the circle. At the last reading, she moved to the south point and turned the page. Once again reading with a different verse for thirteen times around. Then the ceremony went to the west and finally to the north. As she finished, all energy seemed to be drained from the witch.

Casper lay in the center of the pentagram, his chest heaving with every labored breath, as a fine, black mist rose from him.

Looking at the now naked man, Sharlett ordered, "You need to stand and face east." She coughed several times, grabbing onto a dresser to steady herself. "Walk slowly and use your foot to erase a section of the chalk as you go, breaking the pentagram, and circles. Once you start, you need to erase the entire circle." Handing him a man's robe from the back of the door, she sank to her knees. Leaning over, she rested against the bed, nearly unconscious.

~

A few hours later, Wendy and Devon were seated at the kitchen table sipping coffee. "How much longer do you think they'll be in there?" Wendy asked Devon.

He shrugged, looking to the living room. "Do you think Susie is really transfixed by that TV program or just totally bored?"

"I hope it has her attention," Wendy said, shooting a worried glance toward her daughter. "If this doesn't work I don't know what to do. What do I tell Susie?"

"Don't tell her anything until we talk to Sharlett. Hopefully, she can work the magic."

They sat together in silence until they heard the door at the far end of the hall open, and saw a robed figure walk toward them. A strange and pungent odor enveloped him; sweat glistened on his face.

"Daddy!" Susie yelled as she jumped up and ran to him.

In a heartbeat, Wendy was hugging her husband with Susie sandwiched between them.

Devon sat for a moment smiling, then stood and walked to his alpha. "I hate to break this up, but Jacques is getting to be a royal pain. And it's getting close to twilight."

"We will all see what happens before this night is done." Casper turned and looked at the exhausted witch as she staggered along the hall. "Thank you."

"The only thanks I need is for you to destroy those who attacked your family. While you do that, I know of a certain witch who also needs to be destroyed," Sharlett answered, looking at the sheriff. "I would appreciate if you would hold my bag for a few days." Grabbing her coat, she left the room.

"Doesn't she need a ride?" Wendy asked.

Walking outside Devon looked around and reentered the house. "I would offer her one, but she's gone. She seemed like a woman on a mission. I think she smelled another witch when she was sniffing around the house,"

~

Later that evening, as the sky started to show the coming of evening, a group of men gathered outside Wendy's house. They were a formidable-looking crew. Some were unkempt and smelled as if they hadn't washed in weeks. Others looked as if they had just left their offices, but all gave the appearance of wanting trouble.

A tall, unshaven man stood at the center of the group. Looking at the driveway, he sneered at the patrol car sitting there.

"Devon," he yelled. "Get your cowardly ass out here. We got some business to settle."

Darla sauntered from her neighboring house and stood next to the man. "Jacques, you promised me the girl." She looked at the gathering as if she already knew the outcome, a smug grin on her face.

With a gruff voice, Jacques answered, "You can have her, but I get the mother, and what's left of the pack."

"That is our agreement."

Jacques stood and yelled again. Crossing his arms over his chest, his confidence in the outcome was evident in his demeanor.

Another group of men, some of them deputies, walked from the back of the house, forming a line across the front. Each one stood firmly in place. They were expecting the worst and knew they would deal out their fair share when the fighting started.

As the night grew darker and the moon shown brighter, some of the men started to turn. One after the other they fell to the ground as their bodies contorted, then reformed into wolves. Older ones still held human form, being the last to turn.

The front door opened, and Devon walked out. "Jacques, you are about to lose everything." He smiled, as from behind him Casper walked into view.

Jacques looked at Darla and growled, "So much for your magic. I will deal with you later."

Darla lost a lot of her bravado, realizing the spell was broken. She started to walk and then ran back to her house.

Jacques jumped directly at Casper, changing in mid-air into his full wolf form. When he reached Casper, he was met by the large white wolf. The two combatants crashed together in a swirl of teeth and paws. In less than a minute, the wolves from both sides surrounded the fight.

The two alpha wolves fought, tearing and biting each other, neither giving any quarter. As blood sprayed, the white wolf's coat glistened red. Still, the fierceness of the fight continued until the sandy-colored wolf lay on the ground. His breathing sputtered as both packs ceased fighting, to gape at the large tear in his side, exposing ribs and unprotected vital organs. The white wolf stood triumphant over his rival. As the last breath slipped from Jacques, Casper howled in victory.

The wolves from Jacques's pack walked slowly in front of Casper and showed their throats, acknowledging him as their alpha. Casper accepted them into his pack, then stared at the dead wolf. As if an unspoken order had been given the pack turned toward the carcass. A moment later the body of Jacques was torn apart and devoured by the now single pack.

The next day all that could be found of the rogue Jacques was a stain in the front yard of Wendy's house. Even the bones were gone.

"Daddy, are you going away again?" Susie asked.

"No, honey," Casper answered. "Daddy is home."

Wendy smiled and sat down to breakfast with her husband and daughter. "Do you think Sharlett was able to permanently break the spell?"

"I hope so. Wouldn't want to lie to Susie," Casper said, smiling.

Their meal was interrupted by a knock at the door. Wendy let in Devon, who was nodding satisfactorily. "Just thought I would drop in and see how you all are doing."

"Sit down and have something to eat," Wendy invited him.

"Thank you for holding everything together during my," Casper held his fingers in quotation, " 'sickness.' "

"What else would you expect from your beta?" Devon cut a large section of pancakes and shoved the syrup-laden food into his mouth.

"I'm glad you held on for as long as you did." Casper sipped some of his coffee. "Any word on the perpetrator of my illness?"

"I have some men searching for Sharlett. I have a feeling she will find the perp."

The sheriff's cell phone chirped. He listened with raised eyebrows before saying, "We'll be right there."

"What's happened?" Wendy asked, reaching for Casper's hand.

"We found Sharlett and the other woman. They are in some kind of circle that my men can't cross." Devon looked at Casper. "Sharlett says that she needs to talk with us in person."

"Let's go," Casper said. "Wendy, stay here with Suzie. Tell her Daddy had to help the sheriff with something."

Wendy nodded, and reluctantly let go of his hand.

The men got into the squad car and drove to a remote section of woods.

As they arrived at the scene, they found several deputies standing at the edge of a large circle drawn in the ground with a pentagram inscribed within it. Inside, two women were circling along the edge. Their intense stare at each other was not broken as officers tried to enter the circle, but were held at bay by its magic. A strong smell of sulfur permeated the air, causing the men to keep handkerchiefs over their noses.

"That's Darla and Sharlett," Casper said in a whisper, his eyes never leaving the two.

"How can anyone stand this odor?" Devon said, using his own handkerchief to cover his nose.

"They've been doing that dance since we found them," a deputy said. "The one said something about avenging a daughter."

The witches kept sidestepping, and when one thought she had a chance her arm would quickly rise, and lightning would shoot from her fingertips. The lawmen outside the circle were shielded from the intense heat, and the bolts shattered as they hit the edges of the invisible barricade.

"Stand back and away from the circle," the sheriff ordered his people.

As everyone watched, a flash erupted from Darla's hand and appeared to strike Sharlett in the chest. As fast as the bolt hit her, Sharlett twisted a medallion hanging from her necklace. The light returned to Darla more quickly than she had sent it, striking her in the chest.

The light was too bright for any to watch the impact, but Darla's scream nearly deafened all present. She fell to her knees at the edge of the pentagram. Sharlett grabbed the downed witch and dragged her to the center of the inscribed etching in the ground. Immediately Darla started to smolder, then her body burst into flame as a dark entity rose from the earth and pulled the air around her into its hands. Then it returned from where it came, leaving the charred remains with a dark wisp of smoke curling from the body.

Sharlett staggered to the outside of the circle as a bright reddish-white flash flared from it.

Bent over trying to catch her breath, Sharlett spoke. "You can enter now and dispose of her remains."

Cautiously one of the deputies stepped inside the circle, walked up to Darla's corpse, and coughed several times. "This really smells bad." Using his toe to gently nudge the body, he shook his head. "We need something to carry her in; she's disintegrating."

Never taking her eyes off the corpse, Sharlett spoke. "She planned to sacrifice your daughter so that she could retain her youth and power. When your daughter was no longer available, she tried to use me. I let her think I was weak and still exhausted."

"What are we supposed to do with her?" Devon asked.

"I need your help to finish burning the body and separating the internal organs from the rest so that there is no way she might resurrect."

"Do you mean that she can rise again?" one of the deputies asked.

"I don't know. But I don't want to take chances." A cold stare was all she gave the dead witch. "I can't re-enter the circle." Looking at Casper and Devon for the first time since they arrived, Sharlett added, "It's a witch thing."

~

Returning home, Casper told Wendy about Darla and what she had planned: She would get her sacrifice, and Jacques would get the pack. "And Sharlett says the spell is permanently broken with Darla's death," Casper said.

"Now neither one gets anything," Wendy said.

"Daddy promise me you're not going away again," Susie said, running up to her father.

Smiling at his daughter, he answered. "Daddy's home to stay."

# A MOTHER'S GIFT

*Carol L. Wright*

It was time to call the family, they said. My mom, Jane, would not survive this hospitalization.

The news was not unexpected, but terrible all the same. We'd been losing Mom by inches for months—years, really.

First, she had trouble remembering things—even long-cherished family stories. Next, she had trouble remembering people. She asked if I ever heard from her brother who died a decade before. She didn't recognize my brother. She told my sister she hadn't seen me in weeks, when I had just visited her earlier in the day. Each stage was painful, yet each was better than the one to follow.

In recent months, she had stopped speaking. The only real contact she had with others was through hugs. She melted into our arms, soaking up the love. At least we still had a way to reach each other.

Dementia attacked not only her brain but also her body. She became frail, and her ability to swallow was compromised. After inhaling food into her lungs, she contracted aspiration pneumonia. Even with the help of modern science, she was not equal to the fight.

I sat with her in the sterile hospital room with my husband. Our children, who now lived far from home, had gathered close, while my siblings traveled from even greater distances. The rhythmic whoosh of the ventilator reminded us that without its support, Mom would no longer be with us by the time they all arrived. I knew she would have wanted mechanical assistance to help her wait for them, even though she couldn't express consent.

Family was most important to her. She loved children—especially babies. I'd known that all my life. She told me that she had once thought she always wanted to have a baby in the house—but, of course, babies grow.

She was just as in love with her grandchildren, having a special relationship with each. My daughter was her first; my son her second. Their cousins followed, increasing her joy in immeasurable ways. But it had been many years since our family had any babies.

Not long after my daughter, Jessica, married, Mom said to her, "I don't know if you're planning on children, but if you are, could you not wait too long? I want to meet my great-grandchildren."

My daughter assured her they planned to have kids within a couple of years.

"Well, you never know," Mom said. And she had a sixth sense about such things.

~

We never told Mom that Jessica and her husband, Mark, were having trouble conceiving. They started trying when Mom still lived independently. Years passed, and while Mom moved into assisted living, and then to a dementia facility, they still had no success. They consulted a fertility clinic that identified the problem and told them they would need to use *in vitro* fertilization—IVF. There was no other way.

But IVF is expensive and carries no guarantees. Over the past year, they had tried three times. Painful hormone shots forced my daughter's body to produce, in one month, a quantity of eggs that would usually mature over three years. All the while, expenses rose. On the first try, they did not get a single viable embryo. On the second and third, they had embryos that grew, but did not develop into blastocysts—the optimum stage of development for transfer. They transferred some anyway, but none implanted. No pregnancy.

Each failure was, for them, a little death—a death of hope that they would be able to have children. With their insurance coverage exhausted, and their bank account drained, they were losing hope of ever creating life together. They sought counseling to help deal with their grief, and their therapist had them write letters to the child they would never have.

And now my daughter's grief was compounded by knowing that she was losing the grandmother she adored without ever giving her the great-grandchildren they both longed for.

∿

People started arriving. My husband and son went out to meet my sister and nephew in the hall. Jessica and I were alone with Mom.

We had always been a terrific threesome: best friends as well as family. A strong, maternal line of strong, determined women: mother, daughter, and granddaughter. It was a connection we all cherished. And we knew this was the last moment we would ever be alone together.

Although Mom had been nearly unresponsive since arriving at the hospital, I hoped she was still aware enough to hear me as I spoke.

"Mom, I want to tell you something. Jessica and Mark have been trying to have children for a long time, but they have run into an infertility problem. They're getting treatment, but it hasn't worked."

Mom's eyes were open. Was she listening? Was she understanding?

"So," I continued, "when you get to the other side . . . if there's anything you can do to help, it would mean so much."

For the first time since arriving at the hospital, Mom raised her head off the pillow and looked at me. Words were out of reach, but her expression spoke to us in a combination of surprise and pain. She hadn't known about any of this. How could she, when she could barely recognize us? Yet, it was clear to me that, somehow, she had understood.

She laid her head down again as family from the hall bustled in. Each had their moments with Mom, holding her hand and kissing her cheek. After everyone had a chance to say good-bye, the hospital removed the ventilator. Soon after, Mom was gone.

~

A month later, Jessica tried IVF for the fourth time. Mom had left her enough money to make it possible. Compounding her anxiety was the knowledge that this was very likely the last chance they would ever have. Even the clinic didn't support a fifth attempt.

They went through the steps: many days of painful injections, a closely timed trigger shot, egg retrieval, fertilization, pain management. Too weary from disappointment to allow themselves the treachery of hope, they waited for the report from the clinic.

The hardest part for me was waiting for them to call. I wanted to know everything, but I didn't want to intrude on what I knew was a difficult time. When Jessica finally called, I was thrilled to hear that they had a few nascent embryos. But they had produced embryos that looked promising on the first day before. The clinic scheduled a transfer for four days later, but could not promise the embryos would last that long. All anyone could do was hope they would thrive.

As the days passed, the news stayed hopeful. Each embryo was still growing on day two, but fast growers were not necessarily healthy. Sometimes a fast starter would peter out just as quickly.

By day three, there were fewer embryos, but some were coming along in textbook fashion. We wouldn't know anything more until transfer day. The clinic did not disturb the embryos on day four, hoping they might develop better if allowed to rest.

When day five dawned, I startled awake, remembering the last wisps of a dream. In it, Mom was holding a baby who cooed and smiled into her teary eyes. She kissed the baby in her "favorite kissing spot," on the inside of its wrist. Then she looked at me and smiled.

The transfer was scheduled for early that morning. I didn't allow more than a couple of feet between me and my phone, hoping that when it rang, there would be good news. When it finally arrived, the news was better than I could have hoped. Not only did they still have viable embryos, for the first time, they had two healthy blastocysts. They transferred both to double the chance of implantation. But we wouldn't know the results for two weeks.

It was a long fortnight, not knowing whether to encourage Jessie to hope, or help her brace for disappointment. We talked about adoption. We talked about living without children. We shared laughs and tears and the terrible helplessness of waiting.

We stayed with them for part of the second week to be there to celebrate or console them when the day came for the blood test to measure hormone levels. Another early clinic appointment to draw blood. Another seemingly endless wait for results. We baked and settled in with warm cookies and glasses of milk, watching a sappy movie while waiting for the phone to ring.

When the nurse called, she didn't waste time on pleasantries. "You have high levels of pregnancy hormones," she said. "It looks like you're having a baby!"

She'd been so braced for disappointment, Jessica hardly knew how to react. Days later, her first ultrasound confirmed it. One of those precious embryos had implanted.

The doctor was bewildered. "What did we do differently?" she asked.

We knew it wasn't the science that was different. They had a bit of help from heaven.

$\sim$

Less than a year after Mom left us, her great-granddaughter was born—another strong woman in the line. They named the little girl Angela Jane for the angel named Jane who helped her come to be.

The first time I held our miracle child, I kissed her wrist in Mom's sweet spot. That was the first moment I noticed the pale-pink, heart-shaped mark.

"Oh look," the nurse said. "An angel kiss." She couldn't have known how right she was.

We stayed with them for the first week after coming home from the hospital to help with feeding, diapering, rocking, and hugging our tiny granddaughter, who has increased our joy in immeasurable ways.

And to this day, each time I embrace sweet Angela, I think of Mom, who loved babies . . . and hugs.

# THEOBROMANCY

*A. E. Decker*
*first published by Crowded Magazine*

A shaft of early sunlight squeezed through the open door, falling over the chocolate Chinese dragon that dominated Zach's kitchen. Five feet tall and ten feet long, the dragon shimmered with the iridescent green, gold, and rose hues he'd worked into its brown scales. Its delicately ribbed wings unfurled like the folds of an antique parasol.

*Not even Master Terrence can match me in carving,* thought Zach; a sentiment best spoken in the privacy of his own mind. Or at least not in front of Master Terrence.

"Hi, honey. I'm home," he said, opening The Cocoa Dragon's back door a little wider. The rich, heavy scent of chocolate wrapped him in a warm embrace. He sucked it deep into his lungs. "I've been away from this too long."

The dragon seemed to cast him a jaundiced eye.

"Okay, one week," admitted Zach, stepping into the kitchen. His bare arms goose-pimpled at the transition from Baltimore humidity to air-conditioned coolness. "Long for me."

He threw his keys onto the counter by the sink then started towards the dragon, sitting in a splendor of brown coils atop his worktable. *Just a little work on its scales and wings, and it'll be ready to move into the showroom.*

He paused. What was that dark splotch on the floor between his worktable and the main counter? Spilled chocolate he'd forgotten to clean up? Frowning, Zach flipped the light switch.

A round, bristly body the size of a fist. Eight spindly legs. The overhead lights illuminated every hideous detail of the chocolate spider squatting in the middle of The Cocoa Dragon's kitchen tiles.

*Big, brown, hairy* spider! *Oh god, oh god. Big, brown, oh god, hairy spider! Big—*

"Zach?" said a voice.

*Oh god, oh god—*

"Yo, Zach?" The pungent scent of coffee wafted by.

Zach blinked. Coffee? "Casey?" he asked.

"Yep," replied his friend's voice from the open doorway. More coffee fumes wafted inside to war with the chocolate odor. "How'd you get up there?"

"Up where?" asked Zach. The last minute had passed in a panicked haze. He looked around. "Oh." Up on one of the shelves attached to the north wall. The cool smoothness of a jar of Peruvian beans pressed against one arm; he was hugging it like a child snuggling a teddy bear.

Zach risked a glance down. The hairy brown horror still squatted on the tiles, only three feet below his dangling toe-tips.

Asphalt crunched under Casey's feet as he shifted position to lounge against the doorframe. "It's a spider, isn't it? You big chicken."

"Yes, yes." The shelf—a big, sturdy thing, custom-built to hold thick glass canisters—groaned. *Not meant to take this much weight.* Zach shuddered, picturing it coming unmoored, dropping him to meet his bristly, eight-legged fate. "Think you could squash it for me?" he asked, clutching the jar a bit tighter.

Heaving a sigh, Casey pushed off the doorframe. "All right, I'll kill your nasty spider for you." He ambled inside, the two thermal mugs he carried clinking in time to his stride.

He spotted the spider. Stopped dead, his eyes widening until the whites gleamed all around his brown irises. "Shit."

"Shit," Zach agreed. The shelf creaked; it was definitely tilting. "Hurry up and squash it."

"Hell, no." Casey planted himself. "That bastard's magical. I just came to bring you coffee. Squashing magical spiders wasn't part of the bargain."

Fresh groans from the shelf. Zach forced himself to concentrate. "Fetch my mortar and pestle. They're on the shelf over the sink."

The spider clicked its mandibles, a nasty metallic sound reminiscent of an afternoon in the dentist's chair. Shivering, Zach uncoiled his arm from around the jar of Peruvian beans and lifted the lid. Taking out a handful, he rolled them between his palms. The savory-sweet-floral fragrance of raw cocoa clung to his skin.

"Here," said Casey, handing up the mortar and pestle. The spider chittered again as if sensing a change in its fortune. Casey danced back, nearly tripping over the laces on his battered Converse high tops. Setting his jaw, Zach dropped the beans into the mortar. A few brisk strokes of the pestle reduced them to a coarse, brown powder. The spider reared up, boxing the air with its hairy front legs.

*Any moment now the bastard's going to jump at me,* thought Zach. Cold sweat ran down his spine. Hastily, he scooped up a handful of pulverized beans and sifted it through his fingers. The powder spiraled down onto the white tiles, settling in a perfect circle around the spider. With a furious click, it dashed itself against the barrier—and was thrown back.

Releasing the breath that had been congealing in his lungs ever since he'd first spotted the thing, Zach slid off the shelf. The spider, all bitter Nigerian cocoa and malice, hurled itself against the barrier again, and Zach leaped back, jostling against the worktable. Spiders. Magical creatures, even when they weren't made of chocolate. Every time he saw one, he discovered how to teleport. At least he shortly thereafter found himself perched on something high, several feet away.

"Right," he said. He ran a hand through his hair, straightened his shirt, then knelt down next to the circle of crushed beans. The spider hissed. "Who sent you?"

"Has to be one of your Theobromancer buddies, right?" said Casey, crouching beside him. Under the fluorescent lights, Casey's features resolved into the pallor of the night owl and the dark-circled eyes of the near-terminal caffeine addict.

"Yes." Zach reached under his shirt, to where a gilded flower hung from a cord around his neck. "Except for the part about them being my buddy."

Pulling out the flower, he studied it. Ten golden petals gleamed with a buttery shine. The five outer ones formed a pointed star while the rounded interior ones shaped a central pentagon from which half a dozen long stamens sprouted. A gilded *theobroma cacao* blossom: the emblem of a Theobromancer. Less than a hundred aspiring chocolate wizards had been deemed worthy of wearing it.

"Has to be one who knows about your spider thing," said Casey.

"Arachnophobia."

"*Gesundheit.*"

Zach winced but let it pass. "There's James."

"And Alice, of course," said Casey.

"Of course." Zach pretended his heart hadn't just made a little leap at his estranged wife's name. "Lucy knows too, unfortunately." He'd never got on with his sister-in-law. "And Master Terrence."

"Anyone else?" asked Casey.

"One more. Marcel."

Marcel. Master Terrence's other apprentice. Zach nibbled a nail. *Could he still be sore over that prank I pulled at the last Guild meeting? Come on; everyone knows Boy Wonder would never use margarine instead of butter in his truffles.* But, of course, the snooty little shit had no sense of humor.

"You think it's Marcel?" asked Casey.

"Makes sense," said Zach, studying the spider. "This smacks of a challenge. If he beat me in a chocolate duel, he could claim one of my special recipes as a prize."

His jaw tightened. "I always suspected the little bastard was trying to weasel the secrets of my *Tallar Vida* recipe from me. Looks like he's moved on to more direct means of acquiring it."

His *Tallar Vida* recipe. His signature spell, which had earned him a promotion in the Theobromancer's ranks. The very thought of handing it over to Master Terrence's boy-prodigy made his blood boil. Tucking the golden theobroma back in his shirt, he rose. "I'll need evidence to prove it's Marcel."

Casey bent closer to the spider. "Hey, there's a mark on its back." His hand lifted to point.

"No!" Zach grabbed for his wrist.

Too late. Casey's fingertip crossed the air above the circle. The barrier broke. Quick as a blink, the spider leaped onto the back of Zach's right hand and bit.

*Oh, God!* He flung it across the room, shivering with the after-effects of its hairy, prickling touch. *And now comes the agony,* he thought, shuddering down to his very bones. *Please don't hurt as much as the Brazilian wandering spider's bite.* He'd never imagined that shopping for bananas in Rio could lead to a week of agony until it happened. Of course, the black widow's bite had been awful, too. And the brown recluse's.

He braced himself, jaw clenched rictus-tight. Ten heartbeats passed.

The back of his hand itched once.

Ten heartbeats more.

He opened his eyes. "That's all?"

"*No,*" said a new voice.

Both Zach and Casey jumped as the spider stood on its hind legs and grinned—an expression never designed to grace the face of an arachnid, even one made of chocolate.

"*You have eight hours to defeat me, Zach,*" it grated, the words rolling over each other like beans in a grinder. "*When that mark turns violet, I'll claim my reward.*"

*Bang!* The spider erupted in a puff of brown dust. Zach flung up an arm to shield his face from the acrid waft of burnt cocoa. When the red-tinged fumes parted, nothing remained of the spider save a crusty stain on the white tiles.

"That was my fault, wasn't it?" coughed Casey, fanning the air.

"Yeah." Zach studied the small, almost heart-shaped, pink pucker now marking the back of his hand. "Eight hours." He opened a drawer and took out a knife. Dropping to his knees, he scraped spider residue off the floor.

"What are you doing?"

"I need to find out who's behind this," said Zach, brushing residue into a dish. "Marcel might not be the culprit. It could be Lucy trying to humiliate me or one of Master Terrence's crazy tests."

"Slow down." Casey grabbed his arm as he dashed for the pantry. "What about the bite?"

Zach rubbed his chin. "It's not fatal; just a way of putting a timer on the challenge." He looked at the puckers on his hand again. If his time ran out, if he lost—which was *not* going to happen—the theobromancy now coursing through his veins might make him lose his powers for a month. Or turn his skin neon green. Something to add an extra little cherry of shame on top of surrendering his *Tallar Vida* recipe.

"You're right," said Zach. "Nullifying the bite's just as important as finding the culprit." Reaching out, he stroked the dragon's nose. "Sorry, pal. Your scales have to wait."

Plucking a leathery pod of vanilla off an overhead rafter, he turned to Casey. "I'll test the residue while you tend to the antidote."

"Whatdaya mean, 'we'?" Casey drew himself up. "I have my own business to run, you know."

Busy splitting the pod and dropping it into a pot of cream, Zach snorted. Casey opened his coffee shop whenever the whim struck him, closed it likewise, wandered off and left it in the hands of his baristas for hours on end, and lost the keys to the till more often than he ate a hot meal.

"Besides, I don't know how to do your chocolate magic stuff," Casey added.

"Who's the reason I got bitten in the first place?" Zach handed him a wooden spoon.

"Oh, all right." Casey took the spoon. Slouching against the counter, he sucked the last drops of coffee out of his mug.

"All you have to do is stir." Zach set the pot on the stove and added a pinch of dried chilis to the mixture. "Venezuelan trinitario chocolate," he said, chopping up a dark brown block. "When sweetened with Hawaiian white honey, it'll neutralize any spell." He grinned smugly. "It's my own special mixture."

"Yeah, yeah, you're a genius." Casey slouched lower, his body practically forming an *S* curve. "Don't you want your coffee?" he asked, pointing the spoon at the red mug still sitting on the worktable.

"No." Zach dropped the chocolate into the cream. "Coffee contains theobromine, you know. It has its own power. You need to be careful about mixing the two."

"That's mine then." Stepping forward, Casey appropriated the red mug. Zach couldn't help casting it a regretful look. The beginnings of a caffeine headache pounded at his temples. Casey made coffee almost thick enough to cut and chew.

*I'll take it out of Marcel's hide later*, Zach promised himself. "Okay," he said, stepping aside. "Just stir slowly, so it doesn't burn. It'll take about an hour."

"An hour? What if I have to piss?"

"Cross your legs." Zach scraped spider residue onto a block of white chocolate.

Casey flipped him off. Zach reciprocated.

*"You're never going to grow up, are you?"* said a voice in his head. Alice's voice, an echo of that last, dreadful night. He, James, and Casey clutching their video game controllers. She, standing in the den's doorway, tears pouring down her cheeks, fists trembling on her hips.

*I thought you were asleep. I thought you'd cried yourself to—*

*Focus.* Zach banished the memory, but a whiff of rose oil seemed to linger in his nostrils as he heated a silver knife in the flame of a beeswax candle. He used its edge to melt a second slab of white chocolate over the first. Step one, he thought, setting the fused slab on the counter.

It took the better part of an hour to draw a ten-pointed star out of cocoa on the floor near the sink. At last, knees throbbing, the whorls of his fingertips caked brown, Zach sat back to gauge his handiwork. *Pretty good,* he decided. The symmetrical dark lines contrasted beautifully with the pale kitchen tiles.

"How much longer do I have to do this?" called Casey from the stove.

"Just a few minutes," said Zach, going to retrieve the spider-infused white chocolate slab. Returning to the star, he set it in the center, turned it three times clockwise and once counterclockwise, then hefted the small steel mallet he used for cracking toffee.

"Let's find out who's behind this," he said, and let the heavy head fall. The dull crack of impact brought a smile to his lips. A wisp of reddish-purple smoke curled out of the shards of stained white chocolate. Before Zach could make any sense of the pattern, it dissipated.

"Dammit!"

"What?" asked Casey.

Zach stood, knees popping. "I couldn't make out the signature." Snatching up a hunk of white chocolate, he slammed it onto the counter next to the stove. "Whoever's behind this hid their identity well. All I can make out is that the residue is too light to be Master Terrence's work."

"So your list of suspects is down to . . ." Casey scratched an ear. "Four. Marcel, Lucy, James, and Alice."

At the last name, Zach's stomach wriggled again. Grabbing the ladle, he dipped up a scoop of antidote. "I'd say Marcel's still a candidate for Public Enemy Number One, with Lucy next in the running."

*I'll have to devise some other test,* he thought, blowing a wisp of steam off the surface of the melted chocolate shimmering in the ladle. Pure trinitario beans made for a particularly delectable chocolate, with a rich, lingering aftertaste that settled on the tongue like a kiss. Mouth watering, he brought the ladle to his lips.

And a shiny, bulbous shape plummeted from the rafters. Casey yelped, flinging up an arm as a second fist-sized spider swung past his face, suspended on an invisible thread. The lid popped off the red mug, splattering coffee everywhere. The ladle dropped from Zach's hand as he teleported onto the worktable.

Settling on the counter's edge, the new spider folded its front legs under its chin. "Not so easy, Zach," it rasped, favoring him with another of those hideous arachnid-inappropriate grins. "Not so easy."

Then it exploded. A chunk of burnt chocolate spider, a leg still attached, grazed Zach's cheek. Somehow, he managed to control his bladder.

"Much more of this and I'm going to develop a spider complex too," said Casey, fanning smoke out the window.

Zach climbed off the table. "I'm beginning to think it might be Lucy after all," he said. "She always found my arachnophobia hilarious." Fetching a clean ladle, he dipped up another scoop of antidote. He sipped. Silky bitterness mellowed by lush cream—with a slightly sour, aromatic aftertaste.

A cramp seized his bitten hand. "Ooh," he grunted, grabbing his wrist. His fingers flexed and stiffened. The ladle pinged across the floor, dappling the white tiles with brown Dalmatian spots.

Casey whirled around. "What happened?"

"You got coffee in my antidote," Zach snarled as the small pink pucker on the back of his hand darkened to red.

"I did not—oh." Casey scratched his head. "Some might've fallen in when that spider came down." He sniffed the pot of antidote. "Yep. I could smell coffee in a perfume factory."

"What a talent." Zach's hand stopped spasming. Wiping sweat off his brow, he went to the refrigerator, took out a bottle of water, and drank several long swallows.

"Personally, I think coffee improves the taste." Casey dipped a finger in the pot.

Zach refrained from beating his head against the stain-less-steel refrigerator door. "Remember what I said about mixing coffee and chocolate?"

"Sort of," said Casey, licking his finger.

"Well, one of coffee's properties is to speed things up." He let that piece of information sink in, then held up his hand. "See this? Judging by how much the color's darkened, I'd say the addition of coffee to my antidote has *cut my time in half!*"

"Oh." Casey stopped sucking on his finger. "Can't you just make more?"

"No antidote's going to work so long as I have your blast-ed nuclear-strength coffee in my system." Zach scowled at the mark. "At least that second spider—"

"The black widow," said Casey.

"Huh?"

"The second one was a black widow. They're the round ones with the hourglass on their bellies, right?" Casey traced the shape in the air. "Well, the first spider was something else."

That's right; Casey had mentioned seeing something on its back right before the barrier broke. "Was the mark kind of violin-shaped?" he asked.

"Yeah, I guess."

Black widow, brown recluse, and . . .

Brazilian wanderer. Zach swallowed bile. No, his mystery attacker wouldn't forget that one. So, somewhere out there, waiting—oh, god. If he'd known what this day held in store for him, he'd have taken another week off. Now, of course—

The mark itched.

—too late.

He rolled his hand into a fist. "That's a clue. Whoever's sending the spiders must know the order in which they bit me."

"Hey, great," said Casey. He held up his hand for a high five.

Zach didn't slap it. "No," he said. "Not great at all."

Because only three Theobromancers knew the order in which the spiders had bitten him. Having already eliminated Master Terrence, that left—

Alice or James. His wife or his best friend.

*Why?* He squeezed his eyes shut. Why would either of them—?

Unless . . . his eyes flew open. One glance at the calendar clarified everything. "Oh, shit!"

Casey jumped. "What now?"

Pushing off the refrigerator, Zach took down a canister of beans. "Now you're going to go buy some roses."

He may as well have said: "You're going to go stick your balls in a vise." Casey screwed up his face. "Flowers?" he wailed. "No!"

Zach took up his largest mortar and pestle. "Make sure they're yellow," he said as he started to grind.

∾

Fifteen pounds of hand-ground cocoa beans. That, plus one hell of a magical effort, was what it would take to transport himself to London.

"Did you have to move so far away, Alice?" asked Zach, dumping another half-pound of beans into his mortar. Gee, only seven more pounds to go. He didn't even want to *contemplate* how much his shoulder would ache tomorrow.

His ire abated as the pile of uncrushed beans dwindled. Of course, she'd moved back home after the mis— the separation. And at least she hadn't cut him off entirely; Theobromancers needed permission to use their fellow chocolate wizards' ports.

The back door smacked open hard to leave a black mark on the wall. Casey slouched in, a mug in one hand and a bouquet of yellow roses in the other, managing to suggest through posture alone that being forced to carry flowers lowered his masculinity by 17.4%.

"Here," he said, thrusting them at Zach.

Zach poked his chin toward the table. "Put them there," he said, dumping the last of the beans into the mortar. Setting his jaw, he picked up the pestle for the last, agonizing effort.

Casey tossed the roses onto the table and wiped his hand on his jeans. "Man, you're making a mess," he said. A thin brown layer of cocoa dust coated nearly every surface.

Zach grunted. He didn't want to contemplate the cleaning job he'd have tomorrow—*before* opening the shop—either.

Assuming his skin wasn't glowing neon green by then, that is.

There. The last of the beans, ground. Picking up the roses, he rubbed a bright petal between his fingers. Their dusty-spice fragrance tickled his nose. "Hope these do the trick," he said, stepping into the pile of crushed beans. The brown dust puffed up over his ankles then began slowly sliding into his shoes like a horde of curious insects.

Casey sniggered. "Shut up," said Zach, making the necessary passages to transport himself to London. The spell took effect with a faint sizzle, reminiscent of frying bacon.

"Good luck," Casey called. Then The Cocoa Dragon's kitchen melted into streaks of bleary color. A bitter-tasting wind ruffled Zach's hair. A hundred tiny hands, smelling of burnt caramel, slapped the space behind his eyeballs. The world burbled quietly to itself, like a child preoccupied with a lollipop, before re-settling under his feet: a quiet gray London street, a damp gray London afternoon. Staggering, Zach might have fallen if he hadn't caught hold of the edge of a window box. Pink geraniums nodded back at him.

"Hi, guys," he said. His stomach settled enough for him to cautiously raise his head. A disheveled man in a red shirt stared back at him. It took a moment for him to recognize his own reflection in the shop window. Alice's shop? He straightened further. Indeed, it was The Candy Doll, blue-and-white as a Delft teacup. A silver dish of Opera creams sat amongst curls of frothy lace in the display window.

"Here we go." Zach smoothed down his hair and tugged the wrinkles out of his shirt. He assembled a winning smile. A middle-aged woman came out of the grocer's shop next door. Her puzzled glance turned to disdain as it took in first his ponytail, then his earring, and finally the tattoo of a Chinese dragon peeking out of his collar.

"Hello," he said, trying out his winning smile. She ducked her head and hurried away.

"Your loss, lady," he shrugged and pushed open The Candy Doll's door. A little bell chirped. The aroma of melted chocolate, somehow brighter and fruitier than the fragrance that permeated his own shop, wreathed him in a warm cloud.

"Be with you in a moment," called a voice from the kitchen. Alice's voice. His heart tipped over.

"Behave," he told it. Adopting what he hoped would pass for a casual pose next to a basket of pralines, he gazed around the shop. Not bad. Little round tables for patrons to drink cocoa and a blue-and-white patterned floor. Too many doilies and scraps of lace, however. She should get rid of those, maybe paint the walls—

Alice emerged from the kitchen carrying a tray of—oh, not good—those white-tipped, rum-filled confections known as nipples of Venus. The soft swell of her own truffles just peeked above the "v" neck of her blouse, her gilded theobroma glinting between them.

She halted so abruptly it was a wonder the chocolates didn't slide right off the tray. Her already big blue eyes widened. With her petite stature and honey-blond hair, she bore a resemblance to a doll. An edible one, at that.

*Bad thought. No, no!* "Hello, Allie," said Zach.

No hint of reproach showed on her face as she set the tray down on the counter. "Zach," she said, cheeks cotton-candy pink, "how nice to see you."

Maybe she wasn't as angry as he feared. The knot between his shoulders loosened. "Nice to see you, too, Allie. And I'm sorry."

Her brows drew together.

"I didn't mean to forget, especially after all those promises that I wouldn't."

A little crease appeared between her eyes. Taking it as a bad sign, Zach hurried on.

"You have every reason to be angry, but please call off your spiders." Dropping to one knee, he extended the roses with a flourish.

"Spiders?" she asked.

The word hung in the air. So, for a moment, did his jaw. "You know, the spiders you set on me this morning?"

The line between her brows smoothed to mask-like blankness.

"In punishment for my forgetting our anniversary?" he prompted.

Her face came back to life. Clapping a hand over her mouth, she turned away, muffled giggles squeaking out between her fingers. "Did you forget to change your calendar again?" she asked.

What did that have to do with anything? Then an image of his calendar, hanging on the wall beside his copper pots, popped into his head. The album cover of Pink Floyd's *Dark Side of the Moon*.

But that was the picture for June, wasn't it? He vaguely remembered July being Nirvana's *Nevermind*.

Zach shook his head. He'd glimpsed the "Ju" and assumed he was looking at the right month.

Meanwhile, Alice composed herself. "You never could ask for directions. Or dates." She cupped his face. "Today's July the tenth. You're six days early, not three days late."

Her fingers caressed his jaw. He stared into her cleavage, mind blank of all thoughts save one.

"You didn't send the spiders? But—"

His list of candidates fell away to one. James? Why?

"You may as well take these," he said, dragging himself to his feet and pushing the roses into her arms. "Happy pre-emptive anniversary." He slumped into a chair next to one of the round tables.

"Zach?" Alice touched his shoulder. "What's wrong?"

"The spiders, the chocolate spiders, weren't you listening?" He flapped his right hand through the air. "Someone's issued a challenge. I've been bitten. See?"

Catching hold of his wrist, she studied the red mark. "I've never seen a spell like this. Any idea who's responsible?"

"James," he said.

She gasped. "James? Never."

He shrugged miserably.

"Never," she said. "If he sent a spider, it would've been on roller skates or wearing a clown suit."

That wrung a smile from him. Yeah, that sounded exactly like something James would do. But his smile faded all too quickly. "James must blame me for what happened last—"

Her face tightened. Zach ended the sentence before the old pain grew too sharp. "Anyway, my challenger has to be a Theobromancer of my level who knows I was bitten by a brown recluse, a black widow, and a Brazilian wanderer, in that order," he continued. "You and James—"

The pink in her cheeks darkened to a less attractive red. "So your first thought was that I was throwing a tantrum over you forgetting our anniversary again."

He shrugged. "You did say you'd shave me bald and tattoo 'idiot' across my scalp if I forgot it again."

Rising in one sharp movement, Alice stalked to the counter and began arranging her nipples of Venus on a doily-covered plate.

"What?" asked Zach.

She slammed a truffle down hard enough to crack its shell. "That was a joke." She looked up, and Zach caught the full force of three married years' worth of frustration between the eyes. "Hyperbole. I thought humor might get through to you. God knows it worked for your friends."

Zach jumped up, knocking over his chair. "Are you accusing me of neglecting you, Alice?" he demanded, pressing his fists against the counter. "Because I tried, I really did. And I was hurting too, not that anyone seemed to care."

She glared back. "James and I both care deeply for you, and you know it."

"Until you both deserted me in the same month!"

His shout rang echoes off the bell suspended over the door.

Alice cracked another truffle. The small sound might as well have been gunfire in the sudden quiet.

Zach's ears caught up with his mouth. He would have gladly throttled himself to take back those last words.

Alice delicately arranged one last truffle on top of the pyr-
amid then spread her hands to either side of the plate. "You
know why I left."

All the burning rage of a moment earlier turned to mush
in his gut. "Yes, I do."

She looked away. He swallowed, a "sorry" hovering on his
lips like an uncertain butterfly. "You shouldn't sell the cracked
ones," he said instead, taking one of the broken truffles off the
plate. He reached for the other the same second she did. Their
fingers collided. Her wet blue eyes lanced him, and he drew
back, stuffing his hands into his pockets.

"Idiot!" Alice swung away from him, grabbing for a tissue. Some wet, unsanitary sounds followed before she turned
back, pale but composed. "Black widows are more poisonous
than brown recluses, and Brazilian wanderers are worse than
black widows," she said. "Have you considered that whoever's
attacking you is saving the worst for last and it's only coincidence that you were bitten in that order?"

"A coincidence?" The idea spun through his head, sparkling prettily from every angle. "You're right!" he cried, seiz-
ing her up in a rough hug and dancing her around the shop.
"So, it's Marcel or Lucy, then," he said.

"You're accusing my sister?" She pulled free, brushing at
her hair.

Zach smiled. "Does she still refer to me as Satan's bastard
stepchild?" he asked, knowing he could checkmate her where
her twin was concerned. "You know she'd relish winning my
*Tallar Vida* recipe off me."

Her lips pursed. "Sounds like you're convinced it's Lucy."

"Her or Marcel," said Zach, pressing his brow to hers.

He hadn't been so close to her in months. She gazed up at
him, smelling of roses, eyes wide and wondering. It would be
such a simple thing to lean in for a kiss, make it a long one—

He caught sight of his own hand, clasping her shoulder.
From apple-red, the bite mark had darkened to pomegranate.

No time for kisses. There were still some bits of the chocolate black widow lying around The Cocoa Dragon's kitchen;

perhaps he could get an identification off those. "Mind if I borrow some chocolate?" he asked.

"No, but Zach—"

"Thanks," he said, grabbing five bars of dark chocolate off a shelf. Enough to get him home; traveling to one's own port was a simpler matter. "Bye, Allie."

"Wait." Going to the door, she flipped the sign to closed and turned the lock.

"What are you doing?"

"Helping you," she replied, then muttered: "Before you do something really stupid." But she said it quietly enough that he could ignore it. She disappeared into the back room. Something fell with a crash, and she swore discreetly. A little more rattling, then she emerged, carrying a sack.

"You have fifteen pounds of ground beans ready?" he asked as she dumped its contents onto the floor.

"Unlike you, I believe in being prepared," she said, stepping into the pile of powder. "See you in Baltimore, darling."

She blurred and vanished. Alice. Back in Baltimore, after nearly a year's absence. Zach wasted nearly a minute staring at the space where she'd been before a tingle from his hand recalled him to his purpose.

～

"Hi, Zach." Casey waved. He'd fetched his portable espresso machine. He bent over it like a mad scientist tinkering with his chemistry set and an ungodly roar filled the air. Steam rose, and white foam dribbled over Zach's marble countertop. The smell of coffee had temporarily won the battle over the aroma of chocolate.

*What a homecoming.* Zach glanced at his calendar. Nirvana's *Nevermind.* But surely it had been Pink Floyd when he left . . .?

No; he couldn't remember. The images blurred together. "Where's Alice?" he called over the mechanical whines, growls, and rumbles.

"Over there." Casey jerked his head in some vague direction.

"Where?" shouted Zach at the exact the same moment that Casey flipped some lever and the awful noise died. Of course.

"I'm here," said Alice. She stepped out from behind the dragon, her eyes sparkling like colored sugar. "Did you carve this? All of it?"

*She's really here. Here, in my kitchen.*

He forced himself to concentrate. "Of course." He scanned the floor for a chunk of the chocolate widow.

"Wow!" Her fingertips hovered over the curve of the dragon's neck. "Are you going to show this to Master Terrence? He'd be so impressed."

Zach laughed shortly and squatted for a closer inspection of the tiles. "Yeah, right. He'd say, 'Yes, nice whatsit, but just look at those lopsided truffles. What did you fill them with, gravel? Shape up, boy!'"

"Oh, nonsense," Alice said, pulling out a stool next to Casey. "He's tremendously proud of you."

"Proud of me?" said Zach. "When he has Marcel Lepret, boy-genius extraordinaire?" He slammed a fist against his thigh. "Where the hell is it?"

"What are you looking for?" asked Alice.

Zach stood. "I know the black widow exploded around here some—"

He stopped. The antidote pot had been cleared away, the counters wiped clean of cocoa powder. He spun around. Even his ten-pointed star had been mopped up. "The hell?" he said, staring about his sparkling kitchen.

"I cleaned," said Casey, glancing up from a steel pitcher containing enough woolly milk foam to clothe an entire flock of sheep. "To make up for getting coffee in your antidote."

*Cleaned? Casey chose now, of all times, to suffer a fit of conscience?* "And the black widow pieces?" Zach asked, holding his breath.

Casey inverted his thumb. "Down the drain."

"Oh, shit." Zach slumped against the counter. The mark on his hand was taking on rich wine hues. Maybe two hours befor e it turned violet.

"Did I do something wrong?" asked Casey.

*There has to be something I can do.* Zach scanned the kitchen. Copper pots, bins of nuts, canisters of beans, ingots of chocolate . . .

And the dragon, lording over its worktable as if it were the guardian of it all.

The dragon. An idea formed in Zach's head—a mad, desperate, but just-feasible idea. Darting to a drawer, he pulled out his carving tools and a pair of vinyl gloves. Snapping on the gloves, he studied the dragon's unfinished scales.

He didn't have to look to know astonished glances were being exchanged behind his back. "What are you doing?" asked Alice.

"I can't transport directly to Marcel's shop; he locked me out of his portal," said Zach, setting a chisel to the dragon's tail. A tiny curl of chocolate appeared.

Alice sucked in a breath. "You're not . . . you're mad!"

Zach's lips tightened against his teeth. "If he wants my *Tallar Vida* spell, he'll get it. In spades."

"What if it's Lucy?" asked Casey, an edge in his voice. Alice swung round on him.

"It isn't," she said. The tension between them could've melted the whole of Zach's stock.

"I'm locked out of Lucy's portal, too," said Zach, overriding the impending quarrel. "I don't have time to confront them both."

Silence fell over the kitchen, save for the grating tick, tick of the wall clock chopping down the minutes. Zach switched to a curved blade to work on the dragon's wings.

Alice cleared her throat. "Might I borrow fifteen pounds of beans?" she asked.

Zach looked up, blinking. She stared down at her hands, folding and unfolding themselves on her lap. "I'm not locked out of Lucy's portal. I could go ask her—not that I believe she's the culprit, mind."

Casey scoffed, and she shot him a glower.

"You'd do that for me?" asked Zach.

"Of course." Alice's lips thinned. "All you had to do was ask."

Zach winced. It was his turn to stare at his hands. He never did ask, did he? Always assumed he knew best and went from there. *But I often do know best,* he protested internally. The voice sounded tiny and petulant.

Alice was waiting. Clearing his throat, Zach nodded to his pantry. "There are some five-pound sacks in there. Take what you need."

"I'll gather some chocolate for you," said Casey, standing.

After an hour of carving, Zach's right shoulder started clicking in its socket. *Never mind,* he thought, *I'll just cut my arm off tomorrow.* He bit back a laugh of pure weariness. His head swam, and his eyes burned, filled with grit.

On the floor next to the worktable, Alice ground beans, her sleeves rolled past her elbows. Several strands of butter-yellow hair had worked loose from her clip and stuck to her cheeks. Watching her out of the corner of an eye, he remembered falling asleep with his ear pressed against her arm, her pulse singing a lullaby.

"You could say 'thank you,'" she said.

He jumped—fortunately not while carving. He didn't think she'd noticed him watching her.

"Thank you," he said after a moment. "I know you don't want to believe Lucy's behind it."

She dumped another handful of beans into the pestle. "I can't think of a reason why she'd challenge you."

"Except that she's a bitch," said Casey, emerging from the pantry with a stack of white chocolate.

Alice stopped grinding to glare.

"Sorry, Allie." Zach moved around the worktable to start on the dragon's other side. "After what she did to James, I feel the same way."

"What did she do to James?" asked Alice, making every syllable ring in her crisp, British way.

Zach bit his lip.

"It was more what she did to those five or six other guys," said Casey, and stalked back to the pantry.

Alice turned wide eyes and an "O" of a mouth on Zach.

He ran a hand over his scalp. "Yeah." Shit; he'd forgotten about the gloves. Now he had chocolate in his hair. Well, wasn't the first time. "James was about to propose when he found out," he continued, fetching a fresh glove. "Bought the ring and everything. That's why he moved to Australia, to get as far away from her as possible."

He couldn't keep the bitterness out of his voice. "Australia. I was going to visit him there this week. But I couldn't do it. I just knew every funnel web spider in the country would be waiting to greet me. Ended up cleaning the house instead—what a great vacation." He held up his marked hand. "And then I come back here and get bitten anyway. That's irony for you."

"Oh, Zach." Alice's arms encircled him from behind. "I'm sorry. I didn't know."

"James didn't want you to know." He glowered at Casey, who responded with an unrepentant shrug.

"Still sure she didn't send the spiders?" Casey asked.

Zach could have choked him when Alice took her arms from around his waist and set her fists on her hips. "Yes."

"It doesn't matter," said Zach. "You'll confront Lucy, and if she's innocent, no harm, no foul." He checked the mark. Definitely shading more into purple now. *I can't spare more than half an hour,* he decided, selecting another tool.

Beside him, Alice bent back to her grinding. "I'm not convinced it's Marcel either," she said, *sotto voce.*

Zach grunted.

"I know you don't get on, but he's a sweet boy, really," she continued.

Zach's lips curled as he sliced tiny "V" shapes into the dragon's fringe. Alice's fondness for Marcel was another mark in the twit's disfavor, as far as he was concerned.

"He can't help that he's bright."

"Someone has to be responsible," snapped Zach, selecting a gouge. "If it isn't Marcel or Lucy, then who?"

Her sigh blew a damp strand of hair off her forehead. "Well, I see you have it all worked out, as usual." She dropped another handful of beans into the mortar.

His gut twisted. "I didn't mean to—" He had done it again, hadn't he? But who could it be aside from Marcel or Lucy?

The clock ticked impassively on. A quarter of an hour struck down, gone in an eye-blink. Zach willed his tiring hand not to shake.

Five minutes later, the tool slipped from his numb fingers and gashed three scales. Fighting back an expletive, he smoothed the damage away.

Ten. Taking up a brush, he highlighted the scales with edible gold.

Fifteen. Zach folded up his tools and threw off his gloves. The dragon virtually glowed on the worktable.

Was it good enough?

It had to be. He'd be damned before he let Marcel Lepret claim his signature recipe.

"Wish me luck," he said, opening the back door.

"Call me a little slow here," said Casey, watching as Zach tucked the sack of ground cocoa under his belt and slipped bars of chocolate into his pockets. "But what exactly are you intending to do here?"

"Something utterly mad," said Alice, her mouth tightening into a rosebud.

Casey still looked puzzled as Zach dragged a chair next to the worktable. His eyes only widened when Zach straddled the dragon. "You are mad," he breathed.

"That's what the Guild's always thought." Zach grinned then looked across the floor to Alice. "Thanks, Allie. And . . ." He hesitated, unable to think of the words.

She smiled. "Come back and tell me when your brain's working." Her smile wobbled only slightly as she stepped into her pile of crushed beans and vanished.

*I should have kissed her,* thought Zach. Too late now. Stroking his hands down each side of the dragon's jaw, he invoked the *Tallar Vida* spell. A wash of golden light followed his fingertips.

"Rise," he commanded.

❧

The wind blew cold above the clouds, numbing his face until he couldn't feel the sting of his hair whipping against his cheeks. The warm glow of revelry kept him from minding it. *None of you Guild bastards could manage this,* he exulted as the dragon caught an updraft and rose like a bubble.

He managed not to shout, "I'm the king of the world." He'd have hated himself later.

Roads, trees, and houses lay spread out far below him, as insignificant as the toy scenery laid out around a model train. Even the gray fortress of New York City looming ahead seemed no more than a collection of shoe boxes placed on end. The dragon bore him above it all, its sides rippling gently. Its wings didn't creak; they purred with the silken gurgle of melted chocolate being poured into a mold. Strange, how he could hear that sound but not the shouts of pedestrians below as he directed the dragon into the canyons of New York's streets. Times Square passed in a blink of neon lights. He caught a whiff of roses, lilies, and other crushed greenery as he whisked over the flower district. He swerved toward Greenwich Village, where the straight lines of the planned city gave way to a labyrinthine spider's web of old New York streets. A moment later, he crossed Bleecker Street, homing in on Marcel's trendy shop, Doux-Amer.

"There!" he cried, spotting its red brick and glass facade. The dragon swooped, folding its wings to arrow straight through the open front door. The crown of Zach's head just brushed the lintel as they passed inside. The dragon's momentum carried it across the floor, chocolate claws scrabbling for purchase on the ceramic tiles. It finally fetched up against the far wall, toppling an array of decorative boxes.

Zach rolled off the dragon and landed on his back. He lay staring up at the ceiling fan, still gasping with the thrill of the flight. Gradually he became aware of a disapproving gaze. He turned his head. A six-foot-tall white chocolate Statue of Liberty loomed over him, staring disdainfully down her nose.

His wits cleared. "Marcel!" he cried, pushing himself up. The word scraped his dry throat, so he gathered some spit, swallowed, and shouted again. "Marcel!" Where was the little bastard? He glared around the shop. What a poser's paradise: black-and-white checkered floor, scalloped brass fixtures, art nouveau on the walls, and—gah!—modern jazz playing over the speakers. All tarted up in burgundy and gold, like some overblown wine cellar, and stocked with high tables and those tall, tippy stools no one could sit on comfortably.

At the moment, those tall, tippy stools were doing their job of tipping over as the patrons rushed screaming for the front door. The freckled counter boy tossed his cap and apron aside and fled. Through it all, the insipid jazz kept playing. Zach was looking for a way to smash the speakers when the kitchen door banged open.

"What is going on?" cried Marcel, framed in the center of it, his pale blonde hair ruffled, his preppy tie askew.

"Ah, the master of the sneak attack appears." Zach brought out a handful of beans. "Ready for a real fight?"

Marcel puffed out his cheeks. "Have you gone crazy?" He blanched as the dragon poked its head over the counter and breathed two plumes of cocoa powder.

Zach grinned. "Feeling a little outclassed, junior?"

Marcel's jaw tightened. "So it's a challenge? Very well." He curled his fingers, and two pounds of bittersweet chips swirled into the air and merged to form a dog, a shaggy brown Briard, which pounced on the dragon, biting at its throat. The dragon contemptuously swatted it aside with one lash of a claw. It smashed into the wall, leaving a brown smear on the cream-colored paint. Marcel staggered. Zach leaned over the counter, rolling his handful of beans in his palm.

"What's wrong?" he taunted. "Lose the Brazilian wanderer? Bring it out. No mere shadow-beast will beat my dragon."

Give the kid credit; he glared up with no hint of surrender on his face. "I don't need to beat your dragon," he said.

And a perfect circle of agony exploded on the back of Zach's head. He reeled about just as the white chocolate Statue of Liberty lifted her torch for a second blow, her movements stiff and jerky.

"Nothing like my *Tallar Vida*," croaked Zach. That gave life; not mere animation. He raised his hand. Cocoa beans shot out between his fingers like bullets. *Ping, ping, ping!* Splashes of green-tinted white chocolate spattered the wall behind the statue. The arm holding the torch broke off at the elbow. The statue, never losing her expression of placid constipation, wavered a moment then toppled.

But while Zach was occupied with the statue, Marcel darted into place behind the counter, where a pot of melted chocolate steamed over a range. As Zach turned, Marcel dipped his fingers into the pot and flung the clinging drops at him. Brown streaks arced through the air, transforming into small daggers in mid-flight.

*Thinks on his feet*, thought Zach begrudgingly, pulling a slab of white chocolate out of his arsenal. It shuddered under the daggers' impact. One slipped past, touched his forefinger, and immediately clung, immobilizing the joint. Zach deflected the remainder, but Marcel had already spilled a bag of cocoa across the counter. One twist of his wrist, and it shaped itself into a swarm of angry wasps.

*Damned home-turf advantage*, Zach had time to grouse before the wasps surrounded him, buzzing like a thousand tiny drills. Cocoa clogged his nostrils, choked his lungs and prickled his flesh. He could hardly think for the droning of the swarm. *Need to throw Marcel off balance.* He scrabbled in his pocket. His fingers touched something smooth and conical.

*Well, why not?*

Tossing the cracked nipple of Venus into the air, he concentrated. It melted, remolding itself into the figure of a nude woman, her skin smooth as molten chocolate. Throwing back her hair, she winked at Marcel.

She had Alice's face.

Marcel gaped, his cheeks flaming cherry-red. The wasp horde pattered to the floor, its magic undone in an instant.

"Hey," said Zach, pulling one of the sacks off his belt, "that's my wife you're ogling."

As Marcel's face swung round, slack and uncomprehending, Zach threw the sack of pure baker's chocolate at him. It erupted in mid-air, raining jagged brown shards that slammed down around Marcel then expanded rapidly, growing to form a cage. Marcel touched one of the bars, as if unable to believe he'd been defeated so suddenly.

"Checkmate," said Zach. Chocolate Alice winked again, and he hastily disenchanted the nipple of Venus. Some distractions were, well, distracting. "Now—"

A shadow fell over his shoulder. "What's going on here?" boomed a new voice. New, but not unknown. Zach's freshly kindled glow of triumph fizzled. He hardly dared turn around—but he knew it would be worse if he didn't.

He turned. "Master Terrence," he said, staring up into his teacher's impassive ebony face. "I didn't know you—"

The crack to his jaw spun his head around. He couldn't say it surprised him.

"That was for using magic in public view." Folding his arms across his chest, Master Terrence strolled over to the dragon. It ducked its head under a wing.

"Master Terrence!" cried Marcel from his cage. "That madman burst in—"

Master Terrence cast him a single look, and he wilted, slumping against the bars.

"Impressive," said Master Terence, returning his attention to the dragon. The dragon peeped out from under its wing; Master Terrence studied its ears then nodded. "Most impressive." He pivoted on a heel and stared Zach down. "Completely irresponsible, but impressive."

"Thank you, Master Terrence. I realize I broke protocol—"

"Again."

"—but Mr. Lepret challenged me. With spiders." Zach held out his hand, the mark now only slightly redder than grape soda.

"I don't know what he's talking about." This time Marcel returned Master Terrence's gaze steadily.

"Can you prove it, Marcel?" asked Master Terrence.

"*Certainement.*" Marcel pulled his gilded theobroma out of his collar and touched it to a trickle of blood dribbling out of a fresh scratch. "Let the symbol of our craft witness that I did not challenge Zachary Marten," he said.

Zach held his breath. The flower did not wither. Which meant—

Zach released the breath, aching all over. "It must have been Lucy after all."

Thank goodness Alice had gone to confront her. He only hoped she could talk Lucy into ending the challenge.

Of course, Alice didn't think Lucy was responsible. And Alice had been right about Marcel—

Marcel! Zach gestured, and the bars of the cage shivered and cracked. "Sorry," he said, abruptly aware of the state of Marcel's shop; the tipped chairs, chocolate-smeared walls, and shattered Statue of Liberty. "Someone issued me a challenge. With spiders. I thought it was you." He summoned a sheepish grin. Marcel could press charges for an unprovoked assault if he chose.

Marcel rubbed his chin, smearing chocolate across his face. "Spiders, you said? Yes, I remember how you always screamed at the sight of one."

*Just name your punishment, boy genius,* thought Zach, teeth grinding.

Marcel dropped his hand. "In light of your phobia, I forgive you," he said.

Zach's mouth fell open.

"Forgive you. Entirely." Marcel gave a sphinx's grin. Tugging his tie, he walked behind the counter and began setting things aright.

Of all the bitter punishments Marcel could have devised, he had to come up with one where Zach had to live with his guilt.

The clever little bastard.

Inhaling slowly, Zach turned to Master Terrence, who leaned back against the counter, arms folded. "You may have need of more forgiveness before this day's out," he said.

"Why?" asked Zach.

"You mentioned Lucy Cairfax. She recently accepted an invitation to tour cocoa plantations in South America. I suspect she's too busy preparing for the trip to waste time challenging you."

*It wasn't Lucy? Or Marcel? But, but, but—*

Then it had to be James.

Except Alice had insisted it wasn't James either. And his white chocolate test proved it couldn't be Master Terrence. So who could it—?

Zach closed his eyes as the truth socked him smack on the jaw. "I am an utter idiot," he said.

"Yes." Master Terrence patted the dragon's head. "One day I must stop taking on stupid apprentices."

The mark on his hand needed only a little more blue to be termed a proper violet, but Zach figured he could spare a few seconds to glare. Behind the counter, Marcel did the same.

Master Terrence, still petting the dragon, raised an eyebrow. Zach took in a breath—

—and let it all out. "No. I'm not stupid," he said. "But I need to stop acting as if I am."

Master Terrence's lips twitched before settling back into their customary stern line. "I would appreciate it."

Zach nodded. "Look after the dragon for me," he said, digging through his pockets for the five pounds of chocolate necessary to transport him back home. Quicker than flying, and every second counted now.

A tap on his shoulder distracted him. "What?" he asked, looking up. Marcel stood before him, holding out a dark chocolate medallion with a layer of pink filling.

"Use this instead," said Marcel. "*Galette des Voyages.* I perfected them recently."

Zach weighed the tiny wafer in his hand. "I can get back home with this?" he asked, more than a little appalled. Even Master Terrence quickly feigned a cough.

"I am a prodigy," said Marcel, lifting his chin.

"You're insufferable." Zach popped the wafer into his mouth, and his surroundings started to melt around him.

Just before he vanished, Marcel smiled. "But I do not use margarine in my truffles, Zachary Marten."

～

The Cocoa Dragon's kitchen reformed around him, dark and silent. Lingering flavors of bitter chocolate and raspberry wine coated his tongue.

"Hello?" called Zach, switching on the lights.

Footsteps. The scent of rose oil mingled with the coffee smells still permeating the kitchen as Alice pushed through the swinging door that led to his showroom. Casey shuffled after her, mug in hand.

"Sorry, Zach." Alice embraced him. "Lucy didn't send the spiders."

He buried his nose in her hair. "It wasn't Marcel either. Or Master Terrence."

"So you're accusing James?" asked Casey, leaning in the doorway.

"No," said Zach. Alice stiffened in his arms, and he drew back just enough to look her in the eyes. The mark on his hand gleamed deep purple. "You're not responsible either, Allie. You were too angry when I accused you the first time." He tweaked her nose. "I know when you're trying to fool me."

A crinkle deepened between her brows. "Then who?"

He looked over her shoulder. "Casey."

"Hey," said Casey, whisking a hand from his pockets and waving it through the air. "I don't know anything about your—"

"Oh, I have no doubt James was your accomplice," said Zach. Releasing Alice, he faced Casey. "But only one person could've switched my calendar. Gotten coffee in my antidote. Cleaned up evidence. Do you deny that this was your plan all along?"

The clock clicked stolidly on for thirty beats. Then Casey smiled and stuffed his hand back into his pocket. "Hey, Zach."

**279**

"Yeah?"

"Too late."

"What do you mean—" Zach began. Then the mark on his hand tingled. Zach tensed as the sensation quickly grew in intensity. His breath caught in his chest. "Hah . . . ohh, stop!" A thousand tiny, invisible legs scurried up his arm.

"Zach!" Alice gripped his shoulders.

"*Nyuk, nyuk, nyuk!*" A third dark, eight-legged shape plummeted from the rafters. Zach amazed himself by not flinching.

It settled onto a corner of the worktable.

Then stood on its hind legs and bowed.

It was wearing a little clown suit.

"Surprise!" said the chocolate Brazilian wandering spider in a shrill cartoon of a voice.

"That," said Alice, as the spider performed a backflip, "is definitely James's handiwork."

Zach collected his jaw as the tickling in his hand faded. "All this—a practical joke?"

Casey's smile faded. "No joke. I set up this scheme because what happened last year was my fault."

"Your fault?" Zach exchanged a glance with Alice. "But you weren't even involved."

"Oh, no?" said Casey. He set down his coffee mug. The spider leaped onto his shoulder. "I was in the middle of the whole mess. I knew about Lucy's infidelity and Alice's—"

Alice sucked in a breath, her face clenching. Even now, almost a year later, she couldn't bear to hear the word "miscarriage." Casey glanced at her and went on.

"And I knew that trying to keep James's and Alice's respective secrets from one another, trying to pretend everything was okay, was hurting Zach." His shoulders sagged. "I kept telling myself I should sit you all down for a talk. But I didn't, and you two separated. James left."

Zach cleared his throat. "So you arranged this bizarre spider escapade a year later instead of just getting us together for a meal or something?"

Casey shrugged. "You might have refused. Besides, this was more fun." His grin reappeared. "Now. Your forfeit."

Zach's stomach clenched as he braced himself. He'd almost forgotten about the penalty. *Surely Casey doesn't want my* Tallar Vida *recipe?*

Funny, how insignificant the recipe seemed in view of the day's happenings. Alice took his hand, and suddenly he didn't care if Casey demanded every recipe in his inventory.

"What is it?" he asked.

Casey's grin sharpened. "Tell Alice you're sorry for being an ass."

This one was easy. Zach faced Alice. "I'm sorry."

"Promise her you'll listen to her from now on."

Zach hesitated. Alice's face was red, her shoulders shaking. "I'll try," he said.

"Now kiss her. If she's agreeable," Casey amended quickly, holding up a finger.

Zach looked down at her. Reaching up, she hooked her hands behind his neck and pulled his lips down to hers. Sugared rose petals, honey, and—of course—chocolate, flowed across his tongue as a host of silvery bells chimed in his head.

"That works, too," said Casey.

At last, perhaps several perfect decades later, the kiss ended. "Is my debt paid?" asked Zach.

Casey scratched his head. "I suppose."

"Actually," Alice slipped her arm through Zach's, "I quite liked that 'getting together for a meal' idea you mentioned earlier. Does The Fat Abbot still make that heavenly crab chowder and cheddar biscuits?"

He squeezed her hand. "Shall we check it out?"

"Let's."

Arm-in-arm, they walked towards the doorway. Zach paused on the threshold. Casey still slouched against the counter, his mop of black hair shadowing his face.

"Want to come along?" Zach asked.

"You kids have fun." Casey waved then lifted the chocolate spider off his shoulder. "You could take James along, however."

"No, thanks," said Zach hastily. "I'll call him later. You're right. We need to talk."

"All of us," added Alice softly. "Thank you, Casey."

Picking up his mug, Casey saluted her.

As Zach and Alice walked into the hot Baltimore sunshine, Zach glanced back into the kitchen. Casey stood rubbing a thumb over something attached to a thong hanging around his neck. Zach peered closer. A ray of light caught a buttery glint off the object. Smiling, Casey slipped the gilded *Coffea* flower back under his shirt.

Smiling as well, Zach closed the kitchen door.

# ABOUT SALLY PARADYSZ

Sally Paradysz was born on April 15, 1940, and was raised in the Berkshires of Western Massachusetts. She grew up reading, riding horses, and learning a love of and respect for nature from her lumberman father. She married young, and raised three children in the Lehigh Valley of Pennsylvania.

As years passed, her marriage became a struggle against a controlling man who could be quick to anger and all too willing to undermine the self-confidence Sal had once known. Even so, she found a way to seek out higher education by auditing classes and completing course work that, had her husband permitted her to pay the tuition and fees, would have entitled her to a graduate degree.

After a violent rape, about which she feared even telling her husband, Sal wavered in her ability to maintain the status quo. Eventually, she sought counseling through the Network of Victim Assistance in Doylestown, Pennsylvania. With their help she began her recovery from the physical violence, and grew to understand the emotional violence of her marriage. She became an advocate for the self-empowerment of women, drawing upon her own life experiences and bringing the world a message of healing, love, and inspiration. She was ordained into the ministry of the Assembly of the Word, founded in Quakertown, Pennsylvania, and provided spiritual counseling and ministerial assistance for more than two decades.

After thirty-five years, she divorced her husband, and began a new life. In 2000, at age 60, she decided to build a house, partially with her own two hands, in the woods of Bucks County, Pennsylvania.

Sal attended the first-ever meeting of what would become the Bethlehem Writers Group in 2006. She had written several vignettes that she hoped would be inspirational, and brought them to the group for feedback. Here was a bright-eyed, white-haired woman with short bits of writing on several aspects of life and spirituality. The only problem was, they came across as . . . preachy.

All of us who knew Sal know she was never preachy—but that's how her writing came across. And that's what we told her.

Instead of being discouraged, she went home and tinkered with them some more. At the next meeting she brought another draft, then another and another at the meetings that followed. She told us later that after each meeting she would go home and her partner, Mel, would ask, "Did they like this one better?" She just shook her head. "Nope."

But, in true Sal fashion, she never gave up. She kept writing until she finally found her voice—by writing from her heart.

After finding her voice, she wrote about nature. She wrote about recovery. She wrote about strong women, good friends, and spirituality. And then she combined the best of all of them when she wrote about building her house.

It took her years to complete her memoir, *From Scratch: Why I Walked Away from My Life and Built This Home*. At first, it was hard for her to share her private pain with members of the writers group—let alone imagine sharing it with the world. But every time she gave more of herself to her story, she lent it a truth that, when published, helped others in pain to find their own path toward healing.

When she finally published the book, all of the writers group family celebrated. And, in the months that followed, she learned that her words were inspirational to her readers—and anything but preachy.

After a lengthy battle with cancer, Sal passed away while on retreat to the Maine coast, in October, 2017. She was the mother of three, grandmother of eight, and friend to countless more. She lived with her partner, Mel, and their two flamboyant Maine Coon cats, Kiva and Kodi, in the house they built in the woods.

## About Sally Paradysz

She stayed with our writers group until the end of her life. Over the years, Sal became so much more than a fellow writer. She became a cherished friend.

We are so happy to have been part of her journey and feel very blessed that she was a part of ours.

*Carol L. Wright*
*July 2018*

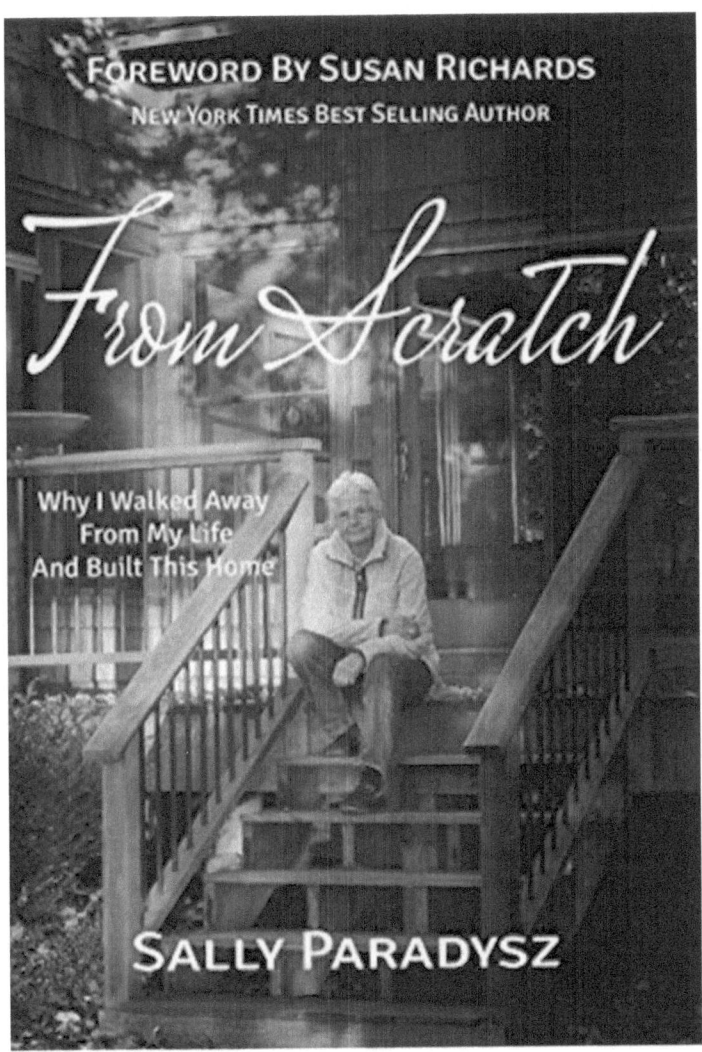

# ABOUT THE AUTHORS

COURTNEY ANNICCHIARICO lives in Bethlehem, Pennsylvania, with her husband, two teenage sons, three cats, and one dog. In her spare time, she bakes well, knits badly, and embarrasses her children by singing in public places.

JEFF BAIRD is a Natural Redhead who has written about the trials and tribulations of Redheads. Lately, he has branched off into musings about hiking through Mother Nature, particularly those with waterfalls or mountain vistas, with his trusty companion, a rescued German Shorthaired Pointer. He resides in the beautiful Lehigh Valley of Pennsylvania.

WALTER BEGO lives in Winston-Salem, North Carolina. Though primarily an editor for Go Figure Reads, he also writes when the mood inspires. His work has appeared in blogs and in the forewords of Headley Hauser's novels, *Trouble in Taos* and *Volition Man*. This is Walter's first appearance in a BWG anthology.

JODI BOGERT is a graduate, artist, freelancer, talkative introvert, and survivor of retail. Her future aspirations include publishing a debut novel and working full-time in either publishing, journalism, or both. To Jodi, creative writing is ever-changing, rebuilding, and reincarnating.

A. E. DECKER joined BWG in 2011. A former ESL tutor and doll-maker turned writer of fantasy, her short stories have appeared in such magazines as *Beneath Ceaseless Skies, Fireside Magazine,* and *The Sockdolager,* as well as in several BWG anthologies. Her YA novels in the *Moonfall Mayhem* series from World Weaver Press, include *The Falling of the Moon, The Meddlers of Moonshine,* and *Into the Moonless Night.* Like all writers, she is owned by three cats.

**MARIANNE H. DONLEY** writes fiction from short stories to funny romances and quirky murder mysteries fueled by her life as a mom and a teacher. She makes her home in Tennessee with her husband, son, and a new puppy. Marianne blogs at *A Slice of Orange.* She's a member of BWG, Romance Writers of America, and Music City Romance Writers. You can also follow her on Twitter @A_SliceofOrange and Facebook @AnOrangeSlice.

**CHRISTINE ESKILSON** received honorable mentions in the 2012 Al Blanchard Short Crime Fiction Contest and the 2012 Women's National Book Association Annual Writing Contest, and third place in the 2017 Women's National Book Association Annual Writing Contest. Her stories have appeared in *Blood Moon* (Level Best Books 2012), *Rogue Wave* (Level Best Books 2014), *Red Dawn* (Level Best Books 2015), the *Bethlehem Writers Roundtable* (September 2014), *Creatures of Habitat* (Main Street Rag 2015), *Over My Dead Body* (December 2015), *Why?* (Zimbell House Publishing 2017), and *Pick Your Poison* (Owl Hollow Press 2017). Christine is an attorney and lives with her family in the Boston area.

**RALPH HIEB** enjoys reading and writing paranormal fiction. He resides in Bethlehem, Pennsylvania, with his wife Nancy. The couple enjoys travel and makes a point each year to take a trip to someplace they have never seen before. In addition to being a member of the Bethlehem Writers Group, he is a member of the Greater Lehigh Valley Writers Group, where he has served as president and a member representative on the board of directors.

**DT KRIPPENE** has roots in Wisconsin and Connecticut. He deserted aspirations of being a biologist to live the corporate dream and raise a family. After six homes, a ten-year stint working in Asia, and an imagination that never slept, his muse refused to be hobbled as a mere dream. DT writes science fiction, dystopian, and alternate-world fantasy. You can find DT on his website, http://dtkrippene.com, and his social media links: Facebook at https://www.facebook.com/dt.krippene, Twitter @dtkrippene, and Pinterest at http://www.pinterest.com/dtkrippene

**JEROME W. McFADDEN** is primarily a short fiction writer who lives in his own deep inner space and occasionally emits paranormal, crime, and wacky stories that are supposed to entertain, frighten, or piss you off. One day he will have his own website and maybe even be on social media. Watch for it.

**STANLEY W. McFARLAND** cares less about form than inviting the reader to think. His first book, *Confessions of a Protestant,* is a collection of biographical and theological poems. His blog, *Confessions of McFarland,* consists of essays of social and religious commentary. His short stories frequently appear in Junk Drawer, the blog of Go Figure Reads, and anthologies. He is currently working on a series of Midrash novels. He lives in Winston-Salem, North Carolina.

**EMILY P. W. MURPHY** is a writer and freelance editor. Her short stories appear in all of the BWG's Sweet, Funny, and Strange anthologies, among other publications. After growing up in Pennsylvania, she has relocated to Maryland with her husband, Adam, their two children, and their two cats. Visit Emily's website at http://emilypwmurphy.com.

**CHRISTOPHER D. OCHS'S** foray into writing began with his epic fantasy *Pindlebryth of Lenland: The Five Artifacts,* recommended by US Review of Books, followed by his mirthful macabre collection *If I Can't Sleep, You Can't Sleep.* Chris writes the gamut from short stories to novels in the veins of myth &

legend, speculative fiction, and other strange tales—all in the hope to reassure himself that his life is normal. See more at http://www.christopherdochs.com and Facebook's @Christopher.D.Ochs.

**SUZANNE PURVIS** is a transplanted Canadian living in the Deep South, where she traded "eh" for "y'all." An award-winning author of long, short, and flash fiction for both children and adults, her work appears in anthologies, ezines, and books. When not writing, teaching workshops, or editing for private clients, she can often be found kayaking in the turquoise waters of the Florida Panhandle. Visit her at: http://www.suzannepurvis.com.

**DIANNA SINOVIC:** A life-long Aquarian, Dianna won her first writing contest in junior high school for a heart-warming story that featured a piece of celery as the main character. So at a tender age, she was already leaning toward paranormal—or perhaps fantasy. Full disclosure: She has never participated in a séance in which a ghost actually appeared or bought a painting that acted strangely. But there's always tomorrow . . .

**KIDD WADSWORTH** believes that it is in our dreams that we find the very best of ourselves. She primarily writes to encourage children to pursue their dreams. However, she also loves to scare people witless. With a flashlight under her chin, she's always ready to tell a ghost story.

**PAUL WEIDKNECHT** is the author of *Native to This Stream: Brief Writings About Fly-Fishing & the Great Outdoors*, a chapbook collection of previously published short stories, essays, and poems. His work has also appeared in *Best New Writing 2015*, *Gray's Sporting Journal*, *Rosebud*, and *Shenandoah*, among others. He is the winner of the Lodestone Prize for Short Fiction and the Peter Barry Short Story Competition. He lives in Phillipsburg, New Jersey. As a life-long Philadelphia Eagles fan and a season ticket holder since 1992, he wants to remind everyone of the 2018 Super Bowl score: Eagles 41, Patriots 33. Philly, Philly!

**CAROL L. WRIGHT** escaped a career in law and academia for one in writing. She loves writing her Gracie McIntyre cozy mystery series (where, unlike in life, justice always prevails). The first in the series, *Death in Glenville Falls,* was a finalist for both the 2018 Killer Nashville Silver Falchion Award and the 2018 Next Generation Indie Book Awards. She also writes short stories in a variety of genres that have been published in literary journals and award-winning anthologies. See more on her website: http://carollwright.com or on Facebook @Carol L. Wright, Author.

# ACKNOWLEDGMENTS

Bethlehem Writers Group extends its thanks to Barnes & Noble store 2259 in Center Valley, Pennsylvania, and especially its Community Business Development Manager, Colleen Gorsky, for hosting the meetings of the Bethlehem Writers Group over the past several years. It is a welcoming and energizing place to work, and we're very grateful for their hospitality.

In addition, we thank the two guest judges of our annual Short Story Award competition. Author Carrie Vaughn selected "Casting Off" by Suzanne Purvis as the winner of the 2017 Short Story Award, and agent-manager Kimberly Brower selected "The Sisters in the Museum" by Christine Eskilson as the winner of the 2018 Short Story Award. We thank them for their time and discernment in selecting these stories to appear in this book.

Last, but by no means least, to our proofreader, Dianna Sinovic, and Executive Committee member Diane Sismour, for their clear heads, sharp eyes, and giving spirits that made this book better.

www.ingramcontent.com/pod-product-compliance
Lightning Source LLC
Chambersburg PA
CBHW031223120726
47905CB00002B/449